PREY

STONE SOCIETY BOOK 4

FAITH GIBSON

**WARNING: This book contains instances of domestic violence as well as non-consensual sex between spouses.**

Copyright © 2015 by Faith Gibson

Published by Faith Gibson

Editor: Jagged Rose Wordsmithing

First e-book edition: August 2015

First print edition: August 2015

Cover design by: Elm Street Design Studio

Photography: Perrywinkle Photography and Shutterstock

Model: Drew Hale

ISBN: 978-1515012962

This book is intended for mature audiences only.

# DOMESTIC VIOLENCE HOTLINE

## 1-800-799-7233 OR 1-800-787-3224 (TTY)

If you or someone you know is a victim of domestic violence, I urge you to call the number above. Please, say NO MORE.

## NATIONAL STATISTICS*

- On average, nearly 20 people per minute are physically abused by an intimate partner in the United States. During one year, this equates to more than 10 million women and men

- 1 in 3 women and 1 in 4 men have been victims of [some form of] physical violence by an intimate partner within their lifetime

- 1 in 5 women and 1 in 7 men have been victims of severe physical violence by an intimate partner in their lifetime

- 1 in 7 women and 1 in 18 men have been stalked by an intimate partner during their lifetime to the point in which they felt very fearful or believed that they or someone close to them would be harmed or killed

- On a typical day, there are more than 20,000 phone calls placed to domestic violence hotlines nationwide

- In domestic violence homicides, women are six times more likely to be killed when there is a gun in the house
- Intimate partner violence accounts for 15% of all violent crime
- Women between the ages of 18-24 are most commonly abused by an intimate partner
- 1 in 5 women and 1 in 71 men in the United States has been raped in their lifetime
- Almost half of female (46.7%) and male (44.9%) victims of rape in the United States were raped by an acquaintance. Of these, 45.4% of female rape victims and 29% of male rape victims were raped by an intimate partner

* Statistics taken from http://www.ncadv.org/learn/statistics

# Dedication

To any man, woman, or child who has ever been abused. You are not alone. May you find the strength to change your stars.

To the man for being the type of person I am proud to call husband.

# Acknowledgements

I want to thank every single person who has read my books. Without readers, an author's world is a lonely place. I hope you all enjoy reading them as much as I enjoy writing them. To those of you who email me, telling me how much you love them, I love you.

My writing posse: Kendall, Jen, and Nikki – thank you for having what it takes to read this kind of book and still find the good in it.

My beta readers: Alex B, Sharon B, Theresa M, Shannon P, Candy R, Tanya R, and Lita T – Your input is invaluable.

The ladies at TaSTy WordGasms, congratulations on your success. You deserve it.

# *Prologue*

2037
New Atlanta High School

"Next up in our talent show is Abigail Swanson. Miss Swanson will be dancing the *Waltz of the Flowers* from *The Nutcracker*."

Troy Quinn got an elbow to the side as his best friend George snickered. "Your girl's doing the nutcracker. She ever crack your nuts?" George was laughing out loud, earning them some stern looks from parents sitting close by. The New Atlanta High School talent show was famous for producing some extremely gifted artists. Troy slouched down in his chair as Abigail twirled around in front of everyone with barely any clothes on.

Goddamnit, he was the only one who was supposed to see that much of her skin. The longer he watched, the madder he got. The song ended and applause erupted throughout the auditorium. Everyone was on their feet clapping and yelling. Fuck. He knew she could dance but this was ridiculous. As far as he was concerned, she wouldn't be dancing anymore. High school was almost over, and by God, he wasn't going to lose her. He had the perfect plan to keep her from going away to that fancy school for dancers.

Abigail bent down to accept a bouquet of flowers one of the senior football players was offering her. The tops of her breasts were spilling over the low neckline of her pink leotard. "Look, I bet Brandon can see Abbi's tits!" George was howling. Troy punched him in the arm and took off toward the front of the building. As Abbi walked down the steps he grabbed her by the arm and dragged her out the side door. "Ow, Troy you're hurting me," Abbi said, trying to pull away from him.

1

"You stupid slut. Where do you get off showing Brandon your tits? And why the fuck is he giving you flowers?" Troy grabbed the bouquet out of her hands and threw it to the floor, stomping the roses until the petals were trashed.

"Stop it!" Abbi was crying now. She wrenched away from him and ran into the girl's bathroom.

"Troy! Hey, Troy!" He turned around to see Brandon Foster coming down the hall.

"What the fuck do you want, Foster? You stay away from Abbi, you hear me? She's mine, and we're getting married." That was a lie, but fuckface didn't need to know it. They had never even discussed plans after high school. Well, not their plans, only her plans to go away to college.

"Married? You're out of your mind, Quinn. She's too young to get married. Besides, Abbi has a bright future ahead of her, one that doesn't include a scuzz like you." Brandon thought he was the shit- big football player sporting daddy's money. Troy punched him in the face. Brandon's head jerked back from the strike.

"What the fuck, Quinn?" Brandon swung at Troy, but he ducked just in time to miss the fist. He came up with a punch to Brandon's gut, doubling him over. Bringing his knee up, Troy caught him in the face, sending him to the floor with a bloody nose.

By now, a crowd had gathered in the hall. Several football players rushed Troy before he could stomp Brandon. Troy swung wildly, hitting as many of them as he could before being grabbed from behind by a truant officer. "You stay away from Abbi, you hear me? She's mine. She's having my baby!" Troy yelled at Brandon as he was put in handcuffs. "She's mine, Foster! Mine!"

Abbi sank down to the floor of the girl's bathroom. Troy had been getting meaner lately, ever since she told him she wanted to apply for the art college and not the community college he was going to. She wanted to be a dancer with the New Atlanta Ballet Company. That had been her dream for as long as she could remember. Her parents had given her every opportunity to achieve her goals, and if her performance tonight was any indication, she could very well receive the scholarship she needed to be admitted to the prestigious art school.

She fully expected Troy to burst through the door at any moment. He was yelling crazy stuff to Brandon. Why had Brandon waited so long to notice her? She'd had a crush on the hottest boy in school since they were in fourth grade. Of course, the captain of the football team only dated the head cheerleader, not some nerdy dancer. Troy was good looking, but his attitude left something to be desired. She tried to break things off with him several times, but he would lose his shit, threatening Abbi if she didn't take him back.

The yelling continued out in the hall, and all Abbi could do was wait it out and pray her dad or some other adult would come rescue her. Hopefully, Troy would give up and go on home. She hadn't seen her parents in the crowd earlier, but surely they had arrived by now. They never missed her shows. Never.

The door opened and her dance teacher, Miss Kelly, came in. "Abbi, you need to come with me, sweetheart. Something's happened."

She stood up, wiping her eyes. "I promise what Troy said isn't true! I'm not pregnant!" She started crying again.

Miss Kelly frowned at her. "Abbi, I have no idea what you're talking about, but you need to come with me. Your parents were in a car accident. I need to take you to the hospital."

"What? No. That can't be right. Miss Kelly…"

Her teacher and mentor wouldn't give her any details. The silent trip to the hospital was the longest ride of her life. When they arrived, Abbi knew something was wrong. Her aunt Judy was standing off to the side of the waiting room. To say Abbi's mother and her younger sister didn't get along was an understatement. For Judy to be there waiting…

The adults who were whispering loudly stopped talking when she entered the room. The hairs on her arms stood on end. Her little brother Matthew was sitting quietly. He never sat quietly. He rarely sat, period. It was all their parents could do to get him to sit down long enough to eat supper.

"What's going on?" Abbi asked no one in particular.

Miss Kelly took Abbi's hands in hers as she explained, "Abbi, I'm so sorry. Your parents didn't make it." Miss Kelly didn't go into the sordid details of the wreck. Or maybe she did. *Her parents didn't make it?* Abbi's brain was foggy. It felt as if someone had stuffed cotton in her head. *My parents are dead?*

"The doctors did everything they could for your mother. Your father died on impact. It appears the brakes gave out." Miss Kelly was still talking, but Abbi wasn't computing it. Not really. How could she and Matt go on without their parents? Who would take care of them? Abbi's life was over.

"If you were already eighteen, you could declare yourself Matthew's legal guardian. Since your birthday isn't for another few months, your aunt is going to step in and take care of you," Miss Kelly stated, rubbing her hand up and down Abbi's arm.

*Her aunt? Judy was going to be their guardian?* She was wrong before. *Now* her life was well and truly over.

# Chapter One

## Present Day 2047

Geoffrey Hartley was standing at the counter of Lion Hart Dojo when the front door flew open. A furious young man sporting a black eye stomped into the gym. Frey didn't hesitate to ask, "What can we do for you, Son?"

That was obviously the wrong thing to say. "I'm not your son!" The young man was pacing like a caged animal, ready to escape his confines and rip his captor to shreds.

"No, you aren't. I apologize if I offended you. I don't know your name, so I cannot address you properly. Let's try this again. What can we do for you?"

"Matt." The teenager stopped pacing and stood in front of Frey, sliding his hands in the pockets of his blood spattered jeans. "Name's Matt."

"Okay, Matt. I'm Geoffrey. Why don't you come to the back with me so we can get your face cleaned up a bit?"

Matt hesitated, taking in all that was Frey. Being the largest of the Gargoyles in New Atlanta, he would intimidate anyone, especially a wiry teen who just had his face pummeled.

"Look, Matt. You came here for a reason. Wanna tell me why you're here, besides the obvious?" Frey had been in this spot too many times to count. There comes a breaking point in everyone's life. You either find yourself and grow, or you lose yourself and wither away. Matt was ready to take charge of his destiny.

"I want to learn to fight." Matt was back to pacing the small area in front of the counter.

"Why?" This might seem like a stupid question, but it wasn't. The reason someone wanted to learn was the most important thing Frey could ask.

"Why? Look at my fuckin' face, man. That's why."

5

"Let me rephrase the question then. Do you want to learn to fight so you can beat the shit out of whoever did this to you? Or do you want to be able to defend yourself next time?"

Matt stopped pacing. "Is there a difference?"

"There's a big difference. If you only want revenge, then you've come to the wrong place. If you want to be able to defend yourself, train, grow physically and spiritually, then you're in the right place."

"I want to protect my sister," Matt almost whispered.

"Who are you protecting her from? The same one that did that to you?" Frey asked while pointing to the bloody nose and black eye. The teen nodded, looking at his shoes.

"Have you been to the police?" Frey had seen too many domestic cases come through the door. Their women's self-defense class stayed full.

"He *is* the police," Matt seethed through his teeth.

*Fuck.* Frey hadn't been expecting that. "Let me guess, he's your father?"

"Fuck no. Her husband."

Frey needed to better understand the situation. "I tell you what, let's go in the back and get your face cleaned up. How old are you?" This time Frey didn't give Matt a chance to refuse; he turned and headed to the locker room.

"Seventeen." The voice was directly behind him, so Matt was following.

Frey removed a first aid kit from a shelf, and once he got the blood cleaned off the kid's face, he placed a small bandage over the cut below his eye. He found a spare t-shirt and offered it to Matt. The interaction had given the young man time to calm down and Frey time to assess his mood.

"Now, if you are serious about training, I'm going to need your parents' consent since you aren't eighteen yet. Just get your mom or dad to come sign the forms, and we'll get you started."

"I don't have any parents; my sister is my guardian. Will that work?" Matt still wouldn't look into Frey's eyes.

"The sister whose husband did this?" Frey was ready to lay into the woman who would allow her husband to do this to her brother. Then again, she was probably getting the same treatment. He needed to find out the cop's name and get Jasper and Dane to check him out.

Again, Matt just nodded, moving his weight from one foot to the other.

"Yes, if she's your legal guardian, that's just as good. When can she come in? I'm assuming you want to get started as soon as possible."

Matt looked at Frey then, "Yes, sir, I do, but I'll have to wait 'til she gets out of her class to ask her."

At least he had manners, something Frey wouldn't have to teach him. "Okay then. As soon as your sister signs the consent form, you can get started. I'm going to warn you, I expect you to listen to what I teach you and do what I tell you to, no matter how odd it may seem. I'm going to be tough on you. Can you handle that?"

"Yes, sir."

"Come on, I'll show you around." Geoffrey walked Matt through the dojo and the gym, explaining the different types of classes they offered. When Frey first opened the place, it was basically a boxing gym. As mixed martial arts became more popular, he expanded training to include Muay Thai as well as other forms of martial arts. Frey was a master in every discipline he studied, holding the highest color belt offered in each. Being a Gargoyle meant he was much stronger than humans. He had to call on his shifter abilities to keep his power in check. It was the reason he was one of the best in the world. His discipline surpassed his strength.

Being afternoon, there were several rooms in the dojo being used. Matt was able to see the different forms

7

being taught. "Why is it so quiet in here?" he asked Frey once they finished their tour.

"That is part of the discipline. When you work on your form, you need to concentrate. Open your mind, close your mouth. When you fight, you will use your voice and your core to help in strikes and kicks. Does that make sense?" Frey was strict when it came to the way his students were taught. He learned many years ago that the mind is the most powerful weapon, much more so than fists.

"I guess. So, which one of those are you going to teach me first?"

"None. You will learn meditation first." Frey knew the reaction before it happened. It was the same response everyone had when he told them they would be sitting quietly in the lotus position.

"I don't get it. I thought you were going to teach me how to fight." Matt was frowning, but he wasn't being disrespectful. He was shifting from foot to foot, as if he was ready to bolt.

"I am. Remember, I just said you have to open your mind in the ring. You must learn how to properly do that. Believe me, it's harder than you think. When was the last time you sat and concentrated on nothing?" Over the years, Geoffrey had taught all his brothers and cousins the art of meditation.

"Honestly, I don't sit. Drives Abbi crazy. My parents used to call me Bean. You know, after those Mexican jumping beans? It's probably why I can eat what I want and not gain weight. I can't sit still."

That explained his constant moving. Frey asked, "Do you play sports?"

"I played basketball when I was younger, but now I have to work. Abbi does the best she can, but I don't ask her for anything if I can help it."

"Is Abbi your sister?"

"Yes, sir."

"I tell you what, why don't we get you signed up? That way when Abbi does give permission, you can start right away." The kid would have to list his sister's name on the paperwork, and he could figure out the husband's name from there. He took Matt to the front, grabbed a clipboard and sign-up sheet. Matt sat quietly filling out the form, his knee bouncing the whole time. He hadn't been kidding.

When Matt finished, Frey took the clipboard and said, "We'll let you try things out for a week, see what you think. If you're still interested, we'll discuss payment at that time. For now, just have your sister come sign the consent form, and you'll be good to go."

"Thank you, I will." Matt reached out his hand and Frey carefully shook it.

"I'll see you soon."

The kid's demeanor was totally different leaving than it had been coming. Now he seemed hopeful. Frey's eyes followed Matt until he was out of sight. He picked up the clipboard and scanned over the information. The address had them living not too far away from the high school. The area was filled with lower income families, mostly those who worked blue collar jobs.

Frey continued looking at the form until he came upon the sister's name. Abbi Quinn. Hopefully there wasn't more than one Quinn working on the police force. He knew better than to get involved personally, but he was a sucker for the underdog. And when that underdog was a skinny kid? Frey was hooked.

Most nights, the gym was going full force until around midnight. Since Frey didn't have much of a life outside his gym and patrolling for Unholy, he stayed late just to be around people. Being only a couple of years younger than Rafael, Frey was one of the oldest in their Clan. He had spent his life protecting others, reinventing himself every so often so he could reenlist in the military. Having Julian as a brother helped when he needed a new identity.

Frey might be the largest, fiercest Gargoyle in their Clan, but he loved humans. He'd spent over five hundred years living among them, interacting with them, learning their ways. To him, there was very little difference in humans and Gargoyles. Both wanted love and acceptance. Both had good and evil. Each had those who were leaders and followers. There were those who wanted complete control over the lives of those around them. Frey was a born leader, but he would follow Rafael to the ends of the earth. He loved his King, but more than that, he loved his cousin. Being two years apart, they had been raised together. Even though they had different parents, Rafael was more like a brother.

Wanting to speak with Kaya before it got too late, Frey left Urijah in charge and headed out early. He arrived to an eerily dark manor. He really should have called first, but it was the middle of the week. Even if Rafe and Kaya weren't home, Jonathan and Priscilla should be there. Frey parked his Jeep and shut the engine off. He reached out with his shifter senses. Nothing. That was more than odd. He dialed the house phone first. No answer. Frey couldn't remember the last time both of the siblings had gone out at the same time. It was usually Priscilla who remained behind. Now that they were getting on in age, neither of them left the manor often. Next he called Rafael.

"Hello, Brother," Rafael answered. He regarded them all as his brothers, whether they were brothers, cousins, or even if they weren't related by blood at all.

"Evening, Rafe. I'm sitting here at the manor, alone. Where are Jonathan and Priscilla? This place is like a ghost town."

"Lorenzo's new housekeeper, Prudence, arrived today from Italy. She is Priscilla and Jonathan's niece, and they are over there now, helping her settle in. What's up?"

10

"I wanted to talk to Kaya about one of her cops. What time will y'all be home?" Frey was one of the few Gargoyles who had adopted the southern style of speaking. While he didn't follow the "good ole boy" mentality, he did talk with a drawl. He had lost his Italian accent a couple hundred years earlier.

"I was just going to call you. I'm afraid we won't be home anytime soon. We are headed to Tennessee with Dane. Julian can fill you in, but shit has hit the proverbial fan. Gregor and Dante are on an airplane headed to Greece. I need you to take care of the patrol schedule until they return."

"Ten-four. Do I need to postpone our sword training?" Frey really hoped not, because he was looking forward to sparring of a different sort.

"No, please proceed. I have a feeling it is more important than before. Listen, I need to go; we have arrived at our destination. I'll be in touch soon. Be well, Frey."

"And you, my brother." He tossed his phone in the cup holder and started the Jeep. "What the fuck is going on?" he asked the cosmos.

# Chapter Two

Abbi's last student left the dance room. It was time to begin planning the fall festival, which meant longer hours after school. Between the afternoon dance classes three days a week and the festival, Abbi would be late getting home every night. She couldn't be happier. Abbi Quinn taught ballet at a local community center. Her class was filled with children from mostly lower income families who wanted nothing more than a babysitter. There were some kids who were truly interested in dancing. Since Abbi couldn't have any children of her own, she relished her time with the little ones, no matter the reason they spent their afternoons with her.

The last child had been picked up, and Abbi was taking advantage of the quiet time to work on the festival. Most of the other classes had let out, so the building was almost empty. Even though it was autumn, the committee had chosen *The Nutcracker* for this year's theme and had appointed Abbi as chairperson. The door flew open and slammed against the wall, startling her. Her husband Troy stalked into the room, his face was furious. *Oh, God. What now?* Troy had a temper, and it was only getting worse. It was all she could do to hide the bruises from her fellow teachers.

Troy rared back and threw a plastic case at Abbi, barely missing her face. She cringed, knowing all too well what it was. "What the fuck, Abigail? You wanna tell me why in the *fuck* I found birth control pills in your drawer?" She stood abruptly as he rushed her. With her back to the wall, there was nowhere for her to retreat. This was a no win situation. If she kept quiet, he would be mad. If she told him the truth, he would be enraged. "I asked you a fucking question!" he yelled.

Troy was in her space now. Toes touching, she could

12

see the fire in his eyes. This never boded well for her. When he was this far gone, she knew it was going to hurt. "I can't do it again," she whispered.

"What was that? I didn't hear you." His breath reeked of whiskey. It usually did when she wasn't home right after school to have his dinner on the table. Some nights he ignored her. Some he didn't bother coming home, and Abbi knew he wasn't spending that time alone. Too many nights he'd come home smelling of someone else's perfume. Those were the nights she appreciated, because then he left her alone.

"I can't do it again, Troy. I can't go through the pain of losing another baby. I just can't!" Traitorous tears she had no control over slid down her face.

"You didn't even ask me. I'm your husband, and you didn't ask me about going on the pill. I want a kid. I don't care if your body is too fucking weak to handle it; we're going to do this until you give me a son. That was the deal, Abigail. You give me a goddamn kid, and I give you your life back."

Abbi wasn't stupid. She knew he'd never let her go even if she gave him a child. She was stuck with him forever. He'd told her as much after high school. He was crazy if he thought she'd hand over her baby to him and walk away. As much as it broke her heart each time, losing those three babies had been a blessing. She could not bring a child into this world to be raised by an abusive monster.

"Hey, Abs, I need to talk..." Her younger brother Matt chose that moment to walk in the door. "What's going on?" He stopped in the doorway, his fists clenched by his side. Abbi tried her best to shield Matt from Troy. Her brother had yet to fill out. He was seventeen, tall, and skinny. Troy was built like a tank compared to Matt.

"Nothing, Son. Your sister and I were having a private discussion. What did you want to talk to her about?" Troy turned so he was between Abbi and Matthew. She

13

peered around Troy's shoulder and shook her head, warning him to keep his mouth shut. The rage coming off Matt was tangible. He hated when Troy called him Son, because he was no kind of father.

When their aunt died, Troy wanted Matt to go live with someone else, and he didn't hide how he felt. As a matter of fact, Troy was extremely vocal on how much of a burden having him around was. Abbi did her best to reassure her brother she didn't feel that way. Matt knew she wanted away from Troy, but with him being a cop, it was easier said than done.

"It can wait. You two are busy. Sorry I interrupted." Matthew wouldn't go far. He would stand outside and listen as he always did. As long as Troy was yelling, he would stay put. If her husband laid a hand on her, Matthew would step in and take the punishment himself.

"What was that about? Are you two keeping secrets from me? You do know I'm smarter than you both, right? I'm a cop. I will have you followed if I think you're hiding something." Troy was back in her face, both hands against the wall on either side of her head.

"I honestly don't know, probably something to do with school. It usually is." Abbi was telling the truth. The only thing Matthew talked to her about was school. Her brother had no real life outside of that and his job.

"You better not be lying. Now get your ass home. I want dinner." Troy moved away from Abbi and bent down to retrieve the plastic container of birth control. He slid it in the front pocket of his uniform shirt. "I'll be keeping these," he snarled. The leer in his eyes let Abbi know what to expect from her husband when they went to bed.

*Please, someone, help me.* She silently sent a prayer to a god she no longer relied on. Where was the Almighty when her husband was yelling at her, hitting her, abusing her brother? She continued to pray anyway. Packing up her things, she hoped Matthew could find somewhere else to

14

sleep.

She locked up the building and was walking to her car when the gravel behind her crunched. Whipping around, she held her mace up and aimed. "Jesus, Matt, I could have sprayed you!" she scolded her brother whose arms were up in the defensive.

"Sorry, Abs. I just wanted to make sure you're okay. Did he hurt you?" Matt cocked his head to the side, daring her to lie.

"No, he didn't touch me. But tonight's going to be rough. Do you think you can..."

Matt cut her off, "No. I'm not staying away. Not tonight. Abs, please. You have to find a way to get out from under him. I know he's a cop, but there has to be someone who can help you."

Abbi had spent the last five years of her life beating herself up for marrying Troy. When her parents died, her aunt had taken control of her and Matthew's inheritance. What Judy didn't spend on drugs, she lost gambling. Abbi had gotten into college on a scholarship. Graduating Valedictorian from New Atlanta High School meant something. At least she'd had the good sense to get her degree and become a teacher. Her dream of becoming a professional dancer died along with her parents. Troy didn't attend the same college, but he made sure his buddies who did followed her everywhere she went. Once he joined the Academy and became a policeman, Abbi saw a change in him. For just a little while, Troy was calmer and more responsible. He made her flowery promises about love and family. She finally gave in and married him. The ink hadn't dried before he began trying to control every aspect of her life, including her bank account.

Judy died of a drug overdose when Matthew had just started his sophomore year. What little money was left in the bank, Troy took as payment for allowing her brother to move in with them. Her parents' house wasn't worth anything after Judy had lived there and trashed it. Matt got a job as soon as he was old enough, never asking Abbi for money for anything: not school stuff, not clothes, not games. Nothing. She was so proud of the man he was becoming. As he took a step into the light, Abbi saw the marks on his face. "Matty, what happened?" She tentatively touched his cheek, noticing the small bandage.

He jerked his head away from her touch. "Got punched. No big deal. Listen, Abs, I want to join the gym, but I need your permission. Will you please go to Lion Hart's tomorrow and sign the permission slip?"

"There's a gym at the high school. Why don't you use it?" Something was up. Matt had never shown an interest in working out.

"You know the jocks have the run of the gym at school. Besides, I want to take a class. Please? I'll pay for it, so don't worry about that." Matt's bottom lip stuck out slightly, giving him a sad, innocent look.

Abbi laughed. "You do that on purpose. Of course I'll sign for you as long as it doesn't interfere with work or school."

Matt bounced up and down on the balls of his feet. "It won't interfere. The gym opens early and closes late. Thanks, Abs. I love you." He crushed her in a hug and kissed her cheek. "I'll see you at home." He jogged off to his junker. It wasn't much to look at, but it was dependable, and he'd bought it himself. He really was a good kid.

She thought back to the bruise on her brother's face. "Oh, Troy. What have you done?" Stalling only put off the inevitable, so Abbi got in her car and headed home. When she arrived, the house was dark except for one room. The light from the television flickered through the window of the living room. Their house was a small three bedroom rancher in a fairly nice neighborhood. Abbi parked in the driveway and entered the house through the side door. She turned on the kitchen light and placed her purse on the

16

kitchen table.

She normally heated up leftovers on the nights she had dance class. If she cooked a meal, it would take a while. The longer it took, the more Troy would drink. One of two things would happen. Either he would get so wasted he'd pass out, or he'd remember why he was pissed at her in the first place and be rougher than usual. Tonight, she would take her chances with him passing out. She chose meatloaf. Between prep and cooking time, it would give her over an hour.

She was mixing the hamburger meat with the various ingredients when Troy came into the kitchen. He walked by her to get to the liquor bottles. Without saying a word, he grabbed her hair and yanked her head back. His black eyes squinted, staring into hers. He crashed his mouth down on hers in a bruising kiss. His teeth grabbed her bottom lip and he bit down. Abbi instinctively jerked back, causing more damage to her lip. She knew better than to say anything. Instead she closed her eyes, fighting back the tears. She should have reheated leftovers.

Thankfully, Troy waited until after supper was over and the table cleared before dragging Abbi to their bedroom where she now stared at the ceiling. Matt was in his room, hopefully asleep. The only noise was the sound of Troy's snoring coming from the other side of the bed. He had gotten what he wanted before passing out. Abbi knew better than to get up before he was deep in sleep. Now that he was out, she eased off her side of the bed and slipped into the hall bathroom. She would make too much noise in the one attached to their bedroom. She closed the door and slid to the floor in front of the toilet. No longer did she have to force herself to throw-up to empty her stomach of the dinner mixed with the come Troy had shot down her throat. His mission to get her pregnant had been forgotten in his alcohol infused lust for revenge.

In the dark, Abbi rinsed her mouth with water

17

before sipping mouthwash from the bottle. She never turned on the light. She didn't want to see her reflection in the mirror. The once bright face of a teenage girl filled with so much hope for the future was gone. All that was left was the haggard face of a young woman who felt anything but young. Quietly, she padded back to the bedroom and slid underneath the covers. She hadn't noticed that Troy was no longer snoring.

"Where the fuck have you been?" he asked her as he flipped back the bedding. He was still naked from earlier, and he was stroking his erection.

"I had to pee," she lied.

"Whatever." He didn't say anything else as he jerked her panties down her legs. With no foreplay to get her at least a little wet, her husband shoved her knees to her chest and thrust himself into her body. Abbi closed her eyes tight, willing the tears to stay put. She lay still, her hands clutching the sheet below her, as Troy used her body for his own pleasure. Not once since they'd been married had he given her an orgasm. He'd never even tried. He pushed her knees higher against her chest and pounded relentlessly until his orgasm came. He didn't call out her name, just grunted a couple of times as his seed spilled into her core. When he was sated, he pulled out, turned over, and went back to sleep.

Abbi sent a silent prayer to every deity who might be listening. *Please don't let me get pregnant.*

18

# Chapter Three

Knowing Julian would still be at the lab, Frey went there after leaving the manor. He let himself into the locked building and found his younger brother in front of the bank of computers where he spent most of his time. Frey didn't know how Julian and Nikolas could sit so long and stare at the screens. Unless he was meditating, he hated sitting still. He needed to be moving. It was one reason he'd opened a gym. He ran a business that allowed him to spar and work out while making money. Not that he needed the money. Like the other Gargoyles, he had more money than he could spend in his long lifetime. Sixx made sure of that.

"Hey, Little Brother. What the fuck is going on? I went by the manor to talk to Kaya, and nobody was home. I called Rafe, and he asked me to rearrange all the patrol schedules. Said you'd fill me in on what's going down." He sat down in Nikolas' empty chair and assessed his brother's mood. Julian and Nikolas were as close as siblings could be without being twins. Julian had to be missing Nik badly.

Jules stopped typing and ran his hands down his face. "How much time do you have?" Julian picked up something that resembled a transmitter and twirled it between his fingers as he spoke. "Talk about a mess. I guess I should start at the beginning. Isabelle has a child, Connor, who has been living with Isabelle's foster family for the last six years. She has been hiding the kid, because she didn't want her former father-in-law to get his hands on his dead son's heir. Someone found out about Connor and sent Isabelle a note. She panicked and called Dane. Having experience in kidnappings, he wanted her to allow him and Kaya to handle the situation.

"Dane has a contact in New Nashville. Corey, the contact, called in a favor with the sheriff's department where the foster family lives. They went to the home and found the foster father, Rico, dead. There was evidence of Maria, the foster mother, being dragged through the house, and her body was found a few blocks away. She is in a coma in a hospital in New Nashville. That is where Rafael is now. There was no sign of Connor." There was a notification on one of the computers, and Julian turned to check it out. Frey kept quiet, clasping his hands behind his head.

Julian returned his attention to Frey. "Somehow, the kidnappers got Isabelle's cell phone information and texted her, telling her to head to the airport. Tessa was going to go in her place, but Isabelle gave us the slip. Long story short, Isabelle is on a plane, and Dante is on the Clan jet going after her."

"So, Isabelle called Dane instead of Dante. I bet he was upset." Frey would be if his mate called someone else for help, even if that someone was her brother. Technically, they weren't mates since they hadn't officially bonded. Still, it had to hurt.

"You could say that. Tessa had a plan, a good one, to disguise herself as Isabelle. Before she could get back with the supplies she needed, Isabelle snuck out and headed to the airport."

"What a clusterfuck. Why can't one of us find a mate that doesn't have a target on their back? Speaking of women, what's going on with yours?"

"Nothing is going on with mine. I am too busy trying to keep everyone else's alive." Julian had one of the most important jobs in the Clan, whether he realized it or not. Frey was often envious of how smart his little brother was. Julian's I.Q. was off the charts. His mind was a weapon all its own, and if the government ever found out what Julian was capable of, he would become a wanted man.

"Truth, Brother. Truth. And Isabelle has a kid? How did Dante take the news?"

"Same way we all did. Shocked at first, but then we all realized we don't know her. Why would we have known

20

she has a kid? I know nothing about Katherine that I haven't read in a file online. I'm sure she has secrets like the rest of us. Dante has already accepted Isabelle, and he's ready for a family. He will do the honorable thing and accept Connor without hesitation. Wouldn't you?"

"Of course I would. We all have pasts, good and bad. We cannot judge others without judging ourselves. I would hate to have stones cast my way for the shit I've done. Besides, I'm ready for a rugrat or ten myself." And that was the truth of it. Frey kept his past to himself. He never wanted his Clan to know the things he'd done during war, the atrocities he'd seen. Meditation helped, but his nightmares sometimes got the best of him. If he was ever lucky enough to find a mate, she'd have to be a strong woman who could put up with his thrashing about during the night.

"Do you ever think about him?" Julian stopped typing long enough to look at his brother. Frey didn't have to ask who Jules was talking about.

"All the time. At least now I can think about the good times and what a good father he was." Roberto Di Pietro, the younger brother of Edmondo, had been a good father, and a great fighter. He blamed himself for Edmondo getting killed, even though he hadn't been around when it happened. He was the reason Frey had joined the military so often, following in his father's footsteps.

When the female Goyles started becoming extinct, Frey had all but given up the dream of having a family. Now that he knew it was possible, it was almost all he could think about. As much as he wanted children of his own, Frey knew he'd never be half the dad his own had been.

"I need to adjust the patrolling schedule, now that Gregor and Dante are out of the country. We are going to continue with sword training. Rafe doesn't want me to postpone working with the rest of the Clan. I am meeting Uri in the morning at the armory, and we will proceed as

21

planned. Dante has already spoken to Oksana and given her an extended vacation. Even though she is in the know about us being Goyles, I don't want her around when we're all half naked and swinging swords. I'd hate to give the old girl a heart attack." Frey grinned at his brother.

Julian barked out a laugh. "Hell, you're enough to give someone a heart attack just by walking into a room. Have you seen yourself?"

Frey knew he was intimidating. Even if he weren't a full-blooded Gargoyle, he would make most anyone stop and take notice. Wanting to turn the attention away from himself he asked, "Heard anything from Nik?" Frey had wanted to go with his brother to help look for Sophia. It had been a long time since he'd been on a mission. Search and rescue was one of his many talents. Rafael suggested Gregor be the one to go since his mate was bound and determined to help find her cousin.

"I talked to him this morning to put him in touch with Ezekiel. Since they're both searching for Sophia, we figure it's better if they work together. Now that Gregor has gone to help Dante, his plan to help Nik has been delayed. Hopefully both outcomes will be positive, and we can get Nik home soon." It was evident by his voice that Julian missed their brother.

They talked about the half-bloods, and how so many of their lives had been connected without them knowing it. Frey mentioned mating with humans which brought the conversation to Kaya. Julian asked, "If you don't mind me asking, what did you want to speak to Kaya about?"

Frey sat up in the chair, leaning his arms on his thighs. "One of her cops. Apparently he's a douchebag that likes to beat on his wife and her younger brother. The kid came into the gym wanting to learn how to fight. I want more intel before I go to bat for him."

"Why don't you just kick the cop's ass and scare the shit out of him?" Julian cocked his head to the side and smiled. Being a shifter, Julian could hold his own in a fight, but he didn't have the extensive training Frey did. If he wanted, Frey could subdue a person just by gripping their shoulder. He could also kill a man with a quick blow to the chest.

"I wish it were that simple. This is something I've got to tread carefully with. Now, I will leave you to your monitors. I've got to hit the skies. Maybe I'll get to kick some Unholy ass instead," Frey said with a grin.

"Here." Julian tossed the item he'd been fiddling with to his brother. "New technology. Tessa got it from Jonas, and I want to test it out before I attempt to duplicate it. It's a transmitter that will allow you to speak to me from wherever you are. No more cell phones while we're flying."

As Julian explained how it worked, Frey turned the plastic over looking at both sides before sliding it over his ear. He pulled a cigar out of his pocket and bit the end off. Pointing the unlit stick at his brother he said, "Call me if you need me. I'll be here."

Julian nodded and turned back to the screens. Unease was rolling off his brother. Maybe he was tired of sitting still after all.

Even though his patrolling had been free of Unholy, Frey hadn't slept well. His thoughts strayed to the young man with the bruised face. Hopefully the sister would sign the permission slip, and Matthew could begin his training soon. Frey opened the gym as he did every morning. He had a couple of hours before he was to meet Urijah at the armory. There were a handful of people that liked to work out before they went to their jobs, but nobody needed a sparring partner this early. So, instead of hitting the boxing ring, Frey hit the speed bag. Even though he didn't need to, he wrapped his hands. If he punched a bag for hours on end with no protection, someone might get suspicious. He began working on the small bag that was located close to the front door, taking care to keep his shifter speed in check.

23

About twenty minutes into his warm-up, Frey started feeling light headed. He grabbed the bag, stopping its motion, when a woman walked into the gym. His stomach churned as he took in her features - mousy brown hair, dull blue eyes, and frumpy clothes. The same hair and eyes he had seen on Matthew. This was Matthew's sister, Abigail Quinn.

"Excuse me. Do you know where I can find Mr. Hartley?" she asked quietly, her eyes not meeting his longer than necessary.

Frey found his feet and forced them to close the distance between him and this broken creature. "I'm Mr. Hartley. Geoffrey Hartley. You must be Abigail." He quickly removed the tape from his right hand so he could shake hers, skin to skin. Dumb move. When she placed her small hand in his, he about fell to his knees. *What the hell?* Frey never got sick, never felt faint.

When she took her hand from his, he felt the loss. As Frey stood frozen in place, he realized he was looking at his mate. *Fuck me. I find my mate, and she's married to an abusive motherfucker.*

"Please call me Abbi. My brother asked me to come by and sign a consent form. May I ask what he's signing up for?" Her voice was soft and musical. Frey wanted to hear it again.

"I'll call you Abbi if you call me Frey." He waited, but she didn't speak; only nodded. Frey was ready to throttle the man who had taken the life out of both Abbi and her brother.

"Matthew wants to take a self-defense class. After seeing his face yesterday, I'd say that is a wise decision. Do you know where he got the bruises?" Frey begged her silently to be honest with him as he stared at her swollen bottom lip.

Abbi shifted from one foot to the other. Not in the bouncy way her brother did. Her movements were timid.

24

She clasped her hands together when she answered, "He's always getting into fights. The bigger boys pick on him. Can you help him, Mr. Hartley?" Her pleading eyes found his. She was afraid for her brother, and she wanted Frey to help.

He couldn't stop himself. The need to be near her was overwhelming. Frey moved a step closer and took Abbi's hand in his, running his thumb across the soft skin of her knuckles. "Yes, Abbi, I can help him." *And you.* Her small fingers curled tight against his, as if she knew instinctively Frey was her lifeline. They fixed their gazes on each other, and he took the opportunity to search her soul. Those beautiful blue orbs staring at him should be filled with love and happiness, not fear and wariness. Abbi blushed and looked down.

"I'm sorry, that was…" She backed away.

"No, I apologize, Abbi. You're stunning. Please forgive me for staring." Frey didn't miss the breath she sucked in when he complimented her. He had seen too many battered women over the centuries to not recognize what he was seeing. Underneath the ugly duckling façade her husband had convinced her of over the years was a beautiful swan just waiting to break through. Right then and there, Frey vowed to break through to the swan.

# Chapter Four

Abbi couldn't think. She had been around a lot of men in her life, mostly fathers of her students. She had even visited the precinct where Troy worked a few times. Never in her twenty-seven years had she ever come across someone as arresting as Geoffrey Hartley. If he was going to be Matt's teacher, she was almost afraid for her brother. This man had to be at least six and a half feet tall. His shoulders were so broad, she didn't know how he found clothes to fit. He would break Matt like a twig. She was reading over the paperwork Matt had already filled out while watching Frey out of the corner of her eye. God, he smelled so good, like an afternoon rain shower and man.

"Is everything all right?" he asked her. Crap, had he caught her ogling him? What was she doing anyway? She was a married woman. Still, just because she was tied down didn't mean she was dead. Anyone would have to be six feet under, toes up, to not take notice of the powerful male that was Geoffrey Hartley.

"I'm fine," she whimpered as she scribbled her name on the designated line. She held the clipboard out and when he reached for it, his hand covered hers. As soon as their skin touched, Geoffrey inhaled deeply, closing his eyes. Did he not know she was married, or did he touch all women that way? She would hate to be the object of his affection. Troy wasn't a small man, and in the bedroom he scared her. She couldn't imagine being underneath a man as large as Frey. She stood quickly, hoping to break the connection. The man's nostrils flared as his eyes popped open.

Instead of releasing her, he reached out with his other hand and tucked a strand of hair behind her ear. His fingers lingered as he whispered, "Beautiful." She searched his eyes to see if he was just messing with her. She knew her appearance was less than stellar. Maybe when she was a teenager and dancing, she had been pretty. Now she was a mess. Troy insisted she dress like her dead grandmother so no other man would think twice about how she looked under the baggy clothes. She wasn't allowed to wear much makeup or fix her hair. She was lucky she had naturally wavy hair, or it would never look decent. The one time she'd gone to the salon and had lowlights put in, he'd gone to the store and bought a box of color and made her change it back that night.

The dark brown eyes staring intently into hers showed nothing but truth. Even a frumpy mess, this man thought she was beautiful. No, no he didn't. He just wanted in her pants. Sighing, she pushed the clipboard into Geoffrey's hand and backed up. "If that's all, I need to get to school. It's my turn for bus duty." Not that he cared about that.

"I take it you're a teacher?" Frey placed the clipboard on the counter and crossed his arms over his chest. His biceps bulged. Why did the man have to be so enticing? She hoped Matt never needed her to come to this place again. The temptation was too strong. *Stop it Abbi. He isn't interested in you. Well, maybe screwing your brains out, but that's what all men want. The only thing they want.*

"Abbi?"

"What?" He had asked her a question.

"I asked if you're a teacher." He was frowning. God, was he mad at her? Oh crap!

She backed up, putting some distance between them in case he was mad. "Yes, I teach second grade at New Atlanta."

"Abbi, please." His hands were out, palms up. "I would never hurt you." He lowered his hands, his fists opening and closing. He was pissed, but not at her. Did he know? Had Matthew told him about Troy? "I am a *real* man. Real men do not harm women. Not their bodies, not their faces, and definitely not their hearts." He shook his head

27

and turned his back to her. His shoulders were moving up and down as if he was having trouble breathing.

"Geoffrey, I…"

He turned suddenly and quicker than she could imagine, he was right in front of her. He lifted her chin gently. "I promise you, I will never lay a hand on you in anger. Do you understand?"

Abbi could only nod. Geoffrey's presence, his body this close to hers, had her stomach fluttering and the juncture between her legs coming to life. She barely remembered being turned on in high school when the captain of the football team kissed her behind the bleachers after a game. Not once since then had she felt alive. Wanted. Frey's nostrils flared again, and as quickly as he'd come to stand before her, he was back a few feet away.

"I will take very good care of Matt, I promise. I hope you have a good day at school." He offered her a smile as he dismissed her. If she never saw another smile again in her life, that one right there would be enough to die happily with. How could someone so large and intimidating have the smile of an angel?

She smiled back. Truly smiled at him. She didn't have to force it the way she did with Troy. This man brought out something in her, something she hadn't known she was missing. "Thank you. You have a good day at…whatever it is you do all day." She blushed and ducked her head. As she rushed out the front door, she heard the deep laughter of a man who was happy.

Abbi arrived at the school and parked in her regular spot. Her thoughts were on Geoffrey. *I'll call you Abbi if you call me Frey.* "Frey…Frey…Geoffrey" She whispered his name out loud, testing it on her tongue. Pounding on her window caused her to jump.

Troy was standing there, hands on his hips, a scowl on his face. "Get out of the car, Abigail."

Abbi took a mental stock of her appearance. She had

28

snuck out of the house while Troy was in the shower, knowing it was the only way she could leave early. Her clothes were the normal baggy ones she dressed in for school. She had on the barest amount of makeup she could get away with. Her hair was just her hair, except Frey had pushed it behind her ear. She absentmindedly touched the spot where his fingers had lingered. "Abigail!" Troy's impatient voice reminded her where she was. Abbi grabbed her purse and briefcase before opening the door. Usually Troy didn't cause a scene in public. He wanted the good people at her school to believe he was a fine, upstanding officer of the law.

"Where the fuck did you run off to? And don't lie to me, Abigail. You know you can't lie to me. I have eyes on you." Troy was in her face, voice low so nobody could hear their conversation.

"I had to sign a permission slip for Matt." Abbi shifted her purse strap higher on her shoulder, keeping her eyes on his. She found out a long time ago looking Troy in the eyes was better than looking away. At least if she was looking at his face, she could see him getting ready to hit her.

"Next time, you tell me when you leave and where you're going. Do you understand me? Sneaking out of the house looks really suspicious."

"I didn't sneak out; I left you a note on the kitchen table." That was the truth. She knew better than to just leave. "I have to get my stuff inside and get to the bus lane. Have a good day at work." Abbi stepped away from Troy, but he grabbed her arm before she could go far. He moved his grip to the back of her bicep, pinching hard. "Owww," she hissed, trying to pull away.

"Where's my kiss, Abigail?" Troy yanked her roughly to him, slamming his mouth against hers. There was no passion, no love in the kiss, only harsh brutality. As soon as he released her, she hurried away. Other teachers were arriving, and she took advantage of their presence to ignore her husband.

Abbi spent the better part of the day thinking about Frey Hartley. Why did she have to meet him now? In the five years she had been married to Troy, not once had she thought about cheating on him. Leaving him? Definitely. But never cheating. She wasn't perfect by any means, but she took her wedding vows seriously, even if Troy didn't. Abbi knew he cheated on her, but that was on him. He had to live with his own conscience. If she were honest with herself, she was glad Troy found other women to have sex with. It kept him away from her. Even if she wanted to have an affair, there's no way she could get away with it. Troy reminded her daily of the people he had watching her.

It was better for her if she just forgot about Geoffrey Hartley. Thinking about him and the way he touched her would only bring about feelings she couldn't follow up on. She had made her bed when she married Troy. Now she was lying in it.

Troy sat in his cruiser outside the school. Abigail shuffled the children off the buses into the building. She smiled at every one of the kids, greeting them by name. Those smiles were genuine, heartfelt. Abigail never looked at him that way. He couldn't remember the last time she had looked at him with something other than fear. If she wasn't so goddamn pretty, he wouldn't have to scare her. If she wasn't so pretty, the other men wouldn't want her, but then again, neither would he. Troy was a good-looking man. He knew it. All the women told him so. All the women except one. Even in high school when they first started dating, it was like he was her second choice. Her first choice would have been that fuckhead on the football team. Troy took care

30

of him, though. Busted his pretty boy face up good. Fucker.

Troy had worried about going to different colleges, but he convinced his buddy George to keep an eye on her. Like the good girl she was, Abigail went to class, work, and back home. If it wasn't for her dipweed brother, she would more than likely have lived in a dorm just to get away from her aunt. That was the only time Troy had been grateful for Matthew. Abigail didn't move to campus because she was afraid of leaving Matthew alone with Judy. Ah, Judy. If Abigail had known the truth about her aunt, she never would have married Troy. It was a good thing his charm worked as well as it did back then.

As soon as his wife had all the kids safely inside the school, she left her post and headed in to begin her day. He really didn't know what she did in there. Didn't care. All he knew was staying in that schoolhouse for seven hours every day kept her out of trouble. Away from the prying eyes of men who might want her. There were a few men teachers, but they were either old or faggots. Yep, his Abigail was safe as long as she was in the school.

Troy walked into the precinct a few minutes late. Normally he looked forward to going to work, but now they had that new queer detective strutting around like a fucking peacock. Speaking of Jenkins, he was headed toward the chief's office. Troy knocked into his shoulder as he walked past.

"What the fuck, Quinn?" Jasper asked, but Troy kept walking, giving him a middle finger. What was the chief thinking, hiring a queer from out West? They were in the South for Christ's sake. The fairy needed to go back where he came from and keep to his own kind, and he needed to take the weirdo from the crime lab with him. What kind of professional had fucking purple hair? The kind that attracted fairies like the detective. He had taken up for the kid yesterday. Fucking faggots. Troy would just have to find a way to make him want to go back West.

31

# Chapter Five

Instead of going back to the speed bag, Frey re-taped his hand and hit the punching bag. If it wasn't so early, he would find one of the Clan to spar with. He needed to release some adrenaline. The bag he was currently attacking had been specially made for him. Too many times he or one of the Gargoyles had taken to a bag and decimated it within minutes, forgetting their strength. Frey could shred the bag if he tried, but that would draw too much attention.

What he really needed was to meditate. If he were at home, he would lose himself in the solitude of his woods or his lake and sit quietly until his mind stilled. Since he was the only one working the counter, he didn't have that luxury. So, he did the next best thing; he hit something. Mason was due any minute to watch over the gym while Frey was gone to sword training. If he were an older Gargoyle, Frey would tell him to glove up and they would enjoy a little morning sparring. At fifteen, Mason was the youngest Clan member. With his Gargoyle blood, he appeared as though he was in his twenties. In just a few years, he would reach maturity and look to be in his thirties. Frey noticed Mason looking a little older every day. He needed to speak with Rafael about that.

Speaking of the young Goyle, Mason walked right by Frey without speaking. His young cousin was definitely preoccupied. Frey punched, jabbed, and kicked the bag several more minutes. He kept watch out of the corner of his eye for Mason to come find him. When he didn't, Frey went looking for him. Mason was sitting at Frey's desk, his chin against his chest. Frey leaned against the door frame, removing the tape from his hands. When Mason still didn't look up, Frey cleared his throat. Mason raised his head and leaned back in the large, leather chair. "What's wrong?" Frey asked as he took the seat across from the desk.

"I'm not sure, to be honest with you. I've been feeling out of sorts for a while, and today's really bad. I've tried meditating, but my brain is so foggy, I just can't sit there. One minute, I feel like I'm going to lose my lunch, and the next..." Mason shook his head.

Frey finished for him, "And the next you feel like you want to annihilate the world?" Frey was pretty sure what was wrong with his cousin. He felt the exact same way, only he had felt that way for the last couple of hours, not days.

"How did you know?" Mason sat up, focused.

"Let me ask you something. Where have you been going, besides the gym?"

"Sometimes I hang out at the lab with Julian. Other than there and home, I go to Rafael's office. When he's out of town, or going to be late, I make sure Willow gets in safely. I know the building's secure, I still have to make sure she's ok, you know?"

Frey did know. It was in their Gargoyle nature to take care of the humans, especially the weaker ones. So, Willow was Mason's mate. Frey couldn't believe how many of the Clan were finding their mates so quickly. The fates must have flipped a switch all of a sudden. Rafael really needed to speak to the other Clan leaders and fill them in on the mating possibilities. "My brother, I do believe you've found your mate."

Mason opened his mouth to speak then closed it. Mason had the appearance of a man, but in truth he was still a boy. Gargoyle lives were so different than humans. When Mason was old enough, he came to live with Rafael to be trained. Several years had passed, and he was growing into a fine young Goyle. His training included fighting and patrolling, not how to handle women. Hell, Frey was almost six hundred years old and still didn't know much about the fairer sex. With Gargoyle females becoming extinct, the males had pretty much given up hope in finding mates.

33

"I don't know anything about females," Mason said as he stood and paced the room.

Frey stood and got in his space, placing his large hands on his cousin's shoulders. "Welcome to the club, Brother. I am pretty sure I found mine this morning as well, and let's just say that's one fucked up mess."

Mason glanced up at Frey's face, grinning. "Yeah?"

"Yeah. Don't look so happy about it either. If I'm miserable that means you're gonna be miserable, because I'm going to need a sparring partner."

"Oh, shit."

Frey laughed, remembering the last time they'd been in the ring together. Mason was strong since he had shifter blood, but he was no match for the older, experienced martial arts expert. "Let's get you out front. I have to head over to the armory and meet Uri." Frey was looking forward to sparring of a different sort.

By the time Frey and Uri reached Dante's estate, the rest of the Clan who were scheduled to train had arrived. Most of the Gargoyles owned large pieces of property in and around New Atlanta. Dante's was the most open, therefore, the most conducive to a training field. Every member of the Clan had access to each other's property in case of emergencies. The gates were secure with voice activated entrance.

It had been almost two centuries since the Stone Society had felt the need to train with swords. There were a few poisons in the world that could take down a full grown Gargoyle, but if you wanted to be certain one was dead, you needed to decapitate him. The females were susceptible to some of the more severe human diseases.

Rafael's father, the previous King, had been slain two hundred years earlier. The cheating bastard of a Gargoyle who took his head thought if he killed Edmondo Di Pietro, he would automatically step into the role of King. He was wrong. The throne would have gone to Rafael, even if he hadn't beheaded the one who'd slain his father. That had been the last time any of the Stone Society had needed a sword. Until now.

With the exception of the Unholy causing chaos, the Clan's lives had been fairly calm. With Gordon Flanagan missing, the Unholy were growing more chaotic every day. Frey was responsible for Flanagan being missing. He shot his helicopter out of the sky when the bastard was gunning for Tessa. His body hadn't been found. Yet.

Uri passed out the practice swords the Clan kept secure at the armory. He learned the art of swordsmithing from his father, who learned it from his. Over the years, the alloys used in the swords changed as each male learned of a better combination for lighter, more lethal weapons. The swords they were using for practice were different than the ones Uri forged personally for each Gargoyle. Julian had found a way to boil high concentrations of hellebore root so that Urijah could add it to the liquid metal. Striking another Gargoyle with their swords would slow their opponent down, giving them an added advantage.

The Goyles paired up. Like riding a bicycle, it didn't take long until the weight and movements of the swords became second nature. Urijah and Frey were sparring with each other. The loud clanging of many swords eventually eased to the sparking of only two. Fairly evenly matched, Frey and Uri entranced the others with their artistic footwork and choreographed movements. When they finally stopped, a loud ovation broke out from the other Clan members. Frey grinned, feeling alive.

Instead of taking the swords back to the armory, they stored them in Dante's garage. Frey got in his Jeep and headed back to the gym. The last few hours had taken his mind off Abbi. She had signed the consent form, so hopefully Matthew would show back up to begin his training soon. When he pulled in the lot, he parked in his reserved spot. It was late afternoon, which meant Matthew could arrive at any moment. The women's self-defense class was underway. Mason was an excellent teacher, even if his good looks often distracted the women. Frey would love to convince Abbi to join one of the classes.

Every time the door opened, Frey anticipated Matthew walking in. He really needed to get his head on straight where the boy was concerned. Even if he was the brother of Frey's mate, he didn't need to show partiality. He definitely couldn't go easy on him. At fifteen minutes after nine, the bell over the door chimed, and this time it was the kid. His face was flushed as if he'd been running.

"Am I too late?" he asked, as he attempted to catch his breath.

"Depends on the reason," Frey told him honestly. If the kid had a legitimate excuse for being so late, he would still start his training tonight.

"I couldn't get away from work. One of the other busboys called in sick, so that left only me. If I can't train, maybe I could hit the weights or something since I'm already here." Matt was shaking his hands out and dancing on the balls of his feet.

An idea popped into Frey's mind, and his mouth spit it out before he could stop himself. "Why don't you come work here?" *Dammit, you're already getting involved.*

"Really? Like, uh, what kind of work?" Matthew raised his eyebrows and stopped bouncing.

"I need help cleaning the showers, washing the towels, things like that. I will pay you whatever you're making now, and that will cut out the drive time between your job and here." Frey didn't need someone doing those chores, but it meant Matthew would have more time to train.

"I don't know what to say. Why would you do that?" The kid was skeptical, and Frey really couldn't blame him. They'd met once.

"Say yes or no; it's up to you. The why is because I

36

like you and want you to succeed. No hidden agendas." *And because hopefully one day, you and I will be family.*

"Yes. Okay, yes! Thank you. I will need to give notice, but after that I'm all yours." The kid was back to bouncing.

Frey laughed at his eagerness. "Then come on. I'll show you to the locker room and you can change. We won't train this late, but we can hit the bags." Frey showed him where to get changed and to stow his backpack. Frey taped their hands before going through a series of stretches. Taking Matt to the speed bag, he showed him the proper technique. It usually took newbies a while to get the hang of the small bag, but Matthew caught on quickly. The teen was a little taller than average but fairly skinny. He would need to change his eating habits, adding in quite a few more calories if he planned on putting on any muscle.

Next, Frey handed Matt a jump rope as he took one for himself. They had only been jumping for a few minutes when he heard his cell phone ring. It was Rafael's ringtone. "Keep jumping, I'll be right back," he told the kid and retrieved his phone. "Yo, Rafe, what's up?"

"I hope I didn't catch you at a bad time. I wanted to find out how training went."

"I'm working out a new client right now, but I have a few minutes. Training went well. Everyone found their groove fairly quickly. Uri was magnificent, as always."

"Well, he should be. For someone as talented as he in making the swords, he should be able to wield one better than the rest of us." Rafael's admiration for their cousin was evident in his voice.

"Truth, Brother. How is Maria? Any word from Dante or Gregor?" Frey hated being out of the loop where his family was concerned.

"We came close to losing Maria. She flatlined, but the nurses brought her back. I had a meeting with Jonas, and let's just say he's on board with whatever we need from him. There's a long story regarding him and Maria, but the short of it is Maria is an old family friend. She's aware of the Gargoyles, and she knows exactly who Jonas is. He is pulling strings and taking over her care. As soon as she's able to be moved, he's bringing her to New Atlanta.

"Jonas has also reached out to Athena for assistance. Since Isabelle was taken to Poros, we believe Alistair is behind the kidnapping. Nobody knows his holdings better than my mother. She has promised to help as much as she can. As for Dante, I spoke to him earlier. They know where Isabelle is, so they plan on rescuing her first. It seems he and Isabelle's son have some sort of mental connection. Hopefully that will allow them to find him quickly and bring everyone home soon."

"Let's hope so. Listen, I still need to talk to Kaya, but that can wait until tomorrow. I'll stop by the station to see her. Hang on a second." Frey covered the phone and told Matthew, "Take a break." He returned to Rafe, "I need to go. Don't want to have my client pass out on the first day. I'll talk to you soon. Be well, my King."

"And you, Cousin."

Matthew was sipping water. "Sorry about that, family stuff," Frey said. Even though Matthew was a teen, he didn't want him to feel as if he weren't important.

"Believe me. I understand about family stuff," Matthew muttered as he tossed the paper cup in the trash.

That, Frey absolutely did believe. Now, he needed to gain the teen's trust and learn all he could about Abbi.

# Chapter Six

Abbi was slow getting out of bed. She'd long given up in convincing Troy it wasn't how many times you had sex but when that determined getting pregnant. She was on bus duty again this morning, so she couldn't be late. However, after school she was going to the pharmacy to buy an ovulation kit. Somehow, she was going to avoid having sex during that time. If that didn't work, she would find a way to go back to her doctor and get one of the shots that lasted six months. Even if Troy found out, there wouldn't be anything he could do to her at that point. Nothing worse than he already did.

"Where are my black socks?" Troy had already showered and was getting ready for work.

"They should be in your drawer." Abbi thought about the laundry she had been folding the night before when Troy grabbed her by the wrist and dragged her into the living room. Being pushed over the back of the sofa and screwed was so much more exciting in the romance novels. Having someone like Troy do it was anything but exciting. It was usually downright painful. "Now that I think about it, they are still in the laundry room. I was folding clothes last night when you decided you wanted to have sex."

"Well, fucking go get them. I don't have all day," Troy demanded. Instead of him getting a pair as he headed to the kitchen, he would wait for her to go get them and bring them back. A long time ago, Abbi had tried growing a backbone. It only took one instance of telling him to do something himself for her to learn it was easier and less painful to do what he said. As quickly as her sore body would move, she retrieved his socks as well as the other clothes she had already folded. When she handed them to him, he grabbed her hand, hauling her harshly to his body. The basket of clothing slipped out of her arm, landing in a

39

messy pile on the floor. "Now look what you did. Can't you do anything right?"

As soon as he let go, Abbi picked up the clothes and shoved them in the basket. She was too tired to refold them and put them away. She would do that when she got home. Luckily, Troy didn't try anything else. He didn't bother saying goodbye, just walked out the door, leaving her to her thoughts. That was dangerous, because her thoughts automatically latched on to the gorgeous man at the gym. Abbi knew it wasn't healthy to dream about someone she couldn't have, but damn if he hadn't gotten under her skin.

When she was looking over the form Matthew had filled out, she noticed all the different classes offered at the gym. Matthew had checked the box for men's self-defense. Right below that was a women's self-defense class. Abbi thought briefly about signing up for the class, but right now she didn't have time. Even if she did, there was no way Troy would let her take a class like that. It would probably just give her a false sense of security anyway. She knew she was no match for someone Troy's size.

Abbi showered, letting the hot water ease the tension in her shoulders. She mindlessly dried off and dressed as she did every morning. While she was choosing her clothes, she wondered what Frey thought about the way she dressed. He called her beautiful, but there's no way he could really think so. He was one of the most stunning men she'd ever seen in her life, in person or on television. Geoffrey Hartley could have any woman he wanted. Maybe that was his deal- he seduced every woman he came across with his beautiful smile, his ripped body. Abbi didn't know the human body had that many muscles in it. Troy was fit, but he couldn't hold a candle to the gym owner.

As she was pouring coffee into a travel mug, Matt bounded down the hall. If he ever heard the noises coming from her bedroom while she and Troy were having sex, he never let on. The times Abbi had looked in on her brother, he'd been wearing headphones. Abbi wasn't loud during sex, quite the opposite. She didn't say a word, didn't make any noises unless Troy got so rough she couldn't help but yelp.

"Good morning, you look chipper," she said, handing the mug of coffee to her brother. He didn't need the caffeine, but he'd been drinking the stuff since he was six. Granted, back then it was mostly milk, but they both loved their joe.

"Guess what?" Matt asked as he grabbed the bread to make toast.

Abbi hadn't seen her brother this animated in a long time. His demeanor was different this morning. "You've met a girl."

"Ew, no. Mr. Hartley offered me a job." Matt drummed his hands on the counter as he waited on the toaster to pop up.

"You have a job. How are you going to work two jobs and go to school?" Abbi was afraid he was getting in over his head.

"Not two jobs, I'll quit the diner and only work at the gym. That way I'll already be there when it's time to work out. I can't believe how nice he is. He reminds me a lot of dad."

Abbi sucked in a breath. They never spoke of their parents. The memories were too painful for Abbi. She shouldn't have been so selfish, though. Matty had been young when they died, but he wasn't too young not to remember. Blinking back the tears, she asked, "Yeah? In what way?" Knowing she was going to be rushing to get to the school on time, she still wanted to give her brother this opportunity to talk about their dad.

"He's just so gentle, but in a stern way. It's hard to explain, really. He is smart and tough, but he doesn't bully or yell to get his point across. I watched him interact with the other people last night, and he was genuinely interested

41

in what every one of them had to say. He knows everyone by name, asks about their kids, their jobs. He's just... nice." Matt spread butter on the toast and took a big bite.

"I'm glad you like him. Honestly, I was worried when I met him. He's just so big. All those muscles, he could really hurt you. But he promised me he'd take care of you." Abbi felt one hundred percent better about Matt working out with Frey. If Matt thought he was nice, maybe he really was.

"I need to get to school. I have bus duty." Abbi grabbed her own to-go cup of coffee. "Matty, if you ever want to talk about them, it's okay. Okay?"

A sad smile crossed her brother's face. "Yeah, okay."

She ruffled his already messy brown hair as she walked by. "I love you."

"Love you, too." Matt turned away, but she didn't miss the tears in his eyes before he did.

As soon as Mason arrived at the gym, Frey left to go see Kaya. He wanted to talk to her before he headed over to Dante's for sword training. The last time Frey had been to the precinct was when they set up the ruse to get Tamian St. Claire arrested so he could go undercover in the Pen. Tessa's cloned brother had all but disappeared once his sister recovered from her horrific car crash.

Frey knew where Kaya's office was, but he couldn't just barge in there and start talking to his Queen. He had to pretend he was there as a citizen. He entered the building behind a cop. The jerk didn't bother holding the door open even though Frey was right behind him. He did stop to talk to the dispatcher, leaning his ass against her desk. "Good morning, Kim. You're looking as pretty as ever."

Kim, not missing a beat, told the cop, "Not gonna

happen, Troy." Noticing Frey, her scowl turned into a seductive smile. "Good morning, sir. How may I help you?"

The cop stood and turned toward Frey. His shitty demeanor at being rejected quickly fell from his face as he got a good look at Frey. Troy wasn't a small man, but Frey was intimidating, even when he wasn't trying to be. Frey ignored the cop and told the dispatcher, "Good morning. I'm here to see Chief Kane."

With her smile glued to her face, Kim asked, "May I tell her your name?"

"Frey," he said, noticing the cop hadn't moved. Frey took the time to study the man. He looked like most other cops with the pressed uniform and the short haircut. This *Troy* was fit, evident when he crossed his arms over his chest. A gold wedding band was on his left hand. So, the douche was married and hitting on the dispatcher.

"Fray, that's an unusual name." Kim obviously didn't like having his attention on the other man and not her.

"Frey is short for Geoffrey. Now, if you would please, tell the chief I'm here."

"Do you have an appointment?" Troy asked. He obviously didn't feel the need to get to work.

"I don't need one," Frey said, crossing his arms over his chest, mimicking the cop's stance. Kim sucked in a breath, and Troy scowled.

"Frey, what are you doing here?" Jasper asked from behind. Thank the gods for a friendly face. He turned and was pulled into a quick embrace with a slap to the back. Frey didn't miss the bigoted remark that rolled off Troy's tongue.

"I need to talk to the chief, but I can't seem to get any service around here," Frey poked at the two people staring with their mouths open. Kim finally picked up the phone to call Kaya, and Troy stormed off.

"Come on. I'll take you to her," Jasper said, not

43

caring that Kim was following protocol. They reached Kaya's office just as she was hanging up her phone. Not bothering to stand, she motioned them both into the small room.

"Rafael said you wanted to talk to me. What can I do for you?" Kaya asked, her face glowing. Something was up, because she looked like she had hit the lottery.

"I'll leave you two alone." Jasper turned to go, but Frey stopped him.

"No, Jas, this involves you, too." As soon as the newest member of their clan was fully in the room, Frey closed the door. "I have a problem, and it involves one of your officers."

Kaya leaned forward and asked, "Which one, and what kind of problem?"

"I had a kid come into the gym; his face was all bruised up. Said his brother-in-law did it. When I asked why his sister hadn't gone to the cops, the kid said the man is a cop. I haven't been able to spend much time with him yet, but I did meet the sister. She had no visible signs of physical abuse, but her demeanor was that of an abused woman. She's beautiful, yet she wears baggy clothes and little makeup. She's very skittish. When she thought I was mad at her, she backed up like I was going to hit her. The kid didn't come out and say the cop's abusing his sister, but he stated he wants to train so he can protect her. He's a wiry seventeen year old who can't even protect himself, yet he's worried about her. I wanted to ask you if you've had any complaints filed against him."

"What's his name?" Kaya asked, frowning.

"I don't know his first name, but his last name's Quinn."

"Motherfucker," Jasper swore. "You've already met him, standing out front."

"*That's* Abbi's husband?" Frey asked incredulously. "Of course he is. The bastard was hitting on the dispatcher

44

when I walked in. She wasn't taking the bait, but he was still trying."

Kaya let out a loud sigh and leaned back in her chair. "I had trouble with him when I first made Chief. He didn't like taking orders from a skirt. He's always been a hothead. I had a couple of complaints filed against him, but before I could do anything about it, the complaints were withdrawn. What do you want me to do? I can't take any action without the brother or the wife pressing charges."

"As far as Quinn goes, I'd like you to put him on second shift. I know that's asking a lot, but if he's on second, that's less time he has to spend at home with Abbi. Also, I was hoping Dane or Jasper could come down to the gym and talk to Matthew. If we can get him to file a complaint, maybe we can get the sister to see reason."

"Does she want away from Quinn? I mean, a lot of women refuse to leave even if they are abused. I've witnessed too many domestic violence cases over the years. I can't understand staying with someone who would intentionally hurt you."

"I don't know. I would hope so. But that's not the worst of it."

"How could it get any worse?" Jasper asked.

Frey sighed and told them, "She's my mate."

# Chapter Seven

Frey couldn't believe the douchebag Troy was Abbi's husband. It took all of his control not to walk out of Kaya's office, find the asswipe, and pummel him until he looked worse than Matthew did. If he did that, Abbi would probably be more scared of Frey than she was her husband. He had to be smart and hope that Matthew would press charges, or at least give them ammunition to go after Troy. Frey would not stop until Abbi was free from her abuser.

Training went by quickly. For a few hours, Frey had been able to think about something other than his beautiful mate and her predicament. Now, he was back at the gym, waiting on Matthew to show up. He had the day off from his diner job, so he was supposed to come in right after school. With that thought, the bell rang as the front door opened. Matthew was keyed up as usual. Frey was looking forward to teaching the teen meditation, showing him how to subdue his energy.

"Hello, Matthew. How was school?" After a lengthy chat the night before, Frey knew Matthew's favorite subject as well as what he disliked. Matt spoke freely about school and about Abbi being a teacher, but became closed off when Frey asked about his past. Matthew mentioned his parents' deaths, but he refused to talk about anything that came after it. Ten years ago, the teen's life irrevocably changed. Now, it didn't seem to be getting any better. Had he been abused for ten years? After they parted ways the night before, Frey had gone home and fired up his computer. Rarely did he do any of his own research; that he left to Julian. When it came to Abbi and Matt, he didn't want to get his brother involved if he could keep from it.

Frey found newspaper articles regarding the wreck. Abbi had been seventeen, a senior at New Atlanta High School, and a promising ballet dancer with a bright future ahead of her. Matthew had been seven. What the article didn't provide was what happened to them afterwards. When he couldn't find the information he sought on his own, Frey called on Julian to do his thing. He wanted any and all information his brother could find on Abigail Swanson Quinn.

"Same as most days, only now we're cracking down for the SAT's." Matthew was worried about his math score.

"If you need help, my brother is really good in math. He'd be glad to tutor you, if you want," Frey offered up Julian's assistance without asking. Julian loved teaching, loved sharing his knowledge, even if it was high school level subjects.

Matthew frowned and stopped moving. He cocked his head to one side, studying Frey. "Why would he do that? He doesn't even know me."

"He knows who you are, and he would do it because I asked him to."

"You told your brother about me?"

"I did. You're a good kid, and I'm looking forward to getting to know you." Frey didn't miss Matthew bristle at the term kid. "You are an interesting young man, and I am honored to be your teacher. Now, before we get started today, I wanted to talk to you about Troy." The bell rang, and a familiar looking face walked in.

"What about Troy?" Matthew seethed, fisting his hands.

"I need to assist this client, but I have someone coming in to talk to you. Please go wait in my office." Frey would not talk about personal business in front of patrons. Matthew turned and looked at the man behind him before walking off to the office as instructed.

"Can I help you?" Frey asked the young man he was sure he'd met before.

"I'd like to work out," he answered as he shuffled from one foot to the other. Where Matthew did this from too

47

much energy, this young man did it from nervousness.

Frey attempted to put the man at ease with a smile. "My name's Geoffrey Hartley, I own the place. You are?"

"Trevor. Trevor McKenzie," he said, politely holding out his hand.

Frey carefully shook the offered hand, firmly but not too hard to be painful. "You look familiar, Trevor. Have I seen you around here before?"

"I don't think so. I work and go home. That's it," Trevor replied as he looked down at his feet.

"Come on, let me show you around. So, what kind of work do you do?" Frey asked him as they walked, certain he had seen the guy somewhere.

"I'm the M.E.'s assistant over at the hospital."

"That's right, you work for Dante. I thought I recognized you." Dante had spoken of his assistant, and how the young man was somewhat of a loner. Frey attempted to lighten the mood by asking, "So, what are you looking for in a workout? You want to build muscle? Bulk up? Get ready for bikini season?"

Trevor's mouth gaped open, obviously not expecting someone of Frey's stature to crack jokes. "I, uh, just want to get in shape, maybe build a little more muscle."

Frey couldn't help but laugh at the look on Trevor's face. Still smiling, he noticed Jasper had arrived. He told him, "Hey, Brother. I'll be with you in a minute."

Frey didn't miss the way Trevor's body stiffened. The young man looked behind him at Jasper. It was obvious they knew each other when Jasper quietly said, "Hi, Trevor."

Frey didn't need Dante's special abilities to know something was going on between these two. Giving them the opportunity for some privacy, Frey said, "Jas, I need to take care of something really quick. Can you show Trevor around until I get back?"

They both looked at Frey like he was throwing them

to the wolves. "If it's okay with Trevor, sure." Jasper told Frey but kept his eyes on Trevor.

"Yeah, it's fine." Trevor's cheeks were pink. If Frey didn't know better, the young man was embarrassed.

Regardless of what was going on between those two, Frey needed to talk to Matthew and let him know exactly why Jasper was there. He found the teen in his office, pacing the floor. "I'm sorry about that. Now, please take a seat." Matthew sat down in the chair across from the desk, his knee bouncing up and down. "Matthew, I want to help you. I have a cousin who is a police detective. One of the good guys. He works with Troy, so he already knows what kind of man he is. What I need you to do is tell Jasper your side of the story. If you want to file charges against him, we'll help you do that. It would be best if Abbi would file charges as well, but I have a feeling that's a long shot, am I right?"

"Yeah. I've been trying to get her to leave his ass, but she says it's impossible since he's a cop. Is she right?" Matthew's face was hopeful. He was looking to Frey to be a savior to him and his sister.

"It is possible, but only if Abbi takes the first step. We can't do that for her. You are a different matter. I don't want to get Abbi in trouble, but as your legal guardian, she is neglecting you by allowing Quinn to physically abuse you. Matt, I have a lot of contacts in this city, and I am willing to go to bat for you, at least until we can get Abbi away from Troy, too."

Matthew stood, pacing the room again. "Why? I know I already asked you this, but why me? I'm just a kid you don't know."

Frey leaned back in his chair and crossed his arms over his chest. He couldn't tell the kid the truth about his sister. "I already told you, I like you. Besides, I can't stand men like Troy Quinn who abuse women and those younger or weaker than they are. Bastards like that only do it because they are on a power trip. Sure, I could tote him an ass-whoopin', but that wouldn't do you or your sister any good. If we are going to get Quinn out of your lives, we have to do it the right way. That begins with you telling us everything you know about him."

"I'll do it. I can handle the bruises, but I'm doing this for Abbi. She's been through too much already."

Frey knew determination when he saw it. The kid had it in spades. "Good, let's go find Jasper, and he'll write down everything you tell him.

Jasper had agreed to talk to the kid that afternoon. Even if they didn't convince him to press charges, they could get more information on Quinn and begin monitoring him closely. The cop was a bigoted redneck. Frey was going to call Julian and have him check the hospital records for any visits Abbi might have made. If there was documented physical abuse, it would be easier to convince her to at least press charges. If she truly was Frey's mate, they needed to get her away from her abusive husband, one way or another. For reasons Jasper didn't understand, the fates chose Abbi as Frey's mate. Whether her being married was a test of sorts, he didn't know. Was he being tested as well?

He had put on a smile around the others, but Jasper's heart was hurting. The look on Trevor's face before he ran out of the morgue haunted Jasper's thoughts. Why couldn't he have kept his hands to himself? Because the mate pull was too strong. Because Trevor was irresistible in his own right. He was smart, and funny, and so very sexy in a geeky sort of way. Just the way Jasper liked his men. Well, most of the time. Craig had been anything but geeky, but he worked really hard to impress Jasper away from the firehouse. He'd stayed after him until Jasper relented. Craig wouldn't come out of the closet around others, saying as firemen their jobs would be on the line.

Julian believed Craig had hacked into Jasper's computer and messed with his employment records. Considering the firewalls Julian had in place, it seemed like a longshot his ex was responsible. The digital trail led back to Jasper's computer, and Craig was the only one with access to it other than Jasper. He hadn't realized Craig was smart enough to hack a system, and even if he was, why would he do that? What did he have to gain by changing the files? Now Craig was missing, throwing up more red flags.

Jasper didn't know what to do about Trevor. How much time should he give him before he apologized? Would Trevor even talk to him? If they never mated, Jasper still wanted Trevor as a friend, no matter how hard it would be to keep his hands off the man. He would worry about that later. Right now he needed to help Frey.

He walked into the gym and immediately felt the pull. Trevor was there. It didn't take him long to find his mate. Frey was laughing at something Trevor had said. He walked up behind Trevor and cleared his throat. Frey eyed him curiously, but Jasper's attention was on Trevor, who tensed up. Was he aware it was Jasper behind him? Was he feeling the effects of the bond?

When he turned around, Jasper whispered, "Hi, Trevor." He didn't know if Trevor would run again, but before he did, Jasper would at least apologize.

"Hi," Trevor responded just as shyly. "I was thinking about joining the gym."

Frey gave some excuse for leaving them alone and disappeared into the back of the building. Jasper hurried and said, "Trevor, I'm sorry. You know, about yesterday."

Trevor, who was giving Jasper's body a good once over, said, "You have nothing to be sorry for. I get it."

"You do?" Jasper wasn't sure he got it himself. And the way Trevor was looking at him, like he wanted to sample the goods, had Jasper more confused than before.

51

Maybe Trevor *was* gay.

"Yep. Just forget it. Do you want to show me around before the big guy gets back?"

Jasper cocked his head to the side, studying Trevor. Maybe he was gay, but Jasper wasn't his type. He was at a loss for how to proceed, so he did what Frey asked him to do. "I didn't know you were interested in working out. Let's start over here."

Jasper showed him machines as well as explained all the classes Frey offered. He ended his tour in the changing room. "So, are we okay?" Jasper asked him when they were alone. He shoved his hands in his pockets so he wouldn't make the mistake of touching Trevor again.

"I guess. I just..." Trevor didn't get a chance to finish his statement. Frey and Matthew came in the room.

Frey said, "There you are. So, Trevor, what do you think?"

Without looking at Jasper, Trevor said, "I would like to take advantage of the trial offer, see how it works into my schedule and all that."

"Sounds good. Jasper, would you please take Matt here into the office. I'll get Trevor signed up and then I'll be right in."

Jasper was frustrated. He really wanted to continue his conversation with Trevor, but he was there for a reason other than his own personal feelings. "Of course. Trevor, maybe we could work out together?" He wanted his mate to know that he was still interested in being around him.

"If you promise not to make fun of my non-badass form," Trevor said, seriously.

Jasper laughed, but his heart also broke a little. He was going to spend the rest of his life making sure Trevor knew just how special he was, mate bond or not.

"I promise," Jasper said with a smile, one he hoped Trevor took to heart.

# Chapter Eight

Even though it wasn't class night, Abbi wanted to go to the community center and work on the fall festival. In her weekly dance classes, she taught simple routines choreographed for young children. *The Nutcracker* involved more elaborate dances, but Abbi would be able to simplify them for her younger group. She could do it at home, but it would be easier in her dance room. Still, she didn't want to take a chance on being caught by Troy. Not again.

Abbi stopped at the grocery store on her way home and bought a couple of rotisserie chickens from the deli. That was something she didn't have to cook, and Troy liked them. She could throw some vegetables on the stove while she worked on the festival, putting her ideas to paper. She wasn't in charge of the decorations, but the committee had asked for her input since she knew the theme better than anyone.

Normally, Troy was home at five on the dot unless he was working out or went out drinking with his partner. It was now half past six, and Abbi knew it was going to be one of those nights. One where he would either be full of testosterone from hitting the gym, or full of alcohol from hitting the bar. Neither scenarios bode well for her. When she heard his car door slam half an hour later, she braced herself for whichever Troy walked through the door. She didn't have to wait long to know it was a whiskey night. Still in his uniform, Troy was livid.

"Fucking cunt put me on second shift. It's the queer detective's fault; I just know it!" Troy yelled as he paced the kitchen. Abbi didn't dare move, didn't say a word. Troy went to the cabinet where he kept his alcohol and grabbed a bottle of whiskey. Abbi didn't drink the stuff, so she didn't know which *man* he chose. Jack, Jim, Johnny… they were all the same to her. "And that Neanderthal? What the fuck was

he on about? I bet he was there to play back up to the fag."
Troy didn't bother with a glass. He took a swig directly out
of the bottle. Turning to Abbi, he pointed at her, bottle in
hand. "Are you even fucking listening to me? I'm going on
fucking second shift. Tomorrow. Bitch didn't give me a
good reason. Just said something about personnel changes
and what's best for the department."

Abbi sat silently at the table. She continued to sit
with the pencil in her hand, scared to move even to lay it
down. Troy paced the kitchen, stopping only to take a drink
from his bottle before grabbing Abbi's bicep with his free
hand. He squeezed her arm to make his point, "This does
not mean you get free rein, you hear me? I will have people
watching you. You are to come straight home. Do not pass
go. Do not collect two hundred dollars. Am I clear on that,
Abigail?"

"Yes, Troy. You're clear." Abbi said nothing else,
because anything else might set him off. As of now he was a
slow smoldering fuse with the fuse several feet long. If she
said the wrong thing, that fuse could be cut short and blow
with her in the line of fire. She wasn't in the mood for
shrapnel.

"Yeah, we're clear. I'm going to bed. Since I don't
have to go to work in the morning, you better be quiet when
you get up and not wake me. You got it?" Troy asked with
the almost empty bottle hanging by his side.

"I got it," Abbi said softly. He gave her arm another
bruising squeeze before he retreated to their bedroom,
slamming the door. Abbi let out her breath, thankful she
had dodged that load of dynamite. She stood from the table
to fix herself a plate of food. Now that Troy was home, she
was allowed to eat. The backdoor opened, and Matt walked
in, or rather bounced in. He didn't say a word until Abbi
gave him the all clear, pointing down the hall. She
mimicked drinking, their code that Troy was drunk.

Matt made his way to the stove to see what was for

54

supper. "Are you hungry?" she asked him, knowing it was a dumb question. Her brother was always hungry.

"Yep," he said as he removed a plate from the cabinet. When he didn't carry on about his day, Abbi grew suspicious. As hyper as he was, he was also as talkative when it was just the two of them.

"Okay, spill. What's up with you?" She crossed her arms over her chest and leaned against the counter.

"Geoffrey's going to teach me meditation. I think it's a crazy idea, but he says it will help channel some of my energy. His brother, some genius, is going to tutor me in math for the SAT's." Matt quieted, and looked down the hall. When he was assured the door to her bedroom was closed, he came back. "Abbi, one of Geoffrey's cousins works on the police force."

Abbi grabbed his arm, moving him farther away from the hall into the laundry room. She didn't shut the door in case Troy came back. "Matty, what did you do? Please tell me you didn't talk to another cop about Troy!" she begged. If word got out Troy was abusing them, he would be ruined. There would be repercussions. Crap! Repercussions like being put on second shift. "Oh my god, you did, didn't you?"

"Abbi, he's not just a cop. He's a detective. He said he can help us. Help you get away from Troy," Matt grabbed her wrists as he whispered. "Let them help you, please Abs. Please!"

Abbi peeked out the laundry room door, listening for any sign of her husband. If he found out she was even considering leaving, his ire would be the likes of which they'd never seen. "Matt, what exactly did you tell the detective?"

"The truth, Abs. All of it. From the time mom and dad were killed up until now," her brother said, unapologetically.

Abbi couldn't stop the tears from rolling down her

55

cheeks. Her precious brother never spoke of their parents, their past, but now he'd laid it all out to a stranger just to protect her. She pulled him into a back-breaking hug. What if they could help her? What if there was a way to finally be free from her prison? Abbi wouldn't let herself get her hopes up. Not yet. Hope was the enemy.

Wiping the tears from her face, she said, "Come on, let's eat." Abbi didn't agree to anything. She couldn't let her brother put any thoughts into her head that may or may not pan out. She heated up both their plates and placed them on the table. She pushed her paper and pencil aside.

"What are you working on?" Matt asked, truly interested in what his sister was involved in. He really was a good kid.

"The fall festival. The committee chose *The Nutcracker* as the theme, and they put me in charge."

"Abs! That's… Are you going to dance? You should totally dance." Matthew's eyes lit up with excitement. When he was little, he would watch Abbi practice. Sometimes he would mimic her moves, spinning and twirling. Once, she even caught him in her toe shoes. That memory of a tiny little boy trying to walk in her ballet shoes, flopping like he had duck feet brought a laugh from her throat. Surprised, she glanced at her brother whose mouth was open. God, had it been that long since he'd heard her laugh?

Just as quickly as the happy memory formed, a bolt of sadness pierced her heart. "You know I don't dance anymore."

"Well, you should. You were the best dancer ever, and you should really think about doing it again. If we could…"

"Hush. Just hush, Matty." Abbi stood and dumped her uneaten food in the garbage. She quickly put the leftovers in plastic containers and shoved the pans in the dishwasher. "I'm going to turn in. Oh, I almost forgot. Troy is going to second shift starting tomorrow, so please be as quiet as possible in the morning."

Abbi didn't miss the grin that quirked the side of his mouth. "I'll be quiet. Love you, Abs." Matt stood and kissed her on the cheek before heading to his own bedroom. He grinned. He flipping grinned. Matt knew about Troy going to second shift. Thinking back to Troy's words, *the detective and the Neanderthal,* it was starting to make sense. Geoffrey Hartley. He knew about Troy, and he had called in his cousin. Abbi didn't know what to make of that. Could there really be a way? Could Frey and his detective cousin help her? And what about his brother tutoring Matty? Why was this man getting so involved in their lives?

Abbi got ready for bed in the hall bathroom. When she entered her bedroom, Troy was snoring loudly, something he did when he was drunk. Still, as quietly as possible, Abbi eased onto her side of the bed. Once she was under the covers, she didn't dare move. Abbi lay still, staring at the ceiling, allowing her mind to drift to the gym owner. Was he responsible for Troy going to second shift? Closing her eyes, a scene played out somewhere in the recesses of her mind. Abbi was dressed in her ballet tights-stretching, jumping, and pirouetting. She ran across the wooden floor, leaping, landing in the arms of Geoffrey Hartley.

When Abbi woke the next morning, Troy's side of the bed was empty. Abbi listened for any sign of her husband in another part of the house. When she heard nothing, she got out of bed and headed for the shower. Normally she would grab a cup of coffee and take it into the bathroom with her. She didn't want to chance running into Troy, so she skipped that part of her routine.

With the shower running, Abbi didn't hear the bathroom door open. Her hair was full of shampoo suds, her hands massaging her scalp, her eyes closed. Cold air skimmed across her back, and she knew. She knew Troy was going to take her right there in the shower. She leaned her head under the spray of water to rinse the shampoo out, but Troy had other ideas. Not giving her a chance to rinse the foam from her face, Troy spun her so her front was against the cool tiles of the shower.

"Troy, please let me rinse my eyes. I can't see," she begged.

"Shut up. You don't need to see. Spread your fucking legs." He kicked her ankle with his foot. She nearly lost her balance when her foot slid too far on the slippery surface. Troy grabbed her hips and jerked her butt back towards him. With no warning, he forcefully pushed his way inside. Abbi was thankful for the lather falling down her back. It substituted as the only lube she would get. Troy shoved his forearm against her shoulder blades, keeping her locked in place as he pistoned in and out of her body. Abbi kept her eyes and mouth shut so the shampoo wouldn't get into either. Her tears seeped out the corners of her eyes, but Troy wouldn't see those. He was too focused on the task at hand to ever look at her face. With a final grunt, he spilled his seed into her body. Mission accomplished. He pulled out and slid under the water, rinsing himself.

Troy stepped out of the tub, and only then did she move. Abbi placed her body under the water, reaching back to turn the heat up as hot as she could stand it. She allowed the tears to flow freely, mixing with the shampoo. When the water turned cold, Abbi got out of the shower. There was nowhere she could go to escape the monster she was married to. She wrapped a towel around her body, not bothering to look in the mirror. She knew she'd see the bruises, and they were just another reminder of what her life had become. *You should totally dance.* Matty's words came back to her, shredding her heart a little more. *You know I don't dance anymore.* Teaching ballet to kids was a balm to her soul, but it couldn't make up for the day her dream was shattered. No, Abigail Swanson was gone, and Abbi Quinn stood in her place. She didn't dance anymore.

# Chapter Nine

Frey tossed and turned all night with Matthew's words floating through his brain. When he finally gave up on sleep, he walked out the back door and down the path leading to the water. As he made his way through the trees, Frey allowed the silence and stillness of the early morning to ease his thoughts. When he reached the end of the pathway, he continued down the dock that jutted out over his five acre lake. Frey sat on the end of the wooden platform, his long legs dangling in the water. He leaned back on his hands and closed his eyes. Meditating would be the best thing for him, but right now, he wanted to think about Abbi Quinn.

Ever since meeting her, he had been consumed with all things Abbi. It was Julian's day to train with the sword. When they were finished, he was going to share with Frey what he called "highly sensitive" information he'd unearthed. Frey didn't like the sound of that. He hadn't liked the sound of anything Matthew told him the night before, either. Matthew shared bits and pieces of Abbi's life as he remembered it from a kid brother's perspective. Frey had to work hard not to become frustrated with the teen when he would skip years of her life. Frey knew digging information out of Matthew was betraying Abbi's trust, but he needed to know what he was up against.

The fates weren't making it easy on the Gargoyles when it came to their mates. Frey learned many centuries ago nothing in life worth having comes easy. He had to be careful with Abbi. Protecting her and watching over her from a distance was one thing. Interfering in her life and convincing her to get a divorce from her abusive husband was another. Even if they weren't mates, Frey would not want to see the beautiful woman abused. He might not be so involved in the outcome, but that was neither here nor there.

The image Frey couldn't get out of his mind was one of Abbi dancing. What he wouldn't give to see the beautiful blonde twisting and turning across a wooden floor. Matthew laughed when he shared how he used to try to wear his sister's pointed dance shoes. He would walk around the house on his tip toes so he could dance like his big sister. Frey hadn't missed the love in the kid's voice as he spoke of their bond or the sadness when he briefly mentioned their parents' deaths. Frey took in all the information, and as soon as Matthew left the gym, Frey had called Julian. He wanted everything there was on Abbi, her aunt Judy, and her dickhead husband.

A turtle not far from the dock walked into the lake and began making his way through the calm waters. Even though the slow animal was causing ripples in its wake, it was not upsetting the peacefulness of the morning. In that moment, Frey knew he was the turtle, and he had to take his next steps with Abbi just as slow as the turtle so as not to upset the peace that could be their relationship.

Training went well with all the Goyles pretty evenly matched, with the exception of Urijah. He continued to hold back unless he was sparring with Rafael. If Frey and Uri had put on a show, the King and their cousin were truly a sight to behold. When training was over, Rafael gave the others the good news that Dante had rescued both Isabelle and Connor. He and his mate had completed the bond. Finally, some good news they could celebrate.

Once the others had driven off, Julian and Frey made their way into Dante's office to access his computer. Frey didn't want to wait any longer than necessary to see the information on his own mate. Julian fired up Dante's laptop. While it was booting up, he said, "I am going to leave you alone to read over the files. I won't leave the property in case you have questions or want to hit someone, but I am going to let you read these alone."

Frey clenched his fists. "That bad?"

"Worse." Julian clicked the mouse and stood from Dante's leather chair.

"Yell if you need me. I'll be outside in the swimming pool."

The first file Frey opened was one his brother had named "hospital visits". Frey reached deep within himself for a calm he knew he would need.

Jasper entered the precinct a few hours later than normal having spent the first part of the morning sword training. If he were a human, his body would be aching. Frey was a relentless teacher, not allowing the Goyles to take breaks other than to work on technique. Jasper couldn't remember the last time he'd held a sword, much less wielded one. Dane had only seen a sword once, and that had been at a Renaissance Fair as a child. That one had been a replica. The half-blood didn't complain, though. He took his training as seriously as the full-bloods and quickly adapted to the weapon. Speaking of his soon to be chief, Dane came through the door right behind him. Kaya had sent in the paperwork for her resignation and Dane's promotion, but she had yet to announce either until they were approved.

As Jasper reached his desk, his landline was ringing. "Jenkins," he answered, pulling out his notepad and pencil, expecting it to be a case. When no one said anything, he spoke again, "Jenkins, hello?" He received no response, so he hung up. On his blotter was a manila envelope. It had his name written on the outside, but there was nothing else indicating who it was from. He was staring at it when Dane approached the empty chair beside the desk. "What's wrong?" his partner asked as he sat down.

Jasper pointed to the envelope without touching it. "That's wrong," he said. Remembering Rafael's recent episode with an unmarked package, Jasper was leery to reveal the contents. "After what Rafe received, I'm afraid of what could be inside." Removing a pair of latex gloves from a desk drawer, he slid them on and carefully sliced open one end of the envelope. Dane sat up in his seat, also curious. Jasper slid the edges apart and peered inside. "Photos," he murmured, turning the package on its end, the pictures sliding out onto his desk. The first one didn't make sense. Using his gloved finger, he slid the top one over revealing the next one in the pile. Jasper continued pushing photo after photo aside until he reached the end.

Dane had stood and was looking over Jasper's shoulder. "Do you know who that is?"

Jasper nodded. "Yes, that's Craig."

"Your ex, Craig?" Dane asked quietly. Jasper didn't hide the fact he was gay, but there were still those on the force who had a big problem with his sexual orientation.

"One and the same." Jasper studied the photos more closely. The lighting was dim, but it was clear someone had his ex-lover tied up, bondage style, hanging from a hook.

"Why would someone send these to you? To make you jealous?" Dane asked, studying the photos more closely.

"That's a very good question. We were broken up before I moved from the west coast." Jasper flipped the photos over, searching to see if the sender had included a message. He wasn't quite ready to share with his partner what these photos meant. Jasper studied the knotwork. In another lifetime, he knew someone who practiced Kinbaku. The art of tying someone up had become popular in the BDSM scenes, but more often than not, it was considered Shibari. The act of knotting and the intricacies of the designs were the draw. Kinbaku went much further into the partner's psyche. There was a level of trust required with both practices. If the trust was absent, the ropes only served as a rough, often painful restraint. The memory of the ropes digging into his skin, the pressure of his balls being separated, the tug of the pins on his nipples; it all came rushing back. Jasper was going to throw up. He grabbed the photos and stuffed them back into the envelope. He couldn't look at these. Not now. Not ever.

"Hey, Jas, are you okay?" Dane asked, gripping his shoulder.

"Yeah, fine," he choked out. He was anything but fine. Jasper needed water. Air. Needed to have never been reminded of what happened so long ago. "I'm going to take these to Julian, see if he can get anything off the envelope. Can you cover for me?"

"Of course. If anything comes up, I'll call you." Dane had a concerned look on his face, as well he should have. If he knew what the pictures really signified, he probably wouldn't let Jasper out of his sight. "I tell you what, I need to go see Julian. Why don't you let me take the envelope when I go?"

Jasper agreed. He took an empty envelope out of his desk and swapped the photos from the original to the new one and placed the original in an evidence bag. If his suspicions were confirmed, only then would he confide in his partner and the techy about the sender, but not until.

Not wanting to go home, Jasper decided to hit the gym. Even after training earlier, he was ready to release his anxiety at seeing the contents of the package. As he pulled into the parking lot, his cell phone rang. He looked at the caller I.D., and it read *Unknown.* Ignoring it, he grabbed his bag out of the floorboard of the passenger side and entered the building. Mason was manning the front desk. He gave the younger Goyle a fist bump as he walked by. After changing clothes, he taped his hands and headed to the specially designed punching bag.

Jasper wasn't as proficient in the martial arts as were Frey, Gregor, or some of the others, but he was a pretty good boxer. Right now, he wasn't worried with form. If Frey were there, he would call him out for it. Jasper didn't care. He just needed to hit something. Hard. Fast. Something to take his mind off those damn photos. Why Craig, and why now? If it was the same person who bound him when he was young, Craig didn't stand a chance.

Getting in a zone, Jasper was unaware of the men and women entering the facility to work out. His shifter stamina allowed him to go for hours without stopping. He should have been paying attention to the time, but he was lost in his jabs. If he had been paying attention, he would have noticed one man in particular staring at him, taking in his form. A wave of light-headedness grasped Jasper, his right fist missing his intended target. He backed away from the bag. The next off feeling had him looking in the mirror. Trevor was there, behind him. His mate was there, not moving, only staring.

Jasper couldn't help the grin that spread across his flushed face. Trevor didn't return the smile, but he did close the distance. "Is it real?" he asked.

Jasper turned to face him and asked, "Is what real?" His adrenaline was still coursing through his veins, and now that his mate was within reach, his beast was tearing at him to be released. He stood still as Trevor moved even closer, until they were almost toe to toe.

Trevor tentatively touched Jasper's right pectoral muscle, more or less poking at him. "This. You. Are you real?"

Jasper gasped as Trevor's fingers traveled from his chest to his bicep. His clinical touch was replaced by a soft whisper against his skin. Jasper glanced around the gym to see if they were drawing attention. He didn't care if people knew he was gay, but Trevor caressing him openly could raise a few eyebrows.

"Yes, I'm real," Jasper whispered. It was all he could do not to grab his mate and drag him to the changing room.

64

Trevor was already dressed in workout clothes, so he couldn't use that as an excuse to be alone with him. He had to get Trevor's hand off his body, or he would ruin their friendship right there in front of everyone. "You ready to work out?" he asked, unable to move away.

"You can still work out after you did that?" Trevor removed his hand.

"I belong to the badass club, remember?" Jasper smiled and winked.

"How can I forget? Yes, let's get this over with." Trevor stepped toward the bench press machine. He set it at more weight than Jasper thought he would, and surprisingly, lifted the bar with no trouble. Jasper admired the way the muscles in Trevor's arms moved underneath his skin. This obviously wasn't his first time in a gym. They took turns on each machine, giving the other time for their muscles to recoup before the next set of reps. Jasper sat down and used the same weight Trevor had. The first time he didn't change it, Trevor called him on it. "I know you can lift more than me."

"Yes, I can, but I've had a pretty strenuous workout already. This is my cool down." Jasper was getting a different type of workout from keeping his beast under control and his cock deflated. He was really glad he was wearing loose shorts. He couldn't help but notice Trevor's were just as baggy. As they were moving to the rowing machine, the bells chimed over the door.

"Jasper, glove up!" Frey yelled as he stormed through the building.

"Oh shit," Jasper groaned.

"What's wrong?" Trevor asked as he put his hand on Jasper's arm, but his eyes were following Frey's movement to the boxing ring.

Jasper sighed, "You're about to see me get my ass handed to me."

# Chapter Ten

Frey read every word Julian unearthed on Abbi, from her parents' car crash, her aunt becoming her guardian, the aunt's death, to Abbi graduating college. He was certain there was much more, but he would have to be patient and get the information from Abbi herself.

The more Frey read, the madder he got. How in the gods' names could a man do that to a woman? At first, it was just a fracture or broken bone that could be explained as an accident. When the red flags began going up, Troy changed his M.O. The visits to the emergency room lessened, but the next few visits, the real tragedies, sickened Frey. Three pregnancies. Three miscarriages. The reports showed stress as the cause, but Frey knew in his soul Troy was responsible. Even if he didn't lay a hand on Abbi, he was the cause of her losing her babies. That probably wasn't all of it, but it had to be the worst of it.

He removed the thumb drive from Dante's laptop and shut it down. Julian was sitting in a lounge chair beside the pool, waiting as he said he would be. "Are you okay?" he asked Frey, concern etched on his face.

"No, I'm not. I need to hit something. I'm going to the gym." Frey stalked to his Jeep with his brother following behind. Frey opened the door, placing his foot on the running board. He noticed the tension in his brother's body. "Thank you, Jules."

Julian opened the door to the Corvette and nodded. Frey knew his brother was torn about something. "What's wrong?"

"I'll do anything I can to help you with Abigail."

"I know you will, but there's something else."

"I need to help Nik get Sophia back." Julian's shoulders sagged as he said, "He hasn't asked me to, but I feel like I have to go."

Frey placed his foot on the ground and walked over to his brother. He wasn't a hugger, so he placed his hand on the side of Julian's neck, giving him a small smile. His brother's heart was warring on doing the right thing. "I get it, and I would be upset if you didn't go help Nik."

"But…"

"But nothing. I got this. Trust me. I have the information I needed, and you gave that to me. It's up to Abbi now; she just doesn't know it yet. Go. Help Nikolas find his female and her parents. When you get back, there will hopefully be two more members of our Clan."

Julian placed his hand on top of Frey's. Nothing else needed to be said.

Frey climbed into the Jeep and headed to the gym. He had almost asked Jules about tutoring Matthew, but when he saw his brother was needed elsewhere, he decided to figure out something else. Julian had done his job, and now Frey would do his. Just as soon as he beat the shit out of something.

By the time he reached the dojo, he was more keyed up than ever. He needed Gregor, but Gregor was in Greece. Then he was off to Egypt. Between him and Julian, surely the two of them could help Nik find Sophia and her parents. He stalked in the door, seeing Jasper. Good enough. "Jasper, glove up!" He didn't wait for the redhead to answer him. Jasper wasn't as proficient in martial arts sparring, so Frey would have to do with plain old boxing.

He didn't bother taping his hands before sliding a pair of gloves on. He climbed into the ring and bounced around, loosening his muscles. Jasper did the same, not wasting any time. They stood in the middle of the mat, tapping gloves, rocking back and forth on their feet, getting a feel for the other. Frey had only boxed with Jasper once before and knew he would have to take it easy, even if the male was a Gargoyle. Jasper threw first, a right jab that Frey easily avoided. Both men punched and jabbed, bobbed and weaved. Neither was landing many punches, but the concentration of the movements was helping to clear Frey's mind.

He really wished Tamian was still in town. Tessa's brother was more proficient than even Frey in martial arts and the best sparring partner he'd ever come across. At the time, Frey hadn't been aware St. Claire was a half-blood. He had worked out at the gym for over three years with no one knowing who or what he was. It wasn't until Gregor found out Tessa was his mate that Tamian's true identity was revealed. Had Frey known the quiet man had Original shifter blood coursing through his lean body, he could have really let loose. Granted, they would have needed to spar when the dojo was closed. Frey was already pushing it now with Jasper.

He'd obviously lost track of time, because he noticed Jasper's punches were coming with less intensity and quickness. Frey backed away, holding up his hands. Jasper leaned over, hands to his knees. "Thank you."

Pulling his gloves off and tossing them in the corner, Frey asked, "For what? I'm the one that should be thanking you. I needed that."

"For not embarrassing me too bad." Jasper grinned, looking around at all the people who had stopped what they were doing to watch.

Frey didn't miss the look Trevor was giving Jasper. "Is there something I should know, Brother?" he whispered so only Jasper could hear.

Jasper followed Frey's gaze until he caught Trevor staring at his ass. He grinned at Trevor and straightened his body. "I'm so fucking confused right now; I'm not sure there's something *I* should know."

Frey removed the gloves from Jasper's hands and tossed them on top of his own. "Truth. The fates aren't going to make it easy on any of us, are they?" he asked as he held the rope for Jasper to crawl through. Following the younger Gargoyle through the ropes to the floor, Frey caught sight of Matthew. The kid was leaning against the wall, arms crossed over his chest, eyes wide.

Frey approached him, worried about the look on his face. "Matt, how was school today?" He wanted the teen to know he was genuinely interested in his well-being.

"It was okay. I want to take you up on that offer for your brother to help me study."

*Shit.* With Julian now going to Egypt, maybe Sixx could help instead. He was a math whiz, too. "I will work something out. Now, tell me what's really bothering you." Frey knew he was reading the kid right when he started shuffling his feet.

"I talked to Abbi, told her Detective Jenkins offered to help. I don't think she was convinced, though. I was hoping you could talk to her. You know, tell her he really can help get her away from Troy."

Frey didn't like the sound of defeat in Matthew's voice. "When would it be possible for me to speak to her? Away from other people?"

Matthew's face lit up. "Tonight. She normally doesn't have class on Thursdays, but she mentioned going to the community center where she could work on the festival. Maybe you can catch her before she goes home."

"What about your training? If I go talk to your sister, we'll have to skip tonight." Frey knew the kid would be on board with that. This was all about his sister anyway.

"I'll double up tomorrow. Please, Geoffrey?" Matthew was standing very still, waiting on Frey's answer.

"I'll go talk to her on one condition. Instead of doubling up tomorrow, you come to my home on Saturday. I want to start you out with meditation, and I have the perfect spot for that."

"Whatever you want. I'll be there. Just tell me when and where."

Frey laughed at the teen. "Come on, I'll get Mason to

work with you tonight." Matthew followed Frey to his office where Frey asked Mason to help Matt on the machines. After a quick shower, Frey climbed into his Jeep and headed across town to the community center. Frey pushed past the speed limits, not wanting to miss Abbi.

Trevor was right. The man of his dreams was part of a badass club. That was the only explanation for what he had just witnessed. Jasper had gone toe to toe, glove to glove with the big guy and was still alive. Not only was he alive, he was joking and laughing. Trevor was so far out of his league with the hot detective he was ready to bolt. Only he couldn't move. The sight of Jasper bent over, hands on his knees, shorts stretched across his fine ass had Trevor glued to the spot. Jasper turned and grinned. Yep, Jasper caught him ogling his ass, and he smiled. That beautiful smile caused Trevor's stomach to do funny things. This wasn't butterflies lightly fluttering around in there. Nope, this was monkeys swinging from tree branches, flipping through the air, catching the next limb one handed. Jasper said something to Geoffrey that Trevor couldn't hear. Geoffrey removed Jasper's gloves and tossed them in the corner. They exited the ring with the owner going one way and Jasper walking toward Trevor. Jasper wasn't even winded or sweating. Yep, badass.

"What are you?" Trevor asked, kind of joking, kind of serious. The Unholy were a type of superhuman monster Trevor had never had the unlucky chance of seeing up close and personal. What if Jasper was some kind of superhuman without the monster part? It was entirely possible.

"I'm hungry, that's what I am. I'm going to go home, shower, and find something to eat. You wanna stop by later?"

Of course Trevor did. If for no other reason than to figure out the mystery that was Jasper Jenkins. "I'm going to finish my workout. I'll need to go home and shower first. If it won't be too late…"

"Not at all. Do you like spaghetti? Or would you rather grill hamburgers? Both are quick."

"Dude, you're cooking, you choose." If either were half as good as the pizza he concocted last time Trevor visited, he would be in heaven. He hated to cook.

Jasper laughed at him, "Okay, I'll figure it out when I get to the kitchen. Oh, I programmed the gate so you can punch in a code to get in. That way you don't have to wait in case I'm in the shower or something."

He had his own code? Was that like having his own key? "What's the code?"

Jasper looked around before answering. He pushed Trevor's bangs off his forehead. "Your birthday."

Trevor didn't know which was more disconcerting, the fact Jasper felt comfortable enough to touch him in public or that he knew when his birthday was. "How do you know when my birthday is?" Trevor didn't tell anyone his birthday, mainly because he wasn't born but created.

Jasper winked at him. "I'm a detective." There was that smile again. Fucking monkeys. "I'll see you later, yeah?"

"Yeah," Trevor sighed, not able to keep his eyes off Jasper's tight ass.

Two hours later, Trevor pulled into Jasper's driveway. Had it only been three nights since he'd first been here? So much had changed in that short amount of time, not all of it good. Trevor wasn't one hundred percent sure Jasper was gay, but the detective didn't have an issue touching him. He didn't know if it was just the man being friendly or what. He really hoped it was *or what*, but if it was, that posed the same question as before- why him? Trevor punched in the month and day of his birthday, and

71

the gate opened.

He parked in the same spot as before, only this time, Jasper wasn't waiting outside. He was probably in the kitchen cooking. If he had decided on burgers, he could be on the back deck. Trevor angled out of his car and made his way to the porch. He knocked on the door and waited. When Jasper didn't answer, Trevor turned the knob. It was unlocked, so he let himself in and called out, "Jasper?" He didn't see his host anywhere, so he walked to the back and looked out. Jasper wasn't on the deck either. Trevor caught the scent of spaghetti sauce wafting through the air and headed to the kitchen.

He helped himself to a bottle of water from the fridge and sat at the island to wait on Jasper who was probably in the shower. A stack of photographs were peeking out of an envelope in the middle of the island. Trevor knew he shouldn't look, but the man in the top picture was familiar. Trevor picked up the photo and stared. This was the creep who'd been looking in the window at the gym. He slid out the next photo, unsure of what he was looking at. The man was tied up in an elaborate system of knots. When he saw the next one in the stack, his breath caught. Was the man being tortured or did he like it? If his hard cock was any indication, he was enjoying it. Trevor turned the picture sideways, taking in the intricacies of the rope.

"It's called Kinbaku," Jasper said behind him, causing him to jump.

# *Chapter Eleven*

Dane and Julian had danced around the Katherine topic long enough. Using the envelope as an excuse, Dane drove to the lab. He didn't bother knocking, as all the Gargoyles had clearance into the building. He entered the computer lab where he found Julian typing away at a keyboard. He didn't know how the Goyle didn't have calluses on his fingers. "Julian, sorry to interrupt," he said as he entered the room.

"Dane, what can I do for you?" Julian turned his way, giving him his undivided attention.

"Jasper received this." Dane held the envelope out, still secure in the plastic evidence sheath. "It's personal, so he would rather you check for fingerprints."

Julian took the envelope from Dane, turning it over, looking at both sides. "What was inside?"

"Photographs. Until he knows who sent them, he wants to keep this to himself." Dane didn't blame Jasper. He wouldn't want anyone to see an ex-lover of his in such compromising pictures either.

"Understood. I'll do my best to find something for him before I leave."

"Leave?"

"Yes, I cannot sit here any longer while Nikolas needs me. I'm leaving for Egypt tomorrow."

"Oh." Dane didn't want to hold up Julian over their disagreement.

"Oh, what?" Julian asked with one eyebrow cocked.

"I wanted to discuss Katherine. Possibly set up a time to have her meet us so we could put this to bed, so to speak."

Julian sighed, "If you can set up a meeting in the morning, I'll do it. I want us to be able to move past this as well."

73

Dane nodded, "Okay, I'll reach out to her, see if she's available. I'll call you tonight or in the morning and let you know."

"Sounds good. And Dane? If she turns out to be my mate, no hard feelings?"

"Of course not. At least I'll know one way or the other." He reached out a hand to Julian who fist bumped him.

"Good. I'll get started on Jasper's envelope."

Dane left Julian to do just that. He exited the lab and leaned against his cruiser. He needed to come up with a feasible excuse to lure Katherine to a meeting.

When Frey arrived at the community center, he noticed there were only a couple of vehicles in the lot. Not paying attention to the cars, he strode into the building. He would have to remember to say something to Abbi about the door being unlocked.

Reaching out with his shifter senses, he heard music coming from the hallway to the right. He followed the sound of tinkling notes floating through the air. Frey wasn't a classical music person, but this tune was familiar. He slowed himself as he reached the door to the only lit room.

Abbi was dressed in dance leotards with a large button down covering the top of her body. How did she dance in that baggy shirt? She was standing at a desk, writing something on a piece of paper. She closed her eyes, swaying to the music. She opened her eyes and wrote something down. Closing her eyes again, she moved away from the desk and spun on her left foot. This time when Abbi opened her eyes, she didn't move to pick up the pencil. Instead, she walked to a closet, opened the door, and stared. Frey couldn't see what had her so entranced until finally she reached her arm in, coming out with a pair of ballet shoes. She clutched them to her chest reverently with her chin bowed as if she were praying. Or remembering. How long had it been since she danced?

Abbi sat down on the floor and placed her feet in the pink slippers. After wrapping the ribbons around her ankles, she tied them in bows. Slowly she stood and removed the too large shirt she was wearing. The first thing Frey noticed was his mate's beautiful body. She was lean like a dancer but still curvy like a woman should be. Troy no doubt insisted she wear the baggy clothes to hide this gorgeous figure from the appreciative eyes of other men. The next thing he noted were the bruises on her slender arms. Obviously, she thought she was alone, or he doubted Abbi would have dared to bare the evidence of her abusive husband. Frey was ready to go to her. He calmed his body so he wouldn't run to her and grab her up, squeezing her in a crushing embrace.

Abbi began to move, slowly at first, as though she was getting reacquainted with the shoes. Frey was mesmerized as this magnificent creature stood on one foot, leaning forward with her right arm extended as she raised her left leg behind her. Abbi held the pose before stretching her leg higher. She lowered her leg then performed the same move with the right one.

Abbi was finding her rhythm. Frey knew from his experience with martial arts, part of the warm up was finding yourself, seeking that place where you are one with your craft. He knew the exact moment Abbi found hers, because she let go. She floated across the room, jumping, turning, spinning, bowing, and stretching. Frey's soul felt as if it had left his body and was moving across the room in hers. He had never seen anything more beautiful in his life. He wasn't an expert in ballet, but he knew what he was observing should have been shared with the world, not stuffed in a closet in a community center to be forgotten.

This creature before him wasn't Abbi Quinn. This exquisite woman was Abigail Swanson.

When the song was over, Abbi stopped dancing and hugged her arms around her middle, her body shaking. Geoffrey Hartley... Gargoyle, soldier, boxer, martial artist... didn't try to stop the tears creeping down his face. What he did want to stop were the tears rolling down Abbi's. Without a thought to the consequences, he closed the distance between them. When she realized she wasn't alone, she gasped, crossing her arms over her chest as if she were naked. Maybe without the large shirt covering her she felt exposed. He stopped inches from his mate, willing her soundlessly to look at him, see the pain in his eyes. The pain for her. He gently lifted her chin and cupped her face in his large hands. Her tears fell faster than his thumbs could erase them. Not knowing what else to do, he kissed her.

Frey expected Abbi to keep her mouth closed tight, to back away and look up at him with disgust. Instead, she opened to him, her tongue seeking his. Her arms snaked around his waist, pulling their bodies closer. Frey put one hand on Abbi's back where the leotard dipped down. Feeling her skin underneath his fingers had his cock coming to life. A moan escaped her mouth into his causing a growl to rise up from somewhere deep in his chest. When she needed to come up for air, only then did Abbi back away. She placed her fingers on her lips. Tentatively, she reached her other hand up and touched the corner of his eye where a lone tear had refused to fall. She studied her wet finger as if the tear was something she'd never seen before. Turning away, she retrieved the too big shirt and slid it on, grasping the two sides together.

"I... what are you doing here?" she asked as she sat down in a chair and began untying the ribbons.

"I wanted to talk to you, and then I saw you dancing... I'm no expert, but Abbi, that was the most beautiful thing I've ever seen. You are so talented."

"What do you want from me?" she sternly asked as she removed her shoes and returned them to their place in the closet.

"I told you, I want to talk." Frey stuck his hands in his pockets, willing his claws to stay put.

"I'm married, but you already know that." Abbi closed the closet door and gave her back to him. She buttoned up the large shirt before turning back around. Digging inside a tote bag on the desk, she pulled out a pair of sweatpants. Of course, they too, were baggy.

"Why?" That was the million dollar question. She could give him every excuse, but none would be good enough.

"Why what?" Her brow was etched with shallow wrinkles. His mate had frowned far too many times.

"Why are you married?"

"That's what people do. Get married, settle down…" Abbi paused. Was she going to say *have kids*?

"Yes, they do. But they usually get married to someone who loves them, takes care of them, has their best interest at heart. Not someone who abuses them, beats up their kid brother, and takes advantage of every bad situation that comes along." Abbi's face paled, but Frey didn't let up. "Let me rephrase the question. Why are you *still* married?"

"It's not that simple. I… He's…"

"You what, love him? He's what? Sorry when it happens? Promises to never hurt you again?" Frey was getting madder with each word he spoke.

"No," she whispered.

"No, what? No you don't love him, or no, he isn't sorry?"

"Both." Abbi walked to the other side of the room. Even when she wasn't dancing, her moves were smooth and graceful. Frey would give anything to see her dance again.

"Then I will ask you again, why are you married to the bastard?" Frey asked, his voice raising.

"It's not that simple!" her voice cracked as she yelled in response. Again, she turned her back on him. And again, she wrapped her arms around herself.

"What if it was?" Frey moved closer to her. Even though she was just on the other side of the room, the distance was too great. Taking care with her bruised arms, he gently turned her body so she was facing him.

Her blue eyes shined brighter because of the tears. "Now it's my turn to ask you why. Why are you doing this? I know Matty is a great kid, and he's told me all about how you're trying to help him. But why me? What do you want from me?"

*Forever.* "Why? Because I see a beautiful woman whose light doesn't shine. I want to give her the sun. I see a talented dancer whose song doesn't play. I want to give her the music. I see a loving sister whose brother is fighting for both of them. I want to give him the lessons. I see someone who deserves the best life has to offer, and I want to give that to her. I can't explain it, Abbi. I was drawn to you the minute I saw you walk into the gym. Yes, you're married, and normally I wouldn't cross that line. I'm not a homewrecker. But from where I stand, your home is already wrecked, and it's your husband who's to blame. What I want from you is a chance. A chance to show you how a woman should be treated. So, I'll ask you again, what if it was that simple?"

Abbi couldn't breathe. She'd been so lost in her dancing she hadn't heard him come in the room. He watched her, saw her. He cried for her. Geoffrey Hartley, the big, badass boxer, cried for her. She couldn't wrap her head around that. Matty had told her all about how nice he was. What if he could help her get away from Troy, what then? She couldn't jump out of one relationship into another. Could she? Was it possible he really wanted to be with her? She so desperately wanted a relationship like the one her parents had, full of love and happiness. Would he really give that to her? He didn't know her, and she definitely didn't know anything about him. Except...

The words, those beautiful words he spoke with tears in his eyes, had her heart humming. There was something inexplicably different about Frey. Some type of tether drawing her to him. If Abbi closed her eyes, she could see the line between them. It didn't stretch from her heart to his. No, this went deeper- soul deep. How could that be? When he kissed her, there was an energy that started in her lips, traveling down through her stomach, ending between her legs. If she wasn't married, she would have been tempted to do more than kiss. If she was honest with herself, she was already tempted, married or not.

Abbi spoke truthfully, "I'm scared, Geoffrey. Honest to god scared. I left Troy once before. I ended up in the hospital for a week. So, you have to understand if I'm a little hesitant. It isn't that I don't want to leave him; I do. I never really wanted to be married to him in the first place. After my parents died, I was lost. My aunt gained control of my parents' money. Mine and Matt's money. If it hadn't been for Matt, I would have rather been dead, too. He was the only thing keeping me going. He still is. Him and all the kids I teach.

"My aunt spent our money on drugs and gambling, before I even knew it was gone. Luckily, I got a scholarship to college and was still able to get my teaching degree. Long story short, I married Troy, my aunt died, and Matt came to live with us. If it hadn't been for one investment my father made that my aunt didn't know about, we'd have been penniless."

She paused to study this man standing before her. His dark brown hair was shorn in a military style. Even

79

though it was late November, he was wearing a short sleeved t-shirt that hugged his chest and stretched over his massive biceps. Black fatigues were tucked into black military looking boots. "Were you in the military?" she asked.

"I was. I did a couple of tours as a helicopter pilot. I retired several years ago and opened the dojo. I've been thinking about opening another one on the west coast."

Her heart sank. Was he moving? Leaving New Atlanta? How could he talk about being with her if he was moving? "So, you're moving?" She sounded like a whiny teen.

"No, of course not. I would travel out there and oversee the building of the structure and the opening, but I would hire one of my cousins to run it. I like New Atlanta and plan on being here for a while. I'd like to think I now have another reason to stay put."

Abbi liked that. She shouldn't, but she did. She needed to guard her heart instead of putting it in the hands of this stranger. His wanting to be with her this quickly didn't make sense. She had heard of love at first sight, but there's no way he could love her. This was all way too sudden.

"How would you like to visit California?" he asked, stepping closer.

"I don't know. I've never been anywhere except Florida when I was younger. Our parents took us to the beach the summer before my senior year. We were supposed to go back when I graduated but..." Ten years later and Abbi still had a hard time talking about it. "I would like to see another part of the country, but I have school. Besides, I can't leave Matt."

"We could wait until school is out for the summer. Then both you and Matt could go with me," Frey said as he closed the distance between them. He reached for her hands, holding them gently in his big ones. "You don't have to

80

decide now, but at least think about it. Abbi, I was serious when I said I want you in my life. I want to show you the world. Hell, I want to give you the world." He raised her hands to his mouth and placed soft kisses on her knuckles. The stubble around his mouth scraped at her skin. The two different textures, soft lips and rough whiskers, together ignited a fire somewhere south of her stomach.

"Can you really help me get away from Troy?" Abbi whispered, afraid if she said it too loudly, someone would hear.

"I can. I have a lot of contacts in this city. You say the word, and I'll help you start the process. I'll set up round the clock protection for both you and Matthew. I'm not saying it won't get messy, because I have a feeling Quinn won't go away quietly. But I will make it as easy on you as possible. You'll have to leave your house for the time being. We'll go get your clothes and anything else you want while he's at work. I'll get you and Matt set up in a secure location where you'll be safe."

There was that feeling again: hope. Then another feeling overrode it: fear. Abbi placed her hand on her stomach, the nausea rolling through. "Oh, god. Oh, crap." What if he'd already knocked her up? What if this was the one time her body decided it wanted to cooperate and she carried a baby to term?

"Abbi, what is it? Look at me, tell me what just went through your head."

"What if I'm pregnant? He's trying to get me pregnant. He'll never let me go. He said so." Abbi tried to pull her hands away, but Frey gripped them tighter.

"Then you will be a wonderful mother, and he'll never see the child if that's what you wish. Abbi, no judge is going to grant that abusive motherfucker parental rights, including visitation. You need to document the abuse, starting now. That means you need to go see a doctor, show him or her the bruises and tell them how you got them."

"I've been to the hospital plenty. Troy's a cop. Everyone believes his lies when he tells them how I got the injuries." Abbi had seen the knowing looks from the doctors and nurses every time she visited the emergency room. If she didn't corroborate Troy's story, she'd be in for even more pain once she was back home.

"That's going to change, starting now. I happen to know the Chief of Staff at New Atlanta. One phone call is all it will take. You go see him, he'll look at your file, and the appropriate documentation will be noted. If you don't want to see him, my cousin's ma... girlfriend is a doctor. She's in Greece right now, but as soon as she's back, you can go see her if you prefer." Frey drew her close and wrapped his arms around her shoulders. In that moment, Abbi felt safe. She allowed herself to melt into the big, strong body holding onto hers. Turning her head, she placed her cheek on his chest, his strong heartbeat loud in her ear. That sound, life thumping, was the sign she needed. She was alive, but she wasn't living. Abbi was ready to start living.

# Chapter Twelve

Troy was beyond pissed. Not only was he stuck on second shift, he'd been given a different patrol. Instead of being close to home and the community center, the bitch Chief had stuck him on the north side of town. He should just say fuck it and drive by the center anyway. When too many calls kept him from being able to do a drive-by, he called his buddy George. Troy had promised his friend a case of beer if he'd keep an eye on Abbi while Troy was at work, especially on the nights she stayed late at the Community Center. Now that Troy wasn't home waiting on her, she could stay later with no reason to be home on time.

When George answered, Troy barked, "Where are you?" instead of saying hello.

"Sitting outside the center. She's still in there."

"Is she alone? At this time of night, she should have already left. Fuck!"

"I see two vehicles in the parking lot. One is hers. Don't know who the other one belongs to, but it's a sweet looking Jeep with about a four inch lift kit, KC lights, big mud tires. I'm getting a hard-on just looking at it."

"Fuck the Jeep. I want to know what she's doing there so late. Get your ass in there."

"I've already been in. All she's doing is listening to fucked up Christmas music and writing stuff down. I'm done with this shit; I got a date. Debbie Cranston's hooking me up with a big-tittied redhead that likes threesomes. When you get off you should come find us. We'll be at Debbie's. I promise not to wear them out before you get there."

"Fuck, at least get the license plate off the Jeep before you leave."

Troy disconnected and quickly forgot about what Abbi was doing. His thoughts turned to after work. "This second shift might not be so bad after all."

"I'm sorry, I shouldn't... Is this a case you're working on because that..." Trevor didn't finish. Was Jasper into pain? Trevor was pretty vanilla when it came to sex, mainly because he didn't have sex. His sex life up to this point was practically non-existent.

"Something like that." Jasper didn't elaborate, but he also didn't put the photos back in the envelope. Instead, he walked to the stove and stirred the sauce. He was quiet while he put water on to boil for the noodles.

"I'm sorry if I overstepped. The reason I looked at all is because I've seen this guy before."

Jasper's head snapped around, "What? When?" He forgot the water and was right in front of Trevor. He picked up the stack and handed it to Trevor. "Please, make sure Trev."

Trevor didn't have to look again, didn't want to look again. "I'm sure. He was outside the gym Tuesday when I went in to sign up. When I walked back outside to my car he was looking in the side window. I thought he was getting his rocks off looking at the women working out. Guess he gets off a different way."

Jasper blanched. Trevor had to wonder if the detective got off that way, too. Jasper took the photos and shoved them back in the envelope. Trevor knew the truth of the photos. "It's not a case is it? This is personal."

When Jasper wouldn't look at him, Trevor had his answer. "That's the ex you were telling me about. That's Craig, isn't it? That's Craig, and he's here. He was watching you at the gym, not the women." Trevor's stomach roiled. Jasper's ex was in town, and he was into some kinky shit. Stuff Jasper was probably into. Stuff Trevor definitely was not. He didn't stand a snowball's chance in hell with this man. "I should go…" He stood, but Jasper was in his space, between him and the door.

"It's not what you think, I promise. Give me a chance to explain before you bail on me. Please," Jasper pleaded. He had his hands on Trevor's arms, squeezing his biceps. He was standing so close to Trevor. Too close. When he was in the same room with Jasper, things were strained. His jeans were strained, always, with a cock ready to burst through the zipper. With him this close, though, Trevor couldn't think. His dick was throbbing, and his brain was absent of blood. Trevor couldn't stop himself. He licked his lips. He wanted this man standing in front of him, but he would not make the first move. Would not make a fool of himself just in case he'd read the signs wrong.

He didn't have to make a move. Jasper's eyes flashed to his mouth, and he took the invitation and R.S.V.P.'d immediately. Tentatively he touched his lips to Trevor's. Trevor wanted more. He wanted to taste this man. Before he got the chance, a cell phone rang. It wasn't Trevor's ringtone, so that meant it was Jasper's. "Fuck," Jasper swore as he pulled his phone out of his pocket and looked at the caller I.D. "I'm sorry, I have to take this."

"Jenkins," he practically barked into the phone, his eyes never leaving Trevor's lips. "I was getting ready to eat... No, I got it; I'll be there in a few." Jasper disconnected, still staring at Trevor's mouth. His eyes drifted up to Trevor's as he asked him, "Can you boil noodles?"

"What?" Trevor was ready to leave since Jasper had to go back out.

"Can you boil noodles? I have to go to work, but hopefully I won't be gone long. I don't want you to leave. If you can boil the noodles, you can go ahead and eat, and I'll eat when I get back. There's salad stuff in the fridge."

"I can boil noodles," Trevor said, not sure if he wanted to, though. He didn't feel comfortable staying at

Jasper's house without him there.

As if Jasper read his mind, he said, "I want you here, Trev. I want you to get used to being here, making yourself at home when you are. I wouldn't have given you your own code if I didn't trust you." Jasper grabbed his belt loops and pulled him so they were chest to chest. He slid his scratchy cheek along Trevor's, the rough friction sending shivers down his spine. Jasper's lips were warm on Trevor's ear as he whispered, "Please."

"Okay," Trevor whispered back.

"I really want to kiss you right now, but if I do, I'll never leave. Thank you for staying." Jasper backed away and headed toward the door. "I'll be home as soon as I can manage."

Trevor's heart had never beaten as hard or as fast as it was now. How was it possible this badass wanted him? He wasn't hungry any more, at least not for spaghetti, but Jasper would be when he got home. Trevor turned to the pot that was bubbling with boiling water and added noodles.

He wanted to look at the pictures of Jasper's ex, then again, he didn't. His curiosity got the better of him, and he took them out of the envelope, spreading them on the island. What had Jasper called it? Kinbaku? He pulled out his cell phone and opened a search engine, typing the term into the blank field. As soon as the pages were populated, Trevor closed his phone. He would read about it later, when he had time to digest it properly. A million questions were going through his mind, most of which stemmed from the photos. Trevor studied every picture of Jasper's ex- his very good looking ex. Each position was more intense than the previous one. His balls shriveled up and tried to crawl back inside his body. There's no way in hell that could be anything but painful. Torturous. There were people who got off on that kind of stuff. He'd seen bodies come across the slab from sex play gone wrong.

He put the pictures back in the envelope and stirred

the noodles. He turned the heat down so the water wouldn't boil over onto the stove and then he took a good look around the kitchen. Last time he was here, he hadn't seen more than the living room and bathroom. He took advantage of being alone and explored Jasper's home. The house was similar to the warden's. Trevor hadn't seen much of Gregor's lodge when he helped get Tessa from the hospital to Gregor's bedroom, but he'd seen enough to know this home was built along the same floorplan, only on a smaller scale.

One would never know Jasper was gay by looking at the interior of his home. With the leather furniture and the wooden accents, this house boldly stated male. Trevor's home wasn't flaming, but it definitely had more feminine qualities than this log structure. He had pictures of Travis and him all around his apartment. Jasper had no photos anywhere, except those on the kitchen island in an envelope. Trevor didn't think those would find their way into a frame anytime soon.

After inspecting every room in the house, he ended up in Jasper's bedroom. He could have found that room if he were blind. The scent was spicy and manly, all Jasper. The bed was made up, just barely. Trevor closed his eyes and imagined the gorgeous detective spread out on the sheets with Trevor straddling his large body. His cock was once again stretching the limits of his jeans. Inhaling one last time, he walked back to the kitchen.

Trevor searched the cabinets until he found a colander. He strained the noodles and returned them to the pot. Deciding he should probably eat something, he fixed himself a plate and settled in to wait on Jasper to get home. Just as he sat down at the table, his cell phone pinged with a text message.

Normally Jasper enjoyed patrolling for the Unholy. Tonight was not one of those nights. He had his mate waiting at home for him. Now that he knew Trevor was gay, he was looking forward to the future. He still planned on being patient with him, especially after seeing his reaction to the photos of Craig. The pictures would be a shock to most anyone not associated with the lifestyle.

When Deacon called, it was all Jasper could do not to tell him no, but it was his duty as a Gargoyle to help patrol and fight the monsters that threatened the humans. Now that several of the Clan were out of the country, he was really needed. He met up with the others and set about corralling the science experiments gone wrong. When the Unholy fought in the streets, the Goyles had to be careful about keeping their shifter selves hidden from the humans.

A couple of hours later, the Unholy were either dead or cuffed and subdued to be taken to the Basement. The special area in the lowest level of the Pen where they kept the monsters was getting full. Rafael had informed them earlier that Gordon Flanagan, "maker" of the Unholy, was dead. Hopefully there would be no more of the creatures created, and they could finally get a handle on them. Jasper was helping Mason load the dead bodies into a van for transport when his cell phone rang. Thinking it was probably Trevor wondering where he was, he answered it. "Jenkins." There was no answer, so he repeated his name, "Jenkins. Hello?" When he didn't receive an answer, he looked at the caller I.D. *Unknown*. Who the fuck kept calling him?

He shoved his phone in his pocket and finished helping Mason. Deacon and Lorenzo had the live ones locked up and ready for the Pen. Lorenzo said, "You get back home. I'll take care of the bodies."

88

"Thanks, Lor. If Trevor wasn't waiting for me I wouldn't put this off on you." Jasper gave the other Goyles a fist bump and took off toward his car. If Trevor hadn't been at his house, he would have just flown. He wasn't ready to explain how he got to work without a vehicle.

As Jasper neared his car, he slowed his steps. There was a tall, well-built man leaning against it; hands in his pockets, feet crossed at the ankles. *Motherfucker.*

Jasper was livid. Why was his past coming back now? How had his ex even found him? Jasper didn't need to get any closer to know the man was Craig. If the way he leaned against the car wasn't enough of a tell, the cologne he wore was a dead giveaway. He always sprayed it on too strong, something that never really bothered Jasper before. Now, it made him want to throw up. He preferred the clean, subtle scent Trevor wore. Trevor. Jasper smiled as he thought of his mate back home, boiling noodles. At least that's what he hoped he was doing. That or playing video games, or wandering through the house, becoming acquainted with it. Anything except looking at those fucking pictures. He wished he'd thought to bring them with him.

Jasper willed his claws to stay sheathed so he didn't take a swipe at the man standing before him. His smile fading, he asked, "What do you want, Craig?"

"Is that any way to greet me? Jas, I've missed you, Baby." Craig smiled, stepping away from the car, but Jasper took a step back.

"Stop. You've got about ten seconds to tell me what the fuck you're doing here. After that, we're done."

The smile was replaced by a frown. "I'm in trouble. I'm in big trouble, and I need your help. Please Jas, you have no idea what I've gotten into, but there's no one else I can turn to." Craig's eyes were dilated, his pulse was racing. The man was nervous, but not in the way he wanted Jasper to believe. Jasper was pretty good at telling when someone was lying. Craig was lying through his straight, white teeth.

He opened his car door and fished out a clean shirt, hoping to mask any blood before Craig could get suspicious. He slid the tee over his head and turned around to find Craig in his space. Before he could stop him, his ex hauled him into his arms and sealed their mouths together. Jasper was surprised, to say the least. He opened his mouth to protest, and Craig took advantage to slide his tongue into Jasper's heat. Jasper jerked away and grabbed Craig's biceps, giving them a hard squeeze.

"If you're referring to being tied up in pretty little knots and then strung up on a hook for someone to have their way with you, I know all about it." Craig's eyes widened. He tried to recover, but he wasn't quick enough. Jasper could see the bullshit being formed before it was able to leave his ex's lips.

"Save it. You walked out on me when I needed you most. I have a new life now, one that doesn't include you. Whatever you've gotten yourself into, you can get yourself out of." Jasper stepped around Craig, but didn't get far before Craig grabbed him from behind, wrapping his arms around his waist.

His cologne was seeping into Jasper's clothes. He turned and with more force than necessary, shoved the other man away from him, sending him sprawling onto his ass. Jasper walked to where Craig was on the ground and seethed, "Listen to me and listen well. You are *nothing* to me. I have someone in my life now, someone who will be around for the long haul. You need to get the fuck out of town, out of my life. Do you get me?"

Craig glanced behind Jasper and grinned. When he returned his attention to Jasper, he snarled his lip, "Yeah, I get you."

Jasper left him sitting where he was and headed home. First he needed to find a way to wash the stench of his ex off his body.

90

# Chapter Thirteen

Standing in the quiet room of the community center with his arms encircling his mate, Frey didn't want to push Abbi, but he didn't want to give her too much time to think, either. "Abbi, if you really want to get away from Troy, let's go get your stuff tonight, while he's at work. You can grab Matt's things for him while you're there."

"How do you know Troy's at work? He just went on second shift today."

"Like I said earlier, I know people, so I called in a favor."

"Where will you take us?" she asked, pulling away from him.

"My place would be safest, but if you don't feel comfortable staying with me, I have several cousins you could stay with, or I can put you up in a hotel. Anywhere you decide to stay will be secure."

Abbi bit her bottom lip between her teeth, thinking. Frey had to look away. He needed to keep in mind what she had been through. Even though she was his mate and he knew they were fated to be together, he had to give her time to get to know him. Having waited almost six hundred years for his mate, he could afford to be patient a few more months, or years even. The first thing he had to do was get her away from her abusive bastard of a husband. Once that was accomplished, she would be free to spend time with Frey.

"I don't know your cousins."

"You don't know me either, but I would prefer you and Matt stay at my home. I have plenty of room, and that way, I will worry less." Frey would worry regardless, until Troy was completely out of the picture.

"Are you sure you can protect me from Troy?" Abbi was frowning again. "Once he finds out I've left, he's going to be hell bent on getting me back. He's going to cause trouble wherever I go."

"I'm sure. I will drive you to and from work. I'll have someone drive Matt, too. Trust me; he won't get close to you as long as I'm around. But Abbi, I need you to do what I ask. You have to file a restraining order, and you have to see a doctor to document the abuse."

"I need to call Matt, see if he's okay with this, but yes, we'll stay with you." Abbi walked over to her bag and pulled out her cell phone. While she was punching in numbers, Frey noticed her phone was an old one. "He's not answering. I'll leave a voice message."

"Tell him to meet us at the gym."

Abbi blinked at him while listening to the message. "Hey, it's Abbi. I need to talk to you. Meet me at Geoffrey's gym as soon as you get this. And Matty, whatever you do, don't go home." She hung up and put the phone back in her bag. "Now what?"

Frey walked over and picked up her bag. "Now, we go get your stuff." He motioned for her to precede him out the door. Abbi locked up behind them and headed to her car. It was an older model sedan that had seen better days. One day soon, she would be driving something more reliable. "I'll follow you to your house. While you pack your bags, I'll stand guard, just in case. If he happens to be home when you get there, just drive on past and meet me at the gym."

"Okay," Abbi nodded and took a deep breath.

"Breathe, Gorgeous. I promise everything is going to be all right." Frey tucked a stray strand of hair behind her ear, his fingertip lingering. Her body shivered. Whether from his touch or the thought of leaving her husband, he didn't know. As soon as she was safely in her car, he shut the door. Frey climbed into his Jeep and fired it up. Letting out on the clutch, he followed Abbi the few miles to her house.

92

Luckily, there was no sign of Troy, and Abbi was able to get her and Matthew's clothes with little trouble. Apparently, the only trouble she had was finding something to put them in. When she walked out the door with several plastic grocery store bags, Frey asked, "Where is your suitcase?"

"We don't have one. We've never been on vacation so…" her voice trailed off as she tossed the bags of clothing and toiletries into her trunk. Frey couldn't imagine not having any type of bag to tote stuff in. He probably had ten gym bags thrown in the back of his closets. First the old phone, and now, no luggage. Did she have anything new? After a few more trips into the house, Abbi assured him she had everything she and Matthew needed as well as some items they wouldn't want to leave behind. He was glad to see she changed out of the baggy sweats into jeans and a UGA sweatshirt.

They drove to the gym with Frey parking in his reserved spot and Abbi parking next to him. He jumped out of the Jeep and hurried around her car to open the door for her. He held his hand out, and she took it. He didn't want to let go but knew better than to be affectionate too soon. When they reached the front door to the gym, he held it open and couldn't resist touching the small of her back, ushering her in.

Matt came walking up from the back of the gym, a load of towels in his arms. "Hey, Abs, what's up?" He laid the towels on the counter and began folding them. Frey laughed at the look on Abbi's face.

"What are you doing?" she asked.

"Folding towels, duh. So, what's going on? Why'd we need to meet here, and why the cryptic message?" He grabbed the pile of now folded towels and looked between his sister and boss.

Frey took the stack from Matt. "Why don't we go to the office to talk?" He didn't wait on them to follow.

As soon as they reached the back, Frey stored the towels in the bin. He walked around to his chair and took a seat across from his mate and her brother. As Abbi explained to Matthew what Frey had suggested, he took the time to observe them together. He knew what it was like to have a younger brother you wanted to protect. Both his siblings would soon be in Egypt, and he wanted to go protect them. Rafael was like a brother, and Frey looked up to the King as the great ruler he was. Frey would lay his life on the line for any of his Clan, blood relative or not. Now he had the opportunity to protect his new family, and he'd lay down his life for them, too.

Frey realized they had stopped talking. "So?"

Matt answered for them both, "Let me grab the garbage, and we'll be ready to go."

Frey nodded, and Matt practically bounced out of his chair.

"Who was that, and what have you done with my little brother?" Abbi laughed.

"That is a young man with a purpose," Frey grinned as he stood from his chair.

Matthew came back, and they all headed for the front door. Urijah was manning the counter as they passed by. He held a fist out and knuckle bumped Frey then Matthew before fisting his heart and bowing his head slightly to Abbi. Frey's heart skipped a beat when his fellow Goyle honored his mate. He grinned again at the look on Abbi's face. One day they would look back on this moment and laugh.

As they approached the parking lot, Frey said, "Abbi, please follow us. Matt, you ride with me."

The teen laughed, "You got a step ladder with you? What does this thing have, a four inch lift kit?"

"Five, and you can climb." Frey turned his attention to Abbi who was shaking her head at her brother. "My place isn't too far. I'll see you there." Once she was securely in her car, he stepped into the tall vehicle and buckled up. If Matthew was going to ride with him, he'd have to remember to put the doors back on.

"Are you going to be okay, or do you want a jacket?" Frey kept extra clothes with him at all times. All of the Gargoyles did. They never knew when they would encounter Unholy, or need to cover up the fact any wounds they received healed rapidly.

"I'll be okay. Man, this is so freaking cool! I've never driven a stick before. Do you think you could teach me someday?" It was a good thing the kid was buckled up. He was looking in the back, twisting and turning to take in the jacked-up ride.

"I'll teach you anything you want to know." There was so much Frey was willing and eager to teach Matt. If Abbi ever accepted Frey as her mate, they would be family. He wanted both of them to know how the man was supposed to treat those in his care. If Matt wanted to learn to fight, he'd teach him. If he wanted to learn to drive a manual transmission, he'd teach him that, too. The most important thing he'd teach him, though, was the right way to treat a woman.

He pulled into his drive with Abbi right behind him. He spoke into the security box, and the gate swung open. "Holy shit! That's some high-tech gate you got."

Frey laughed at the kid but kept his eyes on the rearview mirror. He had driven the whole way home looking behind them more than in front of them, mostly making sure they weren't being followed. When they rolled up to the garage, Frey hit the button on the remote opening the small door off to one side of the massive building. "Is that your garage?" Matt asked, eyes wide. Frey didn't respond. He knew as soon as Matt saw the contents of the building he'd have even more questions. "You have a freaking helicopter? Fuck, man, you have *two* helicopters. Uh, I guess it's too late to be asking this, but are you some kind of commando?"

Frey laughed again and shook his head. "No, I own a gym."

Abbi didn't drive into the garage, so Frey shut the Jeep off and hopped out. He walked outside and motioned for her to pull in beside him. Instead, she shut her engine off and parked outside the garage. "Don't touch anything," he yelled to Matthew, not having to look to know the kid was eyeballing the helos. Abbi's eyes were wide when she noticed the contents of Frey's garage. He opened her door and held out his hand. She took it, not looking at him. She, too, was staring in disbelief at the two helicopters. "Come on," he gestured toward where her brother was walking around each one.

Frey opened the door to the Blackhawk, and motioned for Matthew to climb in. "Just don't..."

"Touch anything, I know," Matthew finished. He sat in the pilot's seat, looking at all the controls.

"Uh, Geoffrey, why do you have a military helicopter?" Abbi was on her tiptoes, peeking in. Frey grabbed her around the waist and lifted her into the bird.

"I was a helicopter pilot in the military. That one over there belongs to the Stone family. I'm their pilot, so I keep it here. Faster access if they need it. This baby, now she's a different story. Maybe I'll tell you some day. For now, we need to get all your stuff inside and get you both settled." When Abbi and Matt climbed out, Frey told Abbi to open her trunk. He handed Matthew as many bags as the boy could carry, and he grabbed the rest. He led them along the path from the garage to the back deck. When they reached the door, he gave Abbi the code to the alarm and asked her to do the honors. Once inside, Frey passed through the kitchen and headed to the staircase leading up.

"I have four spare bedrooms. They all have their own bathroom, so you won't have to share. Pick any room you want, and we'll get you settled in." Frey waited in the hall until they'd both chosen a room. Abbi's was across the hall from his with Matt's being on the other end of the house. He deposited the bags of clothing onto the bed and took the others into the bathroom. "As soon as you're ready, I'll be in the kitchen. Come find me, and I'll show you the rest of the house."

Frey left Abbi and Matt to put away their things. Once in the kitchen, he opened the refrigerator and removed leftover lasagna. He wasn't the best cook in the world, but his food was edible. He stuck the dish in the oven and turned it on. It wouldn't take long to heat up, and there was plenty to go around. He went back to the refrigerator and took stock of the contents. Finding it mostly empty, he made a mental note to go shopping. It would be stupid to do, but he wanted Abbi to go with him. If they were seen in public together too often, word would get back to Troy, and the man didn't need any more ammunition against Abbi. No, as much as he'd love to play the domesticated couple, he'd have to go alone.

He had just popped the top on a beer when his two houseguests came downstairs. "I was just seeing what I had in here," he said, pointing to the fridge. "I'll need to go to the grocery store tomorrow. For now, I have lasagna heating in the oven. If you don't want that, there's sandwich stuff. As far as drinks go, I just have beer and milk." Frey opened a drawer and took out a pad of paper and a pen. "Abbi, please make a list of items you and Matt like. I'm not a very good cook, so if you want to take over the kitchen, feel free. I can grill like nobody's business, I'm just lacking when it comes to using an oven.

"I want you both to make yourselves at home. I don't know how long you'll be staying, but while you're here, I want you to feel free to be yourselves. There's over two hundred acres with a five acre lake, plenty of room if you need privacy. Matt, I have a few older gaming systems, but if there's something different you would like, just add it to the list. Whatever either of you need, I want to provide for you both as long as you're here." Frey stopped talking when he noticed the looks on their faces. "What? Did I say something wrong?" They both looked like they were going to cry.

Matt spoke up first, barely whispering, "We're not used to getting what we want, it's always about what he wants."

Frey had to control his temper. He wanted to find Troy and stomp a mud hole in his ass. "That stops now. While you're here, you will be treated the way a family should be treated. Matt, I expect you to keep your room clean, put your dirty clothes in the hamper, hang up your wet towel. You will need to help with the laundry and dishes, not watch your sister do them all. I already take care of my things, so there's no need for you to worry about that. Abbi works hard. We don't need to make it harder on her by having to pick up after us when we're capable of helping out. Abbi, if you want to cook, please do. If you don't, just tell me. I'm not expecting a cook and maid while you're here. I'm offering my home as a safe haven for you both."

Frey was shocked when Matt walked up to him and wrapped his arms around Frey's waist. Automatically, his arms encircled the teen. How long had it been since the boy felt anything other than scorn from the man in his life? Even if Abbi didn't fall in love with him, Frey knew he would remain in Matt's life as a positive role model. Abbi stood watching her brother, tears leaking from the corner of her eyes. Frey held an arm out, and she stepped into his embrace. He had never been one for hugs, but if this is what it felt like, he could get used to it.

# Chapter Fourteen

Abbi was dreaming; she had to be. The three of them stood in a group hug until Matt broke the moment.

"Are there fish in your lake?" Matt asked, bouncing from foot to foot. The solemn boy was back to his natural, wired up self.

"Yes, there are, and yes, I have fishing poles. I usually meditate on the dock, and that is where you will learn as well. Saturday morning, we will walk down to the lake. Abbi, you're welcome to join us. While you are here, I want you both to enjoy the serenity this land offers. We'll have all day Saturday to look around. Since it's late, I will show you the inside."

Frey was confusing Abbi. She thought back to their earlier conversation at the community center. He asked her to give him a chance, but now he was talking about this being temporary. Maybe he was helping them long enough to get Troy out of their lives, and he expected them to move back home. That made sense, more sense than them just moving in and never leaving. They didn't know each other. He was being a gentleman by letting them stay with him for the time being. Once she was free from Troy, she would move back home. If Frey was still interested, she would agree to date him. She jumped into a bad relationship before; she didn't need to do it again.

After Frey had shown them the downstairs, he declared, "I'm hungry. There's plenty of food if you want to eat. If you aren't hungry, feel free to watch television or enjoy the deck."

Abbi was trying to take it all in, but she just couldn't wrap her head around the fact that she was in this stranger's house, and it felt more like home than her house with Troy ever had. Frey pulled the lasagna out of the oven and turned it off. He set three plates on the counter and grabbed a spatula, dishing himself out a huge helping. Abbi couldn't let him serve them, she wasn't wired that way. She began opening drawers, looking for the silverware. "Thank you," Frey told her as she handed him a fork. He smiled his beautiful smile and set his plate on the table. He opened the refrigerator, grabbing another beer and the parmesan cheese.

"Would you like a beer?" he asked her.

"No, thank you. I'll have water." Abbi opened a couple of overhead cabinets before finding the glasses. She took two down, handing one to her brother. Abbi filled hers with ice and water from the freezer door while Matt found the milk and poured himself a tall glassful.

"I'm sorry I don't have bread or salad to go with the pasta. I wasn't expecting company." Frey seemed embarrassed at the lack of food. Abbi had no doubt when he woke up this morning he didn't imagine he would have her and her brother sitting in his kitchen.

"Please, don't apologize. You're already being too kind by letting us stay here." Abbi took a bite of lasagna, her eyes getting big. "This is delicious," she said around the food. Quickly, she covered her mouth, realizing she was talking with her mouth full.

Frey laughed, "I'm glad you like it. I make it all the time. It's one of those dishes you can make a lot of and it reheats well."

It would take a lifetime to get used to someone like Geoffrey Hartley. He reminded Abbi so much of her father, it was almost unreal. The man, even though he appeared to be early thirties, oozed timelessness. She chalked that up to him being in the military. Abbi couldn't imagine seeing the horrors of war. While they ate, she took advantage of the silence to look around. If there had ever been a woman in his life, there was no evidence of it. The furniture was all male. There were no decorations on the walls that weren't something to do with the military. She really wanted to

100

know if there was or had been a woman in his life.

"Frey, please forgive me if I'm overstepping, but have you ever been married?"

He swallowed the mouthful of lasagna he was chewing and took a swig of beer. "Nope, haven't found the right one, yet. I've spent a lot of years traveling the world, fighting wars. That kind of lifestyle isn't conducive to marriage. It's one reason I retired and opened the gym."

"Speaking of the gym, my car's still there. How am I getting to school tomorrow?" Matt's plate was clean, his glass empty. He was probably still hungry, but wouldn't dare ask for seconds. If Frey really was the nice guy he claimed to be, he wouldn't mind Matt getting more food.

"Matty, do you want more lasagna?" she asked, testing the waters. Her brother's eyes widened as he looked to Frey for permission.

"I've already told you both, make yourself at home. You don't need to ask if you can have more food, Matt. If it's in this house, you're welcome to it," Frey huffed. "As a matter of fact, I'm having a second helping." He didn't wait for an answer. Instead, he grabbed Matt's plate along with his own and dished out more for them both. "Abbi?"

"No, thank you. I'm full." She smiled briefly. Yes, this man was too good to be true.

"Your sister and I have already discussed this, but until this thing with Troy is settled, you and Abbi will have a ride wherever you go. I'm not trying to cramp your style. If you want to go out with friends, that can be arranged, but I'd prefer you hang close to the gym or my house for the time being. Whoever is driving you will be nearby at all times. I promised you I'd keep you safe, and if that means having someone watch your back twenty-four seven, then that's what I'll do.

"Abbi, I'll drop you off at work before I take Matthew to school. Either I or one of my men will be close by all day for both of you. I will pick you up and take you to

101

the community center for your classes. Matt, Sixx will be picking you up and bringing you back here. Abbi, Jasper is going to come over here Saturday and take your statement so you can file a restraining order. I would take you to the precinct, but if Troy has friends in the department, you don't need to be seen down there. He's probably going to figure out you're gone any minute now, and your phones are going to blow up. We'll get you both new phones with new numbers tomorrow. For tonight, you can just turn them off. Actually, it would be better if I could have the sim cards out of them so I can destroy them. That way, he can't track your whereabouts. He is a cop after all."

"I don't know what a sim card is, but here's my phone." Abbi took her phone out of her purse and handed it to Frey. He turned the phone over and opened a compartment on the back, removing a little black disc. Matthew mimicked Frey's movements, and handed his card over. Frey stood from the table and went to the bathroom in the hall. The toilet flushed, and he returned. Instead of sitting, he grabbed his plate and took it to the sink.

Abbi stood and reached for Matt's plate, but he shook his head, "I got it." He took his plate to the sink and just as Frey had, rinsed it and put it in the dishwasher. Frey spooned out the few leftover noodles into the garbage can and put the dish in the sink to soak. With only her plate and glass left, she rinsed them both and placed them in the dishwasher.

"It's been a long day. If you don't mind, I'm going to turn in." Abbi wanted time alone to digest the events of the day. Had it just been that morning that Troy assaulted her in the shower? And now, here she was in another man's home.

"I don't mind. If you hear someone walking around during the night, it's me. I hate to admit, but sometimes I have nightmares and can't sleep. I just don't want you to be alarmed."

"Thanks for the heads up. Well, goodnight, Frey.

Matty, I will see you in the morning."

"Night, Abs," Matt hugged his sister but didn't follow her upstairs. She really couldn't blame him. This was the first time in a long time her brother had a man in his life that paid attention to him. She climbed the stairs to her room. Before she shut her door, she glanced at Frey's room. She couldn't imagine the kinds of nightmares he had, but she bet they had to do with the wars he'd been in.

Abbi took time to look around the bedroom she'd chosen. It wasn't lost on her that she chose the one across the hall from Frey's. For a spare room, it was large, larger than her bedroom at home. As with downstairs, the furniture was masculine yet attractive. The bed was king-sized, and she couldn't wait to sink into the rich looking bedding, but not yet. Abbi was dirty. Even though she'd showered that morning, she felt sullied. Troy always made her feel that way. She didn't want to slip under Frey's sheets with any lingering trace of her husband on her, so she took a quick shower.

She had left every nightgown at home. She refused to bring anything that reminded her of Troy. As soon as she could, she was going shopping for clothes that fit her. She'd seen the way Frey's eyes traveled over her legs when she stepped out of the house wearing jeans. But then again, he'd seen her in next to nothing when he caught her dancing. After putting on a pair of cute pajama pants and t-shirt, she slid between the sheets of the king-size bed. There were no sounds coming from downstairs. If Frey and Matt were still up, they were being quiet. Feeling safe for the first time in forever, Abbi rolled over, hugging the extra pillow to her body and sent up a silent thank you to whoever was listening.

Abbi was wakened by a loud rumbling. She lay still, listening. The noise was low but constant. When the sound continued, she sat up and pushed back the covers, lowering her legs over the side of the bed. When she opened her door, the sound, coming from Frey's bedroom, intensified. He'd said he had nightmares. Was he having one now? As she placed her hand on his doorknob, Matthew's door opened. "What the hell is that?" he asked, his voice scratchy from sleep.

"I think Frey's having a nightmare. Go back to bed." When Matt complied, she turned her attention back to the door in front of her. The moaning hadn't lessened in the minute she'd been standing there. Taking a deep breath, she turned the knob as quietly as possible. The sight of a nearly naked Frey grabbed her attention. The huge man was thrashing about in his bed, the covers tangled around his legs. Abbi didn't know if it was safe to wake him, but she couldn't stand watching the torment he was going through.

"Geoffrey," she whispered as she stepped into his room. "Geoffrey," she said a little louder when her voice wasn't penetrating. "Frey!" she yelled. Before Abbi could think, Frey was out of bed and had her pinned to the wall. His huge body covered hers completely. Her arms were shackled above her head in one of his huge hands. Chest heaving, his breath was coming in harsh pants. Frey's cock grew hard against her stomach. She raised her eyes and gasped. She could have sworn she saw fangs protruding from his mouth. Frey leaned his head in close to her neck, his nose skimming along from behind her ear, down to her shoulder. Abbi closed her eyes and waited for his sharp teeth to sink into her skin.

# Chapter Fifteen

"*Sir, are you sure the building's empty?*"

"*Infrared shows only adults.*"

"*What about women, Sir?*"

"*Son, I gave you a direct order. Fire the goddamn missile.*"

Don't fucking call me Son. "*Yes, Sir.*" *Frey locked on to the target and fired. Direct hit. The pilot flew the jet low over the kill zone. Frey's shifter vision allowed him to see the carnage, drink it in, focus on every last piece of shrapnel. His stomach threatened to come out his throat when he saw the scattered remains of several children.*

"*What the fuck? You said the building was secure!*" *Frey screamed into his com. The tiny, decimated bodies were burned into his brain. He felt the deaths deep in his soul.* "*No, No, NO!!!*"

"Geoffrey."

"*No, I won't do it again!*"

"Geoffrey!"

"*Shut the fuck up! I told you I can't do it anymore!*"

"Frey!"

Frey grabbed his CO by the neck and pinned him to the wall. Oh gods, that wasn't his CO. Fucking hell, he had Abbi. Her body felt so good, smelled so fucking good. His nose was buried in her neck, fangs out. Fuck, he had to let her go, but he needed to get his shifter under control. Had Abbi seen his fangs? *Fuck!* What was she doing in his room?

"Frey?" Abbi's voice was strained.

He didn't remove his nose from her neck as he whispered, "Give me a second."

Abbi remained frozen beneath him, not that she could move if she wanted. Her heartbeat was frantic. He had probably scared the shit out of her, but he couldn't move back. Not yet. The thin t-shirt she was wearing did little to hide her full breasts. Between his fangs popping out and the hard cock in his boxer briefs… Thank the gods he'd put on underwear. If he was completely naked next to his mate, he wasn't sure he could keep his beast under control.

Frey released Abbi's arms and took a step back. He couldn't bear to look at her, to see the fear in her eyes. He walked over to the window, keeping his back to her. He didn't need to push the curtain aside to know the moon was high and full. He could feel it in his soul. The Gargoyles always knew where the moon was. A small hand on his back surprised him. He turned his head finding Abbi next to him.

"Does that happen to you every night?" she asked, removing her hand. Frey immediately missed the connection.

"Not every night, but most." He searched her eyes for fear, but instead he found sympathy. "I'm sorry I woke you." Abbi was staring at his face, his mouth, as if searching for something. *Had* she seen his fangs? He turned back toward the window, this time he did move the curtain aside so it would appear he was looking out. She might find it odd, him staring at the closed drapes.

"I'll leave you alone." Her fingers ghosted across his skin. Frey didn't move, didn't turn around. His cock still hadn't deflated from being pressed against Abbi's body, and the touch of her hand on his arm had him growing harder. He wasn't embarrassed for waking her; he just hoped he hadn't scared her.

"Abbi?" He still couldn't look at her. "I'm sorry if I scared you."

"It's okay," her voice came from across the room. He waited until he heard the soft click of the door closing before he turned around. Scrubbing a hand down his face, he let out a huge sigh. That had been too close for comfort. Instead of going back to bed and risking a repeat performance, Frey slid on a pair of jeans and headed to the lake.

The full moon lit the pathway leading to the dock.

Not that Frey needed the light. Between his shifter eyesight and muscle memory, he could make the walk with his eyes closed. When he reached the end, he didn't bother rolling his pants up. He sat down and dangled his bare feet in the cool, calm water.

Matthew's presence seeped into Frey's mind before he heard the boy's feet tapping along the wood planks. "Mind if I join you?" the teen asked, not bothering to wait on an answer before he sat down.

Frey grinned at him, "I don't guess it matters."

"I figured since you were already down here, maybe you could go ahead and give me my first lesson in meditation. I mean, that's why you're down here. Right?"

"How'd you get so smart?" Frey laughed. "Yes, that is exactly why I'm down here. Okay, first thing close your eyes."

"Don't we have to sit cross-legged?"

"Nope. It's not about a position of your body, but your mind. Now close your eyes." When Matthew complied, Frey continued, "Listen to the sounds. Separate them. Put the frogs in one compartment, the crickets in another. When the owl hoots, put him somewhere else. This will take a while to master, but that's the first thing you have to do, recognize everything around you and put them in different boxes." Frey closed his own eyes and did what he told Matt to do. It would surprise him if the teen could sit still for more than five minutes. When they had been silent for a while, Frey said, "Tell me what you hear."

"Frogs, crickets. I haven't heard the owl yet. There's a dog barking in the distance. Something splashed in the water."

"Very good. Do you hear a heartbeat?"

"Just mine beating in my chest."

There was no way Matt could hear his sister's heartbeat. Frey shouldn't be able to, but with his enhanced senses, he knew Abbi was behind him. He had known the

107

instant she stepped onto the pathway that led to the lake. Instead of calling her out, he allowed himself to feel her presence course through his body. Her pulse was strong as it found his and the two synchronized. Frey couldn't imagine how strongly they would be connected if they were ever truly mated to one another.

Frey was proud of Matthew for sitting still as long as he had. "I'm impressed, Matt. You did very well for your first time. I want you to practice at least once a day. You are welcome to come back to the lake where it's peaceful while you are getting the hang of it. If you get a chance, though, I want you to try and separate the sounds when you are somewhere busy. Eventually, you will be able to push everything out of your mind except what you need to concentrate on. When I get you in the ring, I want you focused solely on fighting... your rhythm, breathing, form. There can be no outside distractions if you are to become proficient."

"Wow," Matt whispered.

Frey didn't think his speech was wow worthy, so he asked, "Wow, what?"

"I've never seen daylight break." Matt was looking around, seeing the lake for the first time.

Frey couldn't remember the first time he'd watched the sun come up. That moment when the darkness gave way to the light, so gradually, yet so suddenly, you didn't realize it had happened. "It's spectacular, isn't it?"

"No wonder you come down here. I..." Matt hesitated. Frey didn't want to push, but he was interested in what the boy had to say.

"You?" he prodded.

"It's nothing. Well, it's something, but it doesn't matter. Me and Abbi won't be here that long."

"Matt, as long as you are here, this is your home. The house, the lake, the woods, all of it. If there comes a day you and Abbi decide you're safe again and you leave, you are still welcome here. Anytime." Frey knew he was getting too close to the boy, but Matt was part of Abbi and that meant he was part of Frey. Even if Abbi never allowed him in her life, he would continue to be a positive role model for Matthew.

Matthew opened his mouth to say something then closed it. He looked away from Frey, his shoulders hunching. Frey wasn't going to push.

Matt cleared his throat, finding the courage to ask his question. "Have you ever killed anyone?"

That had not been what Frey expected to come out of the teen's mouth. "I was in the military, been in several wars. So, yeah, I have."

"How did it make you feel? Did it give you satisfaction or…"

"Taking a life for any reason is serious, Matt. I was in a war; it was kill or be killed. Have you given this a lot of thought?" Was the boy contemplating taking out his brother-in-law?

"Not really. It's just sometimes I wonder if the world wouldn't be better off without some people in it."

"I have to say, I can understand where you're coming from. Not all bad people end up in jail, but we have to try to let the justice system do its job."

"I guess." Matt stared off across the pond, deep in thought.

"I need coffee. Feel free to stay down here as long as you like. Well, at least until you have to get ready for school. I'm going to see about getting you a math tutor for later on, if that's okay."

Matt nodded. "I really appreciate it. I get out of school at three, and I don't have to work afterwards, so any time after that would be great."

Frey was proud of Matthew for willingly spending his Friday night studying instead of doing whatever it was teenagers did now days. "I'll see you back at the house."

109

Frey stood and headed away from the lake, following Abbi's retreating footsteps. She was walking quickly. Every so often her steps would falter, and she would let out a soft curse. Frey figured she was barefoot. He took his time behind her, giving her a chance to either hide out in her room, or confront him in the kitchen. Either way, he was ready for his morning jolt of caffeine.

When he reached the kitchen, Abbi was nowhere to be seen. As he prepared the coffee pot, he reached out, sensing she was pacing back and forth in her room. He took the opportunity to call Sixx. Not only was he going to ask him to keep an eye on Matthew while he was at school but also tutor him. Frey would be the one to watch over Abbi.

After he hung up with Sixx, he called Uri, asking him to hold training by himself, explaining why. When he was off the phone, he checked the refrigerator. Not a lot to choose from. Normally, Frey didn't eat breakfast. Instead he prepared a protein shake at the gym. He would have Abbi add breakfast items to her grocery list, and he would stop at the store later. The back door opened, and Matt came in, more subdued than usual.

"I was just checking to see if I had anything for breakfast. It's slim pickings. I can stop and get you something on the way to school if you'd like."

Matthew pointed at the coffee pot. "That's breakfast enough for me. Besides, I can grab something in the cafeteria."

Frey pulled out a second coffee cup and handed it to Matt. "Milk's in the fridge, but I'm all out of sugar."

"That's all right, I drink it black anyway." Matthew helped himself to the steamy liquid, sipping it carefully. "Ahhhh, the elixir of the gods."

Frey laughed, but he felt the exact same way. "Truth." As he sipped his own cup, his body tingled, his chest tightened. Abbi was close.

"Can I have some of that elixir?" she asked as she

110

entered the kitchen, grinning at her brother. Her smile alone was enough to bring Frey to his knees. He had been through countless battles, nearly getting shot out of the sky, but never had he felt anything like what his mate did to him. This female unsettled him in ways he couldn't fathom. And they weren't true mates. Not yet.

He opened the cabinet and handed her a cup. "Like I told Matthew, we have milk but no sugar. If you would, add whatever breakfast items you'd like to the grocery list." If Frey was honest with himself, he was happier in that moment than he'd ever been in his life. Having Abbi and Matt with him in his kitchen felt like he had a family. He couldn't remember being young, having his parents and brothers in the same house. It was too long ago. With all three of them together, his big house finally felt like a home, even if it was temporary.

Once everyone was dressed and ready to go, they headed toward the garage. Frey had already pulled his truck out of the garage, not expecting Abbi to ride in his Jeep. "Where's the Jeep?" Matt asked.

"In the garage. This will be more comfortable for Abbi." Frey opened the door and held Abbi's bags while she climbed in. Matthew hopped in the back, sliding across to lean forward between the two front seats.

"How many vehicles do you own?" he asked Frey.

"Three for now. Besides the truck and jeep, I have a Harley, too." Frey started the truck and eased down the driveway. The gate automatically opened as they neared and closed behind them.

"You sure do have some cool shit," Matt said as he leaned back.

"Matthew!" Abbi chastised him.

"Well, he does." Matthew sat back, looking out the side window.

Frey laughed softly. He never had to worry about money. He'd always had plenty, but when Sixx came into their lives and started investing the Clan's money, he'd made them all wealthy beyond their wildest imaginations. None of the Stone Society would ever have to worry about their finances. Neither would their kids or grandkids, if and when they ever had them. "I have made some really good investments over the years. Something we need to do is look at getting you some new wheels."

"You can't do that," Abbi declared from her side of the truck.

"Don't worry; I'm not buying him a new Corvette. But you have seen the piece of shit he drives, right? I want him to have something dependable."

"His car may not look like much, but it is dependable, and he paid for it himself. We can't afford anything newer right now." She turned her gaze to the window.

Frey knew he'd just stepped in deep shit and hurt their feelings. He didn't know what it was like to have to scrape by for the necessities.

"I'll make payments. We can set up a schedule, and you can take it out of my check from the gym." Matthew was obviously onboard with having something newer to drive.

"That'll work. We'll go this weekend," Frey told Matt's reflection in the mirror. The kid nodded and smiled. *Fuck.* Just the basic needs being met were putting a smile on the kid's face. Yeah, Frey was going to put a hurting on Troy Quinn.

"We're close to some drive-thrus. Are you sure you don't want anything?" Both said they were fine, so Frey drove on to the elementary. "We are going to drive by slowly, and I want you to look for Troy's vehicle. If he's here, we'll drive around back." Both Abbi and Matthew searched, and neither saw him. Frey pulled up to the front door and let the truck idle. "What time do you get out of here?"

112

"I will be finished by three-thirty."

"Okay, I'll see you then. Abbi, if Troy tries to give you any trouble today, call me immediately."

Abbi smiled and nodded. "Thank you, Geoffrey."

Frey wanted so bad to lean over and kiss her lips. Until she was his, he had to tame his beast. "Have a good day." He waited until Abbi was safely inside before driving off.

"You like her, don't you?" Matthew asked as he climbed in the front seat.

"Yes, she's really nice."

"No, I mean you *like her* like her. It's okay if you do. She needs a good man in her life instead of that piece of shit she's married to. Please tell me you like her."

Frey laughed at the puppy dog eyes Matthew was giving him. For a seventeen year old boy who was almost a man, he could act really child-like. He figured that was because Matt hadn't had a decent role model in ten years.

"Yeah, I *like her* like her. She's pretty, and smart, and one helluva dancer." Frey couldn't help the shit-eating grin plastered across his face.

Matthew gasped. "You've seen her dance? When?"

"Last night when I went to the community center to talk to her. She laced up those funny looking pink shoes and twirled around the room. It was the most beautiful sight I've ever seen."

"Yeah," Matthew agreed, grinning.

When they got close to the high school, Frey pointed out Sixx, sitting in one of his many cars. "That's Michael Gentry. He will be close by all day. When you get out of school, he'll pick you up. Here's his phone number. If you have trouble of any kind, or see Troy before you reach Sixx's car, call him."

"Sixx?" Matthew asked, confused.

"Yeah, Michael worships the old rocker Nikki Sixx. Dresses like him on weekends. It's really funny to see him with his hair all spiked. Don't worry, you'll get a glimpse of the glamour queen tomorrow." Frey couldn't help but smile when his mind brought forth an image of his rocker wannabe cousin.

"Cool. Frey, thanks for this. I still don't get why you chose me and Abbi, but I'm glad you did." Matthew didn't allow Frey to respond. Instead, he jumped out of the truck and gave Frey a backwards two-finger salute as he walked away.

"The fates chose you and Abbi, and I'm also glad they did," Frey told the teen's retreating body.

# Chapter Sixteen

Troy woke with the sun in his face coming through the front window. He'd fallen asleep on the couch when he came in the night before. He had every intention of showering the scent of the two women off his body before taking what was his from Abbi. Shit, he couldn't believe he'd slept so late. She could have at least woken him before she left for school. He'd have to get on to her for that.

His mind drifted back to the previous night's events. Those two girls had been a trip. They had definitely put on a show for him and George. It'd been a while since he and his best friend had tag-teamed the ladies. Before George was married, they did it at least once a month. Then his friend became a little more discreet in his cheating. He wasn't careful enough, though. The marriage lasted all of six months, and once the divorce was final, the threesomes were back on. And now that Troy was on second shift, he could see them happening quite often. As a matter of fact, the four of them had already decided tonight would be a repeat performance.

Troy lay back down on the couch and flipped the television on. He didn't have to be at work for a while, so he was going to enjoy the quiet without his wife banging around the kitchen.

Frey had called Lorenzo and asked if he could watch the school while Frey ran his errands. Mason was manning the gym. He really should be there himself, but Abbi and Matt were too important. He'd close the gym before he'd neglect their well-being. His first order of business was to purchase them both new cell phones. He didn't ask Abbi if it was okay to get Matt a smart phone, he just figured it was better to ask for forgiveness than permission. He was also going to make sure they both had dependable cars, whether Abbi liked it or not.

He pulled into the grocery store parking lot and killed the engine. Before he went inside, he took the grocery list out of his pocket and stared at it. Abbi had written very little on the list. Fuck it, he'd buy what he thought they would like. Once inside, he grabbed a cart and started in the produce aisle. He grabbed the essential vegetables and headed to the meats. By the time he was finished, he had everything on the list plus enough other items to fill the cart. He paid for the groceries, returned home, and put them away. While he did that, he put both their phones on chargers.

He didn't know if they liked steaks or would prefer hamburgers, so he marinated steaks, just in case. If they chose hamburgers, those were easy enough to pat out later. When that was finished, he grabbed both phones off the chargers and headed back toward town. He stopped first at the high school, asking to speak with the principal. The secretary sat staring momentarily before finally gathering her wits about her. Frey had that effect on almost everyone. When the principal came out of his office, he smiled and shook Frey's hand. If they had been in the dojo, he would have bowed.

"Scott, how are you?" Frey asked one of his newest students.

"Doing well. Looking forward to our next class. What brings you here?" Scott wasn't a tall man, but he was stocky, much like Gregor.

"Can we speak in private?"

"Sure, come into my office." Scott escorted him into the inner room and shut the door.

"One of your students is being abused. He came to me for help, wanting to train, and I've taken him under my wing, so to speak. The reason I'm telling you this, is his

116

abuser is his brother-in-law who also happens to be a cop."

"Matthew Swanson. I knew someone was getting to the boy. I've seen the bruises, but he clams up when I ask him about them. He always says it's some punk from work. Dammit, I should have turned him over to child services anyway."

"He's protecting his sister. I wanted to ask you to keep an eye on Matt while he's in the building. I have someone outside watching him. Here is a list of my men with their pictures. If you see any of them lurking around the building, I'd appreciate it if you wouldn't call the cops. They will stay out of the way unless they feel there's a threat to Matthew. If they come in the school, it's for a good reason."

"I'll let the teachers know to be on the lookout. What else can I do?"

Frey pulled Matt's cellphone out of his pocket. "Please give this to Matt. His old one was compromised."

"Thanks for the heads up. I'll do everything in my power to keep him safe inside these walls." Scott held out his hand, and Frey shook it gratefully.

His next order of business was taking Abbi's phone to her and alerting her principal of the dangers of Troy Quinn. Once that was taken care of, he relieved Lorenzo of his post and took up residence in the elementary parking lot. While he waited, he called Rafael and filled him in on what was going on. His King was understanding as well as supportive. They were family, and as such, mates came first. It didn't matter that Frey and Abbi hadn't completed the bond, just like when Dante went after Isabelle and Connor. With any luck, Frey would get Abbi away from her dickhead husband. Hopefully one day, even if it took years, she would feel something other than the mate bond for Frey.

Sixx called relaying he had Matthew safely on his way home. Frey could hear the boy chattering excitedly in the background. "What's the kid going on about?"

117

Sixx sighed. "Apparently, I look like a rock star."

"Well, we all knew that."

"I'll see you later." Sixx cut the connection. Frey laughed out loud, knowing how much of a handful Matt could be when he got going. Frey leaned his head back and smiled. He couldn't remember smiling or laughing as much as he had in the last few days. The kid brought it out in him. He wanted to return the favor.

At three-thirty on the dot, Abbi walked out of the school, looking more beautiful than ever. He had wanted to compliment her clothing that morning, but didn't want to make her feel awkward. There would be plenty of time to build up her self-esteem later. She climbed into the truck and smiled. "How was your day?" he asked as he drove away from the school.

"Same as any other Friday, with the exception of some man bringing me a new phone." She sheepishly smiled and looked away. "Thank you."

"You're welcome. What time is your class at the community center?"

"Normally at 4:30, but I canceled it for today. Troy has a habit of showing up there unannounced, and I didn't want to risk it."

"Very good. Matthew's already home, so let's go see about feeding him."

Abbi didn't respond. She did, however, stare at Frey's profile. He could feel her eyes on him, and his beast was punching him from the inside. *You can just simmer down there big boy. It's gonna be a while before you get loose with this one.* "Do you want to tell me why you're staring?" he asked.

"Do you want to tell me why you care so much? I know there are good people in the world, but you are going above and beyond."

Frey couldn't stop his hand from reaching for hers. She didn't pull away; if anything, she held on a little tighter. "I have already tried to explain it the best way I can. Abbi, I

118

am attracted to you. I'm not going to call it love at first sight, but I felt an immediate connection to you the first time I saw you. If you were single, I'd be asking you on dates, begging you to let me get to know you better. The situation is a little strange, I agree, but I still want that chance to know you and for you to know me." He glanced her way before turning his eyes back to the curvy road his house was on.

Abbi continued staring at his profile. Instead of responding, she threaded their fingers together. The rest of the drive was made in a sweet silence. Frey pulled up to the gate and said, "Open says me." The gate opened and Abbi let out a giggle. He raised his eyebrows at her and asked, "What?"

"You do realize it's 'open sesame', don't you?" She was still giggling when he huffed at her.

"Not at my gate it's not." He pretended to be disgruntled, but Abbi's laugh had him smiling quickly.

As they rolled up to the garage, Abbi asked, "Who's car is *that*?" Sixx had chosen to drive his Bugatti Veyron. No wonder Matt thought he was a rock star.

"That would be Michael's. I'm afraid to let you close to him."

"Why?" Abbi asked excitedly.

Frey cringed. "See, you're already excited, and you've only seen the car. All the women love Sixx. That's what Michael calls himself, after the guitarist, Nikki Sixx of…"

"Motley Crue! I love that band. Does he really look like a rock star?"

"Only on the weekends. Come on, let's get this over with." Frey knew it was a lost cause. Why would Abbi want a big oaf like him when someone as good looking and sophisticated as Michael was around?

The front door opened, and Matthew bound down the steps. "Have you seen this car? Holy shit! It goes like two hundred plus!"

119

"What?" Abbi wasn't impressed with Sixx now. Frey knew there was no way Sixx would have gone that fast with the kid in the car, but he wasn't about to clear that little misunderstanding up.

About that time, the culprit walked out the door, shaking his head. "It does go that fast. *We* didn't go that fast. Hi, I'm Michael." Sixx kept his hands in his pockets and stayed back from Abbi.

"Nice to meet you. Thank you for watching over Matt today." Abbi pulled Matthew into a hug, keeping him away from the expensive sports car.

"You're welcome. Matt, are you ready to study?"

"Yeah, sure. And while we're getting set up, I'm going to show you the lead singer for Cyanide Sweetness. I swear you look just like Desi Rothchild."

"What did you say?" Sixx asked accusingly.

"Man, the lead singer of Cyanide Sweetness. We've already discussed this."

"Yes, but you didn't mention his name. Never mind, let's go."

Sixx and Matthew climbed the steps, disappearing into the house to study, leaving Frey and Abbi alone. "I went to the store, and I have steaks marinating. Is that okay, or would you prefer hamburgers?"

"Mmmmm." Abbi groaned enthusiastically. "I can't remember the last time I had a grilled steak."

Surely she was kidding. Everyone ate steaks. Everyone except those who couldn't afford it or had a fucktard for a husband. Frey knew cops didn't make a lot of money and neither did school teachers. But surely, between the two of them, they could have bought the beef on sale at some point. "Steak it is, then. I will fire up the grill then get started on the potatoes."

"Let me do those. I wouldn't feel right you doing all the work."

"I'd appreciate that. The potatoes are in the pantry.

There's also stuff for salad in the fridge if you want to tackle that too. I suck at peeling vegetables."

Abbi laughed and told him, "I'll have to teach you the proper way to do it then."

Frey wanted Abbi to teach him all sorts of things, and most of them had absolutely nothing to do with food. They worked in tandem, Frey manning the grill, Abbi handling the salad and potatoes in the kitchen. When everything was ready, Frey called out to Sixx.

"There's no way he heard you." *Shit.* He really needed to be careful around her. She was highly observant. Her eyes widened when Sixx and Matt came down the steps.

"What is that smell?" Matthew stood at the entrance to the kitchen and sniffed the air. Abbi laughed at her brother.

"It's steak." She whispered, almost reverently. Frey didn't miss the look between the two of them, nor the one Sixx gave him.

"All right, I'm out of here. I'll see you at the restaurant in the morning." Sixx bumped knuckles with Matt and nodded at Frey and Abbi.

"Man, he's the coolest!" Matthew was bouncing around the kitchen. Frey couldn't blame the kid. Sixx was pretty cool for an old man.

Abbi dished out salad into a bowl, and said, "Yeah, if you like the brooding silent type, which I don't." She glanced at Frey and smiled. His heart soared.

# Chapter Seventeen

The three of them sat at the table, eating, talking, and basically acting like a family after a day at work and school. Frey was afraid to get his hopes up, but dammit, he wanted this. All of it. When they finished eating, they all pitched in and did the dishes. Afterwards, they went into the large living area, and Frey told them to pick a movie to watch. When he opened the hidden cabinet on one side of the wall, Matthew just about had a teenage seizure. Frey could open his own video store with all the movies he had. "If you can't find any on that side, check in here." He opened the cabinet on the other side which secretly housed the video player as well as several different gaming systems.

"Holy shit, Batman!" Matthew began looking through the myriad of video games.

"Matty!" Abbi chastised him for his language, but Frey could understand the teen's excitement. When Matt confided he didn't play basketball, because he had to work, Frey guessed then the teen probably wasn't allowed to have any of the smaller things that would make a kid happy. "You can go through the videos while I'm at work. Go ahead and pick a movie." Even though she was fussing at him, she did it with a soft voice and with love. It was probably her teacher voice. Frey would love to see her interact with her students.

It took Matt about fifteen minutes, but he finally chose a movie they all agreed on. When the credits rolled, they all said goodnight and went to their respective rooms. Before Abbi walked to her door, she stopped Frey and held his hand. "Thank you for everything." She tugged his hand down and stood on her tiptoes, placing a kiss on his cheek.

"You're welcome." When she closed her door, he leaned against the wall, sighing. His cock was trying to escape its confines. He knew then it was going to be a long night.

Frey hadn't been wrong. He willed his hard-on to go away for over an hour and finally gave up. He started off taking a cold shower, but his dick would not deflate, so he allowed his thoughts to drift to the beautiful blonde across the hall as he tugged one out. He woke a couple of hours later, his dick once again standing at attention. Instead of taking another shower, he slid his hands under the covers, removed his boxer briefs, and grabbed his erection tightly.

He reached out with his senses, hearing both his guests were breathing evenly, good and asleep. Once more he brought the vision of Abbi to his mind, her beautiful smile, her toned body, her pert breasts. Gods, she was perfect. Frey closed his eyes and imagined his mate, straddling his body, riding his cock for all she was worth. It didn't take long until he was shooting his load into his underwear. Using the boxers, he cleaned the come off his spent dick. Hopefully, that would sate his need until morning.

Abbi had risen early and cooked breakfast for everyone while the boys had gone down to the dock for meditation. Once again, it had been the three of them eating together, talking about their upcoming day. "I'm ready whenever you are," Frey told Matt when the teen came down from his shower.

Frey so wanted to kiss Abbi goodbye, like he would if she were already his. Instead, he gently gripped her shoulder and squeezed. "Jasper might get here before I get back. If he does, he'll let himself into the gate, so don't be alarmed." Frey had explained their cell phones and the preprogrammed numbers the night before. "I'm going to drop Matt off and check on the dojo. If you need anything before I get back, just call. If I don't hear from you, I'll see you soon."

"Bye, Abs." Matthew kissed his sister on the cheek and followed Frey to the back door. "I'll be glad when my

123

time's up at the restaurant. I can't wait to work for you instead." Matthew climbed up into the jeep and buckled up.

"Won't be long now. You'll be washing stinky towels instead of dirty dishes before you know it." They both laughed. Frey turned on the radio. "Put it on whatever you want."

Matthew gave him a guarded look. "Seriously? Dude, I listen to metal. You don't look like a metal kind of man."

"Oh, yeah? What kind of man do I look like?" Frey regarded him out of the corner of his eye.

"Country. Maybe some old rock, just not the new stuff."

Frey grinned inwardly as he turned up the volume, metal music blasting through the speakers. Matthew's eyes grew wide to match the grin on his face. He just shook his head and started singing. When they reached the restaurant, Frey peered around for Sixx, spotting his car in the lot across the street. Frey turned the volume down. "There's Sixx. He'll probably sit in a booth toward the back, out of the way, so he won't interfere with your job. Just don't leave alone, okay?" Sixx walked in front of the Jeep giving Frey an almost imperceptible nod.

"I still think Desmond Rothchild is that man's love child," Matt said staring after Sixx.

"That's highly unlikely. Now, get in there and clean those dishes. I'll see you at home later." It wasn't lost on Frey that he said *home*.

Matthew held out his fist and they knuckle bumped. "Later, Frey."

Frey waited until Matthew was safe inside the building before driving away. With Sixx there watching, nothing bad could happen to the teen.

Dane arrived at the coffee shop a little before eight. He took a seat at the same table where he'd previously waited for Katherine to show up. That meeting had been at her request. Since then, he'd only seen her on the news or at certain crime scenes. Scenes she shouldn't have been privy to, at least not as quickly as she was. He asked her to coffee under the false pretense that he had some news to share with her.

Julian sat at the next table over, sipping coffee, typing away madly on a laptop. Dane was nervous, and if he was being truthful, feeling a little unwell. Marley, the pretty waitress who served him before, arrived at his table with her usual chipper smile. "Hello, Detective. Having your usual?"

Dane smiled back. He liked that she was attentive and knew what he wanted. "Yes, please." She walked toward the kitchen, tossing him an extra smile over her shoulder. Someone cleared their throat. When he turned around, Katherine Fox was standing beside his table.

"Am I interrupting?" she asked, a little snark in her tone.

"Not at all, please have a seat." Dane stood, pouring on the southern charm as he pulled out her chair. One glance at Julian was enough to have the new half-blood rethinking this meeting. Julian's fingers hovered just above the keys as he glared at the news reporter. Dane knew if Katherine was his mate, he would feel something in her presence. He took in her long red hair, green eyes, the freckles that dotted her cheeks. Was he feeling anything out of the ordinary? Maybe.

"Abbott, are you going to stare all morning, or are you going to tell me why you asked me here?"

"I wanted to let you know Gordon Flanagan is

dead."

"You could have told me that over the phone." She leaned back in her chair, tossing her arm across the top rung. Casually, she asked, "What's this really about?"

"I..." He glanced around to make sure no one was paying attention. "I need to ask you something. You show up at crime scenes often before some of our officers do. Who are you getting your information from?"

Katherine sat up, gesturing for Dane to move in closer. A faint growl came from the next table over. *Shit.* He did as she asked, leaning in. "You know I won't give up my source." She leaned back, the smirk alive on her lips once again.

"If your source happens to be someone inside my department, I need to know about it."

Sliding her chair back, she stood and stepped to his side of the table. "I guess you'll just have to keep on wondering, now won't you?" She turned to leave, and Julian all but jumped from his seat, shoving his laptop in the sleeve as he was headed to the door. That hadn't gone as planned. He mentally chastised himself. If he was going to be Chief, he would need her as an ally more than an enemy.

Marley returned with his latte. The nauseous feeling was back. Shit, could Marley be his mate? She'd been present the last time he'd met with Katherine. He glanced up into her face, a face that was no longer smiling. Not even close to friendly. *Shit.*

Troy cracked open an eye. His second hangover in a row, only this one was worse. He sat up on the sofa, swinging his legs over the side. He leaned his elbows on his knees, placing his head in his hands. "Abbi, bring me some aspirin," he yelled as loud as his head would allow. When his wife didn't answer him, he yelled louder, "Goddamnit, Abbi, bring me some fucking aspirin."

Where the fuck was she? He stood on wobbly legs, pausing to gain his balance. He took stock of his clothes which were rumpled from sleeping in them. They also smelled like sex and booze. What a time he and George had last night. Again, both women had been up for anything. When Debbie suggested he and George suck each other off, that's where he drew the line and called it a night. He wasn't a faggot and never would be. Girls eating each other out was a huge turn on, but two guys sucking dick made him wanna puke.

Troy plodded into the kitchen, looking for a cup of coffee. The pot was empty. "Abigail!" He headed to their bedroom, fully expecting her to be there. When he pushed open the door and saw the empty bed, he lost his shit. Forgetting about his headache, Troy stomped to the door leading to the garage. He knew in his gut before he opened it her car wouldn't be there since she wasn't supposed to park in the garage. He searched anyway. When his instincts were correct, he let out a roar. "You stupid bitch, where the fuck are you?"

He picked up the landline receiver and dialed her cell phone. She was probably back at the fucking community center instead of being there to cook his fucking breakfast. The call went directly to voicemail. He hung up and dialed it again. After the fifth time of receiving no answer, he left her a message. "Abigail, I don't know where you are, but I suggest you get your ass home. Right fucking now." He slammed the receiver down and headed to the shower. He would have to go to the coffeehouse around the corner until she decided to get her happy ass back where she belonged.

As the water sluiced over his skin, Troy thought back to the previous night. Both those girls could suck a tennis ball through an exhaust pipe. He couldn't get Abbi's mouth anywhere near his cock unless he shoved it there while holding onto her hair. Thinking of Debbie sucking him off had his dick getting hard. He reached down for his shampoo and found the bottle empty. "Fucking bitch didn't get my fucking shampoo." Not caring that Abbi's smelled fruity, he reached for hers only to find the bottle missing. "What the hell?"

His cock still demanded attention, so he grabbed the soap and lathered up. When he'd shot his load on the wall, he bathed his body and used the soap to shampoo his hair. As he was drying off, he noticed a nice purple hickey on his neck. "Damn, those girls were feisty," he said to his reflection. He opened the drawer where Abbi kept her minimal supply of makeup. The only reason Troy didn't throw the shit out was in cases just like this one. He'd perfected the art of concealing his infidelity. The drawer was empty. He shut it and opened the one above it. No makeup. Her toothbrush and toothpaste were missing as well. "What *the* fuck?" he spit as he noticed other items missing from the bathroom.

Not caring that he was naked, he strode into the bedroom and began opening drawers. At first glance, nothing seemed amiss. It wasn't until he opened the closet and noticed the clothing that normally hung toward the back was missing. The clothing that really fit her body, showing off her spectacular curves. "You cunt. When I find you, you'll wish you'd kept your fucking ass at home!"

Troy threw on his clothes, swiped deodorant over his pits, and shoved his feet in his shoes. He grabbed his keys and headed out the door to his truck. The first place he would look would be the community center. She was probably teaching some stupid kids how to do the ballet shit she loved so much. First, though, he stopped in the coffee shop. He had to have a jolt of caffeine before he went searching for his wayward wife.

The line to the counter was almost out the door. Why

128

couldn't the fucking place have a drive-thru? It was too far to drive to a chain restaurant, and the convenience store's coffee sucked ass. Troy's stomach grumbled, so he decided to have a seat and order some breakfast. A cute little brunette stopped by to take his order. "Good morning, what can I get you?"

Troy glanced at the nametag attached to her uniform top. A top that was slightly showing cleavage. *Marley.* "Good morning, Marley. You can get me a large black coffee and the bacon, egg, and cheese sandwich."

Her smile faltered when she said, "Coming right up." Her ass swung from side to side as she sashayed off to another table. A table where sat none other than the lead detective at the precinct. Fucking pretty boy Dane Abbott. He was probably gay like his partner. His eyes didn't stray to Marley's chest. No, Abbott kept his eyes on her face, smiling his fake gay smile, laughing at something the pretty waitress said. After taking Dane's order, Marley left for the kitchen, only she turned back, giving him another smile. Bitch.

He did his best to keep out of Dane's line of sight. When Marley brought his coffee and food, she asked, "Can I get you anything else?" She was being courteous, but she sure as fuck wasn't flirting with him like she had with Dane. He started to ask for her phone number anyway when her eyes widened, then scowled. He followed her gaze. When he saw the object of her ire, Troy decided it was time to get the hell out of there. What the fuck was Katherine Fox doing meeting with Abbott? She better not let him know he was the one who always tipped her off when shit was going down.

"Here." Troy pulled out a twenty and said, "Keep the change." He didn't care if the tip was way more than the girl deserved, he needed to leave before that Fox bitch saw him. He grabbed his coffee and sandwich, making a hasty retreat. Once outside, he juggled his food as he unlocked the

129

truck. Sliding into the driver's seat, he placed the coffee in the cup holder and started the engine. It was a little nippy for a November morning. As he waited for the heater to warm up, he devoured his sandwich and made short order of the coffee. He took out his phone and called Abbi again. If it took him all goddamn day, he was going to find the bitch.

# Chapter Eighteen

Troy drove over to the community center, but Abbi's car wasn't there. From there he drove to the school on the small chance she could be there but no luck. As his truck sat idling, he dialed Matthew's number. If the kid knew where his sister was, he'd tell Troy if he knew what was good for him. That call also went to voicemail. "Fuck!" he yelled as he smacked the steering wheel. His next attempt would be going to the restaurant where Matthew worked. He would have to wait until the kid went on break. There was no way he could get away with harassing him while he was on his shift. Troy had a reputation to uphold after all.

When he arrived, he didn't see the piece of shit the kid drove in the parking lot. Troy knew he worked every Saturday morning, so maybe someone had dropped him off. He circled behind the building hoping to catch the kid out back goofing off. Just as he entered the alley, the back door opened, and Matthew emerged carrying a large black bag. *Taking out the garbage, good job for a piece of trash.* Troy threw his four-wheel drive in park and angled out. He caught up with Matthew just as the kid threw the bag into the dumpster. As soon as Matt turned around, Troy was in his face.

"Where is your sister? And don't try to lie to me, Son. You know I don't tolerate lying."

"I'm not your son," Matt seethed, trying to step around Troy.

Troy smacked Matthew with an open hand. "You're right. My son wouldn't be as wiry and worthless as you. Now, tell me where the fuck your sister is."

Matthew touched his face where Troy slapped him, but he didn't back down. Where the fuck was the kid getting a backbone from all of a sudden? "I don't know where she is. If she's smart, she is getting the fuck away from you."

Troy punched Matthew in the gut. The teen doubled over, and Troy brought his knee up catching the kid's face. "I'm only gonna ask you this one more time. Where... *punch* is... *punch* your... *punch* goddamn... *punch* sister?" The kid was bleeding all over the place. Fuck! He had to get out of there before they missed him inside. As Matthew fell to the ground, Troy kicked him in the ribs a couple of times for good measure. "Don't bother trying to convince anyone I did this. It'll be the word of a punk kid against an officer of the law. Besides, if you do tell Abbi, I'll kill her."

Troy kicked him one more time. If Matthew was hurt badly enough, he'd have to go to the hospital, and Abbi would show up to see to him. He'd find his fucking wife one way or another.

Michael "Sixx" Gentry normally dressed conservatively for his job as an investment banker. On the weekends, though, he looked like a rock star wannabe. Today, his clothing was somewhat subdued, but his black hair was spiked and his eyes were lined with kohl. Trying to remain inconspicuous as he sat waiting on Matthew's shift to end was getting harder as his young waitress continued staring and pointing. When she brought him a refill on his coffee he asked her, "Is something wrong?"

Blushing, she quietly asked, "Has anyone ever told you that you look like the lead singer for Cyanide Sweetness?"

Instead of responding, Sixx picked up his coffee and sipped. The waitress opened her mouth to speak but was cut off by someone yelling in the back of the restaurant.

"Matt, Matthew! Help! Someone help!"

Sixx slid out of the booth and ran through the

kitchen, not caring that he wasn't an employee. When he reached the back door, someone was bent over a lifeless body. Matthew! "Someone call an ambulance!" Fuck! How could this have happened? He was given one task, to keep Matt safe. He failed. "Move!" he yelled to the man squatting beside the teen. "Matthew, can you hear me? Matt?"

Blood gushed from the boy's nose as he mumbled, "Abbi." He lost consciousness after that.

"The ambulance is on its way," someone said from inside the door.

"Hang on, Matt. Just hang on. Did anyone see what happened?" Sixx looked around, but there were no spectators or suspects other than the employees gathered round the door.

"I sent him to take the garbage out. When it was taking too long, I went looking for him. I found him laying there, all bloody." Sixx didn't bother to look at who was talking. The police would be there soon, and they could investigate. Right now, he had to get Matthew to the hospital. He was contemplating taking the boy himself when his shifter senses picked up the sirens. Ten minutes later, Matthew was loaded in the ambulance and on his way to get help. Sixx didn't ride along. He ran to his Bugatti and drove like a bat out of hell. As he was driving, he made the dreaded call. Frey was going to have his ass.

Jasper rolled up to the gate at Frey's property and spoke into the security box. The gates opened and he drove on through. His heart was heavy, and he really had wanted to stay at home and mope. When he got home from patrolling the previous night, Trevor had been gone. He had cooked noodles and obviously ate, because there was a dirty plate in the dishwasher. He had not waited on Jasper to get home. He didn't call, didn't leave a note. He just left. Maybe the pictures had been too much. He'd called and texted Trevor but hadn't heard back from him.

Before Jasper could park his car, Abbi came running out of the house. "Abbi, what's wrong?" Jasper threw his car in park and hurried over to her before she could get in her own vehicle.

"Matthew's been attacked!" She didn't elaborate.

"Wait, let me drive you," he pleaded, but she was already in her car, backing away from the garage. "Fuck!" He jumped in his car and took off after Abbi. He hit the button on his steering wheel and dialed Frey.

"Hey Jas, I'm just about there."

"Have you heard from Sixx?"

"No, why?"

Jasper sighed, "Abbi ran out of the house yelling that Matthew has been attacked. She wouldn't let me drive her. I can only assume she's headed to the hospital. Frey, what the fuck? I thought Sixx was guarding the kid."

"Godsdamnit, follow her!" Frey disconnected in his ear. Turning on his police band, he listened for any indication of what happened. When there was nothing about Matthew coming across the air, Jasper called the dispatcher.

Jasper wasn't familiar with the weekend shift, but he called anyway. "This is Detective Jasper Jenkins. Has a call come through regarding an assault on a teenage boy?"

"Yes, Sir. The victim is in route to New Atlanta Hospital. He was beaten pretty badly behind the restaurant where he works."

"Thank you," he said and hung up. He turned on his red and blue flashers, passed Abbi when it was safe, and gave her an escort to the hospital. At least this way he could set the speed limit for her. When they arrived at the hospital, Frey was already waiting at the emergency room entrance with a sick looking Michael.

134

When Jasper turned into the parking lot at the hospital, he noticed Abbi wasn't behind him. She drove right up to the entrance and jumped out, motor still running. He got out of his car just in time to hear her yell at Frey, "I thought you could keep us safe!" Frey reached out for her, but she twisted away and continued on into the hospital.

Jasper told Frey, "Go after her. I'll park her car." From the look on Frey's face, Jasper probably needed to run interference between him and Sixx. They would have to work that out between themselves, though. Jasper had two vehicles to get out of the way.

Frey wanted to pound his fellow Gargoyle into the ground, but more than that, he wanted to comfort his mate. Sixx had already explained what happened, and it couldn't be changed. All they could do now was damage control. Frey didn't wait on Sixx or Jasper. He strode into the emergency room where a frantic Abbi was disappearing through a set of double doors. When he started to follow, a nurse stopped him. "I'm with Abbi," he told the short, stocky bull of a woman standing in his way.

"She said she didn't have any other family, and only family is allowed in there."

Frey pulled out his phone. When recent events outed the Chief of Staff, Joseph Mooneyham's true identity as Isabelle's father, Jonas Montague, all the Gargoyles put his number on speed dial. "Joseph, sorry to bother you. I'm at the ER with my uh, good friend, Abbi. Nurse..." Frey looked down at her security badge, "Nurse Benson won't let me go back with her."

"I take it this Abbi is your mate?" Jonas asked. "What is going on with the fates? Why are you all finding your mates all of a sudden?"

"Joseph..." Frey admonished the doctor who tended to ramble.

"Yes, yes, put her on."

Frey handed the phone to the nurse. "Here, Dr. Mooneyham wants a word."

The nurse grabbed the phone and listened. When she was finished, she shoved it back in his hand. "Follow me."

By that time, Sixx and Jasper had caught up with him. "They're with me," he thumbed over his shoulder.

The nurse, who hadn't been intimidated by Frey, just looked at the other two large Gargoyles and shook her head. "Of course they are," she mumbled under her breath. She opened the door and said, "Third room on the right."

The three Goyles silently strode down the hall to the waiting room. Abbi was pacing the floor, arms wrapped around her waist. Frey's heart knew hers was breaking before he saw the tears falling from her eyes. "Abbi," he whispered. When she noticed the three large men, her eyes widened for just a second before they narrowed accusingly. Before he could stop her, Abbi flung herself at Frey, beating on his chest.

"This is your fault. You said you'd keep us safe, and now Matthew is fighting for his life! Damn you! Let go of me! Get your hands off me!" Abbi was screaming. If he didn't get her under control, they'd all be kicked out. He wrapped her in his arms, pinning her arms between their bodies.

"Abbi I..."

Sixx interrupted him, "No, this is my fault. Abbi, I take full responsibility. I was the one who was supposed to be watching Matthew. Geoffrey isn't to blame."

Abbi stilled in Frey's arms as she glared at Sixx. "Then what the hell happened? *How* did this happen?"

"I was sitting in a booth facing the kitchen. I didn't want to disrupt Matthew's work by sitting in the kitchen

136

with him. Now I know I should have. Every time the door opened, I could see him at the sink, washing dishes. The waitress brought me a coffee refill when I heard the manager yelling. He had sent Matthew to take the trash out. I never thought someone would be waiting on him out back. I'm so sorry."

Abbi wrenched out of Frey's arms. "If this is how you keep someone safe, I'll take my chances at home. I want you all to leave."

"Abbi, no. You have to know that Troy is responsible for this. Please," Jasper pleaded.

"You're probably right, but if I had stayed home, Matthew wouldn't be here. This is my fault, I never should have left." Abbi turned her back on them.

Frey knew the moment she retreated into herself; the moment he lost her. He motioned toward the door with his head, and Jasper and Sixx left the room. He closed the distance between them, but didn't touch her. "I hope you change your mind, but I understand we fucked up. You will never know how much I regret not being there for him today. If either of you get into trouble and ever need my assistance, just call. If I'm not close by, someone will come to your aid, no questions asked. I'm sorry, Abbi. I never meant for this to happen, I only wanted to keep you both safe, and I failed miserably. Just know that I will always be there for you. Today, tomorrow, a week, a year, twenty years from now. Always." When Abbi refused to look at him, Frey retreated from the room.

Jasper and Sixx were waiting in the hall. Sixx looked like a man who was facing the firing squad. Frey did the only thing he could at the moment and walked away without looking back. As he was headed toward the exit, Jonas was walking his way. "I got here as quick as I could. Tell me everything you know."

Frey quietly told the doctor what had transpired, from meeting Matthew at the gym, to the attack earlier.

"That bastard did this to him; I feel it in my gut. Now Abbi doesn't trust me. She was going to file a restraining order and let you document her bruises. Now she doesn't want anything to do with any of us."

"I will go check on Matthew. Once he's in a room, we will station one of our own outside his door so no one but his sister can get inside. As for your mate, let me handle Abigail. You hang tight and don't give up hope." The older Goyle patted him on the arm and strode toward the room where Abbi was waiting. Alone. All Frey could do was trust Jonas to talk some sense into her. Frey walked out into the bright sunlight and closed his eyes. He wanted to stand sentry at Matthew's door, but that would cause too much heartache for both him and Abbi. He called Urijah to take the first shift.

"Frey, wait up." Jasper jogged to the Jeep before Frey could climb in. "What can I do to help? I want Abbi away from this dickhead, too."

"Get with Dane. Find this bastard and follow him. I don't want him taking a shit that we aren't right there watching him wipe his ass."

Jasper dug a set of keys out of his pocket. "These are Abbi's. I forgot to give them to her."

Frey took them from Jasper. "I don't think she'll be needing them for a while, but I'll make sure she gets them. I'm glad you still have them. If she plans on going back home, she's going to need her stuff from my house. I'll go get her things and put them in her car, just in case."

"I'm calling Dane now. Just yell if you need anything." Jasper clapped Frey on the shoulder and turned toward his car. He stopped when he noticed Sixx standing a few feet away, head down, hands in his pockets. Jasper asked, "Has anyone ever told you that you look like the lead singer for Cyanide Sweetness?"

Sixx sighed, "Yes."

Jasper gripped his shoulder and squeezed. He was

138

about to walk off when a car came precariously close to the three of them. "Hey!" Jasper yelled. "Holy shit, that's Trevor. I need to talk to him." He took off jogging after Dante's assistant.

After the detective ran off, Sixx looked up. "Frey, I..."

"Don't. I'm not mad, Michael. It could have happened to any of us. We didn't expect Troy to be waiting on him. Now we know better."

"What do you need me to do? I have to make this up to you, to Abbi and Matthew."

"Julian is heading to Egypt to help Nik find Sophia. I need you to be our computer genius while he's away. I want you to investigate Troy Quinn. I want to know everything about the bastard from the time he was born up to what he had for breakfast this morning."

"I can do that. I'll head to the lab now." Michael fisted his heart and bowed to Frey. "On my honor."

# Chapter Nineteen

Trevor seriously needed to get out of bed. The ceiling tiles were the same now as they had been for the last few hours, and they clearly weren't going to answer his questions. Why did he think Jasper would actually want him? How did he let himself hope there was a chance for him and the gorgeous detective? What did he have to offer anyone, really? When Jasper kissed him, was it out of pity? He'd said he wanted Trevor in his home. Hell, he even gave him his own code to get in. What was that about if he didn't really want Trevor? Jasper had called and texted a couple of times. Trevor just couldn't bring himself to listen to the voice message. The texts were basic, "what happened to you?" questions.

Maybe Jasper had wanted him until Craig came back into his life. Craig, the equally gorgeous firefighter, who was built almost as well as Jasper. When Trevor had received the anonymous text the previous night, he'd arrived just in time to see Jasper in Craig's arms. Jasper probably figured Trevor was not adventurous enough after his reaction to the photos. Whatever. He was used to being alone.

He should probably get out of bed and go to the hospital. Dante had texted him late, letting Trevor know he'd arrived home during the night with his new family in tow. Dante said he'd explain later. He would want to get them settled and not have to worry about the morgue. Trevor didn't have to work on Saturdays, but he didn't want to stay home and have any more of a pity party than he already had with his friend, Jack Daniels, the night before.

The decision to get up was made for him as a knock sounded on his front door. He rolled off the bed and padded to see who it was. He honestly didn't care that his hair was on end or his breath reeked of whiskey. He looked through the peephole. Seeing no one, he unlocked the deadbolts and slowly opened the door. He was just about to close it when he noticed an envelope on the floor. He picked it up and locked back up. The envelope had no identifying marks on it other than his name written across the front. Trevor had a really bad feeling about what he'd find inside.

Instead of opening the envelope right away, he found a bottle of aspirin and popped four of them, chasing them with orange juice. "Yuck," he said aloud to the empty room. He really needed to brush his teeth. He headed to the bathroom and turned on the shower. He brushed his teeth while waiting for the water to heat up. The last few showers he'd taken had been lengthy with thoughts of Jasper filling his head while his hard cock filled his hand. This morning, he rushed through the motions as the memory of Jasper in Craig's arms kept his dick deflated.

Trevor dressed and headed out the door, grabbing the ominous envelope. He drove to a nearby fast food restaurant, ordering two biscuits and a large coffee. He threw in an order of hash browns for good measure. He would just have to work extra hard at the gym, but he needed the carbs to soak up the alcohol. As he was waiting for the cars ahead to move up, he picked up the envelope and ran his finger under the seal. A stack of photos were inside. Trevor knew he should wait until he got to the hospital to look, but curiosity got the better of him. He took out the first picture, and his heart clenched. The second was a little worse than the first, but the third had him wanting to throw up. The car behind him honked bringing his attention away from the pictures of Jasper in various stages of sex.

He paid for his food and drove to the hospital on autopilot. As he pulled into the parking lot, Trevor almost ran over three large men. He mumbled, "Sorry," as he looked out his window. *Fuck!* One of the men was Jasper, one was the owner of the gym, and the other looked like Desmond Rothchild. Instead of stopping, he continued on to his parking spot. Trevor knew he was going to hate himself for it, but he grabbed the envelope along with his take-out bag and headed to the back door. Jasper was yelling his name, but he ignored him. He couldn't talk to him right now. If Trevor ignored him, hopefully Jasper would get the hint and leave him alone.

He unlocked the door to the morgue and entered the cold, sterile room, turning on lights as he went. He sat his breakfast and the envelope down on an empty slab. He turned on the stereo, cranking the volume. His mind was whirling. Did he eat his breakfast first and risk throwing it up when he looked at the pictures later? Or did he look at the pictures first and lose his appetite completely. The smart thing to do was to avoid the photos all together. Trevor had never claimed to be that smart.

Jasper was getting pissed. If Trevor couldn't handle Jasper's past, he could at least be man enough and tell him so instead of fucking ignoring him. He knew Trevor heard him call out to him because he turned around. He didn't have time for this shit. He needed to get with Dane and find Quinn, but he also needed to see Trevor. The music was blaring from inside the morgue. When he walked into the room, Trevor was deep in concentration. He had what appeared to be photos in his hands. Had he taken some of the ones from Jasper's home? Trevor's face paled more with each photo he looked at.

"Trevor," he said, his voice rising above the music. His mate looked up at him before running from the room. Jasper walked over to the stainless table and glanced at the photos. Staring back at him were pictures of himself at various points in time, but all while having sex with Craig. That in itself was bad enough, but the worst part was the

142

date stamp in the bottom corner of the pictures. Every picture was dated at some point that week, including the day before. "Fuck. FUCK!"

Jasper didn't have to turn the music down to hear Trevor puking in the next room. Even though he had no logical explanation for the photos, he couldn't let Trevor think what he was seeing was the truth. He walked through to the next room just as Trevor was wiping his mouth. Tears were streaming down his face, whether from the pressure of throwing up or from what he'd seen, Jasper didn't know. "Trevor, it's not what it looks like."

Trevor glared at him as he harshly wiped the tears off his face. "Really? Because it looks like you've been fucking your ex, and recently I might add." Trevor turned his back on him, sobs wracking his body. Jasper's heart was ripping in two. He closed the distance, placing his hands on Trevor's arms for comfort. Instead, Trevor jerked away from him, yelling "Get away from me!"

"Trevor, please, I can explain." But honestly, he couldn't. "I don't know who gave you those, but I swear to all that's holy, those are not from this past week. I haven't seen Craig in a long time."

"The people in the photos, they are you and Craig, right? You don't deny that?"

"Of course I can't deny it. But Trev, somehow, whoever sent those found a way to date stamp them this week. I haven't been with Craig in months."

"So, you weren't with him last night at the parking lot on Kingsley?"

*Oh shit.* "Yes, but…"

"No fucking buts. Just get out of here, and take those fucking pictures with you. I don't want to see them or you."

"Trevor, please!" Jasper would get down on his knees and beg if he had to.

"GO!" Trevor yelled again, turning his back on him.

Jasper didn't want to leave things as they were, but

143

he didn't have a choice. "I will go, but we aren't finished discussing this," he said to Trevor's back. When Trevor refused to look at him, Jasper grabbed the incriminating photos, shoved them in the envelope, and left. After he found Troy Quinn, he was going to find Craig and get some fucking answers.

Abbi looked at the new phone Frey had given her. How many times had Troy called? If she had just kept her old phone with her instead of giving it to Frey, maybe she could have kept this from happening to her brother. "Oh, Matty. What have I done?" The door opened, and a doctor walked in.

"Mrs. Quinn, I'm Dr. Mooneyham, Chief of Staff."

"How's Matt? Please, doctor, how's my brother?"

The doctor gestured to the chairs and took a seat across from her. "You're brother's a fighter. He has a few broken ribs. From the pattern of the bruising, it appears he was kicked with great force. Other than his ribs, he incurred some superficial bruising. He has been given a heavy sedative, but he'll be waking up soon. The police are going to talk to him, find out who did this. Abigail, I think you already know how serious this is. I also think you know who did this. The police are investigating, and when they find the culprit, he will go to jail. If you allow me to document your injuries as well, he will go to jail for a long, long time."

Abbi gasped. How could this doctor know about her bruises? Frey. "You're Geoffrey's friend, aren't you? The one he wanted me to talk to about..." The doctor pulled her hands into his.

"Abbi, I've been a doctor a long time, and I've seen many cases of abuse come through these doors. I have seen

144

enough of these cases to know that if you don't stand up to your abuser, it's only going to get worse. What happens next time when he doesn't stop at breaking your brother's ribs? What if he hadn't stopped this time? I have to tell you, one of Matt's ribs was precariously close to puncturing a lung. If it had been a couple centimeters over, your brother might not be here now."

"Oh god, no. Oh Matt." Abbi pulled her hands away from the doctor and placed them over her mouth. The tears fell down her cheeks at the thought of losing her brother. The door opened again, and Troy strolled in. The leer on his face fell away when he noticed the doctor. The transformation was instantaneous. "Abigail, I came as soon as I heard. How's Matthew?"

She couldn't speak. This monster had the audacity to nearly kill her brother, and here he was, pretending to care. He should win an award. Before she could speak, Dr. Mooneyham stood and got between Troy and her. Until the doctor stood toe to toe with her husband, Abbi hadn't realized how large of a man he was. He reminded her of Geoffrey and his two cousins. Was everyone Frey knew that large? "Mr. Quinn, I presume?"

"Yeah, I'm her husband." Troy attempted to step around the doctor, but he stood his ground.

"Matthew's condition is tentative. We are keeping a close eye on him. We are also assisting the detectives in charge of this case. I assure you, we will not stop until whomever did this to your brother-in-law has been apprehended."

Troy continued his charade of the caring husband. "I really appreciate that. Now, I'd like to speak to my wife. Alone."

Abbi sucked in a breath. Even though they were in the hospital, Troy wouldn't hesitate to punish her. The doctor had other ideas, though. "I'm afraid that isn't possible right now. I need Abbi to come with me and fill out

145

the paperwork. Mr. Quinn, if you wish to wait here, that's fine. I'll bring Abbi back when we are finished with her."

Troy sneered at the doctor. "I'm her fucking husband *and* I'm a cop. If I want to talk to her, I will." Abbi took a chance and looked around the doctor. The first thing she noticed was the twisted scowl on Troy's face. The second was the huge hickey on his neck.

Dr. Mooneyham didn't back down. Instead, he stood even taller, squaring his shoulders. "And I'm the fucking Chief of Staff of this hospital. You are in my jurisdiction, and what I say is law around here. If you do not cooperate, I will have you removed and banned from these premises."

"You can't do that. I'll call my boss and..."

The doctor interrupted him, "I can do that, and I will. Either you wait here, or I will call Chief Kane myself. Your choice. Nice hickey by the way."

Abbi was impressed. She had never seen anyone stand up to Troy that way. Her husband was livid. His knuckles were white where his fists were clenched. "I'll be back," he seethed before slamming open the door and stalking off down the hall.

Abbi was embarrassed. The doctor had every right to think the worst of her. How could she not press charges against that man? How could she continue to allow him to abuse Matt? She couldn't. She had no idea how she would protect herself from Troy, but she had to try. "I'm ready," she whispered.

Dr. Mooneyham nodded. She didn't have to explain. He understood what she was ready to do.

"Very good, my dear. Please, follow me."

# Chapter Twenty

Sixx's gesture meant more to Frey than any apology in the world. He knew the Goyle felt bad, and now he knew just how bad. Sixx, like Urijah, had given his solemn oath. Frey climbed in his Jeep and headed home. His heart hurt when he thought of Matthew and what he'd endured at the hands of such a large man. Frey was ready to find Troy Quinn and dish out the same punishment to him.

He arrived home to an empty house. When he left earlier, he had been full of hope. He had enjoyed the ride to work, laughing and singing with Matthew. He'd been happy to purchase new phones the day before, knowing Troy wouldn't be able to find them. Even buying groceries had been fun, making sure he bought what Abbi put on the list plus a whole lot of other items he thought Matthew might like. The candles he'd bought for the dining room table would sit in a drawer, unused. There would be no romantic meals for him now.

Frey grabbed some of the plastic bags from the recycle bin and carried them upstairs. As bad as he wanted to place Abbi's clothes and toiletries in a decent piece of luggage, he knew that would be a red flag when Troy saw her stuff. With a heavy heart, he filled the grocery bags and took them to the Jeep. What he didn't do was gather Matt's stuff. Even if Abbi was his guardian, Frey would die a martyr's death before the boy stepped foot in his old house again. He would kidnap him from the hospital if need be. Matt would not be going back to work at the restaurant. When he was well, he would work at the gym where Troy Quinn would not be welcomed.

Frey drove back to the hospital, parking close to Abbi's car. He looked around, making sure nobody was lurking. When he was sure the coast was clear, he deposited Abbi's things in the front seat of her car where she couldn't

147

miss them. He locked the car and headed to Jonas' office. The doctor would make sure Abbi got her keys. As he rounded the building to enter the door, Troy Quinn came barreling outside. Frey stepped back quickly before Abbi's husband had a chance to see him. The man was so irate, he wasn't aware of his surroundings. Frey tracked his movements until he was in his vehicle, speeding out of the parking lot.

Frey called Jasper, alerting him to Troy's whereabouts as he headed into the hospital to Jonas' office. When he was almost there, he reached out with his shifter senses. Even with the door closed, Abbi's sad voice floated into his ears. "But he didn't protect Matty like he promised."

Shit, she was talking about him. Jonas responded, "Please, Mrs. Quinn, reconsider. There is no one more qualified than Geoffrey Hartley and his men to protect you and your brother. I have known him and his family a long time, and I would trust them with my own daughter."

That was good to hear since Dante had just rescued both his daughter and grandson from the hands of Alistair Giannopoulos, an old Gargoyle with a huge grudge against Jonas.

"I...I don't know. He seems nice, but I still don't understand why he's so interested in helping me."

"It's who he is. He and his family are some of the most honorable, uh, people I know. It's in his blood. It should be the way of all of mankind, to help one another, not tear each other down."

After that, there was silence. Frey wanted to barge into the office, pull Abbi into his arms, and reassure her. Instead, he remained where he was: stone still against the wall, waiting for her next words.

"None of that matters right now. I'm not leaving here until Matthew is released."

Frey expelled his breath. He had time, probably not much, but time to set up a security detail for Abbi. Matthew would be coming home with him.

The phone rang and Jonas excused himself to answer it. When he hung up, he told her, "That does it for the paperwork. Matthew is in room 1213. Let's get you up there to see him. We will have a security guard stationed outside of his room. Other than hospital staff, nobody is allowed in to see Matthew other than yourself, not even your husband. If I might suggest, please allow Jasper to continue with the restraining order for both you and Matthew."

Frey didn't hear a response. He could only hope Abbi had nodded in affirmation. When the screech of a chair being pushed back met his ears, he hurried away to call Urijah, letting him know what room to guard. When that was taken care of, he called Jasper, requesting that he or Dane come to the hospital on the chance Abbi agreed to the restraining order. He knew he was asking a lot of his fellow Clan members, but that's what they did. They were family and had each other's backs.

Abbi was scared. She was putting things into motion that could not be stopped. Trusting people she didn't even know. Granted, getting away from Troy was something she'd dreamed about for years, but now that it was a possibility, she couldn't believe it might actually happen. After what the bastard had done to Matthew, there was no way she could continue living with the monster. Dr. Mooneyham assured her she was doing the right thing. The doctor, who was walking beside her, spoke softly to the employees he encountered along the way. He addressed them all by name and with a smile. There was something calming about being in his presence.

When they arrived at room 1213, there was a huge man standing outside the door. She recognized him from the gym. He was another one of Geoffrey's friends. As he and Dr. Mooneyham shook hands, he looked her way, "Abbi, good to see you again."

"I'm sorry; I don't recall your name."

"Urijah. You may call me Uri, if you wish. I am taking first shift watching over Matthew. In the few days I've known your brother, I've become quite fond of the boy. Please rest assured, I will allow no further harm to come to him. To me, this is personal." Uri placed a fist on his chest and gently bowed his head. That was the second time he'd done that. His accent came and went, but she was certain he wasn't from around there.

"Abbi, I believe Matthew has been waiting to see you. Let's go on in," the doctor drew her attention away from the tall guard. She entered the room but stopped short when she got a look at her brother. Her knees grew weak at the battered image before her. Dr. Mooneyham wrapped an arm around her waist, holding her upright. He whispered in her ear, "Shh, he's going to be fine. The bruises will fade. He will heal. He needs you to be strong for him, okay?" Abbi nodded and steeled her spine. She took a deep breath and sat down in the chair next to the bed. She gently picked up Matthew's hand and held it.

Her brother's eyes fluttered open. He saw Abbi and his eyes teared up. "Abs," he managed to squeak out.

"Shh, don't try to talk. Just rest okay?" Abbi had to fight back her own tears that were forming.

"Water," he whispered.

Abbi grabbed the large plastic jug that was full of ice and water and placed the straw to his lips. Matt sipped just a little.

The doctor stepped closer to the bed. "Matthew, I'm Dr. Mooneyham. I know you're still groggy from the pain medicine we've given you. I want you to rest for now. We will keep you sedated for a while so the pain level isn't too much."

Matthew nodded and turned to Abbi. "I'm sorry…"

Abbi couldn't stop the tears. "Shh, Matty. You have nothing to be sorry for. I'm the one who's sorry. I should have tried harder to get away from him. I promise you I'm doing everything I can to make that happen now, okay? Please don't worry about it. You're safe here now. Urijah is outside the door, and Troy can't get you in here."

"No, Abbi," he said glancing to the door and back to her, eyes wide. She turned to see the guard leaning against the door frame, listening. He didn't move from his post, but he did speak, "Hey kid, no one's getting past me, I promise." Matt nodded again as his eyes fluttered.

The doctor placed a hand on her shoulder. "Abbi, your brother will be asleep for a while. We want to keep him knocked out so he doesn't move around too much. Why don't we go back to my office where we will have privacy?"

The doctor had already documented her injuries. Now all that was left was to file the restraining order and begin divorce paperwork. The decision to follow through on both was easy now she'd seen Matthew's face. She rose from the chair and placed a soft kiss on his forehead. "I'm so sorry, Matty." She grabbed a couple of tissues from the box on the bedside table and wiped her face. "I'm ready."

Troy blew through a red light. Oncoming traffic had to slam on their brakes to miss him. "Fuck!" he cursed as he pounded his palm on the steering wheel. Wrecking his truck was the last thing he needed right now. *Goddamnit! I've worked too hard and too long to lose her now.* No, Troy would not lose Abigail. He'd set his sights on her in ninth grade. It took a while, but he finally wore her down. He was forced to take some pretty drastic measures, but in the end they paid off. There was no way all his sweat, planning, and deals with the devil would go down the fucking drain now. If her punk ass brother had just told him where Abbi had holed up the night before, none of this would be happening. And who did that self-righteous doctor think he was, keeping Abbi from talking to Troy? Granted, the man was big, but Troy wasn't afraid of him. Hell, he wasn't afraid of anyone. He was a cop, and his badge afforded him some privileges.

Gravel flew as he pulled into their driveway. He threw the gearshift into park and cut the engine. He needed a new plan. The earlier one would have worked if the doctor hadn't butted in. If he could have gotten Abigail alone for thirty seconds, he would have convinced her to get her ass back home. If he was right, Matthew would have to stay in the hospital at least a day. Troy was pretty sure he heard some ribs cracking when he kicked him. Maybe that would convince the kid to stay away from him now. He never wanted the boy living with them in the first place, but that stupid bitch Judy had to go and fucking overdose.

He sure was glad Matthew had been the one to find her with a needle sticking out of her arm. Troy would've had a hard time explaining why he had gone to see her. Their arrangement had been a good one in the beginning. Judy got the house and half the money for putting up with the kid. Troy knew Abbi would go on to college, so she wouldn't be around enough to figure out what was going on. Thinking of those earlier days, Troy really needed to find those videos they filmed and destroy them.

Enough about Judy. He needed to focus on getting to Abbi. He had to play it smart. He could try the hospital again, but if Matthew was stupid and told Abbi it was Troy who put him there, he'd have to take even more drastic measures. He went into the kitchen and pulled out a bottle of whiskey. He unscrewed the lid and took a long drink, deciding he needed a decoy. He called George and told him what he was planning.

# Chapter Twenty-One

When Frey received the text from Jonas that Abbi was ready to file the restraining order, his heart lightened a little. Urijah had already called and updated him on Matthew. Frey could feel the ire coming over the airwaves as his Clan member spoke of the boy's injuries. He knew they needed to get Abbi away from Troy the right way, but Frey couldn't guarantee the man wouldn't meet his demise if one of the Gargoyles ever got their hands on him.

As badly as Frey wanted to be with Abbi, he felt it best to keep his distance. He needed to go help Mason at the dojo since Uri was at the hospital. Before he headed that way, Frey looked in on Matt. He wanted to see the boy for himself. He and Uri bumped fists as he entered the room. Frey took in the new injuries to Matt's face. The old bruising was covered by fresh splotches. Various butterfly bandages held together some of the lesser cuts. Stitches had been needed for a deeper gash. He pushed a strand of hair off the teen's forehead. Clenching his fists, he turned to Uri. "If that motherfucker comes anywhere near him…"

Uri cut him off, "He's not getting past me. I promise."

Frey nodded. He knew Uri would protect Matthew at all costs. He had one more stop to make before he headed to the gym. He paused outside Jonas' office and listened. Frey was surprised when the voice he heard was Kaya's. His queen had stepped in and was talking to Abbi. The fates couldn't have chosen a better female for Rafael. Instead of sending one of the Gargoyles, Kaya had come to talk to Abbi, woman to woman. She was taking her statement, documenting the bruises, and offering her a place to stay. Frey wasn't shocked when Abbi agreed to go home with Kaya. He'd known in his heart she wouldn't trust him again. The fact she would be staying at the manor brought a big sense of relief to Frey.

"Jonas," Frey whispered, knowing the doctor would hear him.

"Ladies, please excuse me a moment." Jonas closed the door behind him as he stepped into the hallway.

"Here are Abbi's keys. Her clothes and toiletries are in her car. Thank you for all you're doing to help."

"I'm just glad I could convince her to file the order. You go do what you need to do. Kaya and Rafael will take good care of her." Jonas had hidden from Rafael's Clan for hundreds of years. About ten years ago, he had met with Rafael posing as Joseph Mooneyham, but wouldn't declare his loyalty. Now, after the incident with Isabelle and Connor, he was fully on board.

"Thank you." Frey shook the doctor's hand and headed to the dojo. As he reached his Jeep, his phone rang. "Sixx, did you find something?"

"Can you stop by the lab? You're not going to believe this shit."

Abbi had expected to have to talk to Jasper, or another male detective. When the female police chief showed up, she had been pleasantly surprised. Kaya Kane was down to earth and seemed to be genuinely concerned. She had taken Abbi's statement and filled out the paperwork for the restraining order. All Abbi had to do was sign it. Kaya also recommended a divorce attorney since Abbi had no idea who to call. The kicker, though, was when Kaya offered to let Abbi stay with her and her fiancé. She assured Abbi they had plenty of room, as well as a housekeeper who would love to dote on her and Matthew. The place was secure, and no one would be able to find her at Kaya's home.

Abbi wasn't leaving the hospital as long as Matthew was there, but as soon as he was well enough to be released, she agreed to the woman's hospitality. Abbi knew there were kind people in the world. Heck, she was one of them. She just couldn't show it as often as she liked because Troy kept her pinned down.

As soon as the chief left, Abbi returned to Matt's room. She nodded at the tall man standing guard and quietly entered the room. She pushed the chair close to the bed and sat down. She wanted to hold her brother's hand, but she was afraid of hurting him. Instead, she placed her hands in her lap and watched him sleep. Every time she heard a male voice in the hall, Abbi would look over her shoulder, fully expecting Troy to be there.

Her thoughts turned to the divorce. Both the doctor and the police chief guaranteed her she would come out the other end fine, but they didn't know Troy. Even the chief who was Troy's boss didn't really know him. When she asked Miss Kane about Troy's work ethic, the woman had skated around the truth. Maybe she knew him better than Abbi realized. Troy had a way of getting what he wanted. When they were in high school, Abbi had her sights set on someone else, but Troy was always there to interrupt anytime Abbi was talking to Brandon. She never did get to date her crush. They were both busy with their extracurricular activities, and Troy was always up in her business.

Brandon was an exceptionally good football player. He had received a scholarship to play for the University of Georgia. He was their star quarterback for three years before he went on to be drafted early by some NFL team. Abbi bought a second hand UGA sweatshirt at a Goodwill store and wore it whenever she could. If Troy ever found out the true meaning behind the shirt, he'd have ripped it into shreds. Abbi tried to catch the games Brandon played in on television, but Troy hated football. Abbi was pretty sure it

155

was because he was kicked off their high school team for fighting.

Troy had a way of showing up wherever Abbi was, even if he was just sitting in the parking lot in his car. She ignored him as best she could, but he had been relentless. When her parents died and her aunt Judy had been made her guardian, he was always around. Her parents had never let him come over; it was as if they knew what kind of person he was. Her aunt was another story. She seemed to really like Troy. Abbi would find them laughing in the kitchen together. Thinking back on it now, Troy was probably hitting on Judy.

Abbi finally lost her will to fight Troy. When her parents died and Judy took over, the only thing she had the strength for was Matthew. If it hadn't been for her brother, Abbi would have curled up and died from grief. When it was time for her to go to college and her aunt told her all the money for school was gone, Abbi woke up. Her grief induced fog slowly dissipated, and Abbi saw Judy for what she was: a gambling, druggie whore. Abbi found her strength once again, and applied to a small school in town where she could receive grants and scholarships.

Instead of staying on campus and being able to get away from her dreadful home life, she lived at home so she could take care of her brother. That meant not being able to get away from Troy. Even at school, he had his best friend George follow her everywhere she went. Abbi had no idea how he managed to get an education. Thinking about the grown George who was always coming around, she doubted he did. He was always at their house, eating their food, drinking Troy's liquor, sleeping on their sofa.

After she graduated, Troy promised Abbi if she would marry him, they would buy a house where they could start a family. When he made her that promise, it seemed like a good deal. She would finally get Matt away from the hellhole that used to be their home. She agreed, but it didn't take long after the vows to see that Troy had lied. He hated Matt for some reason. Abbi figured it was pure jealousy since she doted on her brother. He was the only one she doted on. So, a broken promise had sealed her fate, and now, five long years later, she was finally getting free.

Even if Troy somehow managed to get everything in the divorce, Abbi would start over from scratch. If it meant getting Matt away from her husband, she'd do whatever it took. She'd had nothing when they got married except her clothes. She could do it again.

"Abs," Matt whispered from his bed.

"Hey, Matty," she smiled at his bruised face. When he reached his hand toward her, she took it. "Don't worry about anything. You just rest and get better."

"I need to tell you what happened," his eyes pleaded.

"I know Troy did this. Don't worry, I'm getting away from him. This should have never happened, but it did and I've filed a restraining order. I'm also filing for divorce. Matt, there are nice people helping us out."

"No, Abs, Troy didn't do this. Please, you can't." Matt was getting agitated.

"Of course he did this. Matt, maybe you have a concussion, or you didn't see him attack you."

"Abbi, no, you can't..." Matthew couldn't sit up without the pain in his ribs hurting too much.

"Shh, Matt, it's okay. Lay back down." Abbi was confused. Matthew was adamant about Troy not causing his injuries. She felt a presence behind her and when she looked up, the big guy, Uri, was standing there. He had closed the door.

"May I?" he asked Abbi, gesturing to the chair. She rose and moved out of his way.

Uri sat down and picked up Matthew's hand. Her brother instantly calmed down. "Hey, Buddy, listen to me." When Matthew looked at him, he continued, "We made a

157

promise to keep you safe. We weren't expecting Troy to find you taking out the garbage. Now, you will be covered twenty-four seven, no matter where you are. Abbi is covered too. Until this is over, neither of you will be without a guard. I'm pretty sure the bastard threatened Abbi since you are trying to convince her he's not responsible, am I right?" Matthew nodded. "Here's what's going to happen. You are going to stay home from school. We will bring your homework to you and take it back so you won't fall behind. If there is anything you need help with, we will video conference a session with your teacher if one of us can't help you."

Abbi couldn't believe that was possible. "How do you know his teachers will agree to that?"

"Because Frey knows the principal, and he assured us they would cooperate." He turned his attention back to Matt. "Your two week notice at the restaurant has turned into an immediate notice. You are now employed by the gym. When you are well enough, you will begin your new job. While you are recovering, you will receive a paycheck same as if you were there. While you are recuperating, we feel it best if you continue to live with Frey. His home is secure. Abbi, if you wish to stay with Kaya that is your prerogative."

"Now wait a minute, I'm Matthew's guardian. He is going to stay with me where I can keep an eye on him." Who were these people who were trying to take over her life? They were almost as bad as Troy.

"Yes, you are, and as such you want what is best for Matthew. Are you going to quit your job? Take a vacation? Be there around the clock for your brother? While we prefer you actually did take a vacation, we realize it probably isn't feasible. You have responsibilities."

"What about your responsibilities? Frey's? The police chief's? You can't put your lives on hold for the two of us."

158

"We can, and we will. Our only responsibility at this point is to keep you and Matthew safe. I know it may seem odd to you now, but one day you will understand. You are family, regardless of whether you feel that way. We do whatever it takes to protect our own."

"You're right, I don't get it." From Frey wanting to be in her life, to the chief taking her in, to this man standing sentry, none of it made sense. People were nice, but they didn't stop everything to be this nice.

"Whether or not you accept our assistance, you're getting it. You may as well be onboard. Abbi, there are those in this world whose kindness overrides the evil. We are reaching out a hand of goodness. Please grab hold."

"Uri," Matthew intervened.

"Yes, Little Man?" Uri responded with a softness foreign to his size.

"I want to live with Frey. Abbi, you should, too. I mean, our stuff is already there, and I want you to be where I am. I don't know the chief, but I do know Frey. Please, think about it."

Abbi never could tell her brother no. She didn't trust Frey, not after he let Matthew down, but she really didn't know the police chief, and she didn't want to be separated from her brother. She may be upset with Frey, but if Matthew felt safe there, then that's where they'd stay.

"Okay, Matty. Whatever you want."

# Chapter Twenty-Two

Frey stared at the screen before him, taking in all the information Sixx had dug up on Quinn. How could one man be so fucking vile? Sixx had already printed everything, so Frey would have a copy for Abbi to give her lawyer. It was going to take some more digging, but Frey knew in his gut Troy Quinn was responsible for Abbi's parents' deaths. From the time of the accident until he and Abbi were married, money that was supposed to be Abbi's and Matt's was transferred from the bank account her aunt oversaw to one in Troy's name. Sixx wasn't quite as good as Julian at digital tracking, but when it regarded bank accounts, Sixx knew exactly what to look for. Frey was impressed with the amount of information he'd found in so few hours.

"I can't figure why the aunt would give him half the money. The only thing that makes sense is they were in on it together from the beginning. What if they both plotted the accident, knowing Judy would be the sole guardian? He sabotages the car, she oversees the estate, and they split the cash," Sixx said as he continued to type, looking at home in Julian's chair.

"But can we prove it? That was ten years ago." Frey wanted to kill someone. Since Judy was already dead, Troy's face came to mind. He vowed then and there Troy Quinn would never get anywhere near Abbi again.   He would find a way to ruin him, his reputation, his name, his face. He was going to make the man suffer in ways he would never recover from.

"Frey, man, reel it in," Sixx said as he rolled his chair backwards. Frey had phased without realizing it.

He retracted his claws and fangs, licking his lip where blood trickled. "Fuck. I really need to patrol tonight. Find some Unholy and let loose."

"I get it. Uri said Matthew will be in the hospital

160

overnight. Normally he would have already been sent home, but Jonas is calling the shots on this one."

"Good. If he's still there, Abbi will be, too. I don't have to worry about either one of them."

Sixx was concentrating hard on a picture on the computer monitor. "What the hell?"

Frey glanced at the screen. "When did you join a band and not tell anyone?"

"That's not me. That's..." Sixx flipped the screen to a website. "I'll be fucked sideways."

"Would you care to explain?"

"I'm not sure I can. I mean, fuck. I think that's my son," Sixx said as he read the article in front of him. "Desmond Rothchild, twenty-three, lead singer of Cyanide Sweetness, was born in New Atlanta before moving to the west coast..." Sixx trailed off, reading silently.

"What makes you think he's your kid? You can't have a child with someone other than your mate."

Sixx paled. "Oh, shit." He looked away from the screen. "I bit her. I bit Rae thinking it was safe because she was human. Fuck, man, I didn't realize it was possible back then."

"What are you going to do?"

"I guess I'll call her and say, 'Hello Rae, remember me? Michael? You had my kid and didn't bother telling me.' I'm sure that'd go over well. And why didn't she tell me? I have a son, and she's kept that from me for over twenty years."

"*If* he's your son. Don't jump to conclusions until you know for sure." Frey was just as shocked as Sixx that he could have mated all those years ago.

"Yeah, you're right. Besides, I need to keep looking into Troy. If Desirae is my mate and this Desmond is my son, I've been in the dark this long. A little while longer won't do any more harm."

Frey's phone rang, interrupting their conversation.

161

"Uri, is everything okay?"

"Yes, Brother. Matthew is awake and talking. He tried to convince Abbi that Troy wasn't responsible, but Troy had threatened to harm Abbi if the kid told the truth. I spoke to him and gave him the rundown of how things were going to go. When he's released, he wants to come back to your home. Abbi's agreed to come with him."

"Holy fuck, are you serious?"

"Yes. She was going to stay with Kaya and Rafe, but Matthew talked her into coming back to your place."

"That's wonderful news. I've spoken to Lorenzo. He's willing to relieve you from guard duty this evening."

"Good. I'm ready to hit the skies and find some Unholy to decimate. Seeing the kid's face and what he's gone through has my beast ready to fight. If I don't take out some of the monsters, I may have to find a different monster and take him out."

"Truth, Brother. I feel the same way. I'm leaving the lab now. I'll see you in the air later."

"Later."

When Frey put his phone away, Sixx asked, "I take it you and Uri will need a clean-up crew tonight?"

"Fuckin-A, we will. The Pen is getting too full. Let's let Deacon rest tonight," Frey said as he stood and stretched.

"I'm going to stay here and see what else I can come up with on Quinn. Call me later, and I'll round up the bodies."

"Thanks, Brother. For everything." Frey wanted Sixx to know he wasn't mad at him.

"Don't. I know you said it's okay, but it's not. He was my charge, and I let him down. I will make it up to him. To you." Sixx was a big ass Gargoyle, but his emotions were evident on his face. Frey would feel the same way, so he let him have that.

He held out a fist for Sixx. Reluctantly, he bumped knuckles then turned back to the computer. Frey left the lab, his heart warring with itself. He was happy Abbi agreed to come back to his home, but when she found out what Troy had been about all along, he was afraid she would be way too hard on herself. At least he could put the bad news off a while. Right now, though, he had something else he had to take care of.

Trevor knew Dante hadn't been home long, but he really needed some time alone. Dante had promised him a vacation after he helped get Tessa home from the hospital. He hated to ask for that time now, but he had to get away. Away from the morgue with all its death. Away from Jasper and all his lies. Away from New Atlanta where nothing good had ever come his way. Well, didn't come his way and stay. He felt so stupid getting his hopes up that someone could have feelings for him. Especially someone like Jasper.

The man was a god. He was in a league of gods. A league of gods who hung out together, worked out together, had sex with other gods. It did not include someone like Trevor. Jasper had fooled him once, made him believe he wanted to spend time with him. Maybe he had just used Trevor to make his ex jealous. No, that didn't make sense. Trevor wouldn't make anyone jealous. He picked up the note that had been included in the photos and read it again.

*Did you honestly think someone like him would want someone like you?*

For a split second Trevor had. He had allowed himself to believe the impossible.

He read the other part:

*Do you even know what he is?*

What did that mean? Trevor's mind was racing and his heart was hurting. He made up his mind to call Dante. He would take a week off as soon as Dante was ready to

163

come back to work. It wasn't fair to ask to leave immediately. His boss had been too good to him already. Speaking of his boss, the door to the morgue opened and the man walked in. Okay, that was just creepy.

"Trevor, how are you?" Dante was part of the league.

"Honestly, not too good. I know you just got back in town, but I was going to call you. I need to take some time off." There. He said it, and there was no taking it back.

"Do you want to talk about it?" His boss pulled up a stool next to where Trevor was sitting. Sitting staring at a piece of paper on a stainless steel slab. A slab that was bare except for the paper. Instead of working, he had been staring.

"Not really. I just need to get away, clear my head. I'm not asking to leave today, but as soon as you are ready to come back to work and feel you can do without me, I'd appreciate it."

"How long do you need?" Dante glanced at the paper on the table then back at Trevor. Even though he was sure Dante couldn't have read the note from that far away, he folded it and put it in his pocket. The move was probably rude, but he didn't want his boss to realize just how pathetic he really was.

"I don't know. A few days, maybe a week?" How long did it take to heal a broken heart?

Dante looked around. "It doesn't look too busy now. Why don't you go ahead? I've got this covered."

"Are you sure? I mean, you just got back." Now Trevor felt bad for asking.

"I'm sure. But I want you to remember something while you're off. I'm here for you. If you feel like talking, I'll listen. No judgment, no words of wisdom, just an ear to listen. Whenever you're ready, come back. I need you here. You are the best assistant I've ever had, and I finally feel comfortable taking a few days off here and there, because I know I have you here taking care of things."

Trevor didn't know what to say, so he didn't say anything except, "Thank you. I'll not be gone more than a week, I promise."

"Take your time. When you get back, I will fill you in on my trip. I think you'll find it fascinating. At least I hope you will." Dante rose from his stool, clapped Trevor on the shoulder and left the room.

Huh. Dante was different somehow. Lighter, happier. Even if Trevor didn't know what true happiness felt like, he could recognize it in someone else. He stood from his spot behind the table and read the note one more time. Yeah, he was doing the right thing by leaving.

Jasper shouldn't mind stakeouts. He was a full-blooded Gargoyle who could sit still for hours at a time and never get tired. Watching Troy Quinn's house for movement, however, was not his idea of a good time. No, the way he felt right now, a good time would be barging into the bastard's house and beating him to within an inch of his life. It didn't bode well for the human that all of the Gargoyles felt the same way. Sure, his responsibility as a Goyle was to protect humans. But when the humans were scum like Troy and Craig, Jasper didn't feel goodwill toward their kind.

What the fuck was Craig up to? Why was he in New Atlanta now? How had he known Jasper was there? Was he the one who sent the photos to Trevor? If so, how did he even know about Trevor? He and his mate had only been together a few times. Jasper could imagine what was going through Trevor's head seeing those pictures. Some of the photos were close ups, taken from the bedroom of Jasper's last home. Craig must have hidden a camera at some point.

For what reason though? He was the one in the closet, refusing to make their relationship public.

The other pictures were taken from far away. Someone had set up outside his home and taken them with a telephoto lens. His previous home sat high on a hill, surrounded by woods. Whoever it was had gone to a lot of trouble. Jasper had to consider that his past was coming back to haunt him. If the one who had tied him up, seduced him, and hurt him was the same one who tied Craig up, were they working together? What if his old lover... no, that wasn't the right word. They hadn't been lovers. Jasper had gone to the man willingly at first, but what happened between them wasn't love. It was sadistic and painful. What if the man had found out about Craig and him and was blackmailing his ex? Maybe Craig hadn't been the one to hack Jasper's computer. Too many scenarios were flitting through Jasper's mind, and he couldn't stop them because they all led back to the hurt look on Trevor's face. Fuck! Trevor already had low self-esteem. These photos were going to do so much harm to his wellbeing. Jasper didn't have to be a psychiatrist to realize that.

He slid farther down in his seat and sighed. All the headway he'd made with his mate had just been tossed out the window, landing in a deep mud puddle. It would take a whole lotta rain to wash the gunk off Trevor's psyche this time.

His phone vibrated. He hastily pulled it out of the holder, hoping it was Trevor giving him a chance to explain. The caller I.D. disappointed him. "Hello, Dante. Welcome back."

"Jasper, how are things?" Dante didn't sound happy which put Jasper on alert. Dante had just returned from Greece after rescuing his mate and her son. Now Dante's son. He should be ecstatic.

"Not too good, if you want to know the truth." He wouldn't lie. Dante would know all of the Clan's business with one phone call to Rafael anyway.

"I always want the truth. Would you care to tell me what happened between you and my assistant that has him leaving town?"

"What? No, he can't. Fuck! Dante, you can't let him leave. Godsdamnit! I'm going to fucking kill Craig. That motherfucker has…"

"Jasper!" Dante interrupted his rant.

"Sorry, but Dante you can't let him leave. Somebody sent Trevor some very incriminating photos, and they somehow date stamped them this week. He doesn't believe me, though."

"The letter probably didn't help."

"What letter?" Jasper hadn't seen a letter. Trevor must have hidden it.

"The letter he was staring at when I walked in to the morgue. He probably didn't realize I could read it, but I could. It said *'Did you honestly think someone like him would want someone like you?'* No wonder he looked like he'd lost his best friend, because he feels like he has."

Jasper closed his eyes. He wanted to hit someone. He wanted to cry. He wanted to find Trevor and kiss him senseless until he convinced him someone was out to sabotage their relationship. "Dante, I swear to you, we were getting to a good place. He's my mate for fuck's sake. I'm not going to let some past piece of ass come between us."

"Trevor's your mate? Are you positive?"

"Absolutely. I know I have to take things slow, make him understand that it is totally possible we are supposed to be together. I already had a long road ahead of me without this shit popping up."

"I wish I could help. He said he'll be back in a week."

"I can't wait a week! I need him now. Need to see him, hold him. Fuck!"

"I'm sorry, Jasper. I wish I'd known before I told him

167

he could have the time off."

"How long ago was this?" Jasper would try to reach him before he got out of town.

"About ten minutes. Jasper, I really think you should give him the space."

"Fuck that. If he has a week to shut himself inside his head, I'll never reach him. No, I've got to find him."

"Good luck, Brother." Dante disconnected, and Jasper immediately called his partner.

"Abbott."

"Dane, Jasper. Are you home?"

"No, I'm at the precinct going over some case files, why?"

"Fuck! Trevor's running, and I need to stop him." Jasper had to get someone else to watch Troy's house. He couldn't abandon his post, not even for love. Wait, love? No, that wasn't right. It was too soon to love his mate.

"Running? And you're going to chase him? You must have it bad, Partner." Dane chuckled.

"You could say that. Remember the pictures you saw? Well there are more, and someone sent them to Trevor. The date stamp on the new ones is this week, even though the pictures are old. I need to convince him I was not with my ex."

"What can I do to help?" Dane asked, realizing the seriousness of the situation.

"Until I can get someone to sit on Quinn's house, I need you to go the apartment complex. Stall him. Kidnap him if you have to, just don't let him leave before I get there."

"I'll see what I can do. I will call you when I get there."

Jasper prayed to all the gods that Dane could put a halt to Trevor's plans, at least until he had time to get there himself. A car turned into Troy's driveway. A twenty-something man got out, looked around, and headed to the

168

side door. Jasper took note of the man's tag number and wrote it down. If he couldn't do right by his own mate, at least he could pay attention and help Frey with his.

The longer he sat there, the more Jasper was convinced he'd lost Trevor. Every second that passed was like a needle stabbing his heart. Jasper lost track of time, thinking about everything happening in his life. His phone rang. "Dane, please tell me you have him."

"I'm sorry, Jasper. He's gone." Jasper disconnected the phone and didn't try to stop the tears.

# Chapter Twenty-Three

Abbi fed Matthew his dinner so he didn't have to move. At first he refused her help stating he wasn't a baby. After the first few bites brought so much pain to his ribs, he gave in. Dr. Mooneyham had stopped by, checking on both Matt and Abbi. He made sure Abbi had something to eat as well knowing she wouldn't leave Matt's room. Since they were going back to Frey's house, the doctor said he would release Matt the next day.

They were watching some sitcom they'd never seen since they weren't allowed to choose what to watch at home. Both of them were laughing at the silliness of it, even if it wasn't really funny. They were enjoying the freedom to watch what they wanted. Abbi caught movement out of the corner of her eye and turned toward the door. Frey and another really large man were in the hall talking to Uri. She couldn't hear what they were saying, but they looked serious.

She didn't miss the fact that Frey had changed clothes. Instead of wearing the faded blue jeans that fit him like a glove, showing off his massive thighs, he was wearing a pair of black fatigues. A tight black t-shirt was tucked in the waist. Instead of his black motorcycle boots, he was wearing combat boots. She thought he was hot before. This Frey was scorching. He was holding a bag of some kind, almost like a woman's overnight bag. As if he planned it, Frey waited until the show was over before coming into the room. She stood so she wouldn't have to crane her neck back so far to talk to him.

Frey's eyes found hers. She didn't know how to feel, exactly. He was a gorgeous man who caused her heart to race. He wanted to be with her, he'd made that clear. Frey had taken her and Matt in, no questions asked, vowing to protect them. Granted, her brother was in the hospital with broken ribs, but that was on Troy. She knew she looked a mess, because she'd left his house that morning with no makeup on. She'd thought she had plenty of time to fix herself up before Frey returned from taking Matt to work.

The man had seen her looking her worst, and he still wanted her. So, while she was conflicted, she was also flattered. She gave him a tentative smile. That must have been what he was waiting for. He came farther into the room and took up residence beside her. He gave her shoulder a gentle squeeze before turning his attention to Matthew.

"I heard the good news. Dr. Mooneyham said you get to come home tomorrow."

"Yeah. I can't wait to get back down to the lake. I guess fishing's out of the question for a while, though."

"You'll be casting a line before you know it. Besides, if I recall, you have some tests to study for." Frey turned to the new man in the door motioning him inside. "Abbi, Matt, I'd like to introduce you to Lorenzo. Lor is going to stand guard tonight."

Abbi took in the new guy's stature. He wasn't quite as tall as Frey or Uri, but he was just as broad. She couldn't help herself when she asked, "Is it a requirement for your friends to be Amazons?"

Lorenzo huffed, "I'll have you know the Amazonians were all female. Are you saying I look like a girl?"

"What? No. I just..." Abbi stuttered then blushed when the newcomer started chuckling.

"You'll have to forgive my friend here. He's full of himself." Frey shoved Lorenzo's arm playfully.

"He's full of something," Uri muttered from behind them.

Grinning, Lorenzo apologized, "Abbi, I'm sorry. It's just my less than serious nature to joke around. It is my honor to stand guard tonight. I will be right outside if you

171

need anything." Just as Uri had done, Lorenzo placed his fist over his heart and bowed his head. She really needed to ask Frey what that was about.

"Okay, then. Urijah and I have work to do." Holding out the bag, he said, "Abbi, I know you've been stuck here all day, so I brought some things I thought you might need." Frey brushed a strand of hair behind her ear. The touch was probably meant to be gentle, but it stirred something in her core. Something she hadn't felt in a long time. Desire.

Her body automatically leaned toward his. She took the bag from his hand, letting her fingers brush his. "Thank you, that was very thoughtful." He continued to worm his way into her soul, one kind act at a time.

"You're welcome. If you need anything else, just call. I have something to take care of, but it shouldn't take long. After that I'll be home. Matthew, get some rest, and I'll pick you up tomorrow."

Matthew yawned and muttered, "M'kay." His eyes fluttered and he was out.

Frey stopped at the door and turned back to Abbi, giving her an odd look. It was quickly replaced with his gorgeous smile and then he was gone. Lorenzo was at his post by the door. Abbi wondered what items Frey thought she might need, so she opened the new looking bag and peered in. He had brought a clean pair of jeans, a long sleeve Henley, a new UGA sweatshirt, a pair of panties, and her toiletries. The panties were a brand new sexy lace number with the tags still on. Did he think she needed sexy panties? It wasn't lost on her that he'd gone shopping. She looked into the bag again. What he didn't bring was makeup. Did he not want her to wear it? No, he said he brought things she needed. He didn't think she needed makeup. Her soul made room for one more piece of him.

Rafael met up with Frey and Uri at Frey's house. It was rare that the King patrolled, but with so many of the Clan taking care of other things, he was needed. He flew in and landed beside the garage. "I've missed this," Rafael said, grinning. Frey knew if he was no longer part of the patrol schedule, he would miss it, too. It was innately necessary for the Gargoyles to spread their wings and soar as often as possible.

As they shook hands, Rafael asked, "So, what did you want to speak to me about?"

"I have an idea I wanted to run by you. I want to build Abbi a dance studio, so she can practice whenever she likes."

"I see. Where did you have in mind?"

"Here. I know I'm jumping the gun, but if things turn out the way I want them to, she and Matthew will not be moving out." Frey toed a rock back and forth.

Rafael cocked an eyebrow. "I take it she is not going to be a visitor at the manor then?"

Frey looked up. "No. Matthew convinced her to come back here. I think the kid's in my corner."

"Is this going to be a new build, or a remodel?" Rafael was the best architect around. Whatever Frey wanted, he'd get. Rafael would do all the research needed to build Abbi the perfect studio, equipped with mirrors, bars, sound equipment, the works.

"I thought about transforming the gym downstairs, but I want this to be all hers. I want a new room built on the west side of the house adjacent to the gym."

"All I need are the dimensions, and I'll get started tomorrow." Rafael loved the process from design to construction, even though he hired out Clan members for the actual build out.

"Thank you, Brother. Now, are you ready to fly?"

"Of course. Where's Urijah?"

"At the lake, where else? Urijah, let's hit it." Frey didn't have to yell. Urijah's shifter hearing picked up the command.

Frey and Rafael phased and launched themselves into the hazy sky. The moon was no longer completely full, but the bright orb cast a beautiful glow through the clouds. Uri met them in the air, and the three of them angled their wings toward the city.

Once they reached downtown, they split off, taking different quadrants. Their teams met them at predesignated locations. Rafael's team was the largest. Even though he was the oldest of their Clan, he was also the most important. His team would protect him above all else.

Frey's team was the smallest, but that was all right with him. More Unholy for him to battle. He adjusted his in-ear transmitter and got busy. Julian had taken Jonas' technology and tweaked it, making the communicators even better for the Goyles. The teams could talk to each other from longer distances. Frey was scanning the busy streets below when he found what he was looking for: a group of monsters just waiting for an ass whipping. "There they are boys; let's have some fun."

Frey and his team landed, making a tight formation around the Unholy. The hybrids stopped fighting among themselves and turned to their new opponents. Frey stood still, allowing the stupid creatures to come to him. He toyed with them, allowing them a few punches to get their egos going. As soon as they started running their mouths, he went in for the kill. After a couple of hours, he called for Sixx on the comm to come bag the bodies.

When Urijah offered to wait on the clean-up crew, Frey told him to head on home. He'd had a long day at the hospital, and Frey wanted to show his appreciation somehow. When Sixx and his team arrived, Frey and Rafael headed home. As they flew, Rafael asked, "How are things with Abbi? Kaya said she was pretty skittish when she took her statement."

"Kaya's right. Abbi's been through hell for a long time. Sixx uncovered a bunch of shit leading back to her husband that she's not going to want to hear." Frey explained what they suspected. "I want Kaya to be safe at the precinct, Rafe. This fucker is a loose cannon."

"She won't be chief much longer. Dane's nomination has been approved by the City Council. I'm ready for her to be home full time, getting the nursery ready. I still can't believe we can finally have kids."

"About that. It might not be my place to say anything, but if Sixx is right in something else he found today, he might have a kid out there who is in his early twenties."

"No shit?"

"No shit. He said he bit his girl in the throes of passion, thinking it was safe. We now know it wasn't."

"Huh. How does he feel about that?"

"He's a little pissed that she kept the truth from him. If he confronts her now, it's going to be a shock that he hasn't aged. But then again, since she's had a kid, she hasn't either. I don't envy him."

"No, I wouldn't either, especially knowing I'd lost that much time with my child. Damn. How are you going to deal with not being able to have kids?"

"What are you talking about?" Frey didn't like where the conversation had gone.

"I mean, Abbi's had a few miscarriages already, and those are human babies. Do you really think she can carry a Goyle fetus to term?"

Frey hadn't thought of it that way. "Honestly? I think it's been an internal defense mechanism. I might be wrong, but I don't think Abbi wanted to bring a baby into the world knowing Quinn would be the father." He didn't

175

tell Rafael that there was a possibility she might be pregnant now.

"That makes sense. I hope for your sake that's the case." When they neared the point they would go separate directions, Rafael said, "I'll pray to the gods on your behalf. Be well, my brother."

"And you, my King." Frey landed on the ground beside the back deck. He was too keyed up to stay home alone, so he showered the Unholy blood off his body, changed clothes, and headed to the gym to relieve Mason. The young Goyle had spent all day manning the gym alone. Even though Frey had decimated some Unholy, he still had nervous energy to burn. He needed to hit something else. The punching bag would have to do. He needed to wear himself out so he got a good night's sleep. He wanted to be well-rested when he brought his mate back home tomorrow.

# Chapter Twenty-Four

Craig grabbed the burner phone and excitedly called the only preassigned number in it. He had done his job and done it well. Jasper was rattled, and his boyfriend had left town. He was ready to collect his payment. After four rings, the phone was answered, "Well?"

"It's done. The kid left town. I followed him for a couple of hours just to be sure."

"Excellent. You have served me well. I will meet you at your hotel in ten minutes." The phone disconnected. Ten minutes? He was close by. Craig's dick began getting hard the instant the man's voice sounded in his ear. That accent alone drove Craig wild. Now that he knew he was so close, his cock was painful against the zipper of his jeans, but he didn't dare touch it. Ten minutes away meant in twenty minutes, Craig would be tied up in those beautiful knots. The large man would not be gentle.

Craig thought back to his time with Jasper. Making his fellow fireman fall for him had been easy. Craig almost developed feelings for the redhead, but the man had sensed it and demanded he end the charade. Craig had no idea why the man hated Jasper so much, but with all the money he received for seducing him, he really didn't care.

Now the man was going to pay him in a much better way. The first time he'd tied Craig up had been scary. Now just the thought of the ropes binding him, holding him hostage, had his dick weeping in anticipation. How long would the man make him wait to come? Half an hour? Two hours? Since he had done a good job in getting the kid to leave town, maybe the man would get him off quickly.

Sundays were family day at the manor. What started off as a once in a while breakfast had morphed into an all-day gathering. It wasn't mandatory, but if the Clan members could be there, they usually were. Priscilla, Rafael's housekeeper, was like a mother to all the Goyles and loved to spoil them by cooking huge spreads.

With so many of the immediate family out of the country, the house was fairly quiet. Kaya wrapped her arms around Rafael and said, "I've never seen them all this subdued. What's going on?"

Rafael placed a kiss on her forehead and protectively placed a hand on her stomach. "Mates, that's what's going on. It seems the fates have been conniving for a lot longer than we realized."

Kaya frowned, but let it go. Rafael would explain everything in due time, and Kaya was learning to be patient with him. When Priscilla announced breakfast was ready, they all headed into the dining room. Kaya was first in line, followed by Rafe, and the rest of the Clan lined up behind them. Once they were all seated, Rafael tapped his coffee mug with his fork. Everyone quieted and gave the King their full attention.

"I wanted to wait until we were all together to make this announcement, but seeing it may take a while for that to happen, I have decided to do this today. It is with great pleasure I tell you I am going to be a father." Rafael waited while the room erupted with shouts of joy, everyone standing and coming around to shake his hand and bow to Kaya. When the room settled back down, Rafael continued, "Since Kaya is going to be a mother, she has agreed to retire from the force. Dane will be stepping into the role of Chief." Dane received congratulations from all around the table.

"I'm not sure what is going on with the fates, but

they have decided we should all find our mates immediately. While this is a positive thing for our future, for some reason they have decided to make it difficult for some of us. Just this week, three of you have figured out who your mates are."

Dane spoke up, "Four."

Sixx answered next, "Five."

Mason slid down in his chair and quietly said, "Six."

If Dane and Sixx had been a surprise, neither was more so than Mason. Rafael looked at their young cousin and asked, "You're too young. Are you sure?"

"If my reaction to her here lately is any indication, then yeah, I'm pretty darn sure," Mason replied, blushing.

Based on the young Goyle's embarrassment, Rafael had a good idea what reaction he was referring to. "Would you care to enlighten us as to who she is?"

Mason looked at the ceiling. "Not really, but you'll find out eventually. It's Willow."

Rafael was delighted. "That's great!"

"How is it great? I'm too young and she's, she's…"

"She's perfect for you. And she's the best assistant I've ever had. Since she's your mate, that means she'll be around a long time." Rafael clapped his hands together.

"She has a boyfriend," Mason reminded him.

"No, she doesn't. They broke up last weekend."

"They did?" Mason was surprised.

Rafael grinned. "Yes, they did. Now, no more excuses. When you're ready, we'll discuss this further." Mason rolled his eyes, Kaya laughed, and everyone else got busy eating.

Rafael took a look around the table. Julian had informed him of the Katherine Fox challenge before he left for Egypt. "Dane, I thought you and Julian figured out that Katherine is his mate."

"Oh, we did. As soon as Katherine was out the door, my mate brought my food to me. The waitress at the coffee

179

shop, Marley? I'm pretty sure she's the one."

"Let us pray to the gods that she is a very boring girl leading a very boring life," Deacon said.

"Here, here," several of the Goyles raised their coffee mugs in agreement.

"That brings us to another topic of discussion. Since so many of us are finding our mates, my plan to visit the other Clans is back on. I cannot put it off any longer. With Julian out of the country, Sixx has agreed to be our information back-up. Dante is home safely with his new family. Frey is meeting with Malakai, another transfer from the west coast. With everything that's going on at the moment, Frey needs another body at the gym, and we need another body in the sky."

"Speaking of bodies, where's Jasper?" Priscilla asked as she brought in another basket of biscuits.

"He had a late night on a stake-out," Dane answered before anyone else could. The rest of them would eventually find out Trevor was gone, but for now, it wasn't anyone's business.

When breakfast was finished, most of the Clan spread out around the manor, either playing video games or shooting pool. Sixx excused himself to head over to the lab. Dane pulled Kaya to the side. "We need to talk about Troy Quinn."

"Let's go to Rafael's office," Kaya replied. Rafael knew this was police business, but Kaya was his business. Now that she was pregnant, he wasn't letting her out of his sight too often.

Frey opened the gym, but instead of working out, he was meeting with Malakai Palamo, a Gargoyle who had recently transferred from the west coast. The newcomer was a martial arts expert, and Frey needed an extra body to help out around the gym. Mason had manned the gym the previous day while Frey and Uri took care of Abbi and Matthew. Hopefully soon, things would get back to normal, but until they did, Frey didn't want to tie Mason down.

Frey grinned to himself when he saw his newest employee. The Goyle belonged on an ad for surfing equipment. He was native Samoan, wearing a tank top, ripped blue jeans, and flip-flops. "Hey, Malakai, welcome to New Atlanta."

"Please, call me Kai. It's good to be here, I think. I don't know about this weather, but at least the scenery's nice." Kai shook Frey's hand and looked around the gym. "So, this is your place? Sweet."

"Yeah, come on. I'll show you around." Frey gave him a tour of the facilities, stopping a few times to talk with some of his regulars. Until he had a chance to spar with Malakai, he wouldn't turn him loose with classes. "So, what do you think?"

Kai smiled. "I'm impressed. This is much larger than the gym I came from. Everything is state of the art. I would be honored to be part of your dojo."

"Glad to hear it. Let's go to the office so we can talk in private." Frey led him to the back and explained some of what was going on with the others. "Urijah is our resident swordsmith. He and I are in charge of the sword training. Mason is our youngest Clan member, but he's maturing nicely. He's getting stronger every day." Since Rafael and Sinclair spoke on the phone often, Rafe had filled him in on what Alistair was up to and the importance of taking up arms once again. Sinclair had already started the west coast Clan training as well.

"Normally, I'm here most of the day, but with my mate's brother coming home from the hospital today, I will be taking the day off. Uri will be here soon to take over. He will teach you everything you need to know. You can

181

shadow us for a week or so. We'll add you to the rotation whenever you're ready."

"Sounds good. I'm glad to be able to continue in the same type of work I was already doing."

The bells over the door sounded and Frey looked at the monitor. Uri had arrived. He introduced the two Goyles and excused himself. It was time to go get Matthew and take him home.

Frey didn't waste any time getting to the hospital. If Matthew had already been released, he didn't want the teen and Abbi to have to wait on him. He stopped at the door and spoke to Lorenzo. "Good morning, Lor. Thank you for standing watch."

"My honor, Frey. Matthew is a good kid. The doctor has already been in to release him. You're right on time."

"Good, good. If you wouldn't mind hanging around, I don't want to take any chances getting them both to the truck."

"I don't mind."

Frey turned to the laughter coming from Matthew's room. He didn't understand their obsession with the old comedies, but if it made them both happy, he wouldn't dare begrudge them their amusement. He rather enjoyed their laughing. He waited a few minutes until the show was over before entering the room. "Hey there, Buddy. How're you feeling?"

"Like I got run over by a tank," Matt said over a smile.

"I hear you've been released. You ready to get outta here?"

"Yes, Sir. I can't wait to sit on the deck, get some fresh air. This place stinks like disinfectant. No offense," he said to the nurse waiting with a wheelchair.

Abbi and Frey laughed at the teen. Frey turned his attention to his mate. "And how about you? You ready to get some fresh air?"

182

"What I want is a shower, but yes, I'm ready to go." She looked tired, like she'd slept in an uncomfortable hospital chair all night.

"Okay, Matt, let's get you in your wheelchair. Abbi, I'll take your bag." Frey had to look away when Abbi bent over to retrieve her bag. Her ass looked too good in her blue jeans.

"Here you go," she said, drawing his attention back to her face.

Once she handed the bag to him, she turned to Matt and helped him transfer from the bed to the wheelchair. He'd already changed clothes, so there was nothing they needed to do except get him seated. Once that was accomplished, they left the room. Frey led the way with Lorenzo bringing up the rear.

When they reached the front exit, Frey tossed his keys to Lor, who went and brought Frey's truck around. Soon, they had Matt loaded in the back seat and were ready to leave. Abbi climbed in the passenger seat and closed the door. Frey could tell she was frazzled. She needed to rest in a good bed. "Thank you, Brother. I owe you one," he said to Lor.

"Nah, it's what we do. You know that." They clasped hands, and Frey pulled him in for a man hug. Lor clapped him on the back and headed toward his own vehicle.

Frey walked around the truck and got in. His cell phone rang. "Yes, Jasper."

"Just wanted you to know that Troy still hasn't left his house. You're clear for the time being."

"Thank you, Brother." Jasper sounded funny, but then again, he had been staking out Troy's house all night. He was probably tired. Instead of responding, Jasper disconnected.

183

Troy was pissed. No, he was beyond pissed. He'd borrowed George's car so he could remain incognito. If Matthew named Troy as his assailant, they would be looking for him. So far, things had remained quiet. He had his portable police scanner and would be alerted instantly if they started looking for him. He had called the hospital to make sure Matt was still there. He was going to wait around at Abbi's car for her to come out and take Matthew wherever she was hiding out, only her car wasn't at the hospital. He parked as close to the entrance as possible without causing suspicion.

He expected Abbi to wheel Matthew out and get in a taxi. If she was hiding, she knew he would be able to spot her car anywhere. What he hadn't expected was for her to wheel her brother out of the hospital accompanied by the big man he'd seen at the precinct, along with an equally big man who brought around a truck. They got Matthew settled into the back with Abbi climbing in the front. The two men spoke quietly and clapped each other on the back.

Who the fuck was this man, and why was he insinuating himself into Abbi's life? First he'd come to the precinct right before Troy was put on second shift. Now, here he was, playing the part of the happy husband to someone else's wife? Fuck that shit. Troy didn't give a damn how big the man was, he was not going to let him take Abbi away. Troy pulled out of the parking lot and followed the truck.

# Chapter Twenty-Five

"I didn't know Jasper was your brother. Y'all don't look alike," Matthew said from the back seat.

"He's not; we're just really close like brothers." Frey needed to be more careful with what he said.

"Do you have any brothers or sisters?"

"I have two brothers, Julian and Nikolas. They are both in Egypt right now."

"Do they live there?" Matthew should be tired from the pain meds, but obviously, they were wearing off.

"No, they live here. Nikolas' girlfriend is there with her parents, and Nik decided to join her. Julian hasn't had a vacation in a long time, so he decided to go as well. Nik and Jules are really close." Frey smiled thinking of his two younger siblings and the way they bantered with each other.

"Why aren't you in Egypt with them?"

"Because I'm here with you and Abbi." That was the truth. He'd had every intention of going to the sandy country until Matt stormed into his life. Abbi was sitting quietly, staring out the window, but he knew she was taking in the conversation.

Matt sighed and whispered, "I'm sorry."

"I'm not. Listen to me." Frey looked in the rearview mirror at the teen. "I have no regrets. You might not realize it, but we're like family now. I wouldn't be anywhere else."

"But they're your real brothers."

"They're my brothers by blood. Jasper's my brother by choice. Doesn't make him any less of one. You're a little young to be my brother, but you mean just as much as if you were. It's hard for you to understand now, but one day you will."

"Frey…" Matt paused, a pained look in his eyes.

"Yeah, Buddy?"

"Remember the first day we met, and I told you not

185

to call me Son?"

Frey's heart skipped a couple of beats. Surely Matt wasn't going there. "Yeah?"

"You can call me Son," he whispered.

Abbi felt more than saw Frey nod his head. She couldn't stop the tears from falling. She had failed her brother miserably. She had allowed Troy to be a part of Matt's life with no positive influence at all. Not only had he been a bad role model, but he'd abused Matt. She was the worst kind of sister in the world. She didn't deserve his love. The man sitting beside her did, though. In less than a week, Geoffrey Hartley had shown her brother more love than he'd seen in the last ten years.

Frey reached across the truck and grabbed Abbi's hand. Now he was offering her his strength. "So, Matt." Frey cleared the frog out of his throat. She wasn't the only one affected by Matt's words. "Some of the guys and I moved your bed and a dresser downstairs to the gym. I figured until you're all healed up, it'll be easier on you than walking up and down the steps."

The man kept surprising her. He not only opened his home to them, he also upended it so Matt would be more comfortable. Still, she couldn't get out of her mind that he had failed him as well. Maybe if Frey had been watching Matt instead of trusting Michael, Troy wouldn't have gotten to him.

They arrived at Frey's driveway, and it dawned on Abbi, "We left my car at the hospital."

Frey rolled the window down and spoke into the security panel. The gate slowly swung open and he drove through. "I brought it back last night after you agreed to come here instead of going home with Kaya."

"How did..." Abbi shouldn't be surprised, but she was. "Is there anyone you don't know?" Was everyone she'd met a friend of his? She bet if she could see the police chief's fiancé, he'd be part of the male Amazon club, too.

Frey pulled up to the garage and parked the truck. "I've been in this town for a long time now, so yeah, I know quite a few people. I'm not going to apologize for having good friends." Frey got out of the truck and opened the back door to help Matt out. He didn't wait on Abbi.

Instead of going in the side door, Matt headed toward the back of the house. By the time Abbi caught up with them, Frey and Matt were sitting side by side on the back deck. Matthew had his eyes closed, soaking in the early morning sunshine. Frey was staring off into the woods, his body still. She had to watch closely to see if he was actually breathing. When he didn't look at her, she continued on into the house. She carried her new bag upstairs and unpacked it. She tossed her dirty clothes in a hamper that hadn't been there the day before.

She opened the closet to store the bag and stopped when she saw the clothes hanging there. She stepped farther into the small space, running her hands over each garment. Tags were still attached, yet none showed the price. The pieces were casual yet stylish. In the very back of the closet was a black leather jacket. Shaking her head, she placed the new travel bag in the back of the closet beside a pair of black riding boots. Ah, his Harley. Abbi had never ridden on a motorcycle. The thought excited her. On a hunch, after seeing the new panties he'd brought to the hospital, she opened the top dresser drawer. There among her plain white panties was a selection of lacy numbers in an assortment of colors. The next drawer held matching bras.

Abbi couldn't wrap her head around the fact that the mountain of a man sitting downstairs had gone shopping for her. The clothes were mostly modest, some in a simple, sexy sort of way. The undergarments were also sexy

187

without being slutty. She grabbed some of her new clothes and took a quick shower. After she dressed, she flopped backwards on the bed and stared at the ceiling. She didn't know how to feel. When she was near Frey, it was like an invisible tether connected them, drawing her to him. Her body hummed, and she constantly wanted to touch him.

When she was away from him, her mind came back to its senses. She was still a married woman. Granted, she was going to file for divorce, but still, she was married. She had known Frey less than a week. Even if he caused a constant throb between her legs, she had to play it smart. She would accept his hospitality, the safety of his home, and his friendship with Matthew. Other than that, she needed to keep her distance. A door closed downstairs, and her two men's voices carried up the stairs. No, not her men. Her brother and her host. She forced herself to get up and go take care of her brother instead of hiding out from the one man who made her feel something other than dread after all these years.

Jasper skipped family day at the manor. He was in a foul mood, and he didn't want to spread it around. Someone else was finally sitting on Troy, even though the man hadn't moved in almost twenty-four hours. Jasper had written down the friend's tag number and instead of calling, had taken it to Sixx. When Sixx picked up on Jasper's unease, Jasper confided in him about everything that had transpired, from the envelope, to seeing Craig, to the new photos being delivered to Trevor. Sixx had seen the envelope in the plastic cover with Julian's handwritten note beside it. The note stated that Julian had found one set of prints on the envelope, and those most likely belonged to whomever had put the envelope on Jasper's desk. Since he had gone to Egypt, he hadn't had time to investigate further.

While the computer was running the license plate number of the car parked at Troy's, Sixx leaned back and clasped his hands behind his head. "I'm sorry Trevor left. At least you know he's coming back in a week. That gives us seven days to find Craig and make him talk. Find out what the hell he's up to."

"I really appreciate it. When I was on the west coast, I didn't really fit in with the Clan. It wasn't anything they did or didn't do, I just didn't feel comfortable with them. Here, I feel like I have a family."

"Speaking of family, I want you to look at something." He turned one of the monitors around so Jasper could see the image that was front and center.

"That's Desmond Rothchild. I see you looked up your doppelganger."

Sixx frowned and dropped a bomb on Jasper, "Not my doppelganger, my son."

"Your son? How the hell is that possible?"

"I dated a girl about twenty years ago. Her name is Desirae Rothchild. One night, during let's say some pretty wild sex, I phased and bit her. She was so blissed out, she didn't realize what I'd done. We dated a while afterwards until one day she disappeared. Now, there's a kid out there with her name who looks just like me. Coincidence? I don't think so."

"Holy hell, and I thought my situation was bad. At least now maybe I can score some backstage passes to their concert," Jasper joked, trying to lighten the mood.

Sixx threw a pen at him. "Right... 'Hey kid, how about giving your old pop, who doesn't look much older than you, some tickets to your show?' I'll ask him right after I see his mom and explain why she still looks twenty-something."

"So, you are going to find them? You know, he's coming here in a couple of months to do a concert." Jasper

189

couldn't imagine how Sixx was feeling. It was bad enough Craig had shown up after less than a year.

"Then I guess I have a couple of months to think about it. Now, back to you. Let's figure out what your ex is doing in New Atlanta and what his agenda is."

The longer Jasper sat, the more agitated he got. "I'm going to head out to the gym. Please let me know if you find anything." They had called Sinclair and gotten every bit of information he could dig up on Craig, which wasn't much.

Jasper parked beside Frey's empty spot. Of course he would be home with Matthew and Abbi. Uri was probably on duty since Mason had worked all day the day before. When Jasper didn't see anyone out front, he strolled back to the office. He walked in expecting Uri, only he found someone else.

"Kai? What are you doing here?" Jasper had been a member of the gym where Kai worked out west.

"Jasper, good to see you, Bro. I'm working here. Had to catch a change of scenery, if you know what I mean."

Jasper did know what he meant. He hadn't wanted to move, yet now he was glad he had. "Yeah, I sure do. It's why I'm on the other side of the States."

"Hang on a sec, someone's at the counter." Malakai stood and headed toward the front of the building. Jasper noticed a bank of monitors that were relaying feed from security cameras. Each one was located in various areas of the gym. A couple were located outside. "I wonder…"

"What do you wonder?" Urijah asked, entering the office.

By now, most of the Clan knew about Craig being in town. Jasper still hadn't shared the fact that pictures of him and his ex were showing up. "Trevor mentioned Craig was looking in the window on the side of the building where the parking lot is. How far back do you keep the security footage?"

"About a year. Are you thinking you might find

190

something on the camera?"

"It's worth a shot. Look at Tuesday afternoon." Jasper sat impatiently while Uri set the parameters for the search fields. Malakai returned, "Are you still a fireman?"

"No, I'm a detective. The quota for hot, alpha firemen had already been met," Jasper joked.

"What was up with your fireman friend, what was his name? Chris?"

"Craig? What do you mean, what was up?"

"After you transferred out here, he came in the gym looking for you. He seemed frantic, too. Like, you'd stolen something of his. I finally told him you'd left town, only I didn't share where you'd gone."

"Here we go." Uri fast forwarded the feed until it showed Craig looking in the window. He froze the frame and rewound. When it came to the point where he got out of his car, Uri stopped it and zoomed in on the tag.

"Gotcha, you bastard." Jasper wrote the tag number down. "Now, let's pray it isn't a rental."

"So, what's the deal with you and your ex?"

"He's a closeted, lying, conniving sonofabitch. He disappeared on me, not the other way around. After almost a year, he finds me, and does everything he can to sabotage my relationship with my mate. So far, he's succeeding," Jasper seethed. "I'm going to call this in to Sixx. Excuse me."

Jasper called Sixx and gave him the tag number. When he returned to the office, he asked, "I don't suppose either of you are up for a little sparring, are you?"

Kai grinned. "If Uri doesn't mind running the show for a bit, I would love to get in the ring."

Uri gestured toward the door. "By all means."

Malakai clapped his hands together, but he didn't realize just how fired up Jasper was at the moment. He was ready to kick some major ass. Malakai borrowed some shorts from Urijah, since they were close to the same size. He kicked his flip-flops off and climbed in the ring. He was

191

used to sparring barefooted, whereas Jasper was not, but he wasn't going to let a little thing like shoes make a difference. Both males bounced around on their feet, warming up their legs. Kai took first swing, and they were off. Neither Goyle was holding back, and it felt great. Jasper didn't intend to hurt Kai, but he wasn't going to worry if he punched a little harder than usual, either. They had sparred together back on the west coast and were fairly evenly matched.

The patrons gathered as they always did when the big guys were fighting. It was a free show, better than anything they could get on pay-per-view. The men stood in awe, wishing they could move that way. The women lusted, wishing they could take the two men home. Neither male paid attention to what was going on outside the ring. That was until Urijah said just loud enough for them to hear, "Jasper, Sixx found Craig."

# Chapter Twenty-Six

Abbi followed the sound of voices into Matt's temporary bedroom. Not wanting to interrupt, she went no farther than the door. Even though her brother was in a tremendous amount of pain, he was laughing and cutting up with the big man. It had been a long time since she'd heard the sound coming from Matt. As if he knew she was there, Frey looked her way, the smile never leaving his face. Even though it was there because of something Matt had said, it was still nice to see aimed her way. Too often she'd been on the receiving end of a scowl.

Her stomach rumbled reminding her they hadn't eaten breakfast. Matt had been too groggy to eat at the hospital, and Abbi had been too nervous thinking about the upcoming days. Living with the tempting, gorgeous man was going to be a walk in the park compared to filing for divorce and staying far away from Troy. She left the two men to do their manly stuff, and she headed back to the kitchen. Her first order of business was to start the coffee pot. Once that was taken care of, she opened the fridge to see what Frey had picked up at the store.

*Holy crap!* Abbi couldn't remember seeing that much food, ever. Not even when her parents were alive. She shook her head and dug around until she came out with all the ingredients she needed to make biscuits and gravy, eggs, and bacon. She hadn't cooked a large breakfast in a while, but she wanted to do something nice for Frey. It didn't hurt that biscuits and gravy were Matthew's favorite breakfast.

The biscuits were in the oven, and the gravy was simmering when the men returned from the gym. "Is that bacon my nose detects?" Matt was practically drooling.

Laughing and pointing at the nearest chair, Abbi responded, "Yes, it is. If you're a good brother, there might just be biscuits in the oven, too."

Frey moaned, "You're christening my kitchen, just so you know."

"What do you mean?" Abbi asked as she stirred the gravy.

"Nobody's ever cooked in here except me, and I have definitely never cooked a breakfast like this. Thank you." The look in his eyes spoke louder than his words could. He liked her in his kitchen.

"You're welcome." She had to look away. She couldn't have her teenage brother realizing what their host was doing to her body. "Matt, do you want coffee?"

"Are pigs tasty? Of course I do."

"Here, I'll get it. You've got your hands full." Frey grabbed three mugs from the cabinet.

There he went again, being nice. There's no way it was all an act just to get in her pants. Frey Hartley was the real deal. He snagged a piece of bacon from the plate, taking a bite and crunching as he talked, "I wanted to let you both know, I'm having a little bit of construction done on the west side of the house. There will be contractors coming and going, but they will not bother either of you. Rafael Stone will be overseeing the project, and he only hires people that are one hundred percent trustworthy."

"Rafael, isn't that Kaya's fiancé?" Abbi asked as she pulled the biscuits from the oven.

"Yes, he's the best there is. Can you keep a secret?" Frey asked them both. When they nodded, he continued, "He happens to be my cousin as well."

Kaya offering her home to Abbi now made more sense. "How do you like your eggs?"

"However you and Matt eat yours. No need in you making two different kinds. I just like 'em cooked." Frey poured everyone a cup of coffee. He handed Matt a cup of black, Abbi a cup with a splash of milk, and took his own black as well.

She scrambled half a dozen eggs, hoping that was

enough. When they were almost done, she added a little shredded cheddar cheese. By the time she had everything ready, Frey had set out three plates, silverware, napkins, butter, and jelly.

Abbi helped Matt with his food so he didn't move around too much. Once they were finished eating, he told Frey, "I really would like a shower before I lay down."

"No problem. We'll get you squared away and then I'll help Abbi with the dishes."

"You don't mind?" Matt was blushing.

Frey shook his head, smiling. "Son, I've taken more showers with men than I care to think about. I was in the military. Besides, I can leave my shorts on. Come on; let's get your stinking ass clean."

Abbi didn't wait on Frey to start clearing the table. There were no leftovers to put away. The next time she made breakfast, she'd have to remember to cook more. By the time Frey returned, she had finished cleaning and was sitting on the back deck enjoying her coffee. Frey had refreshed his cup and sat down beside her. "You should have left the dishes."

"It's okay, you were busy helping Matt. Thank you."

"You don't have to thank me, Abbi. I love that kid. He's funny, smart, and brave. He's everything I would want in my own son."

"You're getting attached to him." Abbi didn't think that was a good idea. When they had to move back out, Matt would miss the connection.

"I am. He needs a good role model. Not that I'm good, but I really care about him. No matter what happens with you and me, I'll always want him in my life." Frey wasn't looking at her when he spoke. His attention was again focused on the trees.

"You *are* a good man, and I appreciate everything you're doing for Matt. And for me." Frey would always want Matt in his life, not her. With everything going on

195

around her, of course he'd changed his mind about wanting her.

Frey finally looked at her. "I don't mean to pry, but I need to know your plans about the divorce. I have to schedule your security."

Abbi's heart sank a little more. He didn't want her divorced so they could be together. He wanted to plan who watched her. *Stop it. You're still married, and even if you weren't you don't need to jump right into another relationship.*

"Hey, look at me. What happened just then?" Frey sat his coffee on the rail and squatted down in front of her. With him being so tall, she was still shorter than him in this position. He placed his hands on her knees and left them there. His touch lit a fire deep inside. God, how she wanted him to move his hands up her thighs. It was wrong, so wrong to feel that way, but he brought out a need in her. A need to be touched, wanted, cherished. Satisfied. Without thought to the consequences, she placed her free hand over his.

She probably imagined it, but she could have sworn Frey growled. He was motionless with the exception of his nostrils flaring. His brown eyes were now almost black, and they were staring at her lips. She wanted him to kiss her. She wanted to feel his mouth against hers, not just on her lips but everywhere. He made her want to feel. She sat her coffee cup down on the deck. If she started something with this man, she had a feeling he wouldn't be able to stop, whether she wanted him to or not. Dammit, she was married. But she was getting divorced, so did that make it okay?

She licked her lips, and there was that noise again. Only this time, she didn't just hear it, she felt it. The deep growl vibrated in her own chest. Frey's hands tightened around her legs, not exactly painful, but strong enough to let her know he wanted more. Before she could blink, Frey pulled her out to the edge of her chair and parted her legs.

196

He didn't move his hands toward her core, but he did situate himself against her body. When he did move his hands, he placed one on her lower back and one at her nape under her ponytail. His eyes flashed with something so primal it almost scared her. Just before he crashed their mouths together, she could swear she saw sharp teeth. When their mouths connected, she expected to feel pain. Instead, Frey's lips were soft, and his mouth was hot as his tongue sought out hers. What was up with her and fangs?

Abbi opened for him. Frey made soft, sweet love to her mouth as his cock hardened against her core. Frey, resting on his ankles, pulled Abbi out of the chair and onto his lap as he maneuvered her so she was straddling him. She wrapped her arms around his shoulders as he held her tightly against him. Frey rose up on his toes, and the movement brought her clit in line with his erection. A jolt of electricity hit her between the legs, a gasp caught in her throat. She wanted more. Had to have more. Clutching his huge arms for leverage, Abbi moved her body against his, wanting the friction, needing the release. The soft kiss turned into a furious frenzy, their mouths no longer making love. She was rocking against him in sync with the motion of his tongue. Before she could stop it, her body convulsed and white sparks flashed behind her eyes. Frey continued the movements of their lower bodies until her whimpers subsided. *Holy shit.* She'd just had the best orgasm of her life, and they still had their clothes on.

Frey muttered, "Fuck." In one swift motion, he returned her to her chair while he picked up his coffee cup and leaned against the railing. She didn't miss the fact that he untucked his t-shirt, trying to hide his still hard cock. She was confused. Was he so disgusted with her that he wanted her away from him? Before she could think about it too hard, Matt opened the back door. How in the world had he known Matthew was going to interrupt them? However he knew, she was glad. She would hate for Matt to have caught her rutting against Frey.

"Have either of you seen my pills? I thought I'd take one and chill for a little while."

Abbi hopped up from her chair, knocking her coffee over in the process. "Oh, crap! I'm so sorry," she braced herself for a tongue-lashing.

Frey grasped her upper arm, turning her to look at him. "It's all right. You go help Matt, and I'll clean this up. Nothing a little water won't fix." His hand on her was gentle, not bruising.

Abbi got Matt settled and returned to the deck. Frey had his hands on the rail, cell phone peeking out from beneath one. It just dawned on her that he was wearing short sleeves. "Aren't you cold?"

He didn't turn toward her when he answered, "No, I don't get cold." She was cold, and it had more to do with his body language than the November weather. "We need to talk." He stuck his cell phone in his front pocket before holding his hand out to her. She placed hers in his, allowing him to lead her down the deck steps onto the walkway towards the lake. After a few steps, Frey laced their fingers together.

"Did I do something wrong?" Abbi asked when the silence was too much to bear.

"What? No." Frey stopped and put his hands on her upper arms. "You are perfect, so please stop second-guessing yourself at every turn." Frey tucked an errant strand of hair behind her ear. It was a move she was getting used to. His fingertips lingered behind her ear as his thumb caressed her cheek. Even though the movement was sweet, it sent a chill over her body. Abbi shivered, and he immediately pulled her into the warmth of his embrace. She didn't allow herself to think how wrong it was. *No, this feels right. This feels like home.* She wrapped her arms around his waist and turned her head so her ear was against his heart.

Frey stroked her hair, over and over. She had no idea

198

how long they stood there, silently, just being. He kissed the top of her head before tipping her chin up so he could see her face. "Perfect," he muttered. He turned them so they could start walking again, this time wrapping a strong arm around her shoulder. "Tell me your schedule for next week."

"I have classes at the community center Monday, Wednesday, and Friday. I need to work on the dances for the fall festival, but I can do that from home. I mean, your house, not..."

Frey squeezed her shoulder and softly said, "This is your home."

"Frey..." Abbi stopped, but he urged her on along the pathway.

"No, don't overthink it. This is your home for as long as you want it. Now, what about seeing an attorney? When are you going to squeeze that into your busy schedule?"

"Kaya gave me a name, but I haven't had a chance to contact her. She's probably you're cousin, too. I swear, you know everyone." Abbi elbowed him playfully in the side.

"Is it Victoria Holt?"

"See, you *do* know everyone."

"One day soon you will meet Jonathan and Priscilla, Rafael's housekeepers. They are more like family, but they keep the manor running like a fine-tuned instrument. Priscilla's the one who taught me how to make lasagna. Anyway, Victoria is their niece, and one hell of an attorney. Also, Rafael is all about keeping things in the family."

"Jonathan's a housekeeper?" Abbi had heard of butlers but not male housekeepers.

"He's so much more than a butler. He takes care of the garden and the grounds. He is a chauffeur and a top-notch mechanic. Where Priscilla is a mother to us all, Jonathan fills the void for those of us who've lost our fathers."

"So, you lost your parents, too?" Abbi knew the pain

199

of losing those closest to you all too well.

"It was a long time ago, but yes. Now, back to Victoria. There are some things I need to talk to you about before you contact her. Things that are going to weigh heavily when she takes Quinn to court."

"Like what? We don't have anything, not really. Just the house, and he can have it. I don't want to live there." When it was all said and done, Abbi wanted a clean break from Troy with no sad reminders of her past.

"Let's sit down." They had reached the end of the dock. There was a bench off to the side that faced the water. Frey put his arm around Abbi's shoulders and kissed the top of her head. She loved the intimacy of the gesture. She relaxed into his side, feeling content for the first time in years.

"Abbi, we've uncovered some things about Troy. There's no way to soften the blow, so I'm just going to tell you. He and your Aunt Judy were partners of sorts. Money traded hands between the two of them. Money that should have been yours and Matt's. We found communications between them that started when you were still in high school."

Abbi leaned away from Frey so she could look up at him. "I don't understand. Judy was broke. She was always coming around asking my mom for money. Dad wouldn't let Mom give her any because she would just spend it on drugs. A couple of months before the accident, they had a huge blow-up. Judy showed up at the house stoned out of her head. She was threatening Dad, saying he'd regret being a selfish bastard."

Frey tightened his grip on her shoulder. "I don't know where Judy came up with the money, but five thousand dollars was deposited into her bank account. A few days later it was transferred to Troy's account. That was two days before your parents' accident. Abbi, I think Troy killed your parents."

# Chapter Twenty-Seven

Frey didn't know any other way to tell her than to rip the Band-Aid off. "I'm so sorry."

"That's crazy. Why would Troy do that? Kill my parents for five thousand dollars?"

"It was more than that, Sweetheart. He and Judy split the money in your parents' account. The money that was supposed to have been yours and Matt's, they split evenly. She got the house, he got you."

Abbi stood and began pacing along the bank. She wrapped her arms around herself, mumbling. Frey wanted to pull her down into his lap and comfort her, but she had to digest what he'd told her. When she stopped in front of him, her body was shaking. He never wanted to see the look she had on her face again. "Can you prove it? Can you prove any of what you just told me?"

"We can't prove he was responsible for the brakes going out on their car; it's been too long. But the money changing hands, we absolutely can. He still has the same bank account he's had since he was a teenager. It is with a different bank than your joint account. You need to call Victoria and set up a meeting as soon as possible. We will hand over the documents regarding the bank accounts. She will take it from there."

"I was so stupid. I always thought something was going on between them, but I turned my head. I told myself they wouldn't do that to me. God! I knew Judy was mad, but that's just twisted. I wish she was alive so I could kill her!" Abbi's body continued to shake. Frey stood and drew her into his arms. He hated seeing her so torn up, and he'd done it to her. No, that motherfucking husband of hers did it.

"I want to see Victoria. Now." Abbi twisted out of his arms and took off toward the house. Frey caught up

201

with her in a couple of steps and quietly followed her inside. She ran upstairs, but Frey didn't go after her. He reached out with his shifter senses and listened to make sure she was okay. Abbi ran back down the steps and sat down at the kitchen table. She had a business card and her cell phone with her.

Abbi placed the call to Victoria, asking when she could meet with her. Obviously Kaya had already spoken with the attorney, because she had been waiting on Abbi to call. "Today?" Abbi looked up at Frey, raising her eyebrows. He nodded. He wanted this taken care of immediately, before Abbi could change her mind. Now that she knew what a piece of shit Troy really was, he didn't think he had anything to worry about. "Today would be wonderful. Where would you like to meet? Okay, can you hang on a second please?" Abbi put her hand over the phone, "She wants to meet at the manor, but I don't want to leave Matt alone."

"I'll have one of the guys watch Matt. Tell her the manor's fine, but give us an hour."

"Ms. Holt, we will meet you at the manor. Is an hour okay? Great, thank you. Yes, see you then."

"Looks like I'm going to see Kaya's home after all," Abbi said when she hung up.

"Let me make some phone calls, get someone on their way over here, and we'll head that way." Frey knew a lot of the guys would already be at the manor for family day. He'd leave it up to Rafael on whether or not they stayed since he was bringing Abbi. Uri was busy with the gym, so Lorenzo agreed to come over.

"Lor is coming to stay with Matt while we're gone. He'll be here in just a few minutes and then we can go."

"Uh, Geoffrey?" The sheepish look on Abbi's face was so cute.

"Yes, Abbi?" He grinned, anxious to hear what she wanted.

202

"I saw a jacket and some boots in my closet, and I was wondering, could we, uh, maybe, take your motorcycle to the manor?"

Frey had bought the riding gear on the hope that one day he would get Abbi on the back of his bike. He never expected her to suggest it. "Absolutely. Why don't you gear up, and I'll go tell Matt we're going to be gone for a little while."

Abbi nodded then jogged upstairs to get ready. Frey was ready to have Abbi sitting right behind him, hugged up tight. Then again, his body was still humming from her getting off earlier. It was probably a good thing Matthew came outside when he did, or Frey would have had Abbi buck naked on the deck, pounding his cock into her pussy. The remembrance of her grinding on his dick would be the only masturbation fodder he would need for a long time. The bliss on her face was embedded on his brain. The scent of her arousal was fresh in his memory. The sound of her sweet moans had been better than any mood music. If he could record the noises she made when she was coming, he'd make millions.

Frey adjusted his cock before he went into the gym. Matt was snoring softly. Frey hated to wake him, but he didn't want him to be alarmed when he woke and neither Frey nor Abbi were home. The rumble of Lorenzo's bike sounded from down the long driveway, and he knew he needed to give Matt a heads up. "Matthew..."

"Hmm?" He blinked his eyes and tried to open them. The pain pills were keeping him pretty zonked.

"I need to take Abbi to see an attorney. Lorenzo's here to stay with you. Is that okay?"

Matt opened his eyes. "An attorney? What's wrong?" He gingerly sat up.

"Don't move, Buddy. Abbi's going to file for divorce from Troy. A friend of the family is a lawyer, and she's willing to meet Abbi today. Are you okay with Lor staying

203

here until we get back?"

"Yes, God yes. Hell, I'd stay with Aunt Judy again if it meant getting Abs away from dickhead."

Frey flinched internally. Matt had no idea what his aunt had done. If Frey had his way, the boy would never find out. It was bad enough that Abbi knew.

"Knock-knock." Lorenzo was standing at the doorway. "Hey, Matt. How are you feeling?"

"Tired. Sore. Sleepy. I'm afraid I'm not going to be very good company."

"That's no problem. I'm pretty sure I can entertain myself while you sleep."

Frey ruffled Matt's hair. "You get some rest. We'll be home as soon as we can."

Matt's eyes closed, and he was out within seconds. Frey and Lor walked back through the house to the kitchen just as Abbi was coming through the other side. Lor let out a low wolf whistle, and Frey let out a low growl. He totally agreed with Lorenzo's assessment of his mate, but his beast didn't like anyone else noticing. Abbi had applied a small amount of make-up, fixed her ponytail, and had donned the boots and jacket. "Is this okay?" she asked, indicating her clothes.

Lorenzo was smart and kept his mouth shut. "It's perfect. You're perfect. Lor, thanks again, Brother."

"No problem. I'm just adding it to your tab."

Frey shook his head, grinning, and took Abbi by the hand. He led her out to the garage where the sleek, black motorcycle waited. "Oh, crap. I don't have a helmet."

Once they were inside, Frey gestured to a shelf where his helmet was stored. "I wasn't sure of your size, so I got one of each." Four shiny black helmets sat side by side on the shelf. He handed her the smallest one. "Let's try this one first. It should be snug, but not so tight it hurts your head." She slid it on and grimaced. He held out the next one, and she swapped with him. She didn't make a face this time. When it was in place, Frey said, "Shake your head no." Abbi frowned but shook her head as he asked. "Is it too loose?"

"I don't think so. Feels good." Abbi shook her head again. "Yep, we're good."

Frey ran the chin strap through both hooks then looped it back through the inner one, cinching it tight. He snapped it in place and straightened the helmet, taking a few seconds to admire the view. "Next time, you'll have to show me how to do that," Abbi said.

*Next time.* Frey was ecstatic she was planning on a next time. He put on his own helmet with Abbi observing his fingers work the strap. He handed her a new pair of sunglasses with safety lenses and put his own pair on. Normally he didn't wear them, but he wanted to show Abbi he cared about their safety.

Frey lowered the passenger foot pegs before straddling the bike. He stood it up and pushed the kickstand up with his heel. "Put your left foot there and swing your right leg over." When Abbi was seated behind him, he told her, "I've never doubled anyone. Never expected to. We'll have to get you a back rest, but for now, you're gonna want to hold on really tight."

Abbi scooted herself forward until she was flush against Frey's body. She wrapped her arms around his stomach and put her chin on his shoulder. Gods, he could get used to this. He turned the key, pushed the run button and then hit start. The massive machine came to life underneath them. Abbi giggled. He looked back to see a smile on her face. "Hang on, Sweetheart." Frey toed the gearshift down into first and eased off the clutch. Her arms were locked around him, her hands splayed across his stomach. When they cleared the gate and were on the road, Frey let loose on the throttle, toeing up through the gears. When the wind hit Abbi in the face, his girl let out a loud *woohoo.* Yeah, he could totally get used to this.

The road Frey's home was on was a winding, two-lane country road that went on for several miles. There were no real shoulders as the land on either side was mostly woods. Frey rarely met another car since there were only a couple of other houses on the road. He knew the twists and turns like the back of his hand, but he didn't want to scare Abbi on her first outing, so he took it easy. When they were about halfway to the turnoff, Frey noticed a car gaining speed behind him. "Abbi, I need you to hang on tight, okay?"

"What's going on?" she asked and tried to look behind them.

"I think we're being followed. Please, Sweetheart, just hang on." As soon as Abbi tightened her grip, Frey twisted the throttle, and the bike rocketed forward. The car sped up as well and got within inches of the back tire. Frey gunned the bike and put as much distance between them and their pursuer as possible. Knowing there was a stop sign coming up, Frey pulled an evasive maneuver that he prayed to the gods wouldn't get Abbi hurt. When they were closing in on the end of the road, Frey slowed the bike. The vehicle behind him got within two car lengths, and Frey swerved into the oncoming lane, braked hard, and the car sped past them.

The intersection wasn't normally busy, and the driver in the car was lucky. He slammed on his brakes at the last moment as he approached the stop sign. There happened to be no oncoming traffic, so he managed to get away unscathed. "That's George's car," Abbi said calmly from behind Frey. It might be George's car, but Troy Quinn had been the driver.

Frey pulled the bike off the road to check on Abbi.

"Are you okay?" he asked, twisting to look at her.

"Yeah, you're a really good driver. It would seem Troy has found me, though."

"I thought you said that was someone named

206

George. Who's George?"

"George Novak, Troy's best friend. When Troy can't keep tabs on me, he has George do it. The guy trailed me all during college since Troy wasn't there to do it himself."

"Are you sure you're okay? You seem really calm about all this." Frey couldn't believe she wasn't freaking out. *He* was freaking out.

"I'm sure. You promised to protect me. Until you prove me wrong, I'm going to trust you."

"But I've already let you down. Let Matt down." Frey should have kept his mouth closed, but he wanted there to be nothing but truth between them. At least as far as their feelings were concerned. He couldn't tell her the truth of the Gargoyles, not yet.

"No, Michael let us down, but I've had time to think on that. He couldn't have known Troy would be out back at the exact moment Matt took the garbage out. Even though I don't really know you, I sense there's something different about you. I haven't known very many men in my life, but I feel something when I'm around you. I've read about gut instinct and women's intuition. Whatever it is, my heart is telling me I can believe you. Believe *in* you. If I had trusted my gut with Troy, I wouldn't be in this mess right now. Until you prove me wrong, I'm putting my trust in you and your tribe of Amazons."

Frey's head was spinning. Between her words and her hands rubbing across the ridges in his abs, he felt like he was in a dream. One from which he didn't want to wake up. He had to wake up. If Troy decided to come back for them, they were sitting ducks. Frey didn't respond, instead he pulled Abbi's hands tighter around his waist and continued on to the manor.

Frey was on high alert, watching for the gray sedan to come at them again. Instead of taking the direct route to Rafael's, Frey took some familiar back roads, just in case. Without further incident, they arrived. Frey rolled up to the gate and stopped beside the security box. Speaking in Italian, Frey said the words *she is the light of my life, my saving grace* into the speaker. At that moment, he knew he spoke the truth. Even during times of war, Frey had never had a more clear purpose than the woman seated behind him. Frey may be protecting her from her husband, but she was saving him from himself. His past.

"What did you say?" she asked, her chin on his shoulder.

"I said *my girl is beautiful.*" Frey couldn't admit the truth to her. Not yet.

He proceeded through the now open gate and rode slowly down Rafael's drive. The manor came into view, and the lack of vehicles surprised Frey. Rafe must have sent most everyone away. One of the detective's vehicles was parked alongside a shiny Mercedes convertible. Victoria was already there. Abbi slid her leg over the bike like a pro. Frey stood next to her and showed her how to unhook her strap. He placed the helmets over the mirrors and took her hand, leading her to the back door.

As soon as they entered the kitchen, Priscilla was greeting them. "Geoffrey, there you are. And you must be Abbi. Aren't you just the prettiest thing? Now come on in. I saved you some cookies. I had to hide them from the rest of the boys. You know how they are about sweets."

Frey laughed at the older lady. He was used to her exuberant attitude, but by the look on Abbi's face, she didn't know what to think. "Abbi, I'd like you to meet Priscilla." Priscilla wrapped Abbi in a tight hug.

Abbi didn't hesitate to return the embrace. When she pulled back she was grinning. "Priscilla, it's a pleasure. I've heard some really nice things about you."

"Priscilla, did I hear you say you hid some cookies from me? What am I going to do with you?" Rafael asked from the doorway.

The housekeeper waved her hand in the air at him.

"If I didn't hide them, nobody else would ever get any. Abbi, it was nice to meet you, dear. If you'll excuse me, I have things I need to take care of." Priscilla removed a sealed bowl from the pantry and placed it on the island. "Cookies," she said with a wink to Frey.

Rafael didn't hesitate to grab and open the container before anyone else could get to it. He held the bowl out to Frey and Abbi. "Cookie?"

Both Frey and Rafael took one and shoved the whole thing in their mouths while grabbing another. Abbi's eyes were huge as she watched these two grown men devour cookies like they would never get more. "Abbi, you better get one before they eat them all," Kaya said as she walked into the room, followed by Dane. Kaya took the bowl from Rafael and offered a cookie to both Abbi and Dane before helping herself to one. Six glasses and a gallon of milk magically appeared in the middle of the island.

"Ah, thanks, Victoria," Rafael said to the newest addition to the cookie eating contest. There was no better way to introduce Abbi to the craziness of the manor than with Priscilla's cookies. When the sweet treats were devoured and the milk was gone, Frey made the introductions. "Abbi, you've met Kaya. This brute is Rafael. The quiet one is Dane, Kaya's lead detective, and this lovely lady is Victoria."

Rafael brushed cookie crumbs off his shirt and said, "Abbi, welcome. While you are here, please feel free to make yourself at home. Kaya and I have family business that needs tending to, so we will leave you in the capable hands of Victoria." Even with the façade of being laid back while eating cookies, the tension in the room was thick. Family business meant something was going on. Frey would make sure Abbi was taken care of first before finding out what else was happening. He helped her remove her jacket and they settled in at the island.

Victoria Holt didn't look like an attorney. If

anything, she looked like a younger, frumpier version of Priscilla. Her looks were deceiving. "Abbi, I'm sorry to be meeting you under these circumstances, but it's a pleasure all the same." She pulled a small laptop out of her bag and placed it on the island. Frey dug the folded papers out of his back pocket, passing them over. "We have already done some digging on her husband. Sixx should have already emailed the info to you, but I brought a printed copy, just in case."

Victoria rubbed her hands together. "I did receive the information, and I have to tell you, I cannot wait to nail this bastard to the wall."

# Chapter Twenty-Eight

Dane had been approved by the City Council to step into Kaya's shoes as Chief. They were going over the transitional period as well as how to handle Troy Quinn when he got a call from Sixx. "Dane, we have a problem."

"I'm with Rafael and Kaya; I'm putting you on speaker. Go ahead."

"You know Jasper's ex is in town and causing trouble?"

"Yes, did you find something?"

"You could say that. I was running his tag number for Jasper. I'm not as good as Julian at this cloak and dagger stuff, so it took me a while. I'm surprised one of you hasn't been called yet. The car Craig was driving popped up on the police server. Someone called in an anonymous tip that a car was off in the woods with the driver's door open. The driver is dead. If my hunch is right, someone is trying to frame Jasper."

"What makes you think that?"

"Because the car is in the woods next to his house. The regular patrol has already been there and they went through the car looking for I.D. Not only did they find the victim's wallet, but they found a video recorder hidden under the seat. It's not good. It shows Jasper shoving Craig and then threatening him."

"Shit, I'm leaving now. Have you called Jasper?"

"Yes, he's at the gym. I told him to head to the manor since Victoria's already there."

"He just can't catch a break. Thanks, Michael." Dane hung up and turned to Kaya and Rafael. "There are some pretty explicit photos floating around of Jasper and Craig. Someone sent them to Trevor, and now he's left town. This doesn't look good for either one of them."

"Keep us posted. We'll talk about work later," Kaya

said.

Dane blew out of the manor and turned on his reds and blues. He hadn't known Jasper long, but he really liked his partner. Too many bad things were happening to the mates of the Goyles. Thinking about Marley, he wondered what kind of trouble a waitress could get into. None, he hoped.

When he arrived at the crime scene, he didn't see the M.E.'s van, but he did see Gregor's Hummer. That was odd since Gregor was in Egypt. He walked into the woods where he found Dante giving orders to the CSU personnel while the officers looked on.

"What's going on?" Dane asked as he approached.

"I couldn't get here in time. One of your cops took the call and found the video recorder. It doesn't prove anything, but it paints an ugly picture since Jasper and Craig fought and someone got it on camera."

"Could you tell cause of death?"

"There are no outward signs, but my guess is a broken neck with the angle his head settled."

"Fuck. Have you heard from Trevor?"

"Unfortunately, no. This is really bad timing," Dante said, frowning.

"Is it worth all this? Finding your mate just to have them tormented or kidnapped?"

"I would give anything if Isabelle and Connor had been spared the trauma they both endured. In the end, I have to hope they feel it is worth it."

"I'm sorry you had to come out here when you just got home. How is Isabelle?" Dane needed to go see his sister.

"She's good, adjusting, but good. Connor's settling in nicely, too."

Dane smiled. "I can't wait to meet my nephew."

"He's the best. I hope when you find your mate, you get lucky like I did. I'm truly blessed with those two," Dante

212

smiled as he spoke of his new family. "Now, let's focus on Jasper and his mate. I still can't believe it's Trevor. With everything that's happening, I hope he can get past what we are and forgive me for keeping the truth from him all this time."

"It is a lot to digest at first. Believe me, I know. I don't think that is going to be an issue, though. The bigger problem for him is he thinks Jasper lied to him about Craig. Jasper's going to have his hands full when Trevor comes home."

"If he comes home. Trevor is a troubled soul, and this didn't help matters."

Dane thought about that for a second. Was he troubled enough to kill Craig? Jealousy was a strong motive.

"No, Trevor didn't do this," Dante said emphatically.

"I didn't..." Dane hadn't spoken aloud, had he?

"No, but it crossed your mind. I know Trevor. He's off licking his wounds."

"Well, let's get in there and get the evidence so we can prove you're right." Dane walked toward the officer who was holding the recorder in an evidence bag. "What do you have, Grady?" he asked the officer.

"Looks like your new boy might not be exactly on the up and up. Seems him and his queer boyfriend had a lover's spat. Might want to call Jenkins and question the fag."

Dane grabbed the cop by the collar before he realized he'd done it. "If I ever hear another derogatory word come out of your foul mouth, I will have your badge. Do you understand me?"

"What the fuck's your problem, Abbot? Quinn was right about you. You're hot for the redhead," the cop said, sneering.

Dane yanked the evidence bag out of his hand and pointed a finger in his face. "Get out of here. If you so much as look at Jasper the wrong way, you won't have a job."

"You can't do that, you're not the Chief."

"Just fucking try me," Dane sneered back. His beast was raging to phase and rip the guy to shreds. He had to get control of himself before he blew it. "Get out of here."

Grady glared at Dane before he stormed away from the crime scene. Dante walked up and placed a hand on his shoulder. He instantly calmed down. "We have to play this one by the books, Brother. Isn't Jasper on a stake-out?"

"He was until sometime in the early morning. He went home and couldn't sleep, so as soon as the gym opened, he went to relieve some tension. I called him, and now he's headed to the manor. Victoria Holt is there talking with Abbi. Might as well get her money's worth. I know we have to be careful, but I'm going to take this to Sixx so he can make a copy of it before I log it into evidence. I have unfinished police business to discuss with Kaya, so I'll be at the manor if you need me. Please call me if CSU finds anything else."

"Will do. Just don't take too long getting this into evidence. We can't play favorites." Dante wasn't telling him something he didn't already know.

When Dane returned to the manor, he parked beside Jasper's car and went inside via the back door. His earlier conversation with Kaya had been interrupted, and they needed to decide how to handle Quinn. When he walked into the kitchen, Victoria was just finishing up with Abbi and Frey. He didn't see Jasper, but knew his partner was somewhere in the house. "I'm sorry to interrupt, but Victoria, I'm afraid we're going to need to speak to you about another matter before you leave."

"No problem. I'm hanging around for dinner anyway."

Dane left them to finish their business and headed to the pool room. When he found it empty, he went to the office. It was empty as well. "They're in the garden,"

214

Jonathan said from behind Dane. "Our Jasper is in a world of hurt, and Rafael led him outside for some quiet time."

"Thank you." Dane had heard the others talk about the garden, but had never experienced it for himself. He walked to the back of the house and out onto the patio. Priscilla was in the process of setting the outdoor tables for dinner. He kissed the older woman on the cheek and continued on down the pathway to Rafael's sanctuary. Even though it was November and the Georgia air was cool, the garden was lush with greenery. Wind chimes tinkled in all directions. Dane stood still allowing the serenity of the moment to wash over him. When he built his new home, he really wanted something like this on his property.

Voices drifted over the air, and Dane directed his feet their way. When he rounded a corner, Rafael and Jasper were sitting on a bench. Rafael's arm was around Jasper's shoulders, and the younger Goyle was baring his soul. "I'm sorry, I didn't mean to interrupt."

Jasper raised his tear-streaked face. "It's okay, Dane. What did you find?" He stood up, obviously glad for the change in conversation.

"Let's take this to the house so we can include Victoria. No need in having to go over it twice," Rafael said, gesturing back the way they'd come. The three men walked in silence. When they arrived in the kitchen, Victoria was chatting with her aunt. "Where's Frey?" Rafael asked.

"He's showing Abbi around the house. She needed a break." Victoria packed up her laptop and said, "Let's head into the office." Priscilla was good about hiding out when they were discussing Clan business, but she was cooking supper for them and needed the kitchen.

Frey and Abbi were coming down the stairs, followed by Kaya. When Abbi wasn't looking, Dane inclined his head at Kaya, indicating he needed to speak with her. Frey got the hint and asked Abbi, "Sweetheart, do you mind talking to Priscilla for a few minutes? Remember

215

the construction I told you about? I need to go over some of the details with Rafael." Frey led Abbi into the kitchen before finding the rest of the group in the office. He closed the door behind him, a little harder than was required.

"What's wrong, Frey? Other than the obvious?" Kaya asked.

"On the way over here, Quinn tried to run us over. He was driving someone else's car. Abbi said his name is George Novak."

Jasper spoke up, "That's the guy who came and visited while I was watching the house. I swear I didn't see Troy at any time."

"Frey, are you sure it wasn't this George? What does he look like?" Kaya asked, now in police mode. Dane knew it would take a long time to get it out of her system.

"I don't know what George looks like, but I damn sure know Troy fucking Quinn when I see him." Frey was pacing the room. Where was Dante when you needed his special calming voodoo?

"Brother, calm down." Rafael didn't like anyone raising their voice to Kaya.

"Please tell me you're going to put his ass behind bars. Abbi has filed a restraining order, and he assaulted Matthew. He is going to flip the fuck out when he gets served his divorce papers. If her moving out caused this type of reaction, I can't imagine what the bastard's going to try then."

Dane spoke up, "We were discussing that very thing before I got the call about Jasper's ex."

"What about him?" Frey was still agitated, but at least he stopped pacing.

Jasper took over pacing the room when he told Frey, "He's dead. Craig is dead, and someone is framing me for it. Oh, and Trevor's gone. Whoever is doing this knows about me and Trevor. They sent him some photos of me and Craig together, and now my mate has left New Atlanta."

"Okay, one thing at a time." Victoria took charge of the conversation. "First, decide what to do about Quinn. If you suspend him for assault, he is going to have all day to plot and scheme. You will need to have someone watching him around the clock."

Frey interrupted her, "He's supposed to have someone sitting on him now." Frey looked to Jasper, eyebrows raised.

"Jasper, who is on duty?" Rafael asked.

"Vaughn. I talked to him on the way over here. He hasn't seen any movement. Other than George coming and going, neither did I."

"What did George look like?" Frey asked.

"He's about six foot, dark brown hair. Average build."

"Same as Quinn, only he's not average. He's a little bulky." Frey dialed his phone. "I'm calling Sixx."

"Are you thinking they pulled a switch?" Dane asked.

Frey nodded and spoke into his phone, "Hey, I need a favor. Look up both Troy Quinn and George Novak's driver's license photos and send them to Rafael's home computer. Thanks."

Rafael opened his computer and waited for the photos to come through. "If Quinn is loose, you're going to have a hard time suspending him," he told Dane.

"What if the bastard shows up to work for his shift tomorrow afternoon. We could catch him then," Jasper said just as Rafael's computer sounded with an incoming email. Everyone in the room stopped moving while Rafe opened the message. He turned the laptop around for everyone to see the side-by-side photos.

"I'll be damned," Frey expressed what everyone was probably thinking. From a distance, the two men could definitely be mistaken for each other.

"Dane, put out an APB on George's car then head

over to Troy's house. If Troy is there, arrest him and bring him in. If George is there instead, ask him where Troy is. If he won't talk, bring him down to the precinct," Kaya said.

When she stood, Rafael grabbed her around the waist. "Just where do you think you're going?"

"I'm still the Chief until I resign tomorrow morning. I'm going to do my job."

Dane was stuck between a rock and a hard place. Before he had transitioned to a half-blood and joined the Stone Society, his first loyalty had been to Kaya, his boss. Now, his first loyalty was to Rafael, his King. Kaya, as his Queen, was second. "I'm on it. Kaya, I've got this." When she started to protest, he held up his hands. "You're stepping down tomorrow morning. There's no need for you to come downtown this afternoon. Besides, you're needed here." Dane glanced over at Jasper who was staring at nothing.

Kaya followed his gaze and nodded. "You're right."

Rafe asked Frey, "Since Quinn knows Abbi's with you, do you think your house is safe? Do we need to put extra security there?"

"Lorenzo is there with Matthew. I think between the two of us, we can handle one human. But I do need to call him and give him the rundown."

Victoria told Frey, "I will have the divorce papers ready tonight. As soon as Dane locates Quinn, I will serve the papers. We might as well hit him with both his suspension and divorce all at once."

"You're going to need security as well," Rafael told the lawyer.

Dane took in everything going on around him. Both Frey and Jasper were in the middle of shit storms all because of their mates. Julian was off to Egypt to help his brother find his mate. Dante had just returned home from rescuing his mate. Rafael was holding on tight to Kaya, who he'd nearly lost. The bright light in all the madness was the

Clan. Not once did they think twice about helping each other. No one said they didn't have time, or they had other obligations. This was family. This was now his family, and he couldn't be more proud.

# Chapter Twenty-Nine

Abbi understood why Frey considered Priscilla a mother figure. The older woman had Abbi feeling right at home amid the chaos that was Rafael Stone's manor. Priscilla kept her busy helping prepare supper. When Abbi asked why she was cooking so much food, the woman said they had a big family. If the people coming and going were any indication, she could believe it. While Frey was busy talking to Rafael, several more of the Amazon tribe arrived. The huge men walked right in the back door without knocking. Somehow, they knew who Abbi was, and they all did that crazy fisting their chest thing Uri and Lorenzo had done.

Priscilla must have seen the odd expression on her face, because she patted Abbi's arm and said, "That means you're family," as if that explained it. Priscilla wasn't the first person to tell Abbi she was now family. How could that be, though?

"I hear you're a teacher. That must be so exciting, to be around little ones all day." Priscilla was a pro at keeping Abbi out of her own head. Anytime Abbi got lost in thought, her new friend would bring her right back out into the present.

"It really is. Too many of them don't get the attention and nurturing they need at home. I try to fill that void as much as possible. It's hard not to get attached to them, though."

"I know exactly what you mean. I never had children of my own, but I have Rafael and the boys."

"So, you never married?" Abbi hoped she wasn't being rude by asking.

"No, I knew my place in the world, and it was always here, taking care of the manor. I have Jonathan. I know he's my brother, and this may sound strange, but I

220

never needed anyone else. He and I have taken care of this household for over thirty years now, so it's sort of like he's been my husband. In a purely platonic way, of course. He and the boys have given me so much love that I haven't missed not having a romantic partner."

Abbi admired this woman deeply. She reminded Abbi of her mother, full of love. Frey and Dane came into the kitchen. "Abbi, may I speak with you a moment?" Dane asked.

"Of course." Abbi washed and dried her hands and followed the men outside.

Frey moved behind her, placing her back to his front, and wrapped his arms around her waist. While it should seem like a sweet gesture, she had a feeling he was offering her strength. If he thought she needed it, she probably did. She placed her hands on his arms and held on.

"Abbi, it has come to our attention Troy was the one driving the car that attempted to run you and Frey off the road. While we assumed he was at home, it seems he borrowed his friend's car. What can you tell us about George Novak?" Dane was in full detective mode, flip notebook and pencil in hand.

Abbi was shaking. She knew Troy would come after her, but try to kill her? Frey's arms tightened around her. "He and Troy have been friends forever. I think they even went to kindergarten together. You rarely saw one without the other. They went on double dates together, and George spent a lot of time at Troy's house while they were growing up. When we graduated high school, George went to the same local college I did. I think he did it just so he could keep an eye on me for Troy. If he'd had a decent father figure, he might have turned out different. Him and Troy both. Anyway, he graduated college, but he never really pursued a career in anything. He's gone from one odd job to the next.

"He was married for a short spell, but it didn't last.

221

He cheated on his wife the whole time. When she found out, she left him. He spends a lot of time at my house on the couch, mooching off us. I mean…"

Frey tightened his arms around her. "It's okay, Sweetheart."

Dane asked, "Is there anywhere you know of that Troy could hide out, other than George's house? Do either of them have any other property like a hunting cabin, or relatives they would go visit?"

"Not that I know of. The only family Troy has left is his mother, but she pretty much disowned him after high school. She lives in a trailer park down in New Valdosta. George never knew his dad, and his mom died a couple of years ago." The hickey on Troy's neck came to mind. "Troy often comes home smelling of other women. One of them might hide him out, but I wouldn't know where to tell you to start looking for them."

Dane snapped his notebook shut and sighed. "I'm sorry, Abbi. I can't imagine what you're going through. Thank you for the information."

"Sorry I couldn't be more help. You'd think I could tell you more about the man I've lived with for this long."

"No, I think it just proves you've been living with the wrong man. Now, if you'll excuse me, I've got an asshole to locate." Dane walked down the steps and disappeared around the house. She was still pressed up against Frey's body, and she didn't want to move. She felt safe in his arms. Content. Abbi leaned her head back against his chest and closed her eyes. Frey pressed his lips to her temple.

"Oh, sorry. Didn't mean to interrupt." Abbi opened her eyes to yet another member of the tribe.

"It's okay. We probably need to get going anyway. Abbi, this is Deacon. He helps run the penitentiary. Deacon, Abbi."

Deacon fisted his heart and bowed his head slightly.

222

"My honor, Abbi." At the other man's words, Frey tightened his grip and placed another kiss to her hair.

"It's a pleasure," she responded. By now, she was getting used to the men in Frey's life all being massive and all treating her like she mattered.

"You two not staying for supper?" Deacon asked as he took the steps to the patio.

"No, we need to get back home to Matthew," Frey told the new guy as if he should know who Matthew was.

"I feel ya. Broken ribs are nothing to sneeze at. Listen, tell Lor if he needs a break to call me. I'd be happy to hang out with the kid."

"Will do. Thanks Deacon." Frey and the man knuckled bumped each other, and Deacon disappeared into the house.

Abbi turned in his arms and looked up at him. "Just how big is your family, anyway? And I don't mean how tall. I realize the gene pool was very selective when it came to you and those you know. I mean, how many of these Amazons are there?"

"Honestly? There's a whole Clan of us. A Society of thousands ready to lay down their lives for you and Matthew. Now, let's go say our goodbyes and get home to our patient."

In that moment, Abbi believed Frey's words to be the truth. They returned to the kitchen where Rafael had Kaya wrapped up much the way Frey had been holding Abbi. The only difference was his hand was protectively placed on Kaya's stomach. Abbi observed the police chief's face and realized she was pregnant. Abbi prayed that was another difference between them.

Before they left, Priscilla dished out plenty of food for them to take home. "We're on the bike, Priscilla; we can't carry all these dishes."

"Here," Deacon tossed his keys to Frey. "Take the truck. I'll bring the bike later."

223

"Thanks, Brother." Frey didn't hesitate to let the other man ride his motorcycle. He must really trust him. Frey and Abbi grabbed the food and headed out the door. When the food was secure on the back floorboard, Frey opened the passenger side door and helped Abbi into the tall four-wheel drive. She liked the way his hands gripped her waist, firmly while still being gentle. While he was walking around to the driver's side, their morning deck encounter came back to her mind. She had never acted so wanton in her life. With Troy, she had no desire to rub against him. Even in their earlier days, he'd never made sex anything other than a means to an end, either him getting off or her getting pregnant.

With Frey, just being in his arms had her wanting to lose her clothes as well as herself. When she first met him, she couldn't imagine being with someone so big. Now that she knew him a little better, she had no doubt he could be gentle while making her feel good. Just thinking about her orgasm had Abbi's core coming to life. "Abbi," Frey husked from the other side of the truck. She started to ask "what" but the feral look in his eyes was the same one she'd seen when she was rubbing against his erection. Could he possibly know what she was thinking about? Instead of answering she bit her lip. A deep growl sounded from his chest as his eyes landed on her mouth. Before she knew what was happening, Frey had her across the cab of the truck, straddling his lap.

His mouth clamped down on hers in a kiss that stoked the fire between her legs. God, the man knew how to kiss. The dance between their tongues was a sensuous samba. Abbi pressed her breasts to his chest, rubbing back and forth. Her nipples ached with a need to be touched. Frey's cock grew hard between their bodies. She wanted to unzip the jeans that held him prisoner and give him pleasure. Sucking Troy had been a chore, especially when he held her head down making her gag. Taking Frey in her

224

mouth would be like worshiping at the Amazon altar.

"Abbi," Frey warned again, breaking the kiss.

"What?" she did ask this time, a little frustrated that he pulled away.

A horn blew answering her question. "Oh, crap," she said as she tried to scramble off his lap. His strong arms banded around her waist, holding her in place. Frey didn't roll the window down to speak, but he did throw up a two finger salute to yet another member of that Society he spoke of. As soon as the man was out of sight, Frey kissed her gently, pecking her lips several times.

"Let's take this somewhere a little more private," he said with a grin.

Abbi climbed off his lap, moving to the other side of the truck, and buckled up. *What the hell is wrong with you?* She took a look at the profile of the gorgeous man sitting beside her, and realized *that's* what was wrong with her. Frey turned the radio on, and asked, "What kind of music do you like?"

"Classical, of course, but that's just to dance to. When I'm in the car I listen to mostly rock, some country. What about you?"

Frey turned the channel to a classic rock station. He put the volume at a level where they could enjoy the music and still hear each other. He reached for her hand and twined their fingers together. "Just about anything really. Depends on the mood. I think I surprised Matt when he turned on some heavy metal and I didn't make him change it."

"Yeah, he's all about that new Cyanide group. Their music's a little harsh for me." Abbi was surprised Frey listened to the same stuff her brother did. She would have pegged him for a country lover. "What's your favorite dessert?"

"Banana pudding. Priscilla's is pretty good, but there was this one housekeeper I wish I'd got the recipe from.

225

Hers was the best."

"Another housekeeper besides Priscilla? You must have been pretty young then. How old are you? I know that's a rude question, but I can't figure you out. Sometimes I look at you and think you're thirty, but you have an old soul, if that makes sense."

Frey smiled and said, "I'm five hundred seventy-one."

Abbi laughed. "Seriously, you don't have to tell me if you don't want to. I'm twenty seven, but you probably already knew that. You seem to know everything else about me."

"I just don't want you to dismiss me because I'm an older man." Frey raised her hand to his mouth and kissed her knuckles.

"Whatever." Abbi couldn't dismiss him now if she tried. He was worming his way into her heart one moment at a time, and she didn't know how she felt about it.

"Before we go home, I want to stop and get Matt something. Do you mind?"

Unless it was a bunch of nudie magazines, of course she didn't mind. Then again, if Matt had asked for the magazines, who was she to say no? "I don't mind."

Abbi had no idea where they were going, but when they pulled into the parking lot of a big sports store, she was confused. "Uh, Matt doesn't play sports."

"No, but he likes basketball." Frey got out of the truck and walked around to her side. He opened the door and put his hands on her waist, helping her down.

"You do remember he has some broken ribs, don't you?"

Frey grabbed her hand, not caring who could see. They walked across the parking lot like any other couple. What if someone from school saw her? She pulled her hand away and crossed her arms over her chest.

"Are you cold?" Frey asked, wrapping his arm

226

around her. He just couldn't keep his hands off her. Before they entered the store, she stopped.

"No, I'm not cold. I'm just afraid someone will see us." She didn't miss the hurt look that flashed through his eyes. "I don't mean…"

"No, I get it." Frey walked into the store without waiting on her.

"Shit," she muttered and ran to catch up with him. "Frey, please stop. Geoffrey!"

"What, Abbi? You don't want to be seen with me yet you yell and bring attention to us. Make up your mind."

"It's not that, at all. It's just, I'm still married."

"Not for long. Are you afraid someone will see you and it'll get back to Troy? I've already told you I'll protect you."

"No, I don't care if he finds out. God knows he isn't faithful to me. But cheating is wrong. What happens if you and I decide to try this thing between us? If you cheat with me, what's to say you won't cheat with someone else?"

"You think I'd actually cheat on you? Abbi, I want you. Forever. *When* you and I try this thing between us, I'm going to make life so sweet for you that you won't ever remember a time before us. I get that you aren't a cheater. I appreciate that."

"Okay then."

"Okay." Frey's mouth twitched. Abbi was sure he was holding back a grin.

"Okay. What exactly are we here for?" She looked around and saw they were in the section that held basketball goals.

"One of these." Frey pointed at a portable stand. A young sales girl wearing short shorts walked up to them and totally ignored Abbi. She had eyes for Frey though.

"Well, hello. What can I do for you?" Her voice was dripping with sugar, and Abbi wanted to choke the bitch.

"I want that one right there," Frey pointed to the

227

goal and portable stand behind the girl. While the girl turned around to see what he was pointing to, Frey pulled Abbi to him, snaking an arm around her waist. As soon as the girl turned back around, Frey tipped Abbi's chin up and kissed her. It wasn't a kiss full of tongue, but it was hot enough to let the salesgirl know where his attention was. When he released her lips, Abbi was grinning. Frey continued to lay it on thick, "It's for our son. Isn't it, Sweetheart?"

Abbi lost the rest of her heart to Frey right there in the sporting goods store. The salesgirl got the message. "If you'll follow me, I'll get someone to check you out." Abbi couldn't hold back her laughter. The girl had definitely checked Frey out. He picked Abbi up and swung her around, bringing on more laughter. The salesgirl couldn't help but smile at their playful antics. Anyone on the outside looking in would swear they were a couple in love.

"Miss Quinn, Miss Quinn!" A small voice coming from a small person wiped the smile right off Abbi's face. Frey put Abbi on her feet just as one of her students yelled her name. Standing behind the little girl was her mom. Debbie Cranston's smirk let Abbi know she'd witnessed the whole thing. Well, damn.

# Chapter Thirty

Jasper's mind was spinning. Too much was happening at one time, and he felt like he was going to have a meltdown. Did Gargoyles do that? Were there psychiatrists who handled the stress of life when it got to be too much for shifters? If there weren't, there should be. He didn't care that Craig was dead. Hell, he'd threatened to do the deed himself. That's what made the situation so bad. Had anyone heard him?

Dante's initial assumption that Craig's neck had been broken led Jasper to believe that their mutual *friend* was involved. Nobody else knew about Jasper's past. Had Craig somehow found out and contacted him? Or had he sought out Craig knowing he and Jasper had been lovers? If so, why now? It had been over a century since Jasper had heard from the man. Even longer since they'd been intimate. Jasper had changed his identity several times since then. None of it made sense. The timing was wrong.

How the fuck did someone find out about Trevor? The only time they were seen together was at crime scenes, and that was in a professional capacity. They had been at the gym at the same time, and Trevor had seen Craig lurking at the window. But they weren't together then, not really. No, someone had been watching Jasper.

Kaya and Dane decided it would be best if Jasper went on administrative leave, pending the investigation. He wasn't suspended since there was no evidence other than the circumstantial video. Everyone in the room knew Jasper was innocent. He had been staking out Quinn's house all night. Now they needed Dante to prove time of death coincided with the hours Jasper had been in his car.

"Jasper, would you mind watching over Matthew tomorrow? Frey will want to keep an eye on Abbi," Rafael requested. Jasper knew it wasn't really an option, but he didn't mind. The kid was funny, and would hopefully keep his mind off Trevor.

"Don't mind at all. As a matter of fact, I might go on over there tonight, if Frey doesn't mind." After the shitty day he'd had, Jasper really didn't want to be alone.

"I don't see why he would. He has plenty of room, and if I recall correctly, about a thousand video games." Rafael preferred shooting pool or throwing darts to video games, but he was well aware of who played what during family day. The competition got pretty fierce.

Normally, Jasper didn't mind being by himself at home, but with Trevor gone, the memories would drive him batshit crazy. "Then I'd say Matthew and I will be able to occupy ourselves quite nicely. I'm just going to go call Frey before we eat. If it's okay, I'll head that way after dessert." Jasper's head might be reeling, but it wasn't bad enough that he would skip one of Priscilla's meals.

Frey had no idea who the woman was, but by the smirk on her face, she was not a fan of Abbi's. Dammit! This was just what Abbi had wanted to avoid. Frey had been so caught up in the moment, he couldn't help himself. Now, Abbi had to deal with the fallout.

Abbi squatted down so she was eye level with the girl. "Hello, Amelia. How are you today?"

"Fine," Amelia replied as she looked up at Frey. She almost fell backwards having to crane her neck so far back. "He's really tall," she said looking back at Abbi. "Who is he?"

If the little girl's mother had not looked at Abbi like she was going to eat her for lunch, Frey would have let Abbi handle it. As it were, he took over answering the little girl but kept eye contact with her mother. "I'm a good friend of

Miss Quinn's. She and I haven't seen each other in a long time, and I told her some really good news. She was happy for me."

The answer seemed to momentarily throw the woman off track, but Amelia was like most children- nosy.

"What's your good news?" the little girl asked, looking up at Frey again.

"I have a beautiful new girlfriend."

"Are you gonna get married? My momma's not married. She just has lots of boyfriends." Frey didn't miss the way Abbi's back stiffened when Amelia asked her question.

"Let's go, Amelia." The woman was no longer smirking.

"I sure hope so," Frey told the girl, smiling.

"I said let's go." The woman grabbed her daughter's hand and practically dragged her away.

Amelia turned back and yelled, "I love you, Miss Quinn!"

Abbi called after the girl, "I love you too, Sweet Pea." She didn't move until they were out of sight. When they were out the door, Abbi's shoulders sagged.

"I'm sorry," Frey whispered. He could feel the torment rolling off his mate.

Abbi scowled at him and huffed out a laugh. "It had to be her. Of all people to run into, it had to be her."

A salesman approached, interrupting, "Sir, are you ready to check out?"

"Yes, I'll be right there." The man walked off, and Frey asked Abbi, "Her, who?"

"Debbie Cranston. I bet she's already on the phone to Troy. She's been trying to get him ever since high school."

"Then you should be glad it was her and not somebody else. He already knows we're together."

"Still, it proves my point about being seen in public." Abbi wrapped her arms around her waist.

231

"You were right, and I'm sorry. Let's go pay for the goal and get out of here. I promise I won't let this happen again." Frey was afraid of what this would do to the headway he'd made with her. He grabbed a basketball off the display and headed toward the cash registers. Once he'd paid, he pulled the truck to the front door so the salesman could load their purchase. Frey searched the parking lot for any sign of Amelia and her mother. When the coast was clear, he opened the passenger door and helped Abbi in.

She was quiet on the ride home, and he let her be. He'd apologized, but he didn't know if it was enough. When they arrived at his gate, he rolled down the window, spoke a prayer to the gods in Italian, and rolled the window back up. This time, she didn't ask him to translate. Frey parked in front of the garage and got out of the truck. Abbi let herself out, jumping down without his assistance. He hauled the box out of the back of the truck and decided to go ahead and put the frame together. He needed something to do while he gave Abbi time to think, or cool off, or whatever it was she needed to do.

Lorenzo appeared a few minutes later. "Need some help?" He grabbed the instructions and started reading over them.

"Yeah, thanks. How's Matt?" Frey asked, walking back from the garage with the tools he needed.

"Okay, I guess. He's still in pain, but that'll go away with time. Hand me the wrench. Abbi looked upset..."

"I screwed up. One of her student's mother saw us in the store together. And when I say together, I was swinging her around making her laugh. The worst part is the woman has obviously been after Quinn since high school. Do you have section C?"

They talked while working, and in no time, they had the frame and goal put together. Lorenzo rolled it over to the side of the garage facing the house while Frey retrieved the new ball out of Deacon's truck. "Oh, shit. I forgot about

232

the food. Here, give me a hand." They got the food out of the back seat and took it in the house. Abbi was nowhere to be seen. Frey stuck his head in the gym and checked on Matt who was still asleep. Once the food was put away, the men headed back outside.

It had been a few years since Frey had played basketball, but it didn't take long to get into a rhythm. He and Lor were pretty evenly matched. After a while, the sound of two bikes rumbled down the driveway. Deacon and Mason rolled up to the garage and parked. "When did you get this?" Deacon asked, sliding off the Harley.

"Today. I bought it for Matt," Frey said, throwing the ball to Mason. "You're on my team," Frey told the young Goyle. Dressed in jeans and leather boots, the four of them played and laughed, basically forgetting their worries for a while.

"Hey, when did you get that?" Matt was slowly making his way toward them. All four of the Goyles walked to Matt so he didn't have to exert himself.

"I picked it up on the way home. I know you're hurting now, but soon you'll be out here showing us how to play."

"Yeah, right. The four of you are fast. Crazy fast. And good. Even if I wasn't injured, there's no way I'd get in there with you guys."

Frey laughed, but he thought back to the game. Had Matt seen them use their shifter speed? When they were home, they didn't worry about holding back. It was possible they'd gotten caught up in the moment and forgot they had humans around. Frey reached out for Abbi, sensing where she was inside. Like a beacon, her body called to his, alerting him to her staring out the window. He looked up, and their eyes met. Her elbow was on the window sill, and her chin rested on her hand. She appeared comfortable, like she'd been there a while. Had she seen something he would need to explain? Returning his attention to her brother, he

233

asked, "Are you hungry? We brought food back from my cousin's house."

"Starving. I think I need a new babysitter. This one didn't feed me," Matt said pointing at Lorenzo. "As a matter of fact, I think he snored the whole time you were gone."

Lorenzo mussed his hair. "You better be glad you're injured."

The four men laughed and Matt smiled. "Abbi was right; all your friends are Amazons."

"What's the plan for tomorrow? Are we still training?" Deacon asked Frey.

"Yes, Mason can cover the gym while Uri is at Dante's. Jas needs to lay low. He can stay here with Matt."

"Sounds good, Brother. Matt, take it easy, and we'll see you soon." Deacon, Mason, and Lorenzo took turns giving Frey man hugs and gently bumping fists with Matt. Deacon climbed in his truck while Mason and Lorenzo straddled their bikes. When they were out of sight, Matthew said, "You're not human. What are you?"

Troy called George every fifteen minutes for an update. The unmarked car was still sitting down from his house. Did they think he was stupid? That he didn't know what a fucking stakeout looked like? He was listening to the scanner, and there was still no mention of him. Good, the kid kept his fucking mouth shut. George was getting antsy, because he was supposed to go see Debbie again. The last time Troy called, George told him he was going to take his truck and go get laid.

While he was trying to figure out how to get another vehicle, his phone rang. He frowned when he saw who it was. "Grady, I'm kind of in the middle of something."

"I just thought you might wanna know that the

queer is in trouble. Seems him and his boyfriend had a little lover's quarrel."

"So what if they fought?"

"His fag friend is dead. I was the first one on the scene, and I found a video camera under the seat. Showed Jenkins pushing the other guy, really fucking hard. Practically threw him across the parking lot. Didn't know pansies were that fucking strong. Anyway, just thought you might like to hear about it before your shift tomorrow."

"Yeah, thanks. Hey, while I got you on the line, I need a favor..."

# Chapter Thirty-One

Abbi was ashamed of herself for running from Frey, running from her feelings. She'd passed Lorenzo on her way in the house and stopped to ask how Matt was. She then shut herself in her room to work on the festival, only her pad was downstairs. Frey and Lorenzo brought the food in from the truck. She waited until they were back outside before she tiptoed downstairs to grab her notebook. Matt was still asleep, so she went back upstairs and attempted to put some dance steps down on paper.

Her attempt to concentrate was futile knowing Frey was outside working on something he'd bought for Matthew. Her mind was on the man and not dancing. She lay down across the bed and closed her eyes. She hummed the tune to *The Sugarplum Fairy* while envisioning the steps the little kids could do. Her mind floated back a few days to the community center when Frey saw her dancing. The tears in his eyes had been real. If he could feel something from watching her dance, it was possible he could feel something more. She wanted him to feel more. Wanted his words to be the truth.

The sound of motorcycles had Abbi walking down the hall to the bedroom that looked out over the driveway. Frey had the basketball goal mounted on the stand, and he and Lorenzo were playing. Deacon had brought Frey's bike back to him, and Mason was with him. They talked and laughed for a bit before the four of them began playing. Abbi propped up on her hand and sat mesmerized at the four huge men. She had never seen so much testosterone in one place. These Amazons were all dressed like bikers, yet they were playing ball like professionals.

Abbi drank in the gorgeous men. All four of them were built with muscles rippling everywhere. Mason wasn't as developed as the other three, but he was no slouch. The speed with which they moved was astounding. At one point, Mason leapt from several feet away, dunking the ball. Abbi gasped. *How is that possible?*

The game went on until Matthew headed their way. The men included Matt in their circle, laughing and joking with him. The smile on her brother's face warmed her heart. It had been too long since he'd had any type of positive reinforcement from a man in his life. Frey had promised he would be that man for Matt. As if he knew she was thinking about him, Frey's eyes found Abbi's. She returned his gaze hoping to convey a little of what her heart was feeling. When he looked away, she decided to heat up the food Priscilla sent home with them. Home. Abbi had to stop thinking of Frey's house as home. By the time she reached the first floor, the motorcycles had started up and were rumbling down the driveway. Abbi reached the window in time to see Deacon's taillights fading.

Abbi took the food out of the refrigerator and set about heating it up. When Matt and Frey didn't immediately come in the house, she went to check on them. Neither one of them looked happy, but Abbi knew whatever it was needed to be handled between the two of them.

At first, Frey thought Matthew was kidding. When Matthew put his hands on his hips and asked, "Well?" Frey realized the teen had seen them using their shifter speed. "There's no way someone can leap flatfooted from that far off and dunk a ball."

"Matt, you're on pain medicine. He didn't jump that far."

Matt threw his hands in the air and hissed from the pain. "You know what? Fucking forget it. I've been lied to my whole life. Why should now be any different?"

*Godsdamnit!* This was all on Frey. Why hadn't he remembered there were humans around? Fuck! "Matt, stop. What do you want me to say? That the guys and I are these shapeshifters with superpowers? That what you saw was real? Would you actually believe something as crazy as that?"

"If it's the truth, yes. I've read about the Unholy. They teach us about 'em in Biology and warn us to stay away from them. If some crazy man can build an army of hybrids who are bad, why can't there be hybrids who are good?"

"They teach about the Unholy?" Frey needed to talk to Abbi about that, find out what exactly was being said.

"Yeah, they do. So, is Abbi right about you being an Amazon?"

Frey ran his hands through his short hair and sighed. Rafael was going to kill him.

"No, I'm not an Amazon."

"Fine. Forget it." Matt turned toward the house.

"I didn't say I'm not different, I just said I'm not an Amazon. That's not even a real thing. It's something Abbi made up."

"Then what exactly are you?" Matt had his hands on his hips, waiting for the truth.

"Let's just say I'm part of a secret society that was put here to protect humans. We…" Frey's phone rang interrupting.

"Jasper, what's up?" Frey listened while watching Matthew's face for any sign of disbelief or disgust. "I'm sure Matt would love to play video games. I think Lor was kind of boring. Come on when you're ready." Frey put his phone in his pocket. "Jasper wants to spend the night. I hope you don't mind. He's going through a tough time and doesn't want to be alone."

"I know how he feels. Now, you were saying?"

"Supper's ready," Abbi yelled out the back door.

238

"Coming," Frey responded, hoping to table this conversation for later.

"So, what you're saying is you are protecting me because it's your duty?"

"No. I'm protecting you because I lo...care about you. A lot."

"Okay, but if you aren't human, what are you?"

"It will be easier to show you than to tell you, but not tonight. I need to talk to someone first. When I get the go ahead, I'll show you. I promise. Just please, Son, don't say anything."

"If you promise then I promise."

"I do. Now, let's not keep your sister waiting."

Dane knew it was futile, but he drove to Abbi's house anyway. Before he got there, Vaughn called him to let him know Troy was leaving in his truck. Dane instructed him to follow the man and report back when he stopped somewhere. If Frey was correct, it wasn't Troy leaving but George. Dane continued on to Abbi's to see if anyone was there.

Coming up empty, he decided to stop in the coffee shop where Marley worked. He would wait there for Vaughn to call in. Dane didn't know Marley's schedule, didn't know anything about her other than she was pretty in a girl next door kind of way. Dane wanted to know beyond a shadow of a doubt that she was his mate. She wasn't really his type, but if the fates had chosen her, they must have had a good reason.

As he was walking to the door, he saw Marley through the window. He paused to watch her work without her knowing he was there. She had a weary smile on her face, but a smile nonetheless. She was taking an order from a man who had his back to Dane. The customer said something to Marley, and she did not look happy. Dane entered the coffee shop just as the man reached out and grabbed Marley's wrist. Dane's beast was ready to tear the man apart. There was no doubt she was his mate at that point.

Marley tried to pull out of the man's grasp, but he was too strong. "Let go of her," Dane thundered as he entered the shop. The man dropped Marley's arm and stood, turning around to face Dane.

"Mind your own fucking business," the man seethed as he stood toe to toe with Dane.

"Are you okay?" Dane asked Marley, whose eyes were wide. She didn't answer, only nodded. Dane stepped back from the man who clearly had no regard for someone else's space. "I think you should leave."

"Like I said, mind your own business." The man pushed Dane, but Dane didn't budge. His shifter strength allowed him to keep his feet firmly planted.

"She is my business." Dane pushed his Henley out of the way to expose the badge he had attached to his blue jeans. "Now, we can do this the easy way, which is you leaving, or we can do it my way, and that ends up with you downtown. What's it going to be?"

The man shoved his way past Dane as he chose the easy way. The other customers clapped and cheered. Dane sat in the vacated seat and ran his hand down his face. He felt Marley standing next to him before she said, "Thank you."

Dane almost said *just doing my job*, but she was more than a job. He smiled and replied, "You're welcome. Are you really okay? Did he hurt you?"

She held out her arm for him to observe. "I might have a bruise tomorrow, but it's all right."

Dane softly gripped her arm, turning it over to see there was no immediate injury. Her skin was soft under his fingers, and his body was humming from the contact. He found himself rubbing her wrist with his thumb. He removed his hand, placing it in his lap to hide the erection growing in his jeans. "Did you know him? Has he given you trouble before?" Dane didn't want to think of other men putting their hands on her, even if they weren't hurting her.

"No, there are just some men who won't take no for an answer. Would you like your usual?"

"Yes, please." When she turned to put in his order, Dane adjusted himself as discreetly as possible. His eyes followed Marley all around the little shop as she waited on other customers. Most were minding their own business, but some were being sympathetic to the incident. Dane wanted them all to hush so she would get back to his table. He wanted to ask her out, take her on a date, and get to know her. The timing was shit, though. He would be taking over as Police Chief the next day, and his responsibilities would increase greatly. He didn't have time to date now, and he'd have even less in the future.

His cell phone rang drawing his attention away from the pretty brunette. "Abbott. Give me the address. Got it, on my way." Troy's truck had been spotted. This just proved his point. If he didn't have time for a cup of coffee, how could he take her out?

"Marley, I'm going to need that to go." She returned with his latte in a to-go cup instead of the ceramic mug. He held out twenty folded up around his business card. When she held her hand out, he placed the money in her palm, holding her hand at the same time. "If you have any more trouble, call me." Dane could feel the pull between them. He really didn't understand how he could be so in tune with her body, so conscious of where she was in the café at every moment, so attracted to her when he normally preferred petite redheads.

Marley whispered, "Okay," and slid her hand out of his, putting the twenty in her apron pocket.

241

"Okay." Dane picked up his latte and left to do his job.

The address Dane was given led him to a row of rundown houses not far from Troy's. The house was deeded to Margaret Cranston, but the odd thing was, she was deceased. It was possible a relative lived there. Dane was about to find out. He parked behind Troy's truck, blocking it in the driveway. He preferred to have Jasper as back-up, but the Goyle was on his way to Frey's. Dane hadn't worked with Vaughn often, but knew him to be solid. They approached the house together, and Dane knocked on the door.

To his surprise, a little girl answered it. "Hello," she said as she looked up at him.

"Are your parents home?" Dane asked.

"I don't have a daddy, but momma's here with one of her boyfriends."

"Amelia, who's at the door?" a woman's voice yelled from somewhere inside.

"Who are you?" the little girl asked.

Dane should arrest the mother on negligence. He could have taken the girl and been gone. "I'm Detective Abbott," he told her.

"He's a detective," Amelia yelled back to her mother. Cussing came from down the hall. A woman appeared from somewhere in the back of the small house, buttoning her shirt as she walked.

"Amelia, can you go to your room, please?" Dane asked the child.

"This is my room," she said as she walked over and sat on the floor.

The mother asked, "What do you want?"

"Ma'am, I'm looking for Troy Quinn. Is he here?"

"Nope."

"His truck's in your driveway. Are you sure he isn't here?"

242

"I'm sure. I haven't seen Troy in a long time."

"But Momma, he was here just the other night."

"Hush, Amelia. Don't mind her. She gets confused."

"What's your name, ma'am?" Dane asked the woman, thoroughly disgusted that her little girl slept in the living room and knew the names of the men who came and went.

"Debbie."

"Well, Debbie, I need you to tell me who else is in the house with you."

"Just a friend."

"I need your friend's name. Please don't cause a bigger scene than this already is." Dane nodded toward Amelia who was drinking it all in.

"I don't have to tell you shit, I know my rights."

Dane lowered his voice and told her, "Look, Debbie, one call to child services will have you so deep in social workers, you will not be able to entertain your men friends for a long time. Or would you like to come down to the station instead?"

"George, get out here," Debbie yelled toward the back of the house.

A door down the hall opened, and George Novak came into the living room with his t-shirt inside out.

"George, where is Troy Quinn?" Dane asked him.

"I haven't seen him."

"But you're in his truck. Care to explain that?"

"He needed to borrow my car to go see his momma. Didn't think his truck would make it that far."

Dane thumbed at the truck sitting in the driveway. "His practically new truck wouldn't make it to New Valdosta, but your piece of shi... junk car would? Try again." Dane wasn't used to being around kids. If Kaya was going to have a baby, he'd need to start watching his language.

"Seriously, I don't know where he is. He asked me to

243

come over, said he needed to borrow my car. He didn't come back, so I took his truck."

"What do you want with Troy?" Debbie asked.

"His brother-in-law was beaten pretty badly. We just wanted to make sure Troy knew about it. If you see him, can you pass that along?" Dane lied, but he was looking for a reaction from the two of them. George didn't flinch. Debbie, however, did. She glanced down at Amelia then back to Dane.

Dane didn't want to be obvious, but he memorized the features of both mother and daughter. Amelia didn't resemble her mother in any way, but had plenty of similarities to the picture he had of Troy Quinn.

# Chapter Thirty-Two

Abbi cleared the table and washed the dishes while Matt, Frey, and Jasper played video games. When she was wiping down the counter, she felt Frey's presence in the room. She glanced over her shoulder to find him leaning against the door frame, watching her. She couldn't help the smile that formed. The man was absolutely gorgeous, in an intimidating "I can kill you with my bare hands" kind of way.

"Will you teach me self-defense?" she asked him. She knew she wasn't strong enough to best someone like him, or even Troy, but she was willing to learn enough to possibly keep her alive.

"Go change and meet me in the gym," Frey told her. He had an odd look on his face as he turned away. Abbi went upstairs and searched through the drawers for something to put on. She found a pair of yoga pants and a t-shirt. That should be good enough.

She padded barefoot into the gym. When she got to the door, she froze in her tracks. Frey was punching a small bag, his fists like fast windmills. He had changed out of his blue jeans and was now wearing a pair of black warm-up pants he'd cut off right above the knee. His legs were massive. His t-shirt was sleeveless, showing off his arms. With each punch, the muscles rippled and bunched. The man was pure perfection. Troy worked out and was fit. Frey was a god. His skin was a golden olive that hinted of an Italian or Greek heritage. The words he'd spoken into the security box at the gate had sounded Italian.

He caught the bag and stopped its motion. When he turned her way, his eyes drank in her clothing. Her t-shirt wasn't tight, but it wasn't loose either. Her pants clung to her legs. Her immediate reaction was to cover herself, but she needed to feel his appreciation for the way she looked.

245

She'd spent too many years hiding her true self behind baggy clothing. Frey cleared his throat. "Come over here." He met her in the middle of the mat. It was cushiony under Abbi's feet as she walked toward Frey.

"I won't pretend that you'll be able to defeat someone my size. For the most part, males are just naturally stronger than females. What you need is the element of surprise. I'm going to show you a few moves that will hopefully allow you to get loose when you're being held certain ways. Our bodies come equipped with internal weapons. Elbows, knees, feet, and head are your best bet for disarming someone."

Frey stepped in front of Abbi and put his hands on her shoulders. "In this position, since I'm so much taller than you, it would be hard for you to effectively strike me in the face, but your knee is perfect. If a man grabs your shoulders, use that momentum to raise your knee into his nuts. It might not stop him, but it'll incapacitate him momentarily. If he bends over grabbing his crotch, bring your knee up again, connecting with his face. When his head pops back, you can strike up with your palm. A good punch to the throat can drop a man as well.

"If he's closer to your height, catch him with your elbow." Frey made a sweeping motion toward Abbi's face with his arm. Next, he turned her body so she was facing sideways. "If someone grabs your arm, use their body as leverage, twisting into them. Here, grab my arm." Abbi grabbed Frey's forearm, and he swung his body into hers, once again striking toward her throat.

"There's an acronym women are taught in self-defense classes: SING. Solar Plexus, Instep, Nose, Groin. If your arms are incapacitated, it's unlikely you'll be able to use your elbow to hit 'em in the stomach. You should, however, be able to stomp their foot. Head butt someone in the nose with the back of your head, not the front. You can knock yourself out if you do it the wrong way. The Groin, we've already covered.

"Another effective move is to take out someone's knee. The whole knee is vulnerable, but if you get in a good strike to the front, you can really incapacitate your attacker, possibly even blow the knee out." Frey went through the motions of the strikes he described allowing Abbi to practice them on him.

"What about flipping someone?" Abbi asked. "Can you show me how to do that?"

"I can, but again, if someone is my size, it will be very hard for you to flip them. Okay, come at me from behind." When Abbi ran at Frey he used her momentum and flipped her over onto the mat. Instead of allowing her to land hard, he cradled her body. "I want to try," she told him after about the sixth time of him flipping her.

Frey shook his head, grinning. "Don't hurt yourself." Abbi waited until he was right on her. She grabbed his arm and bent over, allowing his momentum to keep him going. She forgot to let go, and she ended up on top of him. Frey groaned, but Abbi laughed. It hadn't been pretty, but she'd flipped him over. Sure she had been expecting him, but she was still proud of herself. She laughed at him, "You let me do that."

Frey smiled his beautiful smile and pushed her hair off her face. "Maybe."

She realized where she was and froze. Abbi was stretched out on top of his body, from chest to legs. She started to climb off of him, but he grabbed her ass with both hands, pulling their bodies closer. She couldn't take her eyes off his, even when she felt his cock getting hard. She made the mistake of looking at his mouth. When she did, she remembered his lips on hers.

Frey moved one hand up her back under her shirt, his fingertips barely brushing over her skin. He grabbed her ponytail with the other hand and used it to pull her face toward his. He raised his head, meeting her halfway. Before

247

she knew what was happening, he flipped her onto her back, his large body covering hers, never breaking the kiss. His cock was nestled between her legs, and instinctively Abbi wrapped her legs around his hips. One hand snaked around his neck while the other one found its way into his short hair.

Abbi didn't know who started moving first, but their lower bodies were slowly grinding against each other. She sank her heels into his thighs, needing more. The shorts he had on did nothing to shield his erection from her. The thin barriers of their clothing only added to the friction. The wrongness of being with another man flew into her brain. Frey slid down her body, raised her t-shirt and bra, exposing her breasts. As soon as his hot mouth latched on to her nipple and began licking and sucking, that thought was chased away by how right they felt together. Abbi arched her back, pushing her breast into Frey's mouth. He took her nipple between his teeth, biting with just enough pressure to send a current from her chest to her core.

Her pussy was throbbing, aching. "Frey," she husked, grabbing his hair in both hands. She didn't know if she was pushing or pulling. All she knew was she had to have more. "Frey, I need..." Her words were cut off as he slid back up her body to reclaim her mouth. When they needed to breathe, he broke the kiss. His dark eyes were black, full of lust and need. He rocked his cock against her clit.

The friction was torture, pure and simple. "Frey, please..."

He lowered his mouth to her jaw, running his tongue along her skin until he reached her ear. "What do you need, Sweetheart? Tell me. I need to hear you say it," he breathed. Frey took her lobe between his teeth, giving her a nip. He kissed the soft spot under her jaw and placed bites down her neck. "I can't hold out much longer, Abbi. Tell me what you want."

"You. I want you," she gasped as he scraped his sharp teeth over her skin.

Frey rose up on his knees and lifted his shirt over his head. If she thought he was beautiful before, seeing his chest bared before her had her ready to lick every inch of this Amazon. Speaking of inches, Frey removed his shorts and his long cock sprang free. The man was huge everywhere. It didn't scare her though, knowing how gentle he could be. He grabbed the waistband of her yoga pants and slid them down her legs, slowly. His gaze drank in every inch of her skin as it was revealed to him.

When her pants were off, Frey disappeared between her legs. He raised her knees up, spreading her, exposing her core to him. Frey scraped his teeth along her thigh, biting the tender flesh. "Mmm, Frey..." He bit his way back up her other leg until he reached that spot where she was throbbing, ready. He licked her clit and sucked the sensitive nub. "Oh, god, Frey. Oh, ohhh!" Abbi wouldn't last long with him sucking her like he was. She grabbed his hair, pulling his mouth to her, needing to come but not wanting to yet.

Frey lapped at her folds before sliding his tongue back up, focusing on her clit again. He inserted a finger into her wet heat, then two. While his tongue worked its magic on the outside, his fingers found her spot on the inside. He worked in tandem as her body heated to the point of boiling. "Frey... I can't... Frey, oh god... I'm coming..." Frey sucked her clit hard, and she bucked into his face as she flew apart. He continued rubbing inside while she came, coating his fingers with her juices. When the last shudder left her body, only then did he stop the sweet torment to her clit. He leaned back on his ankles and stuck his fingers in his mouth, sucking them clean. That was the most erotic thing she'd ever seen in her life.

He eased his way back up her body, kissing her stomach, and stopping at her breasts to give them attention.

249

When he placed his lips on hers, she tasted herself on his tongue. It surprised her how much she liked it. Frey's cock was sliding against her wet folds, and he pushed up on one elbow to look at her. "Sweetheart, I need you. Please tell me I can have you."

There was no way she could deny him. "You can have me," she whispered against his lips. With one thrust, Frey was seated all the way to the root inside her body. The intensity was too much with his cock being as large as it was. She closed her eyes against the intrusion, holding back the tears that threatened to fall. Instinctively, her body was ready to protest. When he didn't move, she opened her eyes. The look on his face was a mixture of bliss and worry.

"Are you okay?" he asked. He was holding still, his thickness filling her.

"You're just so big," Abbi admitted.

"Relax, Sweetheart." Frey dipped his head down and kissed her. He licked her bottom lip, waiting for her to open. When she did, he began stroking her tongue with his. He mimicked the motion, moving in and out, slowly, taking the tip of his cock to her entrance then sliding it back in all the way. The discomfort soon changed to pleasure as her body relaxed around him. He rose up on his hands and changed the angle of his movements.

"Oh..." She was amazed how her body reacted to his. "That feels good. I never..." She didn't finish her thought, but she never knew sex could feel so incredible. Or that a man could move the way he was. Frey's movements were slow, sensuous. She bet he would be a good dancer with the way he moved his hips.

He raised one of her legs and put it over his shoulder. He twisted his body so his shaft hit her clit with each down thrust. He closed his eyes as his head fell back. "Fuck, Sweetheart, you are so fucking tight." He began grunting with each thrust. "Fucking hell... feels so good..."

Abbi could feel the pressure building again. "Frey,

oh crap... I'm... oh god..." She didn't know it was possible to have an orgasm during sex, but Frey was making sure she was satisfied, too. Abbi knew in that moment she'd never regret giving her body to him. He already had her heart. He snapped his hips faster, and his grunts became more pronounced. She could feel his body tensing up under her hands as she dug her nails into his skin.

"Come for me, Abbi. Can you do that? Come with me," he begged as he searched her eyes, his thrusts coming harder and more sporadic.

"I'm so close. Oh, god..." And Abbi was coming with him. She kept her eyes on his face. Her core pulsed, squeezing his cock, claiming him. He dropped down, chest to chest, and buried his face in her neck to stifle his yells. Her own sounds were muffled when he caught her cries in his mouth. Frey spilled his seed deep in her body, pumping in and out as his come filled her, mixing with her own orgasm. Frey kissed her neck, her jaw, her lips again. He remained still until neither of their bodies was pulsing. When he slid out, their combined juices ran down her inner thigh.

When Frey once again found her lips, Abbi felt all the love this man had to give. He rose from the mat and said, "Hold still." He walked over to a cabinet and removed a white workout towel, his naked body on full display. He gently cleaned her up before sliding her pants back up her legs. As she righted her bra and t-shirt, she raised her butt off the mat so he could get her pants over her hips. He wiped himself and tossed the towel in the dirty receptacle. He put his shorts on but left his shirt off. Frey held his hand out, and Abbi placed hers in it. When she was on her feet, Frey pulled her body to his, taking her right hand in his left. He began humming a tune, and there in the gym, Frey showed Abbi he did, indeed, know how to dance.

# Chapter Thirty-Three

When Frey descended the stairs, the scent of coffee and bacon wafted through the air. Jasper was standing by the stove, staring at the sizzling pork in the frying pan. "Good morning, Jas. Did you get any sleep?" He and Matt had stayed up half the night, lost in video games.

"Not really," Jasper answered sadly.

Frey hadn't gotten any sleep either. After making love to Abbi, he couldn't shut his mind off, and his beast was trying to claw his way out. It wanted to claim its mate. He'd lain awake all night, replaying every second of their time in the gym. When they came through the house to say goodnight, Jasper and Matthew were locked into video battle. Matthew couldn't believe Jasper had a new game that wasn't even on the market. Both of them had barely muttered "goodnight" and continued playing. Frey walked Abbi to her bedroom door. He knew it was too soon to ask her to sleep in his bed, but he offered anyway.

Abbi politely declined before pulling his head down to hers for a goodnight kiss. The kiss didn't last nearly as long as Frey wanted, but if it had gone on much longer, he wouldn't have been able to contain the beast.

Jasper leaned against the counter, holding his coffee. "I don't think I'll get any sleep until Trevor comes back. It's probably a good thing I'm on administrative leave; I doubt I'd be able to do my job anyway."

"He'll be back," Matthew said as he slowly entered the kitchen. "He's got a hot detective waiting on him."

"What are you doing up? You don't have to go to school," Frey asked as he took out an extra mug. He didn't miss Matthew's comment about Jasper being hot.

"I smelled bacon. I was afraid if I didn't get up, I wouldn't get any. I've seen you Amazons eat." He grimaced as he sat down.

Jasper arched an eyebrow. "Amazons?"

"It's what Abbi calls Frey's band of big, merry men. You're one, too." Matt took the coffee Frey was offering and said, "Thanks."

"Trevor calls us the badass club," Jasper said with a sad smile. "Do you need a pain pill?" he asked Matt.

"That would make my morning almost as stellar as bacon and coffee. The badass club... yep, I can see it."

Jasper left the room and came back with the bottle. He took a pill out, poured a glass of water, and handed both to Matt.

"You're going to make Trevor a wonderful wife someday," Matt grinned as he tossed back the medicine.

"And you're going to get your ass handed to you when you're well," Jasper returned, messing up his hair.

Frey loved watching the banter between the two of them. Matthew hadn't mentioned any friends all week, and with Trevor gone, Jasper could use a friend as well. Frey didn't know exactly how old Jasper was or what he'd endured in all his years. He had come from the west coast where Sin had warned Rafael about the Goyle. So far, he had fit in well with the Clan on the east coast, and Frey enjoyed being around him.

"You don't have to cook, Jas." Frey appreciated him just being there and hanging out with Matthew all day.

"It's no problem. Abbi has to work, and I figured your breakfast normally consists of a protein shake."

"You figured correctly. Between you, Abbi, and Priscilla, I'm going to have to work out more than usual just to keep my girlish figure." Frey patted his rock hard abs, garnering a laugh from Matt. He pulled four plates out of the cabinet and placed them on the table. Right as Abbi came down the steps and entered the kitchen, Jasper was spooning eggs onto the plates.

"Perfect timing." Jasper smiled and winked at Abbi. Like Frey, Jasper had listened with his shifter hearing as

Abbi moved about upstairs and knew when she was close to ready.

"Jasper, you didn't have to go to all this trouble, but thank you. Matty, how are you this morning?" She didn't speak to Frey, but the smile she gave him said it all.

"I'll be better when this bacon gets in my stomach." Matt stuck a slice in his mouth and bit, chewing and biting until it was gone. He totally ignored the eggs and toast until his bacon was demolished.

They ate their breakfast, listening to Jasper and Matt comparing notes from the overnight video fest. Abbi didn't add to the conversation, but she did smile at her brother's antics. Frey mostly laughed. When they'd all finished eating, Abbi stood and started clearing the table, but Jasper stopped her. "I got this. You get to work."

"Thank you, Jasper." Abbi washed and dried her hands before going to the living room for her things. Frey followed her, and when she picked up her coat, he took it from her, holding it for her to put on. She gave him a funny look, then turned around and slid her arms in. He didn't miss the small sigh she let out.

Abbi picked up her purse and worn out briefcase before returning to the kitchen. She told her brother, "Matt, try to behave. I'll see you tonight." She kissed him on the cheek and turned to Frey. "Ready."

"Matt, I'll get your homework and bring it when we come home. Jas, Rafael and a couple of the guys might come by later to lay out a project I asked him to work on. Other than that, it should be quiet."

"Ten-four, Kemosabe," Matt said, stuffing the last piece of bacon in his mouth.

Jasper shook his head, grinning. "Have a good day, Brother."

Frey laughed and shook his head at the teen. He placed his hand on Abbi's back, directing her to the door. When they got outside, rain was sprinkling down. "Stay

254

inside and I'll get the truck." He never thought about needing a covered walkway until now. When he had Rafael build his house, he forewent the attached garage knowing he'd need something much bigger for the helicopters. The way the house was situated, he could add a garage on the west side, but that's where Abbi's studio was going. His best option was a covered walkway leading from the side door to the garage he already had. He'd call Rafe and have him add that to his project list.

Frey pulled as close to the house as possible, and leaned over and opened the passenger door. Abbi didn't hurry. Obviously the light rain didn't bother her. "You didn't have to do that, I'm used to getting wet."

"But I saw a garage at your house. Is it full of junk or something?"

"No, it's full of Troy's truck. I have an umbrella in my car." Abbi settled in and buckled up. Frey wanted to hit something, namely Troy fucking Quinn. How could the bastard be so callous as to have his wife park outside? He calmed himself and reached for her hand. They had done well at breakfast, not letting on that anything was going on between them. Frey knew Jasper could give two shits about it. If truth be told, he probably heard them in the gym the night before. Matthew wanted his sister happy, so he would probably jump for joy. When they got to the end of the driveway, Frey put the truck in park.

"I can't wait any longer. I need to kiss you." He didn't pull her to him. If he did, they'd end up naked within seconds. When Abbi nodded, he leaned over and pressed their lips together. He kept it short and sweet. "Thank you. I knew I couldn't do that when I drop you off, but I also knew I couldn't go all day without it either." He put the truck in gear and pulled out onto the road. Frey immediately checked his rearview mirror for signs of Troy. They arrived at the school without incident.

Frey parked under the overhang where the parents

255

let the kids out. "Have a good day, Sweetheart. If you need anything, you call me."

"I will. See you later." She smiled and grabbed her stuff. Frey didn't move until she was safely inside the school. He parked at the end of the parking lot and got comfortable.

Dane pulled into the precinct parking lot directly behind Kaya. Now that she was pregnant, Rafael was even more protective of his Queen. Like Rafael even had to worry about her with Dane around. He and Kaya had been working together a long time, and he loved his Chief, now Queen, in a sisterly kind of way. He wished Jasper could be there, but Dante was right; they had to investigate Craig's murder by the books.

Today could go down one of two ways: one, with Troy Quinn not showing up for work because he was hiding and felt as though he was going to be arrested for assault; or two, with him showing up thinking the kid didn't rat him out then totally losing his shit when served divorce papers. Dane wasn't sure which one he was hoping for. If Troy didn't show up, they would have a harder time finding him and keeping Abbi and Matt safe. If he did show up, they could follow him, but he would be even more hell bent on getting to Abbi. It really was a no-win situation.

They walked inside together, Kaya greeting everyone as she normally did. "Good morning, Kim. We are going to have our brief a little early. If you can, hold all calls until we're finished."

"What's going on? Is everything okay?" the dispatcher asked, partially out of concern but mostly out of pure nosiness.

"I'll fill you in after the brief." Kaya didn't give the

younger woman time for any more questions.

As they walked through the department, Dane told everyone to meet in the conference room immediately. He and Kaya both poured a cup of coffee before continuing on. Kaya may be pregnant, but she still had to have her morning java.

Normally Kaya went to the podium alone, but today she had asked that Dane stand with her. He was, after all, going to take over as soon as she had her belongings packed. When everyone was in the room, Kaya began. "Good morning. I wanted to meet with you first thing because I have an announcement. Effective today, I will be retiring." There was a lot of chatter and questions being thrown at her all at once. She held up her hand to quieten them. "When I made the decision to leave the force, I didn't have to think hard on who I wanted as my replacement. Dane Abbott has been by my side and had my back for many years now. He knows the department, all of you, as well as the procedures, probably better than I do. I nominated Dane, and the City Council has approved my recommendation. As of the end of today, Dane is your new Chief of Police." There was more murmuring, but mostly congratulations being tossed Dane's way.

"Since we are going to be short a detective, we will be promoting one of you. If you are interested in the position, you will need to write a short essay on why you feel you would make a good detective, and tell what you would want to accomplish. Dane and I will go over all the candidates and choose one by the end of the week."

"Don't you mean you need two detectives? If the fairy's in jail, we'll be short another one," Grady spoke up from the back of the room.

Dane was ready to throttle him. "For those of you who haven't heard, Detective Jenkins is on administrative leave pending the investigation into the death of an acquaintance of his. We have the utmost respect for Jasper.

257

The evidence is circumstantial at best, and I'm going to find the real killer."

"Acquaintance my ass. It was his fag lover," Grady muttered. Dane's shifter hearing allowed him to understand it with no problem.

"Let me make one thing clear," Dane paused, making sure he had Grady's attention. "I cannot tell you how to think, but I can tell you how I expect you to act. You may have bigoted views regarding race, religion, and sexual orientation, but I expect you to keep those views to yourself. While you are wearing the badge that is pinned to your uniform, you will be respectful of the people you work with, as well as any civilians you come in contact with. If you cannot or will not do that, remove your badge and bring it to me. Now." Dane continued staring at Grady. Eventually everyone in the room had turned his way, curious as to whom Dane was so intent on. The man crossed his arms over his chest and leered at Dane, but he didn't bring his badge to the front of the room.

Kaya brought everyone's attention back to her. "I will be here today cleaning out my office. If you have any questions, come see me. I don't want to take any more of the city's time by standing up here chatting, but I do want to say this: it was always my dream to be on the force. Ever since my father was taken out in the line of duty when I was little, I knew I wanted to serve. I never dreamed I would be promoted to Chief, but when that day came, I was never more proud. I thank each and every one of you for the job you do, that you will continue to do for Dane. He has your assignments, so let's get to work."

Normally Kaya would proceed to her office, but Rafael had made it clear she was not to be alone. She would wait until Dane had passed out the day's work before leaving the conference room. The only place she was allowed alone was the restroom, and even then, Dane was to accompany her and wait outside the door. Kaya felt he was being overprotective. Maybe he was, but Dane could see where he was coming from.

Dane called the teams up, leaving Grady and his partner until last. The foul mouthed asshole had been partnered with a rookie a couple of months ago. Dane was going to speak with Kaya about putting the kid with someone less abrasive. Someone who would teach him the right way to be a cop. "Grady, I want you and Chris manning the phones today."

Chris smiled at Dane, "You got it, Chief. Congratulations, by the way." The kid shook Dane's hand, genuine in his sentiment. Grady didn't say a word. He turned on his heel and stalked from the room. "He's not very nice," Chris said to Grady's back.

"No, I'm afraid he isn't." Dane patted the young man on his shoulder. As soon as the room was empty, Dane asked Kaya, "How do you feel about Chris getting a new partner?"

"I think that's an excellent idea. The kid has the right attitude and was top in his class. I'd hate to have his enthusiasm tarnished by that dickhead."

Dane laughed, "I like when you resort to Chief mode."

Kaya sighed, "Yeah, well, I guess those days are over. I think being Queen is going to be a lot tougher."

# Chapter Thirty-Four

Trevor was miserable. Even though he was enjoying spending time with his brother, he was no closer to an answer than he'd been when he left New Atlanta. Dante had texted, asking him to call. He hated not responding to his boss. What if something had happened and he needed Trevor back at the morgue? Surely if Dante really needed him, he'd just say so.

Travis had been really good about giving Trevor his space, but it was evident in the way he continuously peered at him that he was worried. Trevor had always been the goofy one, the one who cut up and made jokes, keeping the seriousness out of life. But Travis was the only one who knew it was Trevor's defense mechanism. Travis knew him better than anyone, and he still didn't know the true depth of his brother's insecurities. It had only been a day since Trevor left home, but he still hadn't told Travis why he'd run.

Travis had wanted to take off work to spend the day with Trevor, but he convinced his brother it wasn't necessary. He wanted the time alone to think, to try and figure out what was going on. Jasper had been honest from the beginning about Craig, about having a relationship with the firefighter, and how Craig had broken things off abruptly. Jasper also told him he held no feelings for his ex. Then why were they together and why was Jasper in his arms? Who knew Trevor and Jasper had spent time together? Craig had been looking in the window at the gym. Had he seen them talking to one another? If so, that's all they were doing, talking.

Whoever it was had obviously followed Trevor, because they knew where he lived, and they had his cell phone number. Whoever it was that sent the text wanted Trevor to see Jasper and Craig together. Was it Craig? Did he want Trevor to know he was in town and there was no way he had a shot at Jasper? Too many fucking questions, and not enough answers. Dante told him he could explain some things. Maybe he would call Dante, but not yet.

Travis' dog, Molly, whined at Trevor's feet. "Hey, girl, do you want to go out?" Molly wagged her butt and yipped at him. Trevor always wanted a dog, but with the long hours he put in at the morgue, he didn't feel it would be fair to an animal. Travis' house was in a small rural neighborhood that was walking distance to the park. He would take Molly for a walk and use the time to try and clear his head. He hooked the leash to her collar and headed outside.

Trevor and Molly walked down the path that bordered the park. Trevor had run in this same park on more than one occasion when he visited Travis. The path was used by runners, bicyclists, people walking their dogs, and couples strolling hand in hand. Trevor always found himself a bit envious of those couples. Even though gay couples had full rights in the eyes of the law, there were still those bigoted people in the world that thought only their kind of love was right. Trevor didn't understand how love could be wrong. He had never been a religious person, but if the god those people worshiped said love was wrong, Trevor didn't want that kind of god in his life.

The park was a beautiful place, lush with green everywhere you looked in the summer. It had enough evergreens that it wasn't completely barren in the colder months. Molly stopped to smell everywhere other dogs had been, scratching and peeing on top of other pee to mark her spot. Trevor didn't mind, though. He enjoyed his time with the black fur ball. They had just stepped back onto the path when Molly started growling. The hair on her back bristled, and she leaned into Trevor's leg. He looked around to find the object of her attention. There were no other dogs in the area, only people. He pulled gently on her leash, "Come on, girl," but she wasn't having it. She began barking and growling, her head now pointing toward the trees off to the side of the park. Trevor turned that way to see a large man staring at him. Molly tugged on her leash, but Trevor kept a tight rein on her. "Molly, hush." When Trevor glanced back up the man was gone.

Trevor investigated the area, but whoever it was had vanished. How could that be? He'd only taken his eyes off the guy long enough to look at the dog. Molly stopped being vocal as if nothing had spooked her. Had Trevor imagined it? Were the events of the past few days wearing on his nerves so much that he was now hallucinating? Why would someone be in the woods where there was no path to walk on? If Molly hadn't caused such a fuss, he would think he was seeing things. When the dog was content to continue on, Trevor allowed her to lead the way. He looked backwards several times, feeling as if someone was watching him. If the text and random photos were any indication, someone had been watching him.

No longer feeling safe, Trevor was ready to head back to New Atlanta and talk to Dante. Hopefully he and his badass club could protect Trevor.

Frey was getting anxious. He was ready for Abbi to be finished with school so he could take her to the community center. They had discussed his presence in her classroom and decided it was best if he waited in the empty room next door. A man his size could intimidate adults, not to mention small children. It was a little past three, and Dane had called letting him know Quinn didn't show up for work. He had called the dispatcher, claiming to be sick. Protocol dictated he call his immediate supervisor. When he didn't do that, Dane and Kaya knew he didn't plan on coming back to work.

What was going through the human's mind? How did he plan on getting out of the mess he was in? Victoria had been waiting at the precinct, but since Troy hadn't shown, she was going to have one of his fellow officers serve him with the divorce papers. Normally, she used a specific civil servant unit for that, but they felt Troy would be more inclined to talk to one of his officer buddies. Soon, Troy would find out his marriage was over. With him assaulting Matthew the way he had, Quinn had to know it was over anyway.

Abbi texted Frey when she was on her way outside. He parked next to the walkway and opened the door for her. She climbed in, smiling. "Hey," she said breathily. Good gods, she couldn't do that to him.

"Hey yourself," he said as he pulled the truck away from the building. "How was your day?"

"Good for the most part. I'm just worried about Amelia. You remember her, the little girl from the sporting goods store?"

Of course he remembered. The little girl stole his heart when she told Abbi she loved her. He had the feeling she didn't feel the same way about her mother. "Sure, cute little girl."

"Yeah, well she wasn't at school today."

"Is she sick? She didn't look sick yesterday."

"Exactly. She misses a lot of school, and it's usually when her mother is on a bender. It breaks my heart that kids have to put up with their parents' addictions when life is hard enough on them as it is. She should be loved and nurtured, not shoved in a corner and forgotten."

Frey could tell Abbi loved the little girl. She probably loved all her kids, but her heart was in her voice when she spoke of Amelia. He didn't have it in him to share what Dane suspected about the little girl. Neither did he want

Abbi to know of the pitiful home conditions the child endured. How would she feel about the child if the girl turned out to actually be Troy's? Would she still open her heart to a child her husband had with another woman when she herself couldn't carry a baby to term? Or would she embrace the child more knowing Amelia had no chance in hell at being loved otherwise? Knowing Abbi's heart, it would be the latter.

"Let's hope she is okay and will be back to school tomorrow." Frey reached for her hand, entwining their fingers. "Dane called. Troy didn't show up for work, and he still hasn't been located. Victoria is going to have one of his fellow officers serve him the papers. Hopefully, that will bring him out of hiding and they will arrest him."

"I just want all of this to be over with so I can move on with my life. I hate looking over my shoulder all the time."

Frey squeezed her hand. "You don't have to worry about that now. I've got your back. As long as you do what I ask you to and be smart about your surroundings, we've got you covered." Abbi nodded and smiled, but it didn't reach her eyes. He wanted to erase all the pain and doubt in her heart. He wanted the smile she gave him when she first got in the truck, before she had time to think about the bad things in her life.

When they arrived at the community center, Frey accompanied Abbi to her classroom, making sure it was empty. He left her to do what she needed to do to prepare for the kids. He made himself scarce, hiding out in the empty room next to hers. One by one the students arrived. Most of the parents left their kids, but there were a few of the moms who sat on the side of the room, watching their little one dance. Abbi went through some warmups before getting into the lesson. All of the kids in her class went to the school where she taught, and they would be part of the fall festival.

Once the music started, Frey couldn't stay put. He made sure nobody was around, and he stood in the shadow of the hall as Abbi showed the children their dance steps. Soon, her studio at home would be finished, and Frey would have the pleasure of watching her dance all the time. He would do what he needed to convince her to dance again. As she smiled at each of the children when they did something right, or even when they got the steps wrong, his soul reached out to the heavens and did something he'd never done before. He prayed for himself. Frey prayed that he would one day have the privilege of seeing Abbi teach their child how to dance.

The time flew by, and soon Abbi was telling the kids she would see them the following day. Since they were all in the festival, Abbi had changed the practice schedule to every day instead of three days a week. Frey hid until all the kids had been picked up. Amelia was among the kids, so Frey had to wonder why she hadn't been in school. He waited for her mother, but saw a stranger walking with both Amelia and another child.

Once Abbi was alone, Frey walked into her classroom. If there weren't other people in different areas of the building, he would ask her to dance for him. Since they weren't alone, he didn't risk it, because when she started dancing, he would want to grab her and kiss her. Kissing would lead to touching, and touching would lead to fucking. No, not fucking. Not with Abbi. They would make love. Even if they got down and dirty, it would always be making love.

On the way home, Abbi was quiet. Frey could feel the turmoil within her. "Abbi," he reached for her hand. "I saw Amelia. Did she say where she was today?"

Abbi responded without looking at him, "She said her mother was sick and couldn't take her to school." Frey let it go, but he was pretty sure there was more to it than that.

When they got out of the truck, Frey offered to carry Abbi's bags, but she took them instead. He really needed to figure out what was going on with her. They walked into the kitchen just as Jasper and Matt had finished eating. Jasper had their supper warming in the oven. He stood and put his and Matt's plates in the dishwasher. "I have some work to do, and I have training in the morning. Mason will be here before you take Abbi to the school, and then I'll relieve him later," Jasper told Frey as soon as they walked in the door.

"I thought you were on leave," Matthew said as he gingerly stood up from the kitchen table.

"I have Amazon work to tend to," Jasper joked.

"Ahh, fighting the good fight," Matthew responded. He had no idea how close to the truth he was.

Abbi put her bags down in the living room and returned to the kitchen. "What kind of training do you have?" she asked as she cocked her head sideways looking at Jasper.

Jasper looked to Frey for help, so Frey answered for him, "He has sword training. The badass club we belong to believes in being prepared for any type of assault."

Abbi rolled her eyes. "It's the Amazon club, and whatever."

"I want to watch," Matt told Jasper. Everyone looked at each other, but he continued, "I would love to get out of the house. If you don't mind, I'd like to ride with you and watch."

"It's fine by me if Jas doesn't mind swinging by to get you. That would save Mason a trip." Frey was going to tell Matthew about the Stone Society as soon as he cleared it with Rafael. The Goyles didn't phase during training, so it should be okay for Matt to go with Jasper.

"Yeah, sure. I'll pick you up at seven-thirty." Jasper shook hands with the men, fisted his heart to Abbi, and said his goodbyes.

"Is he really going to train with a sword?" Abbi asked incredulously.

"Yes, he really is." Frey let it go. If Abbi had questions, she would ask. If she didn't, well, she would eventually find out what was going on. He grabbed two plates from the cabinet and handed one to her. "This smells delicious," he said as he removed a casserole dish from the oven while Abbi reheated the green beans in the microwave.

"I'm telling you, Jasper would make a great husband. He can cook, he's got really great toys, and he's funny," Matt extolled the qualities of his new friend.

Abbi laughed, "It sounds like you're a little smitten with him."

"Nah, he's got his heart set on Trevor. I hope for both their sakes, Trevor gets his head out of his ass and comes back. I hate seeing Jasper sad."

Again, Frey didn't miss the fact that Matthew didn't deny his feelings for Jas. "Matthew, can I ask you a very personal question?"

"Sure," he said as he grabbed a dinner roll out of the basket.

"If Jasper didn't want Trevor, would you be interested in him?"

"Well, he is hot, if you like redheads. But he's too old for me. Besides, I prefer blonds." He stuck the roll in his mouth, tearing off a huge chunk. "Do you have a problem with that?" he asked around the bite of bread in his mouth.

Frey took a beer out of the fridge and sat down at the table. "Not at all. I want you to be happy, even if that means you're going to deprive yourself of the possibility of a great relationship because you won't consider a man with brown hair." Frey wiggled his eyebrows at Matt. "Please pass me a roll." The teen grabbed bread from the basket and threw it, grimacing after. Without thinking, Frey caught the roll with his shifter speed.

"Holy crap," Abbi gasped. "That was... You *are* an

267

Amazon. You all are. Tell me I'm not crazy, Geoffrey."

"You're not crazy. I just have quick reflexes. It comes from years and years of training. Please pass the green beans," he hoped she would drop it. When Frey stuck Matthew's thrown roll in his mouth, Matthew grinned and grabbed another one.

"You really should wait until you're healed before you try out for the baseball team."

"Tell me about it. This sucks donkey balls."

"Matthew Swanson!" Abbi chastised him.

"Sorry, Abs. Amazons are a bad influence on an impressionable young man."

Frey coughed to keep from choking on the bread he'd been swallowing. He sat the beans down and really laughed. He couldn't help it. Matthew was witty and funny, and Frey never wanted the kid to move out. Abbi pointed her fork at Frey. "Don't encourage him," she said, trying to hide a smile.

Frey gave Matthew his homework before he and Abbi cleaned the kitchen in companionable silence. While Abbi worked on the festival, Frey excused himself and headed out to the garage for some privacy. He called Rafael for an update on the construction. They talked about Dante and his new family as well as Kaya's last day at the precinct. When they got to the subject of training, Frey admitted about Matthew seeing the basketball scrimmage. "Rafe, I screwed up, but the boy's going to be my family. He will eventually learn what we are, so, if you have no objection, I'd like to be honest with him."

"Dante and I had the same discussion regarding Trevor. He is Jasper's mate as well as Dante's assistant. He will have to know sooner rather than later, and Dante feels he can shed a little light on Jasper's predicament by telling him the truth of our kind. As long as the boy is trustworthy and can keep our secret, I have no objection."

"He's been lied to for the last ten years by the only

268

male figure in his life. I don't want there to be any secrets between us. I want Matt to know there are good males he can count on."

"I understand, Frey. Good luck with him, although you don't need it. You're one of the best Goyles I know, and I'm proud to call you Brother."

Frey took a second to compose himself. "Thank you. Be well, my King." Frey disconnected and stood quietly, reflecting on Rafael's words. He didn't feel as though he needed luck with Matthew, only time. Speaking of the teen, the back door opened, and he walked slowly onto the deck, enjoying the early evening air. That was one thing they had in common. Even though he owned a gym and spent a lot of time inside, Frey preferred being outdoors. Another way they were alike was in their protectiveness of Abbi. Both men wanted her safe first and foremost. Yes, Frey trusted the teen with their secret, and first chance he had, he would show Matthew the truth of the Gargoyles.

He had bigger concerns at the moment. Like why his mate was in the house throwing up.

# Chapter Thirty-Five

Once Abbi excused herself to her room, she lost it, literally. She had kept her composure on the ride home as well as during supper. Now, she knelt on the bathroom floor, violently retching the contents of her stomach into the toilet. Watching Matthew and Frey together had allowed her mind a brief respite from the earlier news she'd gleaned out of Amelia. The girl hadn't been sick, and her mother hadn't been on a bender. Troy had taken their car and left them with no way to get around. No wonder Debbie had been smirking when she saw Abbi and Frey together. It wasn't because Abbi was with another man; it was because Debbie had accomplished what she'd been trying to do since high school. She had Troy.

That in itself didn't bother Abbi. If she'd been smart and not let Troy convince her to marry him, Debbie could have had him all along. They deserved each other. No, what bothered her was the fact Amelia was the product of his cheating, and he was using the little girl to blackmail Debbie into helping him. Technically, she and Troy hadn't been married at the time Amelia had been conceived, but Troy had expected her to be faithful when he hadn't been. How Abbi hadn't seen it earlier was a mystery. When she stopped and took a good long look at the child, she saw the resemblance. Amelia had his dark hair and dark eyes. She even had his crooked smile. She probably hadn't recognized that trait because the little girl never had a reason to smile, unless she was dancing.

When Amelia showed up for class, Abbi had been happy to see the child, until she saw her dirty tear-stained cheeks. Abbi pulled her aside while the other kids were warming up and asked her what was wrong. The little girl had unloaded a whole lot of information she probably wasn't supposed to know, and obviously didn't understand.

Troy had been to their house, fighting with Debbie. They had argued about a lot of stuff, one being *their child*. Debbie had obviously asked for child support, and Troy had called both Debbie and Amelia names no child should ever hear, much less when it was directed at them. Amelia said she had nowhere to hide since her room was a little corner of the living room. The girl had heard everything. Troy had grabbed the keys to Debbie's car and stormed out of the house.

One of their neighbor's had given Amelia a ride. Since the other mother didn't bother to stay during class, Abbi couldn't confront her about Amelia being upset. By the time class was over, Amelia was smiling and seemed to have forgotten her worries. Dancing did that for a person, no matter their size.

When Abbi was finally able, she rose from the floor and brushed her teeth. As she rinsed, she thought about seeing Amelia every day and being reminded of Troy's infidelity. The thought of him being able to have a child with someone else drove home what he'd said every time she'd had a miscarriage – she was a failure as a woman. She had to remember, it wasn't the child's fault, and she still needed Abbi to show her the love she never received at home. She would have to pretend the familiar face didn't rip a hole in her heart and continue on as she normally would.

Abbi couldn't face Frey or Matt, so she turned off her light and covered her head completely with the bedding. The dark would overtake the sunlight soon enough, and she would hopefully get a little sleep.

A few hours later, Abbi got up. She had lain in bed until both Matthew and Frey turned in for the night. She gave them time to get sound asleep before she slipped downstairs and outside. She sat down in one of the deck chairs and stared at the sky. There were no clouds to obscure the millions of tiny twinkling lights. The last time Abbi had sat outside at night enjoying the sky was when her

271

parents were still alive. Even though their house was in a neighborhood, the closest street light was at the end of the block. She would take a blanket to the back yard, lie on her back, and stargaze. Back then, she had been amazed at the stars. Now, sitting out in the middle of nowhere, the lights were even more spectacular. She couldn't wait until summer when the fireflies would be out in full force.

Would she still be there in the summer? Abbi's head was hurting from thinking about all that was happening around her. Before she met Geoffrey, her life was what it was, abuse and all, but it was her life. She knew what to expect on a daily basis. Matt constantly begged her to leave Troy, but she couldn't. She had been resigned to the fact that she would never dance, never have babies of her own, never know a happy day. Now, in a week's time, everything had changed.

She was still married to Troy, but not for long. Hopefully the divorce would go quickly, but knowing her husband, he'd contest it, dragging it out for as long as possible. Would Frey stick around through the drama? If he decided he was tired of her, where would she go? Her teacher's salary wasn't enough to live on. Troy didn't make a lot of money, either, and they had no savings. There was nothing to split other than the contents of their house. If she couldn't afford a place to live, it didn't matter if she got half the furniture or not.

Abbi sat on the deck, worrying about it all until she could no longer stand the chill. She silently padded back upstairs just in time to turn her clock off and get ready for school.

Jasper picked Matthew up and headed to Dante's. "You hungry?" he asked the teen. The kid was always

272

hungry.

"Does a bear shit in the woods?" Matt always had a smart ass answer, but Jasper enjoyed it. The kid didn't have many friends, and those he did have, he only saw at school. Jasper had enjoyed his time watching over Matt and hoped theirs would be a friendship that lasted a lifetime. At least Matt's lifetime. That was the bad thing about friending humans; their lifespan was so much shorter than a Goyles.

"I honestly don't know the answer to that. I try to steer clear of bears."

"So you, a big bad Amazon, are afraid of a lil ole bear?"

"I'm a badass, not an Amazon. That's a river. Or a rainforest, or something like that." Jasper pulled into the first drive-thru he came to and told the kid to order whatever he wanted. Matt slowly slid across the seat so he could look at the menu. He was practically sitting in Jasper's lap. The teen definitely wasn't shy about being in someone else's space. "What are you doing?" he asked him.

"I'm seeing what they have, duh." Matt stayed leaned against Jasper until he'd placed his order. He dug his wallet out of his pocket and handed Jasper some money. Jasper doubled Matt's order and pulled up to the window.

"Put your money back, I've got this," Jasper said.

Matthew huffed, "I ain't a charity case. Here." He placed the money in Jasper's lap, precariously close to his cock. Jasper picked the money up, added it to the cash in his hand and paid for their order. He passed the paper bag over to Matt, who had finally scooted back to the passenger side. He placed their drinks in the cup holders before driving away from the window.

Matthew took the food out of the bags, divvying it up between them. He placed a napkin with Jasper's food and set it on the seat beside him before starting in on his own burrito. The kid took a huge bite, moaning as he chewed. "God, this is good."

273

"I'm assuming you've never had a breakfast burrito before."

"Not one from an actual restaurant. The cafeteria at school makes some, but they skimp on the eggs, and they don't add all this other good stuff."

Jasper had to wonder at how Matthew lived. He had thrown out kernels of information as they were playing video games, none of which had been positive. At least not since their parents had died. He never dissed Abbi, but he did say he wished she'd never married Troy. If she'd married someone better, neither one of them would have ended up so battered and bruised.

"I'll make these for you any time you want," Jasper told him. "I know we're just hanging out right now while I'm pulling security detail, but after this is all over, you're welcome to hang out at my house, too."

"Really?" The kid's eyes were huge.

He laughed, thinking how much Matthew reminded him of Trevor. They were both so full of life, yet so insecure. Both had shitty family lives. Trevor's parents only wanted him as a back-up in case Travis' heart gave out. Matthew's parents were killed before Matthew even hit puberty. "What about when Trevor comes back? He won't want me around."

"I was just thinking how you and Trev are a lot alike, except for your age. You'll still be welcome, and I have a feeling the two of you are going to be good friends."

They pulled into Dante's driveway, and Jasper rolled his window down, speaking into the security box. The gate opened, and they drove on through. "Do all the Amaz... badasses have those talky things at their gates?"

"Yes. As a matter of fact, Frey's brother Julian designed them. Rafael, who you met yesterday, designs all our homes. My home was already built when I bought it, but he had designed it for the previous owner. You'll find we are a close-knit group." Jasper parked beside the other

274

Goyles' vehicles. "We'll go in and say hello to Dante's mate, Isabelle, and her son, Connor."

"His mate? Don't you mean like his wife or girlfriend?" Matt had his hand on the door handle but waited for an answer. "Look, I know y'all are different. Frey told me that much. He said he would show me rather than explain it to me soon."

If Frey had told him that much, he was going to be honest with the teen. "Yes, we have mates. One person who is chosen for us. Trevor is my mate."

Matthew frowned. "So, even if you wanted to date someone else, you couldn't?"

"Once we find our mates, we don't want anyone else. I have dated before, it just wasn't meaningful. And now that I've found Trevor, I know he's the one."

"So, Abbi was chosen for Frey?" Matthew was trying to figure it all out.

"Yes. Let's talk about this later." Jasper pointed to the door. "It appears they're waiting for us." They got out of the car and headed to the front porch. Jasper had called Dante giving him a heads up that he was bringing Matthew. He was waiting on the front porch with Connor.

"Dante, welcome home. And you must be Connor. It is my honor to meet you," Jasper said as he approached the porch. "This is Matthew."

"Nice to meet you, too," Connor said. He held out his small hand for both guys to shake.

Connor asked Dante, "Da, can I take Matthew out back?"

"You sure can. We'll be right behind you." Dante's face lit up like a new, proud father.

Jasper shook hands with Dante and asked, "Have you heard from him?"

Dante clapped him on the shoulder. "No, I'm sorry, Jas. I've texted a couple of times, but he wanted space. I've been trying to give it to him. He hasn't been gone that long."

"I have a very bad feeling. Someone was watching us. I thought it was Craig, but he's dead. Someone killed him and ...What if they followed Trevor? He's out there, alone and vulnerable. Dante, this is my worst nightmare coming back to haunt me in broad daylight."

"Come on, Brother. Let's get training over with, and after, I'll call him and tell him it's urgent."

The men walked through the house and out the door leading to the back deck. Connor was introducing Matt to the Goyles he didn't know. Matthew greeted them all then asked Jasper, "Just how many badas... Amazons are there?"

Jasper mussed his hair as he walked past, "Thousands."

"Amazons?" Dante asked as they continued on to the open area where they trained.

"You know how Trevor calls us the badass club? Abbi calls us all Amazons. Matthew knows we are different, he just doesn't know the whole truth. Frey plans to show him when the time is right."

"Trevor needs to know, too. I'd already planned on telling him before you declared him your mate."

"Jasper, you're with me," Uri said. He paired the men up, and they went over their technique first. Jasper willed himself to concentrate. Once they began sparring, he let go. His mind drifted back to those days in Ireland where he was fighting for *his people*. Jasper was not practicing with Uri; he was on the battlefield, swift and fierce. His movements were graceful yet deadly. The striking of metal on metal powered his body; the blood spilling at his feet fueled his soul. He was lost in the memory until someone yelling his name brought him back to the present. When he dropped his sword to his side, his chest was heaving. Seven pairs of eyes were locked on him. Uri's was a look of amusement. "Someone's been holding out on us."

276

# Chapter Thirty-Six

Frey had no idea what was wrong with Abbi. After throwing up, she'd gone to bed without a word to either him or Matt. When they went to bed, she got back up. She was avoiding him, but he didn't know why. Something must have happened at the community center, because that's when her emotions had been off the charts. She did a good job of hiding it, but his Gargoyle senses were alerted to her body's fluctuations in breathing and stress. Her being his mate only heightened the intensity with which Frey felt it.

Matthew left early with Jasper, so it was just the two of them in the kitchen. She only spoke to say good morning. Frey had no idea what to say to ease her pain, so he tugged her into his arms and held her. He offered no words because he had none. She didn't pull back from him. If anything, she held on tighter while he smoothed her hair down her back and placed kisses to the top of her head and temple. For a moment, her body calmed as she accepted his comfort. When she released her hold on him, he handed her a travel mug of coffee.

He drove her to the school, holding her hand the whole way. When she opened the door to get out of the truck, she turned his way to say something but stopped. The glimmer of tears shone in her eyes as she smiled. "I'll see you later," was all she said. Frey pulled away from the curb, and seeing Lorenzo in place, he headed to the gym.

Uri was at Dante's, leading the sword training. Mason and Kai had opened the gym, and Frey was hoping to get in a little sparring before the building got too crowded. His shifter was itching to fly, but he would have to settle for a little physical contact instead. Kai was at the front desk when he entered. "Good morning, Kai. Settling in okay?"

"I am, thanks. I wanted to talk to you about getting in on the patrol rotation. The Unholy population has declined rapidly on the west coast, and I miss hunting for the buggers."

"You can go out tonight. With all the shit that's been going on, we're down a few males. It will be nice to have another body in the sky."

"Speaking of which, Uri has been filling me in on some of the situations. This Alistair is bad news, huh?"

"Yes. He's been gunning for Jonas since he mated with a human. Now he's got his sights set on Rafael and anyone in the Clan. That includes you, now. So keep your eyes peeled, and let me know of anything that feels off, no matter how insignificant you think it is."

"Will do."

"You up for a little barefoot sparring? I want to meditate first, but I need to get in the ring and let loose."

"I'm always up for a fight, even if it's the friendly sort."

"Excellent. I'm going to take the back room of the dojo and get my head on straight. I'll see you in a few."

Frey walked to the back of the building where the dojo was. His gym was separated into several sections. The part that held the exercise equipment was the main room most people used. The boxing gym was in the center of the structure. It contained a square ring, punching bags, and speed balls. The dojo was on the right side and was separated from the other sections by a thick wall. This kept sounds from the other parts from penetrating into the martial arts classes. He stopped by the changing room and removed workout clothes from his locker. Since Kai was also into martial arts, they would spar in the dojo where shoes weren't needed.

The back room was dark, and Frey kept it that way. He sat in the middle of the floor and closed his eyes. It took everything in him to calm his body enough to clear his mind. Images of blonde hair flying through the air flitted into his subconscious. Soft pink lips seeped through. The taste of her juices on his fingers and tongue invaded. His cock swelled, making it difficult to relax. Frey lay down on the floor and stretched out. *This is impossible.* He was the master of meditation, yet Abbi's presence in his life was disrupting his abilities. He grabbed his erection, willing it to go away. The instant his hand met the head of his shaft, the vision of Abbi beneath him flashed through his psyche. "Fuck," he muttered.

Frey listened to make sure he was still alone in the back of the building. He lowered his black shorts, freeing his cock. Instead of fighting the visions, he allowed them free rein. He stroked slowly at first, but the memory of her tight pussy clamping down on him as she came had his balls aching and his fist stroking faster. He pulled his shirt up as hot spurts of come coated his stomach and chest. He bit his lip to keep from yelling her name. Pain from his fangs added to the pleasure of his release.

When the pulsing subsided, Frey removed his t-shirt and used it to wipe up the mess. Jacking himself wasn't anywhere close to the real thing, but hopefully it would calm his beast until he could make love to Abbi again. He headed to the changing room and took a quick shower before going in search of Kai.

Troy drove around his neighborhood several times to make sure nobody was sitting on his house. Being able to use both Grady's and Debbie's cars made it easy to give anyone looking for him the slip. When he didn't see anyone watching, he parked Debbie's car down the street in the driveway of a vacant house. All the neighbors had already left for work, so he didn't have to worry about anyone seeing him as he stayed to the backyards to reach his own house. When he was inside, he went to the kitchen and grabbed a new bottle of whiskey.

This hiding out bullshit was getting on his nerves, and it was all Abbi's fault. He loved being a cop. Carrying a gun and badge gave him the credibility and respect he'd not had before joining the force. Now that was ruined. He would have to move where nobody knew him to get another job. Being married to the prettiest girl in town should have been a boon, but she'd turned out to be a prudish, selfish bitch. But she was still his. Would always be his. At least he had any other woman he wanted whenever he wanted. Crazy, cheating bitches were good in the sack. He hated every fucking one of them.

The craziest of all was Debbie. Fucking cunt, trying to bribe him, *him,* for child support. Fucking brat wasn't his, it didn't matter if she did look just like him. No way was he paying for a kid that could belong to any man in New Atlanta. She could be George's spawn for all he knew. No, Troy wouldn't claim any kid that didn't come out of Abbi's body.

Fucking Abigail. He needed to find her, bring her back home. He would convince her that he would change. Promise not to hit on her or her fucktard brother. He just needed the chance to get her home, fuck her nice and easy a couple of times. Buy her a bracelet or some shit. Women liked that kind of stuff. Then when he had her, he'd never let her out of his sight again. She was fucking his.

His pacing and drinking was interrupted by the doorbell ringing. He glanced through the window to see Grady standing there, holding something in his hand. He took in the empty street, and wondered what the fuck his fellow cop was doing there. Troy opened the door to the man.

"Hey. I uh…"

Troy searched the area again before jerking Grady

280

into the house. "What are you doing here?"

"Look, man. I don't know what this is, but the Chief told me to bring it over here."

Troy took the offered letter. Grady didn't hang around while he opened it. He shut the door and relocked it, taking another swig of whiskey.

The return address was from the Law Office of Victoria Holt. He didn't know any Holt. Maybe Abigail's parents had some money he didn't know about, but then it would have been addressed to Abbi, not him. He ripped the envelope open and read the letter. Divorce. He didn't get any farther than that one word. Fucking bitch thought she could divorce him? He took a long pull of the amber liquid, not caring it was spilling down his face.

"Fucking cunt! Who the goddamn does she think she is? Fucking bitch! I'll kill you!" Troy yelled to the empty house. He threw the letter into the kitchen sink and found a lighter in a drawer. He set the document on fire. He drank long swallows of whiskey while he watched the papers burn down to ash. When his bottle was empty, he threw it across the room, shards of glass flying in all directions.

"Fucking, no good, can't give me a goddamn baby cunt. You don't want me? Fuck you. If I can't have you, nobody can!"

Everywhere Trevor looked, he saw a large man with dark hair and dark eyes. He had no idea of their true color, but could imagine they were black. He'd left Travis a note explaining he needed to get home. He somehow felt if he traveled at night, he'd more easily be able to tell if someone was following him. He was wrong. Every pair of headlights behind him had his body tensing up. He was ready to get out of his car and somewhere safe. Where that was, he didn't have a fucking clue.

His first instinct had been to call Jasper, but he was the reason Trevor was in this mess. He knew only one person to call that he absolutely trusted: Dante. His boss had given him space, mostly, but if anyone could offer Trevor sanctuary, it would be the big guy. He called Dante's cell phone and it went to voicemail. "Dante, it's Trevor. I think I'm in trouble, but I'm not sure. Please call me back." All he could do was wait. He was about an hour outside of New Atlanta. Surely his boss would get the message before he arrived into town. The night had shifted into morning, and the sun was in his rearview mirror making it impossible to see if someone was trailing behind him.

Trevor had just reached the New Atlanta city limit sign when his phone rang. "Hello, Dante?" he asked without looking at the caller I.D.

"Yes, it's me. Where are you?" Dante asked, but there were other voices in the background. He definitely wasn't at the morgue.

"I'm on 75 just hitting the exit for the hospital. Are you there? Dante, I think I'm being followed."

"No, I'm at home. Listen to me; don't go to the morgue. I want you to come straight here."

"I don't know where you live. I need an address."

"You do know where I live. I live on the same road as Gregor. Do you remember how to get to his place?"

"Yes," Trevor was shaking now. It was still a half hour drive to get to the warden's property.

"Go past his driveway for half a mile. I'm the only property on the left side of the road. I'll be watching for you and the gate will be open."

"Dante I'm..." he wanted to say scared, but his boss probably already knew that.

"I know, Trevor. Just be careful, and if you see anyone tailing you, don't stop. Call me back and I'll come get you."

282

"Okay. I'm sorry." He didn't know why he was apologizing.

"It's what friends do, Trevor. Just get here safely."

Trevor disconnected the phone so he could concentrate on where he was going. He drove well over the speed limit, not caring if he got stopped. Hopefully the police would deter anyone that was following him. He continued on with no sign of any cars close by until he turned on the road leading to Dante's. A black SUV was pretty far behind him, but it didn't make him feel any better. The road was secluded with very few houses. If the SUV didn't turn soon, Trevor would know he was being followed. He passed Gregor's driveway, using the odometer to gauge half a mile. The SUV was gaining on him, but he'd slowed down so he wouldn't miss his turn.

Trevor found the driveway, and true to Dante's word, the gate was open. As soon as he cleared the metal barrier, it automatically closed behind him. The SUV had stopped and was sitting in the road at the entrance to the driveway. Trevor couldn't see if it was the same guy from the park. He traveled on down the driveway to Dante's house where his boss was waiting for him outside.

"Trevor…" Dante looked like he wanted to hug him but refrained.

"Were you followed?" Jasper asked as he ran out of the house. He did hug Trevor. Hauled him into a tight embrace. When he finally let him go, Jasper gently grasped his face, looking him over.

"I think so. There was a black SUV that got behind me once I was on this road." Trevor focused on Dante as he talked. He couldn't look at Jasper. Not yet.

"Jasper, why don't you check it out?" Dante suggested. Jasper started to object, but he backed away from Trevor and took off running down the driveway.

"Come on, let's go inside. There's much we need to talk about." Dante led Trevor inside his home where several badasses were gathered. The room was filled with way too much testosterone. Along with the big men were a little boy and the teenager he'd seen at the gym. The teen was staring at him like he had somehow pissed him off. The little boy, however, was smiling. Dante introduced everyone, and when he got to the child, he said, "Trevor, I'd like to introduce you to my son, Connor."

"Your son? I didn't know you had a woman."

"I do. Her name is Isabelle. She's at work right now, but you'll meet her later."

Trevor was afraid to ask *what else*. But what else was there Dante had failed to tell him?

Before he could ask, the front door opened and a pale looking Jasper walked through. He stared at Trevor before looking to Dante.

Dante asked, "Did you see who it was?"

Jasper nodded, "It was Theron."

"Who's Theron?" one of the badasses asked. Trevor had already forgotten his name.

"Alistair's son," Dante responded. From the looks on their faces, that explained it all.

# Chapter Thirty-Seven

Frey and Kai sparred in the dojo away from the people who were working out. Normally Frey didn't mind onlookers, but today, he needed to let loose a little. In the privacy of the back room, he could do that. Kai had really good form and control. He was quick, even without his shifter advantage. Frey would definitely feel good about letting the new Goyle lead his classes. Once they were finished, he took another shower before going to pick up Abbi. As he stood under the hot water, an odd feeling ran through his consciousness. He stilled his mind to see if he could pick up on it, but it was gone as quickly as it arrived.

As he was headed out the door, his phone rang. "Geoffrey, it's Victoria. I wanted to make you aware that the divorce papers were delivered to Quinn's home about an hour ago. I just received the notification, or I'd have called you earlier."

"Thank you for calling Victoria. I'll handle it from here."

He didn't waste any time in getting to the school. He pulled out his phone to call Dane and notify him of Troy's whereabouts when it pinged with a text message from Dante. He called Dante first.

"Dante, is everything okay?"

"Actually, no. Trevor returned early from his trip, and he was followed. It seems the one who is after Jasper is Theron."

"Your cousin, Theron?"

"Yes, it took me a while to get the information out of Jasper and confirm they are one in the same, but it's him. Alistair isn't the only one who holds a grudge against our Clan. It must run in the family."

"What does he want with Jasper?"

"They have a history together. Jasper wouldn't

285

elaborate with Trevor in the room. Trevor is clearly shaken and wants nothing to do with Jasper. I have sent Jasper and Matthew back to your house. That's why I'm calling. Is there anyone else available to stay with Matthew? I'm afraid Jasper's mind isn't where it should be at the moment."

"I'm headed to the school to relieve Lor. I will see if he's free."

"I would offer to help, but I have my hands full on this end. I'm calling Rafe so he can alert the others to Theron's presence."

"No, I get it. Fuck, Brother. You just got back from dealing with the bullshit, and now it's come to your front door."

"Until we cut the head off the snake, I have a feeling we're all in for more of the same. All we can do is train and remain vigilant. Go protect your mate. I'm going to call mine."

"Be well, Dante."

"And you, my brother." Frey disconnected. He had met Theron centuries ago. When Rafael's father was slain, his body was taken back to Italy to the family tomb. Frey had accompanied Rafael to the Italian villa while Dante and Gregor remained in the states running the Clan. Alistair and Theron had shown up to allegedly pay their respects to Athena. Knowing there was no love lost between Athena and her brother, Rafael told Alistair the memorial service was a private, family affair and asked them to leave. Frey would never forget the hatred coming from both father and son.

How in the world had Jasper been involved with Theron? It wasn't really any of his business, but if Theron was after Jasper in any way, Frey wasn't sure he wanted him hanging around Matthew.

He rolled into the vacant parking space next to Lorenzo and rolled down his window. He asked Lor, "Is everything good here?"

286

"Yes, nothing out of the ordinary." Lor asked, "What has happened?" The normal jovial Goyle was very attentive.

Frey explained what little he knew about the situation with Jasper and Trevor. "Speaking of Jasper, he's not in a good place right now. Can you head over to my house and watch Matthew? I don't mind Jasper staying so he'll have company. I just don't trust that his head is fully in the game right now."

"No problem. Maybe I'll take them up in the helo. It will give Matthew a thrill and possibly help get Jasper's mind off things. That is, if you don't object."

"I think it's an excellent idea. Just be careful of Matt's ribs. We don't want to jar anything loose in there."

"I'll guard his ribs as well as the rest of him with my life. You have my word."

"Thank you." Frey wondered how humans got along without a support system like the Clan. He had watched them over the five centuries he'd been alive, and not once had he seen any of them bond together in such a way. Sure, there were good people like Priscilla and Jonathan who proved their loyalty daily. But for the most part, humans were a selfish bunch.

While he was waiting on Abbi, Frey called Dane, telling him about Troy. If the man's previous actions were any indication, he was probably plotting his revenge at that very moment.

Abbi's stomach had been upset all day. She had an old nausea prescription in her purse from when she was pregnant the last time. It had been less than a week since Troy had forced her to have sex without the pill, but her body was behaving like it had the last three times she'd been knocked up. She could hope and pray all she wanted that this wasn't number four, but she knew better. Knew her body. She was carrying the spawn of Satan in her stomach.

She really shouldn't think that way. She glanced over at Amelia who was concentrating on a picture she was coloring. The little girl was the product of Troy, and she was an angel. Abbi had no idea how the little girl could be so sweet with her home conditions what they were. If Abbi could, she'd kidnap Amelia and give her a loving home. The first bell rang indicating it was time to pack up and get in line for the bus or parent pick-up. When Amelia continued sitting at her desk, Abbi told her to put her things away.

"Miss Quinn? Can you give me a ride to dancing?"

Abbi shouldn't be surprised at the question, but she was. "Honey, I can't just take you with me without permission. Where's your mom?"

Amelia pulled a crumpled piece of paper out of her backpack and brought it to Abbi. It was a note from Debbie saying she had no way of getting Amelia to the community center on time. If Abbi could give her a ride, the neighbor would bring her home. Abbi stared at the handwriting. It looked legitimate, but she was still leery. Something about it felt off. Could it be that Debbie wanted time alone to be with Troy? Now that Abbi had left him, he was probably spending all his time with her.

"Okay, Honey. I'll take you. Get your stuff together."

The little girl wrapped her arms around Abbi's legs before doing as she was told. When all the other kids were where they were supposed to be, Abbi took Amelia by the hand and led her outside to Frey's truck. When he saw them together, he got out of the truck and came around to help them in.

"Hello, Amelia. How are you?" he asked the girl while giving Abbi a *what the hell* look.

"I'm fine Mr. uh… I don't know your name."

Frey picked her up and placed her in the back seat of the truck, buckling her in. "You can call me Frey."

"Okay, Mr. Frey," she said, giggling. "That rhymed."

"Yes it did," he said, tickling her side. Abbi stood in awe of this huge man who in one moment, made this little girl's eyes shine. She knew the feeling. She smiled as she climbed in the front seat. When Frey got in, Abbi laid the note from Debbie on the seat between them. She met his gaze and raised her eyebrows.

He frowned and slid the note back to her. She put it in her purse then reached for his hand. She needed the comfort only he could give her. Amelia sat in the back seat, singing softly to herself. It was some country song Troy played over and over at home. The nausea was building in her throat, and she told Frey to pull over. He barely got to the shoulder before she slung the door open and lost what little was left on her stomach. Frey was there, holding her hair away from her face, rubbing small circles on her back. She was mostly dry heaving, but it burned her throat nonetheless. When she was no longer spasming, he handed her a bottle of water so she could rinse her mouth.

"Thank you," she said, taking his offered hand and straightening from the crouched position.

He placed his hand on her forehead but didn't say anything. When the tears burned the back of her eyes, she didn't stop them from falling. He pulled her into his arms on the side of the road and held her while she cried. "Shh, Sweetheart. It will be okay, I promise," he whispered into her hair. When she composed herself, she moved back, and he swiped at her cheeks with his thumbs. "Abbi, I'm here for you. Every step of the way."

Her heart was torn in two. One half was breaking for the child in the back seat, for her brother who'd endured nothing but pain at the hands of her husband, and the little bean in her belly she had prayed wouldn't come to be. The other half was rejoicing at the warmth and compassion she received from the man standing in front of her. She reached way down deep in her soul and grabbed on to the good half.

289

Frey helped her back into the truck, and Amelia asked, "Miss Quinn, are you all right?"

"Yes, Sweet Pea, I just have a stomach bug." She wished that was all it was.

When they arrived at the community center, Frey turned in his seat to Amelia. "Can you do me a big favor? Can you look around and see if your mommy's car is in the parking lot?" Amelia unbuckled and searched out her window before scooting to the other side of the truck, making a big show of looking all around.

"She's not here."

"Thank you. Come on, let's get you two ladies in here so you can dance." Frey helped the little girl out of the back seat, holding her hand while they walked across the parking lot. Abbi committed the sight to memory. Instead of working in the class today, Abbi decided to put the kids on the stage. One, it would help them get a feel for their places in the dance, and two, it was closer to the restroom. She had taken another nausea pill right after throwing up. She hoped it would work its magic long enough for her to get through the next hour.

She took all the kids to the auditorium and placed them where they needed to go. She went over and over the steps with the kids, amazed at how quickly most of them got them right. Abbi removed her cell phone from her back pocket to check the time. They were about halfway through the class when the lights flashed off and back on. The kids squealed when the lights went out then giggled when they came back on. That happened two more times, about five minutes apart. Abbi knew Frey was somewhere close by, watching. She could somehow feel his presence. That tether she'd noticed the first time they were alone in her dance class had only gotten stronger. She clapped her hands, getting the children's attention when the fire alarm sounded.

The mothers who were watching jumped up from

290

their seats, and Abbi directed the kids their way. "Stay in a straight line and stay with Bethany's mom!" She counted heads as the kids marched by, and she knew instantly who was missing. "Where's Amelia?" she asked the last few kids. Bethany said, "She went to the bathroom."

Abbi had a really bad feeling about what was going on. She had promised Frey she wouldn't go anywhere alone, but she couldn't leave the child in the building when the fire alarm was blaring. She ran down the side of the stage and out the door that led to the hallway. When she reached the bathroom, she opened the door, and her face was covered with a rag. The cloth had been doused in noxious smelling liquid. Abbi fought with all her might. Her training with Frey flashed through her mind briefly, but it was no use. She was fading fast.

# Chapter Thirty-Eight

Fuck, Abbi! Where was she? Frey asked the mothers if they'd seen her, but they were too intent on getting the children safely outside. He looked around for Amelia and finally saw her coming out of the building, alone. He ran to her and knelt down, "Hey, Little One, have you seen Miss Quinn?"

The little girl's eyes were wild. She was crying and nodding. "She went to the bathroom," she said on a hiccup.

"Why are you crying? Has something happened to Miss Quinn?" He knew that answer before it left her quivering mouth.

"He took her," she whispered. "He said if I didn't do what he told me to, he'd kill my momma."

Frey could not believe the levels this bastard would sink to. He lifted Amelia into his arms. He pulled his cell phone out of his pocket and dialed Dane. "He's got Abbi. I need an APB on Debbie Cranston's car. I'm not sure that's what he's driving, but recent events make me believe he is." He didn't say goodbye before hanging up. He called Lorenzo next.

"Where are you?"

"Getting ready to put the bird in the sky, why?"

"The bastard has Abbi." Amelia's little body started shaking in his arms as her sobs became louder. "I need to you come to the community center. Dane is putting an APB out for the possible vehicle she is in. I have no idea where he'd take her, but I'm hoping Sixx can get a lock on her cell phone."

"Ten-four. We'll be there in fifteen," Lorenzo said. He was barking orders to Jasper and Matthew before the line went dead. Shit, Matthew. He didn't need to be here for this in case it went sideways. No! Nothing was going to happen to Abbi. Frey would die before he let anything happen to his mate.

As firetrucks and police vehicles arrived in the parking lot, one of the mothers walked up to Frey with a frown on her face. "Who are you exactly?" She was looking between him and Amelia. He appreciated the fact someone had the kid's best interest at heart.

"My name is Geoffrey Hartley, and I'm a friend of Abbi's. Can you please take Amelia while I speak to the police?" He handed the crying little girl over to the woman who tried to calm her down. He dialed Sixx and had him try to locate Abbi's phone. Unless she had powered it off, he would find her. He had to find her.

Frey was relaying what happened to one of the officers when Dane arrived. "I'll take it from here, Grady," he told the cop. Frey didn't miss the look the older man gave Dane.

"What was that about?"

"He has a chip on his shoulder. Now, tell me what happened."

Frey told Dane everything from the note Amelia gave Abbi to the fire alarm. He kept his eyes on Grady who sent a text to someone. Afterwards, he didn't stick around the crime scene. He got in his cruiser and headed toward the back of the building. "Where's he going?" Frey asked Dane, pointing at the car.

"Who knows with him, probably going to take a piss." Dane directed the other officers to stay with the women and children while the firemen checked the building. When they got the all clear, everyone made their way back inside to wait for the parents to pick up their children. The woman who was holding Amelia walked toward Frey and Dane. "She keeps asking for you," she said to Frey. Amelia held her arms out, and Frey immediately took her.

The little girl wrapped her arms around his neck, muttering, "I'm sorry. I'm sorry." Over and over.

Frey hugged her tight and whispered into her hair as he stroked it, "It's not your fault, Little One. We will get Miss Quinn back, I promise." He prayed to all that was holy he could keep that promise. The sound of helicopter blades registered in Frey's ears. Lorenzo would be there soon, and Frey still had no idea where Abbi had been taken. He called Sixx back and lit a fire under his ass.

Abbi came to, another rank smell infiltrating her nostrils. This was ammonia. She blinked her eyes and came face to face with a monster. Her husband slapped her so hard her head jerked over her shoulder. "You stupid fucking bitch." Since she was tied to a chair, she couldn't raise her arm to block his hand. The next strike was with his fist. Same cheek, only harder. "Did you honestly believe you could get away from me?" This time it was a punch to her stomach. Abbi wished she hadn't taken a pill. She'd love to throw up all over her hus… no, not her husband. The man standing before her was someone different. Someone pure evil. Any shred of humanity that was in Troy Quinn had left the building.

Troy paced the floor, his hands sliding through his dark hair, making it stand on end. A low moan brought Abbi's attention to the other side of the room. In a corner, Debbie was in the fetal position. From this angle, it looked as though her face was badly beaten. Abbi knew how that felt. Her cheek was throbbing. "Shut up. Shut the fuck up!" he yelled as he kicked the other woman with the toe of his boots. Abbi knew from experience they were steel-toed. Debbie reached out, grabbing his pants leg, muttering, "Amelia. Your daughter… Amelia…is…your…daughter." Troy rared back and kicked Debbie in the head. No sound came from the woman again.

294

"Abigail, my beautiful Abigail. What am I going to do with you? Look what you made me do. All you had to do was love me and give me babies. Even that whore could give me what I asked for." Troy pointed to the lifeless body in the corner. "But I didn't want her fucking kid. I wanted yours. I wanted you to give me a baby. That's all I asked for, wasn't it, Abigail?" He spit her name. She closed her eyes and willed the wetness on her cheek to dry. She would not give him the satisfaction of seeing her cry.

"I asked you a fucking question!" He grabbed her long hair and yanked her head back, so she had no choice but to look up. His face was a mask of hatred, the likes she'd never seen before. "Why could you not give me a goddamn baby?" he yelled.

"Because I fucking hate you," she seethed. "I pity any child that has you for a father." He released her hair and caught her on the left cheek with a fist. That one had her seeing stars. At least the bruises wouldn't be one-sided. Abbi had been through the pain before, but nothing like this. She shouldn't poke the bear, because this time she was pretty sure he wouldn't stop before he killed her. She thought about it: dying. If she had to go, now was a good time. Matthew had found a father figure in Frey, and he would be okay. Frey would find a beautiful woman without baggage to give his heart to. After all, he'd only known her a week.

She smiled when she thought of the big man and how in the short time she'd known him, he'd shown her enough love to last a lifetime. She held on to the memory of his beautiful face, his gorgeous smile, his Amazon body. A punch to the stomach stole her breath. "What the fuck are you smiling about? That big motherfucker you think is gonna come save you? A cold piece of fish pussy like you can't keep a man satisfied. Even if you already fucked him, I know from experience it wasn't any good. Stupid fucking cunt. I was going to take you back. Forgive you. Then you go and file for divorce. Haven't you figured out by now I'll do anything to keep you?

"Your daddy wouldn't let me see you, so I took care of that, didn't I? Me and Judy figured that shit out together. You were so fucking smug, looking at that goddamn pretty boy football player. Wouldn't give me the time of day. I didn't need your virgin pussy. I had a real woman warming my bed every night." He stopped pacing and got in her face. "I took your parents, I took your money, and now, I'm gonna take you."

*Please, whoever is up there, please let him kill me now.*

Troy punched her really hard, knocking her out. When she came to, she was naked from the waist down. He had his cock in his hand. It was hard, and he was stroking it even harder. Abbi tried to squeeze her legs together to keep him from entering her, but he'd tied her ankles to the chair.

"Troy, no. Please no. I'll do whatever you ask, just please don't do this. If you ever loved me, please don't rape me!" Abbi's sobs were uncontrollable. She thrashed her head back and forth, jerking her body trying to rock the chair.

"Rape? Baby, it's not rape when you ask for it. I know you want it." Troy grabbed her face in his hand, holding it still while he lowered himself to her legs. Somehow he got his dick into her body. She wasn't wet but he'd never bothered with that anyway. He shoved his cock into her dry core and started pounding. She moved her head and bit his hand. He stopped raping her long enough to grab her throat. "I'll kill you, you fucking bitch. But not before I get what's mine." Troy squeezed her neck as he fucked her. It didn't take long before his body jerked, and he orgasmed into her. "You're mine, and I take what I want," he hissed into her ear, never releasing the pressure on her neck. She was ready to die. Abbi brought up an image of Frey and Matthew together as she floated into oblivion.

296

Sixx got a location on Abbi's cell phone, but it wasn't static. It had moved, stayed static for about half an hour, and was on the move again. By that time, several of the Clan had arrived including Isabelle and Kaya. When they heard a child was involved, both women came offering their support. Frey was thankful, because the little girl wanted nothing to do with the mother who had been holding her. When Frey introduced her to the two women in his Clan, the little girl finally stopped crying and allowed them to take care of her. That was one less worry on his plate.

Lorenzo landed the helicopter in the parking lot and Frey jumped in, sliding a pair of headphones on. "Sixx has a lock on her phone. She's headed north on Guntersville Road." Matthew was sitting in the seat next to him, his hands clenched, knuckles white. Frey reached over and enclosed his big hand over Matthew's smaller ones. He didn't make any promises. Too much time had passed. He had let Abbi down, again. Even if he got her out of this alive, she'd never forgive him.

They patched Sixx through to the onboard communication system so he could give them immediate change in directions. "Her signal has stopped. She is on the bridge at the Brockton train yard."

In less than five minutes, the helicopter was hovering over the bridge. "Fuck, there they are!" Jasper pointed to the railing of the bridge. Troy had Abbi over his shoulder like a sack of potatoes.

"What the fuck did the bastard do to her?" Matthew screamed. "Frey you have to stop him; you can't let him do this, Frey! He's going to throw her over!"

Frey's heart stopped when Troy laid Abbi's lifeless body on the edge of the bridge, and with one flip, sent her falling to the tracks below.

Frey jerked the cans off his head and dove out of the helo. He phased in mid-air, begging his body to fly faster and harder than it ever had before. Frey reached her body with no time to spare. In one motion, he grabbed her, wrapped her in his wings, and flipped his body over just as the last grain of sand hit the bottom of the hourglass. His body smacked the ground, knocking the wind out of him. Frey hit the side of a rail and flipped, never loosening his hold on his mate. His body was battered, but he would heal. He reached out with his senses, searching for a heartbeat. There was none.

Frey let out a roar. His precious mate was gone before he'd had a chance to claim her. If she was going to die, she was going to do it as a fully bonded mate. He knew there would never be another female for him. With tears flowing down his face, Geoffrey sank his fangs into Abbi's neck, sealing the bond forever.

# Chapter Thirty-Nine

Jasper was out of the helo before Lorenzo landed. Troy fucking Quinn was not getting away. Jasper had no idea if Abbi was dead or alive or how badly damaged Frey was. Lorenzo would check on them. This motherfucker was going to jail. Death was too good for the bastard. He would sit in a box in the lowest level of the Pen. Alone. Gregor and Deacon would make sure he never saw daylight again. Troy had momentarily been stunned at seeing Frey flying through the air. When the helicopter landed, he saw Jasper headed toward him, so he took off for the car. Jasper used his shifter speed and caught up with him before he could get away.

Troy started yelling, "What the hell are you? Stay away from me you faggot freak! Get your hands off me."

Jasper held back on the first punch to his face, but being a Gargoyle, a pulled punch still packed a lot of power. "I'm going to do to you what you did to Abbi." He punched him in the stomach. Troy doubled over, gasping for breath. Jasper brought a knee up, snapping Troy's head back so hard, he landed on his ass. Jasper picked him up off the ground, holding him by his collar and the waistband of his pants, so his feet weren't touching the ground. His eyes grew wide as Jasper released his fangs. "You are a worthless piece of shit. You killed Abbi's parents, you abused Matthew, you raped Abbi, and now you've murdered her, too. You don't deserve to live, but death is too easy for a worthless maggot like you." Jasper threw him to the ground, his head cracking on the concrete.

"He killed our parents?" Matthew asked from behind Jasper. Matthew glanced at Jasper's fangs. Ignoring them, he turned his attention to Troy who was writhing on the ground in agony. He ran at his brother-in-law and kicked him in the face. Jasper knew he was damaging his

299

ribs in the process, but the boy deserved to dole out whatever punishment to the man he chose. "I hate you! I hate you! You stupid, evil fuck, I hate you! All I ever wanted was a father. You couldn't be that. You were so fucking jealous of Abbi's love for me that you hated me. I hate you back, you fucking fuck!" Matthew kicked Troy until his body gave out. Jasper gently hauled him away, holding him in his arms while the boy cried.

Red and blue lights flashed in the distance. Sirens interrupted the sound of sobs coming from the teen in his arms. Jasper had no idea who all had arrived and were now watching the interlude between him and his friend. He didn't care. He would hold onto the boy as long as he needed.

"Gun!" When Jasper heard the warning, he turned his body so he was between Troy and Matthew. With no thought to who could possibly see, he phased, wrapping the teen completely in the safety of his wings. The bullets smacked his back, and the shell casings pinged against the pavement. Troy was unloading his magazine into Jasper's body. The sound of another gun rent the air, this one coming from the opposite direction. Jasper's head snapped up at the sound. When he saw who had fired the shot, his heart stopped. Trevor was holding a service pistol like it was a part of him. Only one shot was fired. That's all it took. Trevor had put a bullet right between Troy's eyes.

Trevor handed the gun to Dane and headed straight for Jasper. When he'd closed the distance, Trevor reached out to touch his wings, but Jasper phased back so he could check on Matt. A flash of confusion and hurt passed quickly across Trevor's face. Still, he knelt down and wrapped his arms around them both. Jasper searched his eyes, "Trev…"

"We'll talk later. Right now Matt needs us." Trevor leaned his head against the teen's and closed his eyes. Jasper had no idea what to think until he saw Dante. He gave Jasper a small nod before phasing and diving over the

300

railing.

"Frey," he whispered.

Abbi never really thought about death before. She'd heard there would be a white light with your loved ones waiting for you if you were good. She'd heard the horrific tales about your soul burning in an eternal flame if you were bad. She must have been neither. There was no light, only pain. Not the pain of being burned, but the pain of being hit multiple times. The pain of your stomach being ripped out through your navel. The pain of heartache at never seeing those you loved again.

*Matty. My sweet Matty. You are why I'm not seeing the white light. I am so, so sorry, my sunshine. My bean. What I wouldn't give to see you bouncing around just one more time. Eating the last piece of bacon. Singing that heavy metal music at the top of your lungs when you think nobody is listening. Wearing my toe shoes and trying to do ballet.*

*Frey, you beautiful man. You tried to save me. I know it was my mind playing tricks on me. There's no way you could fly. Men don't have wings. And those fangs. I saw those before, you know. A couple of times. You thought you were hiding them, but I saw them. Then I felt them. You bit me! Why did you do that? Not that it hurt. Well, maybe a little, but when your body's already hurting so badly, what's a little nibble between lovers?*

I love you, Sweetheart.

*Yes, you did love me. I know it. I felt it in the way you held me, the way you looked at me, the way you made love to me. I loved you, too. I can say it now that I'm dead. Even if it was only after a week, I love you Geoffrey Hartley...*

*I love you.*

Frey didn't leave Abbi's side until he heard the sad wailing of a little girl- Amelia. Her mother was dead. The man who brought her into this world was dead, too. Kaya had somehow kept social services out of it. For now. Debbie Cranston had no immediate family, and now they were searching for some not so immediate relatives. Frey kissed Abbi's forehead, "I love you, Sweetheart." He stood and walked into the hall where Isabelle was having no luck in quieting the child. "Here, give her to me," he told Isabelle. As soon as Amelia was in Frey's arms, she tucked her head into his neck, and the sobs lessened to quiet tears.

"Come on, Little One, let's go sit with Abbi." Frey refused to call her Miss Quinn. As soon as possible, he was going to convince Abbi to change her name. Whether she went back to Swanson or moved forward to Hartley was her decision, but one he would allow her to make on her own. Frey sat back down in the hard hospital chair where he'd been keeping vigil for the last forty-eight hours. Jonas was monitoring Abbi closely. She had suffered fractures to the left side of her face and internal bleeding from a miscarriage. According to the tests, Abbi had been two months pregnant.

When Frey explained to the doctor that Abbi hadn't been breathing, Jonas suspected the bite to her neck was the only thing that saved her. "I don't understand," Frey said. "I thought the bite only served to seal the bond."

Jonas rubbed his chin, "I have been testing a theory. Our Jasper is not the first Gargoyle to prefer men. While most of the older males have kept their sexual proclivities under wraps, a few have not. There are two cases I know of where males have found their mates in other males. Human males. They cannot procreate, yet their lives have been extended somehow. I do believe the saliva being released into the bloodstream is the cause."

"Since I bit her and she lived, Abbi is now truly my mate?"

"Yes. You will want to have the discussion with her, because it should ultimately be her choice. But I would have done the same thing had I been in your shoes."

Abbi's injuries weren't life-threatening. Jonas explained that her coma was a self-induced defense mechanism. When her mind was ready, she would wake up. Frey would be there when that happened. His chair was next to the bed so he could hold Abbi's hand. He needed to be touching her constantly. His beast was howling to be near its mate. Frey stayed in the chair during the day, but at night, he slid into the bed with her, holding her, watching over her. When the door was closed and the lights were off, he reached out with his mind, talking to her, telling her he loved her and needed her.

The little girl in his arms was quiet, her body going slack. Her soft, sleeping breaths were puffing against his skin. Frey had always wanted children. Even when he was flying a helicopter in the worst parts of the world, seeing humans decimate each other, his mind was never far from the future family he secretly dreamed of. Back then, it had been nothing but a fantasy. Females were nearly extinct, and the chance at finding a mate was dwindling closer to zero. Still, he longed to have a female to share his life with, fill his home with children. The fates, it seemed, had other ideas for him.

When Abbi came out of her coma, he would allow her all the time she needed to fall in love with him. If she never did, he would live with it, but the little girl in his arms was his. He had already called Victoria and put the paperwork in motion. Even if relatives of the mother were found, Frey was going to make it worth their while to allow him to adopt Amelia. Abbi might hate him for keeping Troy's child. She might not be able to handle being around such a harsh reminder of her husband's infidelity, but it was something he had to do.

Matthew came into the room, quietly leaning against the wall as he stared at his sister. Frey loved the boy; not because he was Abbi's brother, but because of what type of person he was. He might still be a teen, but the person inside the young body had the heart of a good man. He had wanted to protect his sister against someone older, tougher, and meaner. He didn't let his age or size stop him from trying. Frey respected the hell out of the kid. He would love to adopt him too, but since he was older, Frey would simply remain in his life as a father figure and provide for him as if he were his own son.

They had spoken about all the things Matt had seen when they rescued Abbi. He had promised he would show Matt the truth of the Gargoyles, he just thought it would have been in a planned setting. The kid took it all in stride and listened intently when Frey told him about the Clan. From what Dante told Frey, Trevor was having a harder time with the truth. Not because of what they were, but because Jasper hadn't told him. Jasper was still on administrative leave which was a blessing for Frey. He had saved Matthew's life, and Frey was indebted to him. While Frey was at the hospital with Abbi, he trusted no one more with Matthew's well-being than Jasper.

Matthew pushed off the wall and came to stand on the other side of Abbi's bed. "Any change?" he whispered.

"Not yet. We have to keep talking to her and encouraging her."

"Can… I know you don't want to leave her, but can I have a minute alone with her? I have something I need to tell her." Matthew's voice cracked as he looked down. Frey could see the tears rolling down his cheeks.

"Of course. I'll be right outside." Frey stood with Amelia in his arms and stepped into the hallway.

Frey didn't use his enhanced hearing to listen in on

their private conversation. Whatever Matthew needed to say was between him and his sister. Instead, Frey focused on the little girl in his arms. He could envision her in Abbi's dance studio, wearing a little pink tutu, twirling in circles while giggling. At least he hoped the child could overcome her trauma and one day laugh again. The way Troy had used Amelia set Frey's soul on fire. If he could dive into the human's hell, he would go after Troy Quinn and rip the motherfucker to shreds.

"Frey, get in here!" Matthew yelled. Isabelle ran out of the waiting area and took the sleeping child from his arms.

He hurried into Abbi's room. The beautiful sight before him came close to knocking him to his knees. Abbi was awake and smiling at him.

# Chapter Forty

Abbi's heart hurt. She was the one who failed Matty, yet here he was pouring his heart out to her. He told her everything that happened from the time the helicopter landed up until this moment. At first, she thought she was dead. Her eyes had flickered momentarily, and she'd seen Matthew standing by her bed. She was in the hospital, and she was in a whole lot of pain. Pain that radiated from her heart. Didn't they give patients morphine or something? Maybe she had been given drugs, because she had heard Frey say he loved her. Now, Matty was going on about how much he missed her and needed her. He told her she'd been a great mom to him, but now there was a little girl who needed a mother. As much as he wanted her to come back for him and for Frey, if she couldn't do it for them, could she please come back for Amelia.

Troy was dead. He would never bother either one of them again. It was time to start healing for both of them. Time to put the past behind them, and look to the future. With Frey in their lives, the future looked really good. Matthew loved Frey and wanted them all to be a family. Not just for his sake, but for all their sakes. Frey loved Abbi and needed her.

God, she loved her brother. She could do this. She could wake up for him, for Amelia, and for Frey. And yes, she would wake up for herself, too. She willed her eyes to open. The lights weren't too bright, so after a few blinks, she was awake and focused on the beautiful, bruised face of her sunshine. "Matty."

"Frey, get in here!" he yelled. Ouch, that hurt. "Oh, god, Abs, oh god..." Matthew leaned his head on the side of her bed and wept. She reached her hand out and ran it through his hair.

Abbi was aware of Frey before she saw him. Her big,

strong man. Her savior. She smiled at him, "You bit me," she whispered. Matthew's head popped up, and he looked from Abbi to Frey.

"I'll just leave you two alone," he said, blushing. Abbi wondered what that was about.

"What exactly do you remember?" Frey asked as he sat on the bed next to her leg, taking her hand in his.

"I was at Debbie's and Troy..." Abbi couldn't say the words. Not to Frey. She turned her head and let the tears fall.

"Hey, look at me." Frey touched his index finger to her chin and gently directed her face back to his. "You don't have to tell me what you went through. I already know. I'm not talking about that, anyway. I want to know what you remember about me." He brushed the tears off her cheek and placed kisses where his thumbs had wiped.

"You can fly. I was falling but you caught me. And you bit me. Is what Matthew said true? Are you special?"

Frey nodded. "I don't know about special, but I am different."

Abbi knew she'd seen fangs. "I knew it!"

Frey laughed, "What did you know?"

"I saw your fangs. When you had your nightmare, then again when we made love. I thought it was stress playing tricks on my mind, but I saw them, didn't I? Can I see them now?" She was curious as to how he looked with them.

Frey picked up her hand and kissed her knuckles. When he lowered her hand away from his face, two sharp fangs protruded over his bottom lip. Abbi reached out to touch them. "Careful, Sweetheart. They're really sharp." Abbi tentatively touched one, making sure they were real. Before she realized it, they disappeared into his gums.

"What else is special? I want to see it all. The real you. That is the real you, isn't it?" Abbi wanted to see Frey for what he really was. The medicine was probably giving

307

her a little extra courage.

"Abbi, can it wait until we're home? I promise, I'll show you everything when you're stronger," he said wiggling his eyebrows. She laughed even though it hurt her face. "Seriously, though, there are things we need to talk about. Things that you probably aren't ready for."

"Frey, do you love me?" Abbi blurted out the only thing she needed to know.

"I do, Sweetheart. I know it's soon, but I love you with everything I am."

"That's all I need to know." She reached out, grabbing the front of his shirt and drew him in for a kiss. "Ouch," she said as their lips touched. "Oh my god, my face! Frey, how can you look at me?" She covered her face with her hands.

He pulled her hands away and kissed her on the forehead. It must be the only spot that wasn't bruised. "Because you're beautiful. Always beautiful."

"Mr. Frey!" Amelia's little voice came from the door. A woman Abbi didn't know was holding the girl's hand.

"Come here, Little One." Frey held his arms open, and Amelia ran to him. He picked her up and kissed her cheek. "Look who's awake."

The little girl blinked at Abbi. To be seven, she seemed much younger. Her eyes welled up with tears and she whispered, "I'm sorry."

Frey shushed her, "I told you, nothing is your fault. Abbi's going to be just fine. Her face looks a little funny now, just like Matthew's, right?" Amelia looked from Frey to Abbi and nodded. "She's going to come home in a few days, and you two will be dancing together before you know it."

Abbi's heart soared. Frey loved her, and he obviously loved Amelia. That poor child. Her mother was dead. Abbi didn't want to think what would happen to her. If Abbi was in a better place financially, she'd adopt her.

"Is she going to come home with us? I want her to live in your big house, too."

Abbi was stunned. "Frey, what's going on?"

He didn't answer. He motioned for the woman standing in the door. "Amelia, can you go with Isabelle so I can talk to Abbi?" The little girl hugged his neck, and he put her down. She stopped at the door and turned back, "I love you, Miss Quinn."

"I love you, too, Sweet Pea."

Frey's brow dipped between his eyes. Whatever he was going to say was serious. "I'm adopting Amelia. I probably should have waited and talked to you about it, but I couldn't wait. I needed to put the process in motion before the state came in and took her away. Abbi, I'm sorry if that bothers you. I know she's Troy's kid, and she'll be a reminder of what kind of man he was every time you look at her. But she needs a good home, someone to love her and show her what a real family is. I want to give her that."

"Geoffrey Hartley, I love you."

"If it bothers you... wait, what did you say?"

"I said I love you. Yes, Troy brought her into the world, but instead of being a painful reminder, seeing her with you every day will be a loving reminder of how there are good men in the world."

"Every day? Does that mean you want me?"

"Yes. You saved my life, in more ways than one. Since I can't adopt her myself, I'd love to be part of your daughter's life."

"How about if we adopt her together? Are you willing to accept me for the different kind of male I am and be tied to me forever?"

The tether connecting them not only drew their souls together, but it tied itself in a knot she knew would never come undone. Abbi whispered, "Forever."

309

Things around Frey's house got back to normal. Not the previous normal he'd endured for almost six hundred years of living alone, but the normal of having a family and friends around constantly. Abbi came home from the hospital and immediately moved into Frey's bedroom. She had some bad days when the memory of the rape and Debbie's death wouldn't leave her mind alone. She joined a support group full of those who had been through the same type of trauma she had.

Matthew's injuries healed, and he began working at the gym. Sixx helped him study for his SAT's which he passed with almost flying colors. Amelia settled into her new home, and after a few days, began to smile. She and Connor had play dates on the weekend. Even though the little boy was borderline genius, he absolutely adored Amelia and doted on her like crazy. He was teaching her to draw, and in her own cute way, she was teaching him to dance.

With Troy dead, all his assets were turned over to Abbi. He'd had several bank accounts where he'd stashed money over the years. The amount of cash was close to two-hundred thousand dollars. Since they were still officially married, it all went to Abbi. Sixx invested the cash for both Matthew's and Amelia's college fund. Abbi refused to step foot in her old house, so Frey hired a crew to go in, clean it out, and give all the belongings to charity. Abbi wanted absolutely nothing that reminded her of Troy with the exception of Amelia.

The car he had driven to the train yard belonged to his fellow officer, Grady Pine. Grady confessed that he arrived at the community center just as Troy abducted Abbi and texted him when the coast was clear. He was now on the other side of the badge, having been arrested for accessory to attempted murder. Being in lock-up at the Pen meant he might have been on the receiving end of an irate Goyle or two.

Abbi had finally gone back to work once her face was free of bruises. The fall festival had been postponed due to her absence but was now back on track. Frey continued to hang around the community center while she was teaching, but it was more for his enjoyment than her protection. He loved to see his woman dance. Rafael had completed her studio, and Frey was ready to show it to her.

Friday night, after they arrived home from her class, Matthew took Amelia into the living room to watch a kid's movie. Frey picked Abbi up and carried her through the gym.

"Frey, what are you doing?" she laughed as she leaned back in his arms.

"I want to show you something."

"But the kids…"

"Not that, you dirty woman." He kissed her quickly. When they were on the far end of the room, he placed her on her feet with her back to the door. "I have a surprise for you." He opened the door and turned her around.

Abbi walked into her brand new studio and froze. Her eyes were large as she took in the equipment and the details. While she walked to the middle of the room, Frey grabbed her toe shoes he'd placed by the door and stuck them in the back of his jeans. He found the remote for the stereo system and clicked it on. Soft music filled the air, and Frey walked to where she was standing. Getting down on one knee, he removed her toe shoes from behind his back and placed them around his neck. "Abigail Swanson, you are the sunshine that fills my days, the moonlight that fills my nights. You are the missing piece of my soul. From the first time I saw you dance, I knew I had to see it again and again. I'm offering you a place to dance, to teach, to love. I'm offering you my home, my love, my heart." Frey pulled

311

a small box out of one of the shoes and opened it, presenting her with a cushion cut diamond. "Abbi, will you marry me?"

Before she could answer, a little voice yelled, "Say yes!" Amelia ran into the room and grabbed Abbi around her legs begging, "Please marry my daddy so you can be my mommy."

Abbi knelt down in front of Frey and nodded, "Yes. I'll marry you." She leaned in and placed her lips to his. When she pulled back she smiled at the little girl. "And yes, I'll be your mommy," she said to Amelia as they all fell in a pile on the floor. They hadn't told Amelia about their plans for Abbi to adopt her as well in case it didn't go through. Now, there was nothing to worry about.

"Is this a private party?" Matthew asked from the door, smiling. Frey held his arm out and Matthew joined the group on the floor.

The wedding was a small gathering down by the lake. The weather was cool, but nobody cared. Frey stood with Victoria at the edge of the dock while he waited on Abbi. Frey had closed the gym early for the first time ever. He wanted his Clan there with him. Dante, Isabelle, and Jasper had helped set everything up while Connor and Amelia kept each other occupied inside. Chairs filled with their family lined the bank of the lake. White lights were strung through the trees, casting a magical glow. All of the local members of the Stone Society who weren't off in Egypt were there. Sixx had a video feed set up, and Julian was streaming the ceremony on his laptop in Egypt.

The music started, and Frey held his breath. Abbi was already his mate. They had discussed all aspects of the Gargoyles, and he had shown her his true nature. He didn't need this ceremony to know she was his, but he wanted it for her. He wanted her to have his last name and to be a Hartley in the eyes of the world. Amelia came down the dock first. Instead of wearing a dress, his daughter insisted she wear her pink tutu. She was adorable as she tossed the flowers around her. When his gaze reached the other end of the dock, his breath hitched. Matthew had been working out, and he wore his suit nicely. That wasn't what had Frey choking up. Matthew had come to Frey asking if he could change his last name to Hartley so all four of them could be a real family. Frey went a step further and adopted him as well as Amelia. Frey now had a son.

The woman on his son's arm was breathtaking. Literally. Her long blonde hair was swept up in some fancy hairdo that Frey couldn't wait to untangle. Her dress was pale pink, soft and flowy. Perfect for a dancer. Matthew presented his sister to Frey and took his place beside him as best man. Amelia stood to Abbi's left. Victoria performed the short ceremony, including both Matthew and Amelia in the vows Frey had written especially for all of them.

The reception had been set up in Abbi's dance studio. When it came time for their first dance, Abbi held up her hand. "I have a surprise for my husband. Frey, if you would, please stand here." She directed him to the middle of the floor. "I'll be right back," she said before disappearing into her changing room. Soon, the music started and Abbi returned wearing her toe shoes underneath her wedding dress. Frey stood immobile as his wife, his mate, danced all around him. He thought back to that first night he'd seen her dance. When he thought it was the most beautiful thing he'd ever witnessed, he'd been wrong. So very wrong.

This creature before him wasn't Abigail Swanson. This exquisite woman was Abbi Hartley, and she was his. His beautiful dancer launched herself into the air, knowing he would catch her. He did. And he would. Every single time.

313

# *Epilogue*

Abbi had never been so nervous in her life. She glanced in the mirror one more time, smoothing the soft material over her stomach. She allowed her hands to pause over the barely visible bump. Four months. For four months, she had willed her body to be strong. For four months, she had not been sick. For four months, she had hidden this little tidbit of enormous news from her husband. She had never successfully carried a baby past the first trimester. This time she had. This time, she had a good feeling about the little miracle growing in her stomach. She would tell her husband, soon. Frey was a worrier. A very protective sort of Gargoyle, but Abbi had learned that was part of being what they were– Alpha male, badass Amazons who protected their mates and family above all else.

"You're on in five," the production assistant announced. Abbi took one last look at her reflection and fitted her tutu on over her baby. At Frey's urging, Abbi had quit teaching school and had begun teaching dance full time. She kept her classes at the community center and added classes at the gym during the day while Amelia was in school.

She had come a long way since high school. Even though this was a limited engagement, she was finally going to dance on stage with the New Atlanta Ballet Company. Abbi had been approached to fill in when both the principal dancer and her understudy had fallen ill. She'd had little time to practice, but she felt good about her abilities. Now, she would see just how good she was. She waited until she heard the music cue and took her place on the stage. She knew Frey, Amelia, and Matthew were sitting in the front row. Others in the Clan were there as well. It warmed her heart to be part of such a large, wonderful family. Knowing they were all in the audience helped calm her nerves. She

314

blocked out everything but the music and allowed it to fill her senses completely.

Before she knew it, her dance was over, and the roar of the audience was deafening. The lights came up, and to her disbelief, everyone was on their feet. Just like in high school, the boy of her dreams was standing at the stage with a bouquet of flowers in his hand. Unlike in high school, Abbi knew the man of her dreams was indeed a reality as he stood smiling up at her with Amelia and Matthew by his side.

The week flew by, and Abbi brought the house down every night. On the final evening, Matthew had stayed home with Amelia, and Frey was in her dressing room, acting as her personal security guard. At least that's what he claimed. Dancing turned her male on. There was a knock on the door, and the director of the Ballet entered, oblivious to what he'd almost interrupted. "Abigail, you were marvelous! I would like to extend an offer to you. We would be delighted if you would join our company."

Frey picked her up and swung her around. "Abbi, this is great, Sweetheart!"

She wrapped her arms around his neck, hanging on for dear life. When he sat her on her feet, she told the director, "It is a wonderful opportunity, and I sincerely appreciate the offer, but I must decline. I have a family to raise."

The director took her hand in his and kissed her knuckles. A low growl came from Frey, and Abbi had to laugh. "It has been an honor. If you should change your mind, please give us a call." The man bowed and left them alone.

"You are so bad," she said, smacking Frey on the arm.

"I don't like anyone touching you. You're mine. All mine. I can't wait to get you out of this tutu. Have I told you how sexy you are in pink?" he asked as he bent down and nibbled on her neck. When Abbi let out a moan, Frey was lost. He ripped the frilly skirt from her body and pointed at her leotard. "Take it off. Now." He stalked to the door and locked it. By the time he was back, Abbi was naked. Frey didn't bother removing his clothes. He unzipped his pants, releasing his erection. He grabbed Abbi's ass in both hands and lifted her. She immediately wrapped her legs around his waist. With the swipe of his arm, he cleared the dressing table, placing Abbi on it.

She leaned her back against the mirror as Frey grabbed his cock and directed it to Abbi's opening. She was slick and ready for him. She was always ready, always wet for her Amazon. He slid home and pushed her knees up, opening her body further for him. Abbi cupped her sensitive breasts. She rolled her nipples between her fingers, sending an extra spark down to her core. Frey had shown Abbi how good sex could be when you had love between you. She had no inhibitions when it came to making love. If it felt good, they did it, and right now, it felt fantastic.

"Oh gods, Abbi, I love how you grip me...feels so good."

"Pick me up, Frey," Abbi commanded. She wanted to be closer. "I want to feel you," she moaned as he drew her body to his, her bare breasts rubbing against the jacket of his suit while his dick thrust into her pussy. Abbi wrapped her arms around his neck and found his mouth. Frey could make her come by kissing alone. She bit his bottom lip, "Frey... god, oh...god yes..." She latched on to his mouth again.

"Abbi...gods fuck." He was close.

"Bite me, Baby, please, oh god, Frey," she begged as she offered her neck to him. It wasn't something she did often, but every once in a while, she needed the pain of his fangs as they latched on to her skin.

With a deep growl, Frey allowed his fangs to drop, and he gave her what she wanted. They came together with

Abbi yelling his name and Frey's release muffled in the curve of her shoulder. He held her steady while she pulsed around him. When the aftershocks subsided, Frey licked her neck where he bit her and gently lowered her to her feet. "Fuck, woman," Frey breathed against her ear. Yeah, she felt it, too.

As Abbi found her clothes and dressed, she told him, "I'm ready to be home. I have a surprise for you." Abbi was ready to give Frey the good news.

"Surprise, what kind of surprise?" he asked as he tucked himself into his dress pants and zipped up.

"You'll have to wait and see. Please grab the flowers." Frey picked up the bouquet he'd brought. The rest of the flowers Abbi had given to the other dancers. She appreciated them all, but she only wanted to keep the ones from her husband.

Frey had borrowed Sixx's Veyron. He wanted his beautiful dancer to arrive in style, not in a pick-up truck. When they arrived home, Abbi immediately led him upstairs. "Close your eyes," she said as she stopped in front of the spare bedroom. When he complied, she opened the door and moved out of the way. "You can open them." Frey walked into the middle of the room and froze. While they were at the ballet, Isabelle and Kaya had miraculously turned the room into a nursery. The three of them had been planning it for days, and her friends had pulled it off perfectly. When Frey didn't move, Abbi's heart stopped. "Frey?" When he finally gave her his eyes, he was smiling.

Geoffrey Hartley... Gargoyle, soldier, boxer, martial artist, mate, husband... didn't try to stop the tears creeping down his face.

# Author's Note

Music has played such an important role in my life, getting me through the bad times, adding to the good times. Music is powerful.

Have you ever heard a song that just did it for you? One that stopped you in your tracks and grabbed your soul? I have, and it is the basis for Frey and Abbi's story. I had heard "Shatter Me" by Lindsey Stirling probably a hundred times. I love the song, and I put it on repeat often. Lzzy Hale's voice along with the haunting lyrics and powerful violin grabbed me one day. I stopped what I was doing, listened to the song, and sobbed.

Once I regained my composure, I went to the computer and wrote the Prologue for Frey. I hope you take time to listen to the song that still gives me chills.

## Frey Playlist

Shatter Me – Lindsey Stirling, featuring Lzzy Hale
Hush – HELLYEAH
Caught in the Sun – Course of Nature
True Colors – Cyndi Lauper
If You Only Knew – Shinedown
My Demons – Starset
Waking the Demon – Bullet for My Valentine
Everlong – Foo Fighters
Bully – Shinedown
Song of the Caged Bird – Lindsey Stirling

# *About the Author*

Faith Gibson is a multi-genre author who lives outside Nashville, Tennessee with the love of her life, and her four-legged best friend. She strongly believes that love is love, and there's not enough love in the world.

She began writing in high school and over the years, penned many stories and poems. When her dreams continued to get crazier than the one before, she decided to keep a dream journal. Many of these night-time escapades have led to a line, a chapter, and even a complete story. You won't find her books in only one genre, but they will all have one thing in common: a happy ending.

When asked what her purpose in life is, she will say to entertain the masses. Even if it's one person at a time. When Faith isn't hard at work on her next story, she can be found playing trivia while enjoying craft beer, reading, or riding her Harley.

Connect with Faith via the following social media sites:
https://www.facebook.com/faithgibsonauthor
https://www.twitter.com/authorfgibson

Sign up for her newsletter:

http://www.faithgibsonauthor.com/newsletter.html

Send her an email:  faithgibsonauthor@gmail.com

319

## *Other Works by Faith Gibson*

## The Stone Society Series

*Rafael*

*Gregor*

*Dante*

*Nikolas*

*Jasper*

*Sixx*

*Sin*

*Jonas – A Stone Society Novella*

*Julian*

*Urijah*

*Dane – A Stone Society Novella*

## The Music Within Series

*Deliver Me*

*Release Me*

*Finding Me*

**Tap Dancing with the Devil** *– Standalone MF Suspense*

**The Samuel Dexter Books**

*The Ghost in the Mirror*

*The Ghost in the Water*

*The Ghost in the Desert – Prequel Short Story*

**The Guardians of Truth –** YA Fantasy
(writing as Andi Copeland)

*Oracle*

Made in the USA
San Bernardino, CA
28 June 2018